THE ROYAL WIZARD

DAWN OF RAGNAROK BOOK 1

BOOKS BY ALIANNE DONNELLY

BLOOD AND SHADOWS
Blood Moons
Blood Trails
Blood Debts
Blood Hunt

DAWN OF RAGNAROK
The Royal Wizard
Dragonblood
Prince of Deceit

THE BEAST
Bastien
The Beast

OTHER TITLES
Wolfen
Virtual
Function: L1VE

ALIANNE DONNELLY

Dreams open the windows through which in our waking hours we seek to see. They are the worlds we create when reality fails to live up to our expectations, and the secret lives we wish we could live. They are the stories we write for ourselves, with no thought of critics or audiences, knowing that, whatever they might be, they will always be well received.

PROLOGUE

Through the Veil of light and shadow, a moment away from time, the great raven's croak announced a coming rift. Each beat of his black wings sent ripples through the air, disturbing a world that wasn't a world and beings therein and not.

Freki, awakened from her slumber, raised her head and growled, making the earth shiver beneath her master's feet. Laying a hand upon the she-wolf's head, Woden, son of Borr, the All-Father and ruler of Asgard, hummed to soothe her ruffled fur. "Muninn," he said, heralding his friend's arrival. Freki huffed and settled her head on her paws, but her watchful eyes traced the raven's flight until he perched on Woden's arm.

Muninn beat his wings, cawing madly to relay his news, and Woden's brow furrowed in concern as he cast his sight inward to remember what he'd forgotten. The past splayed out before him, a vast wilderness he'd traversed many a time, seeking wisdom on paths taken and paths abandoned. He flew across its plains and meadows to the present as it wove into the Web of Becoming.

There, in the subtle weave, a snarl of crossing destinies arose. Woden traced a lifestring, then another, and another, searching for the one to cause such turmoil, a being so central to a future its very life would alter the world to make it converge. He found it in a most unexpected place. In water. A young girl knelt where a cottage used to stand, staring at the driftwood remains of a great flood. She called for her caretaker, wept for the old woman, screamed her sorrow until she could scream no more. And when she rose again and began walking away, the snarl pulled tighter and thrust Woden into another place and time.

Frastmir, the castle seat of King Manfred of Wilderheim. Not precisely the castle itself. A chamber deep beneath, in the earth's embrace, where an old wizard scryed the air, seeking wisdom beyond his time. His visions showed him dozens of futures and for a moment at least, the human with magic flowing in his veins saw in the way of the All-Father. War and peace, a kingdom destroyed, a vain, selfish king demanding livelihoods with an imperious gesture, visions of dark futures, one worse than the next…and through it all, a single path, one precious thread of hope for something better. It meant a great risk to everything he held dear, the king he'd sworn his life to and the prince who would one day take his place.

Nico's old shoulders slumped as he realized what he had to do. For the good of Wilderheim, its king and his only heir, he would have to betray Manfred's trust and place in harm's way the very boy he hoped to save. He would have to send the child prince into war. "Forgive me," he whispered, as he would many times again until Prince Saeran returned to his father's side.

But there! The prince and his following already riding out to Lyria, even as the Aegiran armies gathered to march from the south. *May your horses be swift and your will strong*, the old wizard thought in blessing. He knew what was to come. Saeran's guard would see Aegiran arrows fly before they reached King Halden's keep. Nico sent a prayer to the gods that the prince would pass safely through his uncle's gates.

Woden caught the prayer in his fist and flipped it across his fingers like a coin, sensing through it the prayer's truth. The wizard was old. His body could no longer carry the weight of his mind and soul. Nico had seen three generations of rulers sit the throne of Wilderheim, and he knew he would not see the fourth. But how could the wizard dare leave him without counsel?

He needed to school an apprentice, but not just anyone would do. It had to be someone strong of magic and pure of heart, with a quick mind and wise soul. Someone who would one day stand at the young prince's side and guide his hand to be just and fair. But years, decades of searching for the right person, have yielded nothing, and he was losing hope.

Muninn cawed, shifting the vision sideways, and Woden spotted a familiar face. Perhaps the old wizard's hope was closer at hand than he realized. With a thought, Woden bent the flow of destiny. The snarl of lives groaned beneath the weight of his command, pulling tighter, resisting, until it gave way and a shining thread of power sprang free, aligning the others alongside itself.

A pot broke in the kitchen. The cook screamed and chased the thief outside, but the wily youth escaped with a loaf of bread to fill a painfully empty belly. The wizard noticed and Woden smiled, savoring his reaction. There again, the girl who'd mourned an old woman's death. She was the one. She would change everything. If only the wizard and his king could accept the counsel of a woman.

Another shift and there was the young prince, barely thirteen years old, strapping on armor and climbing the stairs to the battlements. He gravely surveyed the armies before him and directed the archers in their assault. A shout went up too late. Saeran's faithful general grabbed the boy, shielding him with his body as a massive boulder struck the wall. The two of them fell off the battlements into the courtyard while pieces of the castle wall rained down on them.

The boy lived. The general did not. Seeing his friend and protector take his last breath, Saeran closed the general's eyes, and mounted those same stairs back again, calling for the archers to light their arrows.

Years passed in a blink. Lyria had won the war brought to its portals and young prince Saeran stood at king Halden's side, rebuilding what had been destroyed, healing what had been hurt. People looked to him and saw their savior, for it was because of the young prince that his father, King Manfred had sent his armies to aid Lyria. To protect his only son, he had sent Saeran the means to save a kingdom.

And as the prince laid down to rest in Lyria, in a candle-lit chamber deep beneath King Manfred's hall, the wizard's new apprentice cast a spell. There was more than magic in Nia. Like all things Other, she held power in her soul and so an illusion became real and a stone wall shivered into being, locking her in the dark. "Nico!" she called.

With a gentle chuckle, her mentor appeared beside her. "Easy, child. There is nothing to fear." Waving a hand, he uttered an ancient word and the wall disappeared.

Nia allowed Nico to pull her to her feet. "You couldn't have warned me?"

"I thought I was teaching you an illusion." He led her to the table and pressed a chalice into her hands. "Drink."

She coughed as the watered wine slid down her throat. "That was *not* an illusion."

"The wall should have been nothing but mist, an image to fool others," he said by way of apology. "But you made it real." He beckoned to his chair, and it slid over to him so he could sit next to her. Taking her hands in his, the wizard waited until she was calm enough to meet his gaze.

"I don't know how much time we have left, child," he said, "no one knows that. The gods will do as they will. But this you must remember always. Words hold power. Far more than you will them to, more than you would ever expect. Do not use them foolishly. A word can save a life or destroy it. It can cut as well as any blade. Never underestimate the power you hold. Never give voice to an angry thought. You must learn that all actions have consequences and, once spoken, words can never be taken back."

Nia nodded, wide eyed. Nico would never say so, he knew better, but there was more behind his simple lesson. Something that made Nia feel again like the starving, abandoned child she'd been ten years ago. He was saying good-bye.

Woden sighed and let the vision go. Three futures now lay before the kingdom of Wilderheim, all waiting for two people to make a choice. The All-Father resettled Muninn on the arm of his seat and stroked his beard, deep in thought. What would become of this land where humans mixed with beings Other? What would an Other do, given the power to rule humans?

So engrossed in his musings was he that he almost missed the shadow slip away. Almost.

PART ONE

A Meeting of Souls

 1 

Midwinter was celebrated by all in Wilderheim, rich or poor. It was an entire week of revelry and good food, a time to forget how cruel and bitter winter could be. The lands were covered with snow, the roads all but impassable, yet in Frastmir and the villages surrounding it, there was nothing but joy in everyone's eyes.

Nia kept pace with Nico's tired gait across the courtyard. She worried he might fall on the uncertain ground. Several maids and hostlers had slipped on icy patches just this morning. Looping her arm through his, she steered him toward a more even part of the walkway.

Nico sighed. "Enough for now, I think," he said wearily.

Nia nodded and walked him over to a bench, sitting down beside him. No one acknowledged them as they passed. Unlike Nia's sloppy shadows, Nico's cloaking spells always worked the way he wanted them to, however long he needed them. In all her time in Frastmir, no one had ever seen her in his company, save disguised as a boy.

"The prince returns tomorrow," she told him.

Nico nodded. "And none too soon."

The young prince had not expected to arrive at his uncle's keep during the first wave of attack. Despite having not yet reached his majority, Saeran and his army had managed to turn the Aegiran forces back and restore peace to Lyria.

But it had not come without a price. Everyone in Frastmir remembered King Manfred's rages as news continued to pour in about the war, the casualties. He'd turned on everyone, but most of all Nico whom he blamed for sending Saeran away.

It had been necessary, Nico would say each time. And then he would show Manfred the vain, cruel, heartless king Saeran would have become had he not left. Saeran needed to see war so he might value peace. He needed to learn the cost of a life and soul so he might never take either for granted. And he needed to prove he could stand against an enemy and defend his people, for Wilderheim was rich in something far more valuable than gold or silver. This kingdom was steeped in magic, filled with creatures Other, who lived on the borders of the human realm. Wilderheim, some said, was the closest a human could get to the realm of the gods, a bastion between Otherlands and the world of humans. And as such it could not fall.

King Manfred didn't believe in old wives' tales. Even with a powerful wizard as his advisor he was too human to See. Nia prayed Saeran would show more respect to their gods.

"Are you certain they will accept me?" Nia asked, worrying the edge of her cloak.

Nico chuckled. She'd been asking him the same question for five years, and he'd always answered the same way. This time, however, he spoke slowly, chose his words with care. "The king trusts me."

While there was no uncertainty in what he said, there was caution. Manfred's steadfast trust had been broken the day he realized Nico had sent his only son into war. It had to be earned back, and though Saeran was returning safe and sound, a hero already beloved by his people, whether Manfred's faith in his wizard was also restored was yet to be seen.

"When I tell him you are worthy of this office after I am gone he will accept you without question. Besides, is there any man alive capable of resisting your charms, my child?"

Nia blushed. "My charms, as you know, still need a lot of work, but I doubt I will ever be able to charm anyone to do my bidding."

Her master laughed. "They will do it for the asking."

"I wish you would be serious," she chastised. Even after all her time in study, even at her age of ten and nine, Nico had more faith in her than she had in herself. "What of the prince?" She asked, tracing circles in the snow with her toe.

"What of him?" Nico returned.

Nia sighed as the wind picked up, ruffling her rebellious hair. She brushed it back and readjusted her hood as she spoke. "The king will not be king for much longer, you said so yourself. I will be in the service of Prince Saeran, and I know nothing about him."

Prince Saeran's accomplishments were commendable, but what should she expect from a man raised in war?

"Who is to say he will heed my word when…when you're…" She looked away. Her greatest fear was not for herself but for all of Wilderheim if its ruler and wizard were always at each other's throats. This land thrived because of the balance of justice and magic. If that balance became disturbed, everything would suffer, and that weakness would call to those hungry for its secrets.

Nico patted her hand. "Prince Saeran is a good man. I have sworn to provide counsel to the rulers of this kingdom, and I will bring them someone whose judgment I trust and value more than my own. But by that same token, Nia, I swear to you that I would not bring you to a king unworthy of his crown and your magic."

"You have great faith in him."

"As I do in you."

She smiled. "Tell me about him."

Nico sighed. "It has been a long time since I've played games with the young prince. He used to love seeing me weave illusions. I would show him pictures of heroes and horses when he was a child, and he would laugh in delight and say that one day he would grow up to be just like them."

A gust of wind snatched Nia's hood off her head. Pulling her cloak closer around her, she helped Nico to his feet and led him back inside the castle.

"Once," he continued, "there was a great celebration and the castle was filled with foreigners. They came from faraway lands, bearing gifts that dazzled the king and his son. The prince walked among them, looking at everything and asking hundreds of questions about them until the merchants became unsettled, fearing the prince's displeasure. Then an old woman with a veil hiding her face beckoned to him and placed a simple wooden box in his hands. 'What is it?' he asked. The woman waved her hands over the box and opened it. It was empty. The prince laughed and thanked her, then returned to his seat at his father's side."

Nia frowned. "I don't understand. What was the box for?"

Nico chuckled as he lowered himself into a chair before the hearth. A fire sprang to life and he sighed in pleasure as its steady warmth seeped into his old bones. "It was only a box. But as she waved her hands over it, she slipped a colorful stone into his hand. Saeran spent the rest of the night trying to learn the trick."

"I assume there is lesson to be learned from this story," Nia encouraged. She filled a basin with hot water and placed it on the floor for Nico to soak his aching feet.

"The lesson is, child, if you keep searching for answers about the obvious, you will miss the true treasure. There is no point to worrying about the prince's reaction to you. What you should be worrying about is what sort of king he'll make."

The way he looked at her as he said it, Nia knew he'd seen that very fear in her mind. Rather than confirm her insecurities, she said with confidence, "A good one."

Nico raised a brow in question.

"He will have me to advise him, will he not?" She grinned with humor she didn't feel.

Startled by her answer, Nico laughed, shaking his head at her impudence. His apprentice had grown into a unique woman. Though she hid beneath her cloak most days, she was beautiful as few women were. She had the easy charm and playfulness of a child, yet her mind was as ancient as his own. She worried, at times too much, about things that rarely plagued even the king himself. Nia had become like a daughter to Nico, and she was more than worthy to serve as Saeran's advisor.

But would the prince be worthy of her advice?

Nico had glanced into the future, and what he'd seen troubled him.

Nia poured wine into two goblets and gave one to Nico. "It's strong.

I think this should be a day of celebration."

"Wisely said," Nico praised, bringing the goblet to his thirsty lips. He ached. In his body as well as his mind. For Nia's sake he had stayed longer than he should have. He wanted to be there to present her at court as his successor. Nia should not have to face that on her own. But the effort was taking a toll on him. It wouldn't be long now.

Glancing at his apprentice, he felt at peace. Not because his worries left him, but because Nia exuded serenity. She was the calm in a raging storm. She would do the same for the prince and help him lead the kingdom. Nico had chosen well when he'd brought her under his care. At the age of nine, small and starved, an orphan with no recollection of where she'd come from, she'd proven herself capable of much more than either of them had anticipated.

"They've not yet hung the mistletoe," he remarked absently.

"They will do it before the prince's arrival," Nia told him. "Would you like to see?" As with any ritual at Midwinter, the hanging of mistletoe would be a celebration all on its own.

Nico shook his head. "Not tonight," he said, closing his eyes to hide his sorrow. "I think I will rest awhile before the prince's banquet." Before he would present Nia. As much as it pained him, he could not wait any longer. After tomorrow, Nia would no longer be his charge and he would no longer be needed.

Nia kissed his brow. "Sleep now," she said, covering him with a blanket. "I will wake you when the time comes."

~

"Stable the horses," the cloaked rider said, and without waiting to see his orders obeyed, he ran up the stairs into the great hall. The guards changing shifts grew wide eyed when they beheld him. He smiled in greeting and held a finger to his lips to silence them.

It was good to come in from the cold. The sun had set not long ago, but when it did it took all warmth and comfort with it. Stripping his gloves and cloak, he paused by a hearth to warm his hands. The journey had wearied him. He glanced at the chair nearby, wanting nothing more than to rest awhile, but he knew he'd be asleep the moment he sat down and there was important business to attend to.

Shaking off some of the winter's chill, he continued on his path, up the stairway and to the royal wing. A long hallway stood dark before him, all the torches extinguished for the night, but he could see well enough by the light of the moon. He traced the tapestries with a reverent hand as he passed, recalling fond memories of hiding behind them. The servants always pretended they couldn't see his feet poking out.

At the very end was a set of double doors. The guards who stood watch before them during times of war and unrest were gone, no longer needed now that peace had been restored. He grasped the handles and shoved the portals open.

As he'd suspected, the chamber was lit with candles and the king himself paced before the hearth, tugging at his beard.

"What weighty business troubles your mind, my king, to furrow your brow this late at night?" he asked, deepening his voice and biting back a grin.

King Manfred started and spun around to stare at him, but the moment recognition dawned, the ruler of Wilderheim rushed forward to embrace him. "My son," he cried. "My boy!"

Ceremonies were for kings. There would be time enough for them tomorrow and the next day, and the next. After ten years, this was all Saeran had wanted. To embrace his father without crowds of witnesses watching their every move and gesture.

"I'm home," he said as his father wept with joy.

 2 

It was late. Nia was exhausted, but she couldn't sleep.

Tomorrow the prince would arrive and Nico would present her at court as his apprentice. He would expect her to stand tall before them and be worthy.

Worry gnawed at her.

What if they turned her away or shunned her? Women, as all mothers, shared a connection with the earth, and female witches with gifts of foresight, truthsense and the like were common enough. But it was rare for any woman to carry raw magic like Nia did, let alone so much of it.

She would have to prove herself, if the king deigned to allow it. If even one of her spells went awry…

Nia set aside the scroll she'd been studying and took another tome from the shelves. Yawning, she read spell after spell, committing it to memory. She wiggled her fingers, playing with magic while she read. Not enough to work the spells, only enough to create sparks in the palm of her hand. It helped her concentrate. The ancient language was no longer a mystery to her. The words were clear, and she understood their meaning no matter what dialect they were in.

To learn magic is the same as learning anything else, Nico's voice guided her, *You need only open your whole self to it. Open your mind and let the words in. Their meaning will follow.*

She immersed herself in her studies, allowing nothing else to distract her. She read the spells and repeated them to herself, letting her voice echo softly all around her. Once she knew she'd not forget one incantation, she moved on to the next one, and the next.

She shifted in her seat when it became uncomfortable; stood to walk back and forth. The words came faster and faster as she chanted with her eyes closed, her concentration absolute.

Then, all of a sudden, a strong wind whirled around her, raising her hair and making her cloak billow. Just as quickly, it was over. Nia opened her eyes to total darkness and sighed, listening for the sound of all her scrolls and parchments fluttering to the floor. But she couldn't hear the rustle parchment. All she heard was the walls whispering in rushed words she couldn't quite catch.

At the very least, their voices assured her she was still inside the castle. Scowling, she clicked her teeth together, trying to remember what incantation she'd been saying to make all the torches and candles go out.

It made no sense. Recalling the symbols in the scrolls, she tried to match them to the words she'd chanted. She couldn't. The spell she'd chanted wasn't the one she'd read. One small mistake in pronunciation and something like this happened. "Bah," she whispered. This was precisely what she was trying to avoid!

Something stirred in the darkness, and she turned her head toward the sound. Had she conjured something else besides the wind?

It stirred again and this time, Nia was certain she heard cloth swishing.

"Who's there?" a male voice demanded and Nia started. The man sparked a flame on one of the candles and brought it around to look at her. Without thinking Nia blew lightly and the candle across the room went out.

But it had been enough for her to see she was no longer in her study and for the man to catch a glimpse of her. She was in someone's bedchamber!

"I wish Father had told me he was sending someone to me," the man said, a grin in his voice. "I would have been better prepared."

Nia drew back a step. *What?*

He was moving again. He'd risen from bed and was coming toward her in the darkness. His step was somewhat unsure, but he seemed to know which way to go. Nia had no such advantage. She didn't know where she was, or what was around her, and she didn't dare conjure light. It would make it too easy for him to find her.

Closing her eyes, even though it was dark in the chamber, she tried to create an incantation to take her back. Nico had said something about reversal spells a fortnight ago, but she couldn't remember his exact instructions. Frantic words slipped over her lips in a hushed whisper. A transportation spell needed words to be voiced, not thought. Nia needed a place to appear and a way to get there, and neither of those would help if she didn't know where she was in the first place!

He must have followed her voice, for she suddenly sensed he was in front of her, so close her nose almost touched his chest. His breath stirred the hair at the top of her head and she could hear his heartbeat. Gasping, she took a step back, but encountered a wall. The contact threw her off balance. Nia began to tip to one side, her hands flailing for something to grasp on to.

The man caught her waist and turned her so she was trapped between the wall at her back and him.

"Release me," she hissed, funneling a small thread of magic into her voice to charm his compliance. It didn't work.

"My, aren't you in a temper," he said with a chuckle. "Not to worry, my girl, I'll take good care of you." As his lips brushed her temple, his hands slid up from her waist until they were level with her breasts.

Nia slapped his hands away and shoved as hard as she could at his chest. It didn't make him fall back as she'd intended, but he did move to give her room. She sensed he only did it to humor her, which only frustrated her further. Anger made her magic boil, and she gritted her teeth to keep it contained. "Don't touch me."

Silence answered her. Nia felt the moment he sensed a threat like a charge in the air. His alarm, however muted, sparked her own, and she felt along the wall, moving sideways to get away from him while racking her brain for something to help her get out of here.

What came to her was nothing so structured as a spell. It was a sloppy invisibility cloak she'd used as a child. It never lasted long, and it took more magic and concentration than she'd had back then, but it was something. Reaching deep inside her, she called up her magic and drew darkness and silence around her.

Completely cloaked, she moved another step to the side and winced when her hand struck a rickety table. The water jug and wash basin on top of it rattled together and in a blink the man was in front of her again, caging her in. "If you aren't here to warm my bed, girl, then why are you here?" His hand braced on the wall next to her head, but it was his other hand that worried her for in it he held a dagger which scraped along the stone wall, making her cringe. Her cloak dissipated.

"By mistake," she said hoping the man didn't decide to stab that dagger into her heart. Nia could hurt him if she needed to, she could even kill him if he forced her hand. Magic filled her palms, ready to be used, but caution kept her still.

"Mistake," he repeated, his deep voice strained, as if he was trying to hold back laughter. "You came to the prince's bed chamber by mistake? And how, pray tell, did you manage to appear here without me hearing you enter?"

"What prince?"

"This prince," he replied. "Son of King Manfred of Frastmir, heir to the throne of Wilderheim. Are there so many princes around you need clarification?"

"The prince is not due to return until tomorrow. You're lying to me."

He leaned in closer. "Are you certain of that?"

Scowling, Nia quickly cast her senses down through the walls into the earth to orient herself. She went two stories down and through the underground study before she touched packed earth and bedrock. She found the leylines running north and south and determined she was in the south wing of the castle. The royal wing, where only the king, his heir, and visiting nobility slept. Flowing back to the chamber, she followed the floor stones out into the hallway and traced it left and right. Not far to the left, she felt a different song. Wood. A great wooden portal which could only be the king's bedchamber.

Oh, no.

"P-prince Saeran?" she asked weakly. Who else would be sleeping in the prince's bedchamber?

"Who are you?" he demanded. "Did you come through the window? Where are the ropes? Who helped you?" The tip of the dagger ran up the crease in her cloak to her neck. "Why are you here, little bird?"

"It was an accident. Please, I mean you no harm," she implored reaching out. She didn't need to touch the dagger to make the blade disappear; she could work the spell through him.

He breathed in deeper when her fingers curled into his night shirt. The blade was gone. He wouldn't see it disappear in the darkness, but he might feel the weapon's balance change. "So you're not here to warm my bed," he said, "but you want to. Is that it?"

Nia sputtered.

"If I were you, I'd choose my words wisely."

"Release me," she told him.

"And if I do not?"

"Then…then I will…" She would what? He was the royal heir, the future king to whom she was supposed to be swearing her fealty tomorrow. What could she do? Maim him? Enchant him? Turn him into a bumbling idiot? "I'll turn you into a toad," she finally said and winced.

He chuckled. "A witchling, then? Turn me into a toad, you say?" She felt his lips by her ear as he whispered, "I'm fairly certain they jail people for that."

They would do more than jail her if anyone found out. "Don't make me do this," Nia said, willing him to step back and release her.

Instead he leaned in even closer, his nose to her neck and inhaled. "I can make you relent. I can make you want me."

At her wits' end, Nia did what she had to. "And I can make you regret this for the rest of your life." She shouted three words, hoping they were the right ones. There was no flash, no great boom of magic, only silence. Nia reached out but encountered only air where the prince had stood. "Prince Saeran?"

Nothing.

With a thought, she conjured light and looked around. The chamber was grand and worthy of a prince, but it was cold in its opulence. He had yet to make it his home again. "Prince Saeran?"

Croak.

Nia looked down and her light flared brighter as relief washed over her. She hadn't killed him!

There at her feet was a bewildered toad, staring at his hands, his eyes wide and mouth open. Then he looked up at her. He croaked and jumped, landing on his side and rolling onto his back. His wild struggle to right himself made Nia wince. He kicked his legs and made a sound no natural toad would make. It might have been a panicked scream.

Taking pity on him, Nia picked the creature up and brought him to her face so they were at an equal level. "I did warn you," she said. "No, don't struggle, you will hurt yourself. I will turn you back but you have to stay still, or I cannot release you."

The kicking continued. He even tried to bite her, not realizing toads had no teeth. The clamp of his soft mouth over her fingers was little more than a tickle but when his long tongue shot out at her face, he almost struck her eye.

"All right," she said, holding him a little farther to evade his continued attacks and spoke the words to reverse her spell. The air shifted, her light flickered, and the toad grew and transformed back into a man, which left Nia holding his face. Any doubt she may have had as to his true identity disappeared when she recognized him by the light of her magic. Dread settled in her belly. *Gods protect me.* She'd turned the crown prince into a toad!

Saeran blinked his eyes rapidly, panting as his heart fluttered in his chest. His feet tingled and his arms and legs were shaky. But at least he had feet. And legs, and arms! Saeran pushed away from the accursed witch and immediately tripped over his own feet. He hit the floor hard, but the pain was nothing to him while his heart tried to beat its way out of his chest. He stared at the witch with his eyes open so wide he thought they might fall right out of his head, but he dared not blink even once for fear of what she might do to him next.

There was still light in the room, little orbs of it floating in the air between them like giant fireflies. Breathing hard to keep from fainting like a girl, he stared at the woman, truly seeing her for the first time.

She wasn't very tall, but she carried herself with the air of someone much bigger and nobler than her dress would let on. He'd caught the merest glimpse of her before his candle went out earlier, but now that he saw her Saeran had no doubt she was powerful. He could see it in her eyes.

"Are you all right?" she asked, wringing her hands together.

"All right? I…" That was when he saw his dagger. Or rather, the hilt of it because the blade was gone. His favorite dagger! The one gifted to him by King Halden, which he kept at his side all the time and beneath his pillow when he slept. It was ruined. And it was her fault! "You changed me into a toad!"

"You thought I was a whore!" she returned with righteous indignation.

"Who the bloody hell are you?"

She took a deep breath and absently waved a hand. All the torches and candles in the room flared to life. "Ah!" When she took a step toward him, he scrambled back, grabbing the ruined dagger hilt and waving it at her. "Stay away from me!"

She stopped, looking unsure. "I am Nia," she said, bowing at the waist like a knight. "Nico's apprentice."

The wizard's name stirred a memory, but as awake as he was at the moment, Saeran was still exhausted from the journey. He'd only gotten to bed moments before this stranger appeared, having spent long hours talking to his father. "My father did mention something about an apprentice," he said, trying to recall his exact words. "He did not say it was a woman." But he had said he'd never met the apprentice himself.

Nia blushed, appearing much younger than she had when he'd seen her through the eyes of a toad. "He doesn't know, Highness. I am to be presented at court tomorrow."

In the silence that followed, Saeran's mouth quirked. "He doesn't know?" Sitting there on the floor of his bed chamber, dressed in nothing but his night shirt while a cloaked woman with hair like sunshine caught in gold looked at him as if she expected him to shout for the guards and have her beheaded, Saeran's dagger hand lowered. Of all the things he'd imagined coming home to, this had to be the most ridiculous.

As the panic he'd felt slowly melted into irrational hilarity, he imagined this Nia appearing before him and his father tomorrow and suddenly he couldn't contain his mirth. The chuckle turned into a laugh, and when she looked at him as if he'd lost his mind it got worse. "Gods, I can't wait to see his face!" He fell back, lying spread eagle, laughing until he couldn't breathe. "Ahahahahagirlhahahahahwizardahahahah…"

If anyone saw him in that moment, they would think him mad. Every time he tried to stop, he would look at the girl and start all over again. His sides began to hurt and his eyes watered, which only made him laugh harder.

Finally he struggled to raise himself off the ground, his insides still tickling, but he tried hard to make himself stop. He grinned at Nico's chosen apprentice and had the satisfaction of seeing her completely confused, which he would wager his future crown didn't happen often.

She drew back when he approached, another spell no doubt on the tip of her tongue. He liked her already.

"Calm yourself, Nia," he said, his grin turning crooked, "I know better than to make you angry twice. Who knows what you would turn me into next?"

After an uncertain moment, Nia returned his smile. "I was considering, a caterpillar. Or some other kind of worm."

Saeran chuckled. "I could not have asked for a more fitting advisor."

"*Nia*," Nico's familiar disembodied voice whispered through the chamber, and Nia's smile fell away.

"I must go."

"No, wait!" But she was already gone, dissolved into mist and then nothing at all.

Saeran sighed, disappointed.

She'd turned him into a toad. He smiled. The woman had courage. He needed that. Someone who wouldn't be afraid to tell him the truth, no matter how unpleasant. He'd spent too much time in a place where no one could afford to be above another. To come back here, where even as a child no one had ever told him anything but what they thought he'd wanted to hear was something of a disappointment.

How was Saeran to trust someone who couldn't look him in the eye?

But Nia was already proving herself different. Even unsure of herself in the presence of the royal heir, she hadn't hesitated to put him in his place. Curious that it ended up being at her feet. Even more curious was that while she'd bowed to him, he'd wanted to bow to her in return.

Nico would not have groomed a fool, let alone presented one at court as his successor. If he had enough faith in a female to have her take his place, it meant she had to be not only powerful but learned as well. The wizard Saeran knew would have made certain his successor was everything he himself had been. He would have taught Nia all he knew and groomed her to put the welfare of the kingdom before anything else.

Saeran had no doubt Nico's faith in her would be justified, and that intrigued him immensely. He would have kept her here with him until morning had she not disappeared. He wanted to talk to her, get to know the woman who would be his right hand when he took the throne.

During the hours he'd talked to his father, the king had informed him of his decision to step down in a few months' time. The years he'd been away had taken their toll on his father. The once proud king was now tired, eager to relinquish his crown and all its responsibilities. With Saeran returned healthy and hale, he wanted nothing more than to be a father to his son.

Saeran would be king before he'd even had time to reacquaint himself with his kingdom, and he would need Nia more than she realized if he was to justify Manfred's faith in him.

There would be argument, but Saeran didn't care. He couldn't wait to stand up in front of the assembly tomorrow and thumb his nose at tradition and all those old goats on Father's advisory council by accepting her as his.

3

Nia spent the day avoiding Nico. Since she couldn't go outside and the study was too obvious, she hid inside her room, locked and warded so he couldn't get in. Of course, that wouldn't stop him if he was really determined; he'd taught her those wards, after all. But at least he respected her wishes and left her alone. The king no doubt kept him busy, seeing as the prince arrived ahead of schedule. The entire castle was talking about it. Not just the servants, but the walls as well. Nia was mortified. If the walls knew, then Nico definitely already knew.

Nia moaned and hid her face in her pillow. "How am I supposed to face any of them?"

The walls laughed at her.

At noon, Nico knocked on her door.

"I don't want to see anyone!"

"Very well," Nico said. "Stay there if you wish, but do not be late for the ceremony. Your dress robes are ready."

When she was certain he'd left, Nia cautiously opened the door and looked at the garments hanging there as if a person stood in them. "You are not dress robes," she said.

The garment shoulders raised in a shrug.

Nia rolled her eyes and stepped back, allowing the clothes to walk in.

These were the clothes that took months to be decided on? She supposed it could be worse. As a wizard, Nia had no rank. She wasn't a commoner so she could not wear the dresses they wore, nor was she a noble to wear gowns and jewels. Instead, Nico decreed a wizard should dress so no one would see her as one of them, but everyone would know to come to her when needed. Nia would wear a pair of breeches, a blouse and a long jerkin. The breeches were wide for modesty but while the jerkin was long, it would mold to her figure, leaving no doubt in anyone's mind that she was female.

Nia had spent the last ten years dressing like a boy, and modesty wasn't something she'd spent too much time thinking about. What worried her more was that people would be looking at her and really seeing *her*. Their eyes wouldn't glance off her to look at something else, and at the king's right hand on the dais she would be the center of attention right along with him. Come what may, there would be no more hiding from anyone.

Nia touched the clothes, and they flew away from her, pointing at the bath tub before laying neatly out on her bed, ready to be donned. Nia considered running away. She could fly out the window and be long gone by the time they came to summon her.

But she couldn't do that. Nico had saved her life. He was the only family she had and the only one who hadn't turned her away. She owed him more than she could ever repay, if she lived to be a hundred years old. This had always been the price for his hospitality, friendship and tutelage, and Nia had accepted it knowing this day would come.

All too soon the bell tolled for the evening meal. It was time for Nia to get ready. She washed in the tub, scrubbing her skin until it was pink and rinsing her hair with flower-steeped water. With a thought, she dried herself and dressed and then paced the room trying to come up with an excuse not to go down to meet her mentor.

But when Nico summoned her, he gave her no choice but to obey, and she appeared at his side in front of the great hall. The doors were closed, but the sound of revelry still reached them. So many people. From all over the kingdom and beyond.

They had come here tonight to welcome the prince back home, but they would also be there to witness her presentation. Laughter rang clear over the strains of music. The jugglers were performing in the corners, she knew, but the center of the room was for dancing. There would be long tables lining the walls, laden with food and so many torches and candelabras that it would seem like daylight.

Nia knew exactly how it looked. She'd seen the preparations of the great feast.

Movement in the corner of her vision had her spinning to face the tapestries. She just caught sight of something small before it ran off again. Nia followed its mad flight to the main castle door.

There, standing in shadow, was a whole family of them. Wispy creatures, childlike in stature, their overlarge eyes the color of gemstones. They watched her and whispered, and the vines growing out of their heads like hair spread wildly around them as if for cover.

"Seedlings," Nico said. "They've come to see you take the crown."

"What crown? I'm a wizard, not a queen."

"To them that is precisely what you are. Their rulers and guardians will look to you when there is need, not Saeran. They will seek your magic. Humans cannot see creatures Other unless they make themselves seen. They have their own kingdoms and lands within Wilderheim and they rarely concern themselves with human affairs unless something we do encroaches on their well being. When it does, we…you will be their intermediary."

Nia's eyes widened. "You never told me this!"

"I never expected I would need to," he said and while she recognized the truth in his word, she also heard there was something he was holding back. "They never appeared to me. Not in all my years. This is a great honor, Nia."

The seedlings blinked their big eyes and melted into the walls. But they opened Nia's Sight to all the rest. Everywhere she looked creatures large and small appeared for just a moment and then hid from her once more. Tall, regal Sidhe glided in pools of torchlight, away from the shadows. Winged creatures perched in the rafters, their talons digging grooves into the wood. Animal spirits with wise eyes roamed the hallways, watching her with suspicion. Shadowy forms moved across the floors, horned things with tails like snakes. They hissed words she couldn't understand, but the sound of it sent chills up her spine.

"There are so many." There one moment, gone the next. In an instant the hall was empty again, and Nia was so terrified she couldn't move. "I don't think I can do this," she managed to say. "I cannot be the royal wizard. Please don't make me do this."

"You can and you must," Nico insisted. "Now look at me. There's a lass. Help will never be far for someone like you, Nia. You have friends and allies all around you. All you need to do is call out to them, and they will come to your aid. But you must do this."

"It is too much."

"It will never be less. Only more."

Nia shook her head, looking at the seal on the great hall door to give herself something else to focus on. "You should be in there. Your place is by the king's side." Something had to be wrong. The prince must have told his father who she was, what she'd done.

She would walk into the great hall with Nico and kneel before the king, and then he would rise from his throne and point a finger at her. The guards would rush forward to seize her, and she'd be dragged to the edge of Frastmir to the waiting noose. They would hang her and leave her there to be devoured by wild thing.

"You worry for nothing, child. All will be well, wait and see."

The music quieted suddenly and Nia froze with a gasp. "Why have they stopped?"

"The king is making a speech, no doubt." Nico rose to his feet and came to her, pulling her to the side. "We will have our turn soon enough. But first..." he nodded toward the staircase.

Nia followed his gaze just as prince Saeran hurried down the steps, still working on the fastenings of his jerkin. He spared her a brief glance, his gray eyes twinkling as he passed them. The timing was impeccable. Saeran never slowed in his step, yet he reached the door just in time to walk through it as the guards on the inside opened the great portals.

A cheer went up in his honor and Nia watched with her mentor as Saeran made his regal way to the dais where his father sat waiting. The crowds parted at his approach, smiling faces following his progress with affection.

On the dais, Saeran leaned over the king to say something in his ear and then faced the people and nodded his thanks. He would make a speech of his own before seating himself to his father's right.

The great door closed, shutting out the sight of it and Nia strained to catch something of what was said. She needed to know. He could be calling for the guards this very moment. She stood there for untold moments, oblivious to everything but the silence in her mind. It was as if the castle was holding its breath in anticipation.

Then Nico took her hand and squeezed, bringing her attention back to him.

"Take a breath," he said, letting go of her hand. He turned her to face the door just as it opened and added, "Walk."

The crowd was silent. Not a word was uttered as Nico strode toward the dais with the help of his staff. Nia wanted to help him, to provide a shoulder for him to lean on, but she sensed this was the way he wanted it to be.

She did not look at anyone as she walked, keeping her gaze on a point at the foot of the dais. Any lower and she would look meek. Any higher and she would see the prince.

At last they reached the dais. Blood roared in Nia's ears as both she and Nico lowered themselves to one knee before the king.

"Rise, old friend," the king said before they knelt completely. "It is no good for men of our age to kneel to anyone." There was warmth and friendship in his voice, their strife buried now that Saeran was home safe and sound.

While Nico stood, Nia remained where she was. She was not to raise her gaze until Nico called her. Her palms were moist and her mouth dry. What was the pledge she was supposed to make? What were the words? She couldn't remember! Her throat became tight, but she willed herself not to lose control. If she was to be banished, flogged, or killed, Nia would submit with whatever dignity she possessed.

"My liege," Nico was saying, "Accept my humble welcome to prince Saeran and my deepest commendation for the aid you both have rendered to our Lyrian neighbors."

"We thank you," the king said formally. There was a pause in which Nia held her breath. When next he spoke, the king sounded hesitant.

"What news have you, Nico?"

"Most honored great king," Nico started. It was almost time. They had practiced this endlessly in the past week. Nia knew she had to do this, but it frightened her. What if the king refused Nico's choice?

Oblivious to her rising panic, her mentor continued speaking, his voice strained, but strong. "All things come to an end, but with each end there is a new beginning. I have served your family for many years, and it has been the honor of my life to stand guard over Wilderheim and its kings. But I fear I can no longer, in good conscience, uphold my oath to you, nor swear another to your successor. I am old, my body weak. The time has come for me to retire from your service. Tonight I bring before you the one whom I have chosen to take my place and perform my duties from now on. I present to you my apprentice."

Those were the words. Nia took a breath and stood, taking the two steps that would bring her to Nico's left. Her entire body shivered as she raised her chin and looked up. She made certain her eyes revealed nothing of her apprehension.

A low hum went through the crowd, but the king waved his hand and all fell silent at once. He studied Nia for a moment and then transferred his gaze to his aged wizard. "A woman," he said with a note of question in his tone. "This is the one you would have replace you, Nico?"

Nico half nodded, half bowed in answer. "She is, my liege. Nia is in every way equal to the task and will serve you as faithfully as I have."

A spark jumped from one of the torches behind the king. It floated like a feather through the air, and as it did, Nia noticed it had a shape: long, pointed ears, crackling wings, and long insect-like arms and legs. The spark perched on Saeran's shoulder and gazed at his profile for a moment before it whispered something in his ear. Nia didn't hear what it said, she doubted anyone but Nico noticed. Saeran himself showed no sign of being aware of the creature.

More of them separated from the torch flames, circling King Manfred's head.

"You are certain of this?" Manfred asked.

The sparks crackled as if in argument with each other and then, before Nico could say a word, Saeran spoke up. "Father," he said, rising from his seat to join the king. As he did, the sparks flared and burned out. Nothing remained of them, not even ash. "You know Nico's judgment to be beyond reproach. Has he not proven that countless times over the years? In your service, and your father's, and his father's before that?"

Manfred grunted his reply, eyeing Nico with something very close to reproach.

Saeran took the noise as agreement and said, "Then why do you question his decision now?" There was no disrespect in his tone, only mild curiosity and perhaps a little mischief.

The king turned to him, an imposing, though aged figure. "You have known the wizard all your life. Do not let friendship cloud your judgment in this, son. The apprentice will serve you in the future. It will be your choices she will guide."

Saeran nodded. "I understand, Father. That is precisely what compels me to speak. Should not I be the one to approve or disapprove of Nico's choice?"

Whatever secret message those words contained, they did not please the king. Nia could see him weighing a difficult decision in his mind as he studied his son, and she knew just what he was thinking. Saeran had been a boy when he left, but he'd returned a man. As much as Manfred wanted to treat him as his son, he had to show him the same respect he would expect from everyone in the kingdom. If he humiliated Saeran now by taking away a choice that was rightfully his, it would look as if his own father had no faith in his ability to lead, and Saeran would spend his entire rule defending his claim to the throne of Wilderheim.

If the smile Saeran was biting back was anything to judge by, the prince knew quite well that he'd left his father no choice but to agree.

Manfred's mouth quirked, but he schooled his features, appearing to contemplate the situation. "I am not sure you are ready for such a choice," he said, eyeing Nia. She dropped her gaze just enough to not look into his eyes. "It's one thing to turn away a raging army of marauders, but quite another to resist the charms of a beautiful woman."

The assembly chuckled, making Nia blush. But when she dared a glance at Saeran she saw that he did not appreciate his father's insinuations. His handsome features became hard as stone, but he tempered his voice when he said, "Though I am young, I would think I have acquired enough sense by now to hear words of wisdom, no matter who speaks them. We look to our fathers to make us strong, but we have our mothers to make us wise. No woman should have to use her charms simply to make herself heard. And having grown up without a mother, I would be a fool to turn away a woman's counsel now."

There was silence after his speech. Saeran's mother died not long after his birth, and some said the king never recovered from the loss. He never took another woman to wife, and he cleaved to his son all the more because Saeran was all he had left of the woman he loved. It was the reason why Manfred lashed out against Nico with such vicious anger for sending his only son away, to his death for all he knew.

Everyone in the great hall knew the story and their pity for both king and his son was a palpable thing. But as Nia looked around at the Others hiding among Manfred's court, she saw something else. Pride. Acceptance.

At last, the king sighed. "Very well, Saeran. Since it is your choice to be made, let it be thus: The apprentice shall be yours to accept or not. Should you accept her, she will speak her oath to you, not me, and you alone shall live with your decision from this moment on."

Another hum went through the crowd, and Nia glanced nervously at Nico.

He remained calm, nodding his own acceptance of the king's decree and bowed to the prince. "I present to you, then, Prince Saeran, my apprentice, Nia."

Nia prepared herself for the harsh words she knew she deserved.

Saeran, however, merely looked at her for a moment, his lips tight as if he was trying not to smile. Then he spoke. "A man would be either witless or a toad to disregard the wisdom of his elders. Since I am neither witless, nor a toad"—he winked at Nia—"I receive your apprentice, Nico, with full confidence in both you and her."

Nia almost fainted.

"Come forth, Nia, and make your pledge."

Her tongue darted out to moisten her dry lips. She glanced at Nico as she came forward, kneeling on the first step of the dais.

"No," the prince said suddenly and her heart sank. But he continued speaking in a milder voice. "Rise," he told her. "I would have you say the words to my face, not to my feet."

Terrified, Nia's mind raced in all directions, blanketing the great hall and bringing back thoughts she ought not hear. She felt the shock of everyone there. She felt Nico's pride in her and Saeran like the warmth of sunshine, and Saeran's solemn dignity as he stood before her, waiting for her to rise and speak.

She felt the king stand from his seat, but he stopped himself from interfering. There was admiration in his mind as he stood witness to the ceremony. He even glanced at Nico, wondering if the wizard thought him a lesser man than his son, for he had adhered to tradition when Nico had given his pledge. An old man already, Nico had struggled to rise once he'd knelt.

Nia took a breath as she rose to her feet, pulling back inside herself. She searched for the words and spoke them with all the confidence she could find. "I swear my life to your service, my liege," she said. "My wisdom and magic are yours. I swear to advise you as best I can, for the good of the king and kingdom. I swear to defend your life with my own and serve you faithfully for as long as need be, until death or longer."

Saeran nodded acceptance. "I honor an oath with another," he said. "Truth for truth, loyalty for loyalty, sword for spell. From this day forth, your place shall be at my side, as my right hand. Until death or longer." Then, though the ceremony was almost over, all the necessary words spoken, he added, "And you shall kneel to no one more."

He grasped her shoulders, as was custom, and sealed the pledge with a kiss on each of her cheeks. "I thought you'd have me beheaded," she whispered at the first kiss.

"Ribbit," he replied at the second.

Once he stepped back, Nico approached and turned her to face him. "I have raised a magnificent wizard," he said, affection shining in his eyes. "No father could hope for a better daughter. Nor wizard a better apprentice." He pressed a kiss to her forehead and then moved his hands in the air between them, conjuring a robe. When it came into being, it floated in the air, billowing on an invisible current of magic. He settled it over her shoulders, closing the clasp at her throat. "I shall miss you, child," Nico whispered and then released her. "Now go take your place."

She nodded and woodenly walked up the stairs to stand behind the prince's seat. From there, she watched Nico bow once more to the king and prince and walk away. As he retreated to the great door, Nia balled her hands into fists, refusing to let the tears fall. She would not cry out, or run after him. This was the way it had to be.

As the door closed behind Nico, the Others disappeared and Nia's hands slowly uncurled. Who would take care of him now? Who would support him over the icy patches? Who would warm water for him to soak his feet? Who would make his tea?

For the rest of the night, Nia was not alive. She watched the banquet with vacant eyes, listened with deaf ears as the musicians played, and the king and his son conversed. She nodded when she ought, spoke when it was required, yet in her heart, she searched for Nico.

He was gone.

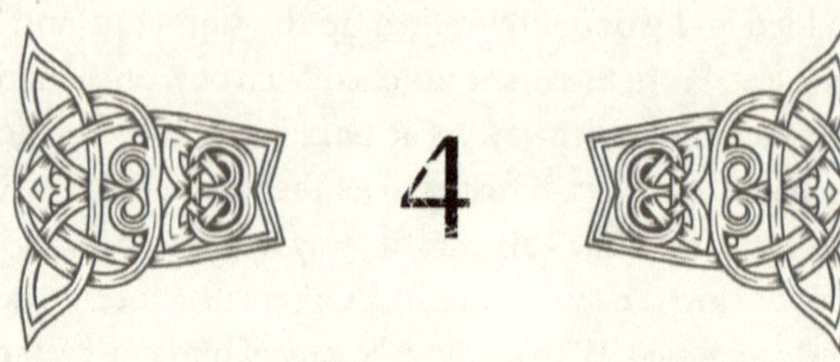

The next day King Manfred announced he would be stepping down and relinquishing rule of Wilderheim to his son.

The news was unexpected, and Manfred, with Saeran and Nia at his side, spent the day assuring the nobles that Saeran was, indeed, ready and worthy of taking the throne.

"But he is just a boy!"

"Barely a score of years to his name!"

While the king tried as he might to tell them all again about his son's great deeds and Saeran vowed all those things kings always vowed, Nia wanted to make herself deaf to escape all the noise, which kept getting worse the longer they talked. No platitudes would ever be enough to appease these people because their outrage had nothing to do with Saeran's age or Manfred's wishes. With Saeran just returned, they hadn't had time to assure themselves of his favors. And they would do all they could to stall until those favors could be secured as Manfred's had been when he'd taken the throne upon his father's death. And with each moment the king tolerated their insolence, the nobles grew bolder, louder and even more insolent.

When she couldn't stand it any longer, Nia strode forward. "Quiet," she said, and all the noise stopped. The nobles still bickered, but nothing came out of their mouths.

"Thank the gods." Saeran sighed, not realizing everyone could still hear him.

Manfred was not amused. He glowered at both Nia and Saeran. "These are your people," he said. "Will you ignore them this easily when you take the throne?"

"No," Saeran replied. "But neither will I condone rebellious drivel that serves no purpose other than to fill the hall with noise. I am your son and heir. No one should be questioning my claim to the throne. Has such blatant bait to treason become accepted among your court since I last sat by your side?"

Nia smiled, watching the nobles' mouths stop moving. "Well, they heard that last part, if nothing else," she told the king and his son. "And as words go, it seems those were the only ones truly necessary." Nia returned to her place behind Saeran and took apart her spell. When the two royals only stared at her, she nudged her chin to urge them to face their people. "They're waiting."

Saeran raised an eyebrow at his father, grinning smugly.

Manfred harrumphed and, keeping his laugh in check, Saeran faced the nobles.

He didn't need to say another word. One after the other, they all dropped to one knee before him.

The following weeks passed with excruciating slowness as the preparations began for Prince Saeran's coronation. King Manfred wanted everyone worth noting to attend the celebration. It was to take place in the spring, when the snow thawed and the roads were safe to travel.

Nia went through the motions, spoke when spoken to, but her mind was elsewhere. She missed Nico terribly. The study seemed so empty without him there. The servants had moved her belongings to his old chambers, one floor beneath the royal bedchambers, but Nia refused to sleep there. What if he came back one day? In her heart she knew he was gone, but magical things happened every day. Nico could find his youth again, and when he returned, he would need his own bed.

But no one had seen the wizard since he'd walked out of the great hall. Worried for his well being, the king had sent messengers in all directions, looking for him. He'd meant to reward Nico for all his years in the king's service and never got the chance. If Nico was still alive, he was hiding somehow, from everyone including Nia because even scrying for him proved useless.

She had little time to stare into water with the coronation keeping her occupied. While the prince prepared with his father and all those in charge of orchestrating the celebration, Nia met with guards and cooks, maids and servants, everyone who had a function to perform in the castle. She spoke with them at length, learning about them and their trades. She enjoyed the conversations for the simple reason that she missed having someone to talk to.

They seemed to like her well enough. After she helped the butcher's sick daughter and resolved a dispute between the milliner and baker, showing her willingness to aid commoners and merchants as well as nobles and kings, the townspeople embraced her as one of their own. And the more time she spent with them, the more at ease she began to feel. While she was in town, trading stories and jests, she didn't have to be anyone but who she was. The Others didn't show themselves anymore and soon she forgot there was more to being a wizard than standing by the king's side all day long.

As winter continued, Nia acquired more work. There were more oaths and rituals to learn. As the royal wizard, she would be the one to place the crown on Prince Saeran's head. It was a great honor, usually bestowed upon someone much older, but she wasn't worried. The only one with the power to dismiss her now was the prince, but instead he seemed to have already gotten into the habit of asking her thoughts even after he'd spoken to his advisory council.

One day, when a great winter storm blew in, keeping everyone in their houses and in front of their hearths, Saeran summoned her to the meeting room. "I want to see my kingdom," he said.

"I am sure after the coronation there will be a procession planned—"

"No, Nia. I have been gone for ten years. I want to see what's become of Wilderheim. I need you to show me what the others won't say."

Nia bowed. "As you wish." She knew of only one way to show him what he wanted to see. Closing her eyes, she drew on her magic and started writing in the air. The runes etched in light floated in a circle between them until she drew the last. Then the circle solidified and in its center an image took shape.

Saeran came closer, gazing at the castle as if from a great height. "This here, what is it? I don't remember it being there before."

"It's an armory, Highness. Your father commissioned enough weapons to arm several battalions should they be needed. He also reinforced Castle Frastmir's defenses. Here, here, and here, you see? That is for oil. The channels run through the walls to pour out around the perimeter."

"He expected me to fail."

"At first, perhaps. You were only a child, Highness. No one expected you to take command as you did, let alone lead Lyria to victory."

His eyes darkened at the memory. "Halden couldn't do it. Have you ever been to Lyria, Nia?"

"No, Highness."

"It's beautiful. The entire kingdom is a work of art. People journey there from all over the world. They have the greatest masters of music, art and poetry. It's a place of peace and knowledge, meant to be open to those who seek it. They didn't stand a chance against Aegiros. Halden is a great king, but he's no warrior. All he knew to do was close the gates, and I thank the gods he had at least that much presence of mind."

"Why didn't the guard take command? Why did you?"

"Halden's queen was expecting their first child, and he was not about to leave her side for even a moment. With them unable to do anything, I was next in line. My father forced the issue when he gave his order. Three thousand Wilderheim soldiers came to aid Lyria because of me, but only on the condition that they follow no one's orders but mine under the threat of death to their families. He never meant for me to lead them. He only wanted to make sure no one would use me to bring down a kingdom—his or Halden's. The soldiers were to protect me even at the cost of their lives. Many of them did.

"I would not have survived without them. They were the ones drawing up battle plans and leading the troops. Until the Aegirans were turned back, all I did was learn from them, issue the orders they themselves came up with, and watch them die carrying them out."

"It must have been terrible."

"Yes," he said at length. "It was. Can you show me our borders?"

Nia turned back to her window spell and altered the view. For the rest of the day and half the night, she showed Saeran his kingdom and told him everything that happened and changed since he left. The prince proved to be an attentive student, genuinely curious about everything and concerned with the welfare of his people. While he made sure Wilderheim was properly guarded and defended, he also asked about the crops, the forests and game, the merchants and their trade routes.

When she told him the roads had been neglected, he took a quill and parchment and began writing down what needed to be done. Widerheim didn't have a mountain of gold and jewels in its coffers, but it had skilled stone masons and a young wizard willing to lend her magic to the task.

By the time she finished explaining about the cycles of flood and drought along one of the major rivers, Nia was exhausted and Saeran looked to be no better. The candles had almost burned down. They'd go out soon, leaving only the hearth fire to light the chamber.

"Nia," Saeran said.

"Hmm?"

He smiled at her, and she noticed the window spell had quietly dissolved, leaving individual symbols floating through the air between them. She must have dozed off. "It's late," the prince said. "You should get some sleep."

She nodded and rose from her seat, wincing at the pins and needles assaulting her legs. "Good night, Highness."

"Good morning, Nia."

~

Saeran sat irreverently across a chair, only half listening as the master of ceremonies explained the coronation rituals for the hundredth time. He gazed out the window which overlooked the courtyard. This far up, he could scarcely see its edge, but instead he saw over the castle wall. The fields stretched in that direction, all of them covered with snow. The sky was dark with heavy clouds. One storm may have passed but another was brewing in the distance. It wouldn't be long before it reached them.

He shouldn't be here. These meetings served no purpose other than make him restless. The council never discussed anything of import. All they did was give him lists to approve. Supply lists, food lists, lists of entertainers, lists of dignitaries, and lists of complaints. All centered around the coronation. Why couldn't he simply take the crown now and move on? Why did everything have to have celebrations and feasts and revelries attached to it? A celebration for his return. One for his coronation. Another for his father, in remembrance of his reign. When did it end?

When was he supposed to do his duties as king? Or was this what his father had done all these years behind closed door? No, he wouldn't believe that.

Saeran had yet to set a foot outside. If not for Nia, he would have no inkling of what Wilderheim truly looked like. He was slowly going mad trapped in here. His entire body hummed with the need to do something. Roll around in the snow like a child or ride for hours on end.

"Your Highness? Your Highness."

Saeran looked at the master askance. There was a map of the castle on the table and several little flags dotted it. This meeting was to plan where the guests would be housed. Celebrations of this magnitude sometimes lasted a month, perhaps more. It would not do to place a crown prince next to an impoverished noble. The prince looked over the map and then back up at the master.

The man attempted a brittle smile, his voice tense with strained patience. "Would you care to finish the thought?"

The thought. What had he been talking about? There were so many thoughts and sayings the master fancied. Sometimes he had entire speeches composed of proverbs. He could have been talking about any number of them, one more useless than the other, but he stood on the ceremony of uttering them because it seemed to be his purpose in this room.

Saeran dropped his feet to the floor, straightening in his seat to stall for time.

"I am sure he would," the king's voice intruded on the tense silence, "if he had any idea what the beginning was." He stood in the doorway, his eyes bright with amusement.

The master bowed so low his forehead almost touched his knees. "Your Majesty, what an unexpected surprise."

King Manfred smiled. "Enough for today I think, Master Samson. We would not want the prince's head to explode. Where would he wear the crown?"

Saeran almost jumped out of his seat. He tensed in anticipation, ready to kiss his father for freeing him from the clutches of this goblin. Yet he waited for his father's words. He was not free to leave until the king said so. At least that was how it should have been. In truth, the king indulged his son perhaps a little too much.

"Oh, but your Majesty!" Samson sputtered, his rounded cheeks turning red. He was one of the more well-fed masters, those the king retained out of deference to their long service. As soon as the crown was his, Saeran would compensate them handsomely for their service and send them on their way. It was time for fresher minds. "There is still so much to review," he was saying, but the king waved his words aside.

"Later," he said with royal finality.

Master Samson bowed. "As you command, my liege," he muttered and made his exit as if the king had delivered a great affront. Or perhaps it was Saeran who'd done that.

He rose from his seat, heaving a great sigh of relief. "I will never be able to thank you enough, Father."

The king chuckled. "I remember my days before I got my crown. I thought perhaps you might need some help."

Saeran grinned sheepishly. "You were not wrong."

"Off with you, then. Go do something I would not approve of. And if anyone tries to stop you, tell them you are the king's heir."

Saeran was out the door almost before he'd finished speaking. Shaking his head, Manfred took the seat his son had left and gazed at the castle's map. Things were progressing even better than he had expected. His brother had not lied to him about Saeran. The boy had a gift for making people love him, a gift a king could not do without. He was more than able to rule this kingdom, and already he had little need for a father's advice.

Though Manfred still had doubts about the new wizard, he'd seen her shoulder her duties with as much dedication as Saeran carried his. Nico had trusted her, and she was already proving worthy of Manfred's trust. Saeran was well met by her.

Ah, he missed his old friend now. All his messengers have returned empty handed. There was no trace of the wizard since the day he'd presented his apprentice. It seemed as if Nico had disappeared into thin air.

Manfred couldn't say he begrudged Nico his peace. Not after the way he'd treated him these past few years. He only hoped Nico would forgive him a father's devotion. It seemed to Manfred that the wizard's final decision had been as wise as his very first, and each one in between. Nico had trained a successor and trusted her enough that he had not stayed to oversee her conduct or meddle in her decisions.

Now Manfred would have to do the same. Saeran was a clever, eager boy, a king already before the crown was even his, but each time he made a decision on Manfred's behalf, he looked to his father for confirmation and support. He had all the makings of a great leader, but he also had love and respect for his father. Manfred worried that as long as he was by Saeran's side, his son would spend his days looking over his shoulder for approval.

If he wanted Saeran to thrive, and Wilderheim to accept him, Manfred could not remain a shadow over his son's reign.

Perhaps it was time for him to pay a visit to his brother, one long overdue. Ten years, in fact. Ten years in which Halden had weathered a war, fathered three children and good as raised Manfred's own. Now that Saeran was here to sit the throne, Manfred was free to see for himself how Halden was faring. They had much to talk about.

After the coronation, he would make the arrangements. He might not disappear as completely as Nico had, but he would give his son the chance to show what he is capable of.

Nia watched with apprehension as three servants scaled up a tall ladder to hang a banner above the archway. They were arguing and gesturing wildly, the one on the bottom jumping up and down, throwing the ladder off balance. Not one of them seemed to notice what they were doing. It would only be a matter of time before the ladder tipped away from the wall.

She moved closer, preparing to stop them from falling such a distance, should it be needed. Opening and closing her hands, she waited, watching the top of the ladder as it shuddered and shifted ominously.

"Good morning."

Nia jumped and turned, almost butting her head against Saeran's. The prince smiled, his gray eyes twinkling in his handsome face, a lock of dark blond hair falling over his forehead. "Good morning, Highness," she replied. "I thought you were meeting with the masters."

He flashed a quick grin. "Come with me." Without waiting for an answer, he turned and walked away.

"I…" she started, glancing at the ladder. The prince took precedence. Sighing, she turned to follow him and winced as she heard the servants give a shout and crash to the ground behind her. Nia shook her head and hurried to catch up with him. "Where are we going?"

Saeran stopped inside the stables, looking around in indecision. "You there," he pointed to one of the hostlers, "saddle two horses. I and the royal wizard are going for a ride."

Nia glared at him. "His name is Micah," she scolded as the man scrambled to obey.

Color stained the prince's cheeks. "Forgive me," he said. "I have not yet learned everyone's names. Many of them are new to me."

When the hostler led two readied horses to them, Saeran nodded and gave him a coin. "Thank you, Micah. You do fast work. That is always appreciated."

Micah's eyes grew wide at the praise, and he bowed away at once.

"Now then," Saeran said, swinging up into the saddle with ease. "Shall we?"

Nia swallowed hard and cautiously approached the huge gray stallion. "Hello," she said with a tentative smile. "I am Nia. Please don't throw me off."

The animal snorted a laugh. *Nico has neglected his duties to you, child.*

Nia's smile turned sad. "He did the best he could."

"What was that?"

"Nothing, Highness."

"Mount up, then," he urged. "I intend for this to be a long ride."

The stallion snickered. *You will come to despise chairs. Hop up then. No good to keep the princeling waiting.*

Nia did as she was told, following the horse's directions to mount. She'd seen others do it many a time, but it was a different matter to have to do it herself. It only took her three tries to find her seat. Nia was proud of herself.

Hold on now, he said at the same time as Saeran shouted, "Let's go!"

The first jolt would have had her flying through the air, had her mount, Satardust was his name, not kicked out with his hind legs to set her upright once more. Before she could even draw a full breath, they were out in the open, galloping across the frozen fields.

Hold on with your legs and lean forward, Stardust advised. *See how the princeling rides?*

Nia took a chance and looked to her left. Saeran rode beside her, moving in rhythm with his mount's gallop. Nia mirrored his pose, grinning as the new position gave her much more balance and control.

They rode for a long time until the wind chill made Nia's face go numb, and her legs became so sore she didn't know how much longer she could keep her seat. When the castle was so far in the distance they could barely see it and they approached the forest's edge, Saeran slowed their pace and then stopped to catch his breath. His eyes were feverish, his face alight.

He dismounted at once, lifting his face to the sky. "This kingship will be the death of me," he muttered.

Nia grinned and swung her leg over to dismount as well.

Careful, Stardust urged, but it was too late. Her knee buckled and she yelped, tumbling to the ground. With her foot still caught in the stirrup, she gazed up at Stardust with her mouth hanging open. "That hurt!"

Saeran peeked at her from behind her mount. "Nia?" He came to her and freed her foot from the stirrup, holding his hand out to help her up. When her legs still refused to support her, he laughed and slid an arm beneath her shoulders to brace her against his side. "You should have told me you do not ride."

"Your Highness?"

"Yes?"

"I am afraid I don't ride."

"Thank you for telling me. Perhaps I should have a carriage prepared instead."

She returned his easy smile with an awkward one of her own. Her rump felt numb and her legs were wobbly. As mortifying as it was to be so helpless, it was made a thousand times worse by Saeran's helping her. But though she could have restored her sapping strength in moments, she didn't. It didn't occur to her while Saeran had his arm around her and was smiling the way he was. Nia forgot she was a wizard, and his vassal. For that small moment in time, she was nothing more than Nia.

Stardust suddenly tossed his head with a snort and paced sideways right into them. The other stallion backed away from the forest's edge, both animals' eyes wide. Saeran frowned. "What in Thor's name…"

He ascertained her balance before he released her. Grasping onto his mount's reins, he settled the beast with a soft touch and then drew his long dagger, returning to Nia. "Handsome does not spook easily," he told her. "There is something there."

Fangs, Handsome said, *and claws.*

"It's an animal," Nia translated, taking a couple of uncertain steps toward the trees. "Put that away."

"What are you doing?" Saeran hissed. "Get back here. Get behind me."

She looked over her shoulder at him. "Behind you?" she repeated, puzzled. "I am supposed to protect you, Highness."

"Nia, stop," he said.

She didn't listen. Not even when something rustled a short distance off. The prince swore and came to her instead. Nia could feel him at her back, his blade shining next to her. She put her hand over his on the handle and made him lower it.

Neither of them wore gloves and the touch of her warm hand on his cold one jolted Saeran. He didn't know what to do first. The horses needed calming before they panicked and trampled them to death, or ran off and left them here. It would take a day to get back to the castle on foot. The snow came up to Saeran's knee in the shallow parts.

But he couldn't leave Nia unprotected. She had no armor or weapons, and when she lowered to her knees in the snow, he was certain she'd lost her mind. "What are you doing?" he demanded. Brandishing his dagger, wishing he'd taken his sword instead, he waited for the beast to appear.

"Come forward, brother," Nia called out. "You will not be harmed."

"Must you?" Saeran growled at her.

"I must," she returned, her gaze never leaving the trees.

A massive gray wolf stumbled out of the shadows, easily half the size of a draft horse. No wonder the animals panicked. Handsome reared and Saeran had to duck to escape his hooves. He expected to be trampled, but then Stardust slammed into Handsome from the side, somehow subduing the mount and moving him out of the way at the same time.

Saeran didn't know what was going on, but he turned his attention back to the bigger threat. The one with a maw large enough to crush a man's skull in a single bite.

But something was wrong. The wolf was licking his snout again and again, his legs stumbling over each other. If Saeran didn't know better he'd say the beast was drunk. He moved forward raising his blade. "Get back, Nia."

"Put that away," she told him again, never taking her eyes off the wolf. "He couldn't harm us if he wanted to."

As if to agree with her, the beast whined, almost falling over with the next step. Nia held out her hands in a sort of welcome, and to Saeran's utter shock the wolf came to her, ears flat. The beast sat down as soon as he was within reach, shivering and huffing as the whines continued.

"Tell me what ails you, brother," Nia said, and if he hadn't seen it with his own eyes Saeran never would have believed. The wolf was weeping.

At a loss for words, he lowered his blade and watched as woman and beast stared at each other. The wolf licked his snout and shivered, and his front legs were bowed as if he could barely support himself.

Nia sucked in a sharp breath. "Will you allow me to look into your mind?" she asked.

Another soft whine.

Nia placed her hands on either side of the wolf's head and looked into his eyes. "He has been poisoned," she said for Saeran's benefit. "He ate from a carcass left in the woods. It's…killing him. I can't…I…" Nia released the wolf and circled her arms around him for a moment. "I am sorry, brother. Will you let me take your pain away?"

The wolf lied down with his head in Nia's lap, one of his paws reaching for her hand. Tears in her eyes, Nia grasped his paw and placed her other hand over his eyes. "Sleep," she whispered. "I will see to it your pack does not suffer as you have. Be at peace."

The great beast closed his eyes with a sigh and Saeran watched his chest rise and fall while Nia stroked his fur. It didn't take long. Within moments the wolf became still, expiring quietly beneath the wizard's touch.

For a while, Nia sat there, cradling his head, as her tears slid down her cheeks. She mourned him as she would a true brother. Saeran was amazed at her compassion. Kneeling in the snow beside her, he touched her shoulder.

As if awakened from a dream, she looked at him with fire burning in her blue eyes and said, "Huntsmen did this."

She brushed off his touch and moved the wolf off her lap, pushing to her feet.

All at once, the sky became dark with storm clouds. Thunder rolled in the distance as she walked into the woods, and Saeran pushed to his feet to follow.

"Nia!" he called after her. Anger trailed in her wake, so thick it choked him. A terrible wind picked up, lashing at her robes, but the branches that hindered Saeran's progress bent out of her way to allow her passage. Within moments they reached a clearing. By then the sun was gone and the forest was pitch black, yet somehow he could still see her. She almost glowed in the darkness, drawing his eye, his only guiding star in the unnatural night.

Nia reached her hands to the sky and lifted her face to it. Saeran felt magic wind around her like a cloak, twisting around her arms. She spoke a series of words, reached higher.

When the rustling started anew, Saeran raised his blade. They were surrounded by the sound of it, and there were too many to fight by himself. "Nia," he tried again, but she didn't answer.

To his left something exploded out of the bushes. Saeran turned, dagger at the ready, but what landed at his feet was a piece of meat. Dozens more came flying out, all of them piling together around them.

When the last of the carcasses fell, Nia lowered her arms and faced him, her eyes sparking with terrible light. "Your huntsmen did this," she told him, furious red lights flashing around her. "They were all around, in every corner of the wood. Just tossed on the ground for any beast to feed on and die." She gritted her teeth as tears slid down her cheeks. "The poison tore through their bodies and it took days."

Rage simmered in his veins. He saw from Nia's reaction that she could see it in his eyes. "Show me," he said tightly.

Nia weaved her hand through the air between them, drawing on the red light and pulling it in. Mist following her movements until it formed a circle. She said a word of command to make it glow like a torch and in its depths images took shape. Four huntsmen argued in the woods. Saeran knew them. They'd brought in a great boar only yesterday, boasting of the hunt's thrill. Telling him he'd have loved it. In the vision their words were drowned in silence, but their meaning was clear. They had just evaded a pack of wolves. The forest was full of them; they could not step foot past the creek without hearing their howls. But hunting them was forbidden unless they attacked livestock, and that had not happened in too many years to count. For the safety of Frastmir and its inhabitants, they proclaimed loftily, something had to be done.

If there were fewer wolves, they mused, there would be more game for them to hunt, more mouths to be fed with such bounty. In truth, they thought only of the people. But disobeying the order to spare the beasts was punishable by a lashing and imprisonment. Two of them had wives and children to feed, one was courting a shopkeeper's daughter, and the last was quite sought after by the tavern wenches. None of them could chance being caught.

They looked from one to the other, each weighing his comrades and all alighting on the same idea at once.

All it took was a wild boar or two, a vial of poison, and a sad shake of the head when the palace guards asked after the day's trophies. No one had to know.

With a swirl of black smoke, the vision changed and Saeran found himself in the castle, looking at the huntsmen's drunken faces. Their beards were greasy with food and their hands filled with meat. One took a bite from a succulent pig's leg and threw the rest to the dogs. They fought over it viciously, tearing into each other as much as the meat, and the huntsmen laughed, entertained by this. "Enough," Saeran ground out, unable to watch anymore. "I've seen enough."

The images faded back into mist and then disappeared. As they did, the carcasses all around him burst into flames. The smoke they emitted reeked of pain and death as the poison burned off. That was Nia's doing. She was a distance off, staring into the dark forest, her back to him. The lights were gone, her magic darkened once again.

"They will pay for this," he said, joining her on the other side of the pyre. She wouldn't face him.

"There are still others out there," she said weakly. "Many more, and all suffering the same." Her hands were clenched at her sides and somehow he knew she'd felt the wolf's pain. Just as she felt the pain of the others now.

"Can you help them?"

Nia shook her head and he could see it break her heart to say the words. "Not from this far away. They are too weak to come to me and it would take too long to find them." She swayed on her feet and Saeran caught her, sitting down in the snow with her. "Nico would have known what to do," she sobbed.

Saeran pulled her closer, but though she allowed the touch, she didn't lean on him. "I swear to you I will see them hanged."

When the fires died down, Nia stood, wiping her sleeve across her wet face. "We have to go back," She said, pushing to her feet. "We'll freeze out here." She waited for him to stand and then turned in the direction they had to walk in.

"Wait," Saeran said. He went to a raspberry bush and ducked under it, pulling out a large piece of wood. "I saw this earlier," he told her, handing it to her. It was curiously even from one end to a large, twisted knot at the other. "You'll need it. Even Nico had one."

Nia curled her fingers around the wood and tested its balance. It fit into her hand. Saeran couldn't see any obvious weaknesses; it would be sturdy enough to lean her weight on and with some work, a fine staff, indeed. "Thank you, Highness," she said, managing a small smile.

They returned to the castle in silence, and said not a word to anyone about what they had seen, but Saeran knew something needed to be done. And when he met her gaze in front of the great hall, a moment before going his own way and leaving her to hers, seeing the pain still there, he knew he would be the one to do it.

6

Nia would not leave her chambers again until the day of the coronation. It was not by choice. The spell she'd worked that night drained her so completely that when she returned to the castle, the staff proved to be invaluable. It would take some time for her to recover both physically and magically.

What happened outside her study doors, however, did not escape her. Nia could feel the walls shiver with whispers. Rumors of things she would not have believed—had she not expected them.

The walls gossiped to her of the prince. How he'd marched through the castle courtyard, bearing a heavy beast in his arms, a small group of guards following close behind. How he'd kicked down the door on the huntsmen's cottage, tossed the furry heap at their feet and demanded, "Is this your work?"

How the huntsmen had stared in fright at the prince's countenance, unsure of which answer would bring his wrath down upon their heads. Ah, but the prince needed no answer, for he knew it already.

The walls described how he made the four men tie each other's hands and lead each other outside the castle. And then it was the earth itself who whispered to her of Saeran's angry words. "Were I to be fair, I would give you that selfsame poison to drink and watch you writhe in pain. And you would drink it again, for each animal that died from it, shaking in agony."

The huntsmen, the earth told her, shuddered and fell to their knees begging for mercy, but the prince had none to spare them, for he knew they'd had none for the beasts.

And so, a great oak groaned, the four huntsmen were hanged from his branches, dancing in the wind.

Such was the prince's justice.

But then the breeze slipped through a crack into her study, hissing a secret in her ears. For as the prince had stood before the men preparing to be hung, as he'd watched them weep and pray, he'd whispered it to the winds: "For Nia."

"Enough," Nia told the walls, the earth, and the breeze. "No more rumors. No more death or secrets." And she closed her eyes, willing herself not to dream when sleep claimed her.

Dreams found her anyway, childish memories grown into a nightmare to haunt her day and night. She sat in her tree, telling it all her woes. Eirwen was being cruel again. She'd heard a merchant caravan passing not far from their cottage and Nia wanted so desperately to see them, but Eirwen refused to let her. It was too dangerous, she said. They had no business with those people, she said.

But she could hide, Nia argued. They wouldn't even know she was there!

Eirwen would hear none of it. One day Nia would understand. Eirwen had promised she would keep Nia safe.

In her anger, Nia screamed at the old woman, ugly words she'd never meant to say and, ashamed of herself, she ran here. But then it got dark, too dangerous to walk through the forest on her own. Instead, Nia fell asleep in that tree and dreamed of singing. She sang to a river and its waters rose up to her, tendrils of it caressing her cheek like a mother's touch. Then more of it rose, reaching to her, cradling her, answering her voice with a melody of its own. A song of home to drown out Eirwen's cry...

Nia started awake, then again when she saw Saeran right next to her.

She sat up on her pallet. "Your Highness!"

"Wizard," he replied. "Why do you sleep under the castle when there are dozens of much nicer places you could rest your head?" He looked around the dark room. He wouldn't see more than shadow, the large table and the overflowing bookshelves behind the archway. No point wasting candlelight when all she did was sleep.

Nia struggled off the pallet, her legs unsteady. She was fully dressed but felt raw and exposed with Saeran watching her. No one but she and Nico ever stepped foot in the underground study. "What are you doing here?"

Saeran caught her elbows to steady her as he led her to sit at the table. He was smiling, and she couldn't fathom what might have amused him. "Calm yourself," he said, "I am the prince, remember? I can go wherever I please."

Nia sparked the torches with a thought and a small burst of magic. They flared to life, filling the chamber with light until she could see him clearly. He looked worn, tired. His clothes were disheveled as if he'd slept in them, and though he smiled, it was a weary smile.

"What princely business brings you to my private study?" she asked, glancing at the pitcher of water some distance away. She was so thirsty her lips stuck together, but the pitcher was too far. If she tried to call to it with her magic still so weak, it would fall and shatter halfway to the table.

"At first," the prince said, following her gaze, "I looked for you in Nico's old chambers." He left her to retrieve the pitcher and poured her a goblet of water. "But it looked as if no one had stepped foot in it in months. Then…" He handed her the goblet and resumed his seat. "I inquired among the maids where the wizard was housed, and they pointed me to another chamber, across from Nico's. But that one looked the same, so I asked, very politely, where my royal wizard might be found, and they pointed to the ground."

"Hmm." Nia drank from the goblet, feeling her strength return a little more with each sip.

Seeing she would not speak, Saeran grinned. "And so I found my way here to give you something and found you sleeping. I knocked, mind you. And called your name. Several times. You did not move at all, so I came closer to find you were barely breathing. Naturally, I became worried. But you looked so peaceful I was loath to wake you.

Instead I decided to wait for you to awaken on your own."

Nia blushed. It was a wizard's sleep she'd slept, something a body forced on the mind when one's strength was depleted. For a wizard to drain herself of magic completely meant death. To restore herself, Nia needed rest and time. She would not have awakened, even if he'd tried to rouse her. "And how long have you waited?" she asked, dreading his answer.

Saeran shrugged. "Not long. Half a day, perhaps."

Nia choked. "Half a day?"

The prince's good humor faded. His eyes grew serious and his lips compressed into a tight line. "I want you to teach me," he said. "Every spell an incantation you know, I need to learn. What happened with the huntsmen can never happen again. They could have poisoned the streams and killed us all."

She stared at him agog. "You want me to teach you magic?"

Saeran nodded.

"I…I'm not sure I can." Rather, she wasn't sure it was wise to try. True, no one knew what they were capable of until they attempted it. Magic could be found in the oddest places and many went through their entire lives changing the world in subtle ways without being aware of it. But there were also those hungry for power which would forever be denied to them. What if Saeran didn't have any magic in him, no matter how much he wanted it? What if he blamed her?

"You can try," he said.

He was in earnest! Nia shifted in her seat, wincing at the ache in her back. Could she defy a royal order if he gave it? "You mentioned you've brought me something," she said, stalling for time. "It wouldn't by any chance happen to be food, would it?"

Saeran grinned. "Wait here. I will call for a tray."

Nia sighed when he left the study, looking around for guidance. "Nico," she whispered, "what have you gotten me into?" She fancied she could almost hear him laugh at her in gentle mockery.

The prince returned, placing a stack of parchment on the table. "We begin now."

"Wait, I have not said yes."

"I told the runner to bring two trays. I am starving. We can eat here, can we not?" he asked, reaching for the pitcher again to pour himself some water.

"Yes, but I—"

"Yes is spoken. You may begin your instruction." He sat down facing her like an eager school boy, waiting for her to speak.

Nia glared at him. "Very well. We begin."

"Excellent!" Saeran nodded. "What do I do first?"

"You close your mouth and listen."

"What—"

"Shh!"

He quieted.

"Listen until you hear everything. Every movement of the air as you breathe, every beat of your heart, the hum of the candle flame, the chatter of mice…everything."

Saeran shifted to find a more comfortable position and strained his ears to listen. "I hear nothing."

"You are not listening hard enough. Concentrate. It helps if you close your eyes." She closed her own to demonstrate. "Put everything from your mind but the sounds, and listen not only with your ears, but with your heart."

Saeran breathed in deeply and held his breath, counting heartbeats. He could hear them getting louder, but only because they were thrumming in his head now. Expelling the air from his lungs in an explosive sigh, Saeran shook himself and tried again. He drummed his fingers on the table—that he could hear. He tapped his foot. Also a sound his keen ears were able to pick up. Besides that, he heard nothing. "This is boring. When can I work a spell?"

"When you learn to hear what is around you," she said without opening her eyes. "A thing will tell you how it wants to be changed. It will know your intent and help you achieve it. A pitcher will know when you want it to float next to the table instead of sitting on it. It will do as you command. But a flower will not obey a command to grow if it knows your only intent is to pluck it."

There was wisdom in her words. She sat unmoving, composed, but still at ease. Saeran's backside was starting to ache from sitting on the hard chair, yet Nia didn't show any discomfort at all. Her control over herself was astounding.

She knew what to do and was the only one who could teach him. He would have to learn on her terms and trust she would lead him true. Saeran closed his eyes again and quieted his mind. For a long time, nothing happened. He heard nothing but his own breathing, felt nothing but his weight sinking into the chair.

But then it began to change. Slowly, he began feeling lighter, almost floating. His hands felt warm, his head swam. The flicker of torchlight cast shadows on his eyelids, and he followed the movement as if he could see the real flames dancing.

Suddenly he heard them. Two torches, then three, and then all of them. They were singing! Not in the sense of a human voice, but it was a melody nonetheless. They sang in the direction of the book shelves, as if performing for them, and Saeran's awareness floated toward the dark alcove. The scrolls and tomes there whispered. He could hear words so ancient and powerful they sent a chill up his spine, and he knew such knowledge in the wrong hands could destroy with impunity.

Wary of it, Saeran withdrew.

He pictured Nia in his mind, sitting in front of him, regal as any queen, and suddenly he heard her breath as he did his own. He heard her heart beat like a drum to the rhythm of life all around him.

Saeran opened his eyes, amazed when the sounds didn't dull. He saw Nia there, and she was so beautiful it pained him. She hadn't moved, sitting quietly with her eyes closed. Saeran had faced armies, felt warriors' souls leave their bodies and seen peace at last in their dying eyes. He'd met with great kings, masters of every trade, wizards and holy men; sought their knowledge and wisdom. Nia's silence was more profound than anything those men had ever taught him. Her serenity seeped into his bones and made him feel as if no ill or plight could touch him as long as she was there.

He leaned toward her, captivated by this strange, beautiful dream, and reached out to touch her. His fingers brushed through her hair, and the golden strands chimed for him a harmony of countless strings. Nia tensed. But she didn't move. Saeran felt like a master musician, playing the silken strands to yield a melody that shamed the most accomplished bards.

The music all around him grew louder to compliment his movements. He did it again, savoring the sound as clear as crystal, and then he leaned closer still and touched his mouth to hers.

The song quieted. His ears became deaf to everything but the beat of his heart, thumping in perfect unison to hers. He kissed her softly, reverently, and Nia yielded to him with a sigh that shivered through his soul.

In that moment, Saeran sensed everything stop and wished it could stay that way forever. Shrouded in silence, hidden in the depths of time itself, Nia looped her arms around his neck and he pulled her closer still. The table was gone. They floated together in a warm current of air that folded around them like a blanket.

They had no anchor to latch on to except each other. Saeran held Nia so tightly he could feel her heartbeat against his chest, yet it still wasn't enough. He needed more. Her heart set the rhythm of his. Saeran wanted inside her skin, to touch her soul and bind it to his.

Sounds began to intrude. Someone was approaching.

A sharp knock at the door rang out in deafening echoes, jolting Saeran and Nia out of the trance and they fell to the ground several feet apart.

Nia stared at the prince, frozen in shock, unable to look away. Her heart was racing so fast she couldn't catch her breath. Saeran seemed similarly incapacitated. He looked as if he wished to say something, but couldn't find his voice. And neither of them dared to blink.

The knock came again.

"Enter," Saeran managed to say, pushing to his feet. The last contact broken, Nia exhaled at last.

The servant opened the heavy door and entered, stopping just inside, his mouth agape. The table was overturned and the chairs lay in broken heaps against the walls opposite each other. Candlesticks were strewn all over the floor among piles of parchment and scrolls, the tapestries half torn off the walls. It looked as if a storm had raged through the study, catching the prince and his wizard in its path.

"I..." Liam began but never finished. He offered the large tray instead. "Food."

"Thank you," Saeran said, reaching for the goblet at his feet but the pitcher he sought was shattered by the book shelves. "You may set it down on the floor there."

Liam looked concerned. "You Highness, I could send for maids to straighten up—"

"That won't be necessary," Nia said, grateful to have found her voice. She rose and tried her best to smooth her hair back. "Thank you, Liam. That will be all."

Doubtful but obedient, Liam set the tray down, bowed and retreated to the safety of the castle above.

There was silence for long moments after he was gone. Nia didn't trust herself to look at Saeran, but she felt his gaze on her the entire time. The he swallowed hard and said, "Time really stopped. I did not dream it, did I?"

Nia nodded. "Time stopped."

"Was that supposed to happen?"

Nia met his gaze uncertainly. "I don't know," she admitted.

Saeran looked away, searching through the mess on the floor. He retrieved the bundle and came toward her.

Nia shrank away, making him stop in his tracks. "I came to give you this," he said, placing the bundle on what used to be her pallet. "It did not seem right to leave it lying in the woods. I burned the rest." Then he turned on his heels and left, closing the door behind him with a gentle click.

Only when he was gone did Nia move again. She took the bundle and carefully untied the cloth.

Inside was the wolf's pelt.

"Something is bothering you."

Saeran looked away from the window at his father. "What?"

"I said something is bothering you," Manfred repeated. "And before the crown has even touched your head. This does not put my mind at ease about leaving, son."

"Oh. It's nothing, really." He looked back out at the children playing in the wet, melting snow. "Only…time."

"Time?"

"Yes, time. It comes, it goes. Never stops. Have you ever thought about time, Father?"

"I don't believe I have. Time, you say?"

Warming to the subject, Saeran came to the table covered with long sheets of cloth. "Is this the whole of time or only a part of it? Is there an end to time? Where is the beginning? Does it move from past to present, or is it still and we are the ones who move? And what if it stops?" He crumpled the fabric together. "Does anyone else notice?" He looked to his father for an answer. "What do you think?"

"I…"

"Because if all of time stopped, nothing should have moved." He wasn't certain anything had moved. But everything had. There hadn't been a single thing in Nia's study that hadn't shifted, flown, fallen or shattered. How had that happened? The lack of answers maddened him, especially when he couldn't ask the one person who might have the answers.

But would she? Nia had looked just as stunned that day. Then again, a wizard probably encountered stranger things every day. She would have already forgotten about it. No doubt. Put it right out of her mind.

How could she? Time had stopped! Or they had stopped. Or the world had, or…something. He'd kissed other girls before, and that had never happened. And one or two of them had been witches.

"Well, I see you are otherwise engaged. I will leave you to it, then."

And that kiss! What had he been thinking? Why for the love of Freya had he stopped?

He couldn't be thinking this way. It was exactly the sort of thing his father had accused him of being too weak to resist. "When are you set to depart?" he asked Manfred. "Father?"

The king was gone.

Saeran frowned and followed him out into the hall, watching his beloved father hurry away as fast as dignifiedly possible. Shaking his head, Saeran returned to his window.

Spring was coming. Soon all the snow would be gone and everything would be green again. The ceremony was to take place in a fortnight, and the dignitaries from other lands were already on their way. Halden wouldn't be among them. News had reached Frastmir that his youngest child had the fever. Less than a year old, the boy probably hadn't lasted long enough for the message to arrive.

Another reason for Manfred to go to his brother. As soon as Saeran had the crown on his head and the burden of a kingdom on his shoulders, his father would be gone and there would be only him and Nia to look after Wilderheim. People would bow and come to him with their concerns and disputes, expecting him to know what was best and what was needed. He would never again walk through the villages without an escort, and people would forever see him as only a king.

Saeran didn't know why that suddenly seemed like such a bad thing. Everyone wanted to be king, or at the very least noble. He smiled, watching a little girl scoop snow and water into her hand and dump it down the back of a boy's neck. All he'd ever wanted was to be at peace. After so many years of destruction and death, just peace.

Perhaps with Nia at his side, he might finally find it.

~

The ceremony was a short affair. No grand speeches or oaths. It consisted of presenting the new king and Nia's placing the crown upon his head. To make up for the lack, Manfred had commanded a feast to be held afterward in celebration of all good things.

The grand hall was filled to the brim like a giant treasure chest of jewels, and Nia didn't know where to look first. Colors swirled all around her as jugglers, performers, flame breathers, dancers, and guests moved about. There was soft cloth everywhere, covering the walls and ceilings like a tent, and it billowed in the breeze coming in through the topmost windows, giving the illusion that everything moved.

Wine flowed freely and there was food aplenty. The tables were laden and bards played in honor of the newly crowned king. Important guests had come from all over the kingdom and beyond to witness the coronation. Two kings had come, allies of King Manfred, to witness the occasion, bringing with them their entire courts. Those who had no room in the castle took up residence with wealthy nobles in the realm. Knights set up tents in the outer bailey, leaving the inner courtyard open for fairs and more revelry.

In the chaos of merry making, rules seemed to be forgotten. Nobles mingled with commoners, men took liberties behind the cover of columns and tapestries, queens drank their fill with no regard to decorum, even allowing touches that should not have been allowed. No one seemed to mind.

Nia rose from her seat at the crowded table to find a more open spot from which to view the festivities. She found refuge in a dark corner and cast a spell to shield it and herself from sight. Safe inside her hiding place, she could see everything without being part of it.

Faces paraded before her, carefree and joyous, paying no heed to anything but their own revelry. Several times a juggler passed in front of her, or a flame breather displayed his art. Nia admired their skill. Their discipline was astonishing.

Saeran himself seemed to be everywhere at once. Several people have already commented within her hearing how unseemly it was for a king to be so restless. It was tradition for the king to sit his throne and observe the revelry, not walk about and be part of it.

Saeran happened to overhear one such comment. He turned to the man who'd spoken and raised a brow. "If you think you can sit that throne all night, take it. I will find myself a more comfortable seat."

Nia eyed the royal seat and had to agree. It was made of black metal, its back and armrests covered with grooves and thick knot work which formed the symbols of Wilderheim. There was a thin cushion on it, but it looked no more comfortable than the rest of the throne. No wonder Saeran refused to sit on it.

Having settled that, Saeran turned to move on. He was three paces from her when he stopped and looked around, frowning. He couldn't see her. Nor hear her, quiet as she was. Her spell was perfect. Nia had spent weeks making certain of it.

Saeran tipped his head and stepped back, looking at the wall on either side of her.

"Is something wrong, your Majesty?"

Saeran took the noble by the arm and pulled him closer. "Lord Dunbar, look at this. What do you see?"

The portly man wiggled his ruddy moustache. "Nothing, your Majesty."

"You see the wall, do you not?"

Dunbar squinted. "Yes, your Majesty."

"Then you do not see nothing."

"Yes, your Majesty. I mean, no, your Majesty. Is everything all right, your Majesty?"

Saeran grinned and Nia scowled at him. "Thank you, Dunbar. You have confirmed what I thought. There is nothing here to be seen."

The celebration went on and on, even after the king and his father took their leave of the festivities. When the noise rose to an unbearable pitch, Nia left as well. She wasn't yet ready to sleep and instead went out to the courtyard. The moon was full in the clear night sky.

She lifted her face to it and breathed of the spring air. All around her everything was returning to life. The night had music of its own, and Nia could almost dance to it.

Countless stars twinkled and winked at her. They called to her, beckoned her closer. *Come fly with us,* they said, and Nia was tempted. But she knew better than to succumb to that temptation. Those who dared to fly up to the stars never returned. Some scrolls said it was because the night sky was the gateway to Valhalla, others that such beauty and splendor was unbearable and it burned the poor creature to ashes.

Yet there were stories of a wizard so pure of heart that he was accepted among the stars and became one of them. But when he began to miss his beloved, the stars returned him to the ground and he brought a piece of one with him, to gift the one he loved.

"Can you command the moon closer?"

Nia smiled, without turning to face the new king. "Of course. What sort of wizard would I be if I could not? But simply because a thing can be done does not mean it should be done."

"A flower will not bloom simply to be plucked," he quoted in passing.

Nia gaped at him and then laughed. "What are you wearing?"

Saeran grinned. Now lying on the bench, he inspected his tattered sleeve and breeches torn off at one calf. He looked absolutely bedraggled. "A disguise," he told. "Someone should have told you, child, I am the king. The only way to do anything without being noticed is to wear a disguise."

"My sincerest sympathies, your Majesty," she said. "And yet…" Without warning she pushed him off the bench to the ground. "If you insist on dressing as a commoner, you'd best get used to being treated as one." Then she regally seated herself on the bench he'd vacated.

Saeran pulled on her hair in retaliation as he sat next to her from the other side.

"I smell sheep's dung," she noted absently.

"It is part of the disguise," he replied in kind.

"I'm sure."

After a moment of easy silence, Saeran shifted with a wince. "I would like to continue my lessons."

Nia nodded. "You have practiced on your own." He had somehow known where she was hiding in the banquet hall. "You notice things now that not many others do."

Saeran shrugged. "Well, I notice the obvious. When a hall full of people shifts to leave a sizable portion of empty space, one tends to wonder why." Nia pushed at him, but the grin he gave her faded too quickly. "I tried to…the time. I could not make it stop again."

Nia didn't look at him. "Neither could I." Though she doubted her methods were the same as his. She wasn't as oblivious as she might sometimes appear. There were several maids and ladies tittering to others about the young king's robust spirit. While she'd searched her books and scrolls for the smallest hint to explain what had happened, Saeran had gone around kissing strange women, and Nia did not like it. Not at all.

But that was neither here nor there. Unknown magic was unpredictable. Something like this could happen again, trap them in time somehow, and what if they never got out?

She drew her knee onto the bench to face him. As she did so, she changed. Her robes disappeared, replaced by a simple peasant's dress, her hair pleated itself into a rope to hang down her back and shoes melted from her feet. "I tried to find an explanation in the scrolls. There isn't one. Any reference to time always says the same. It cannot, and should not, be tampered with."

"Then how do you explain what happened?"

"I don't," she said, frustrated at her own shortcoming. "I can't."

"Perhaps we should try to do it again."

"Again? I don't even know how we did it the first time."

We kissed. Neither of them said it. The knowledge was simply there.

"We cannot," she said, straightening in her seat again.

Saeran swung his leg over to straddle the bench and face her. "Why? Keep in mind, Nia, you speak to a man from a royal lineage. A king. And I do not like being denied."

"In your place, I would start getting used to it. I am not here for your amusement. If that is what you want, there is a bevy of willing bodies for you to seek out. I hear you have already given some a try. I am sure they would welcome you back with open arms."

Saeran reached out to her face, but a small blue spark burned his fingers, her way of refusing his touch. Saeran pulled back with a huff. "Nia, face me."

She didn't move.

"Please," he said.

Nia hesitated, but as much as she felt like a spurned lover, she wasn't. Saeran was her king and she'd sworn to serve him. A tantrum was not acceptable behavior from a wizard. Once she had convinced herself of this, she turned only her face toward him.

"You misunderstand my intentions. A bevy of willing bodies? That is not what I want. Not from you."

"Then what do you want?"

"I want you to look at me and see a man, not a king. I want you to laugh with me and talk with me, to be my companion and friend."

He shouldn't be saying such things. There had to be balance between justice and magic. Her duty was not only to the king, but to all of Wilderheim, and Nia had to be able to put the needs of the kingdom above Saeran's if it came to that. Her heart was not hers to share.

"I need your magic, Nia," he said, "but I also need you. Let me be your friend. Let me hold you when you need to be held. Like that day in the woods." He reached out again. "Let me kiss you—"

"Why?" Nia cried. He had to know this couldn't be! He would have to take a wife soon, a princess or noble who would give him more land and wealth, make him a stronger king and give him heirs. Saeran had far more obligations as king than he knew, and no matter how sincerely he looked into her eyes now, Nia had no place in his future, except as a wizard.

"Because," he said fiercely, cupping her face in his hands, "the first time we kissed time stopped. That has to mean something."

Humans ever lived at the whim of the gods. They toyed with lives, gambled for destinies. They could be unrepentantly cruel or generous beyond one's wildest dreams. But one never knew which of the two would be their lot.

Nia had felt something when Saeran kissed her. Something too powerful to be imagined and too subtle to be the result of a spell. Time had stopped, and she had a sinking feeling it wouldn't have if anyone but Saeran had kissed her.

How was she supposed to explain that?

She wasn't. The kingdom had to come first. As much as she wanted to believe Saeran cared for her, a deep sense of unease held her back. Something was coming and she wasn't sure either of them was truly prepared for it. Saeran would need a wizard at his side, a weapon and a tool. Not a friend. Not a lovesick girl dreaming of a star she would never be allowed to touch.

When he leaned closer, Nia covered his hands with hers and pulled them away. Stroking his cheek, trying to ignore that bewildered, hurt look in his eyes, she pressed a chaste kiss to his lips. "May Woden smile upon your reign, your Majesty. May you never have the need to go to war again, and may your kingdom love you and prosper. Let Freyr send you a woman to love and cherish and give you heirs. For it can never be me."

Rising to her feet, Nia became the royal wizard once again, her robes flowing around her and her hair shining silver in the moonlight. Her gait was fluid as she walked away, carried by magic when her step faltered.

"What about my lessons?" Saeran called after her.

"Tomorrow," she replied, not trusting herself to face him again. "In the glen."

8

Nia returned to her study, never so grateful to have a sturdy door between her and the rest of the world. The torches were cold, but two dozen candles burned bright to illuminate the space. In the past, this must have been a prison, perhaps even a torture chamber. There were still metal rings embedded in the stone walls from which shackles could be hung. The archway had hinges on one side and a hole on the other where the cage door would have locked.

Instead of thieves or murderers, it now held ancient words scribed on parchment spelled to withstand the test of time. Instead of torture implements, there was a makeshift washstand, a small altar to the gods, and a table with but two chairs to it and its surface reserved only for manuscripts and tomes.

Nia had done what she could to set everything back to rights. She'd managed to repair many of the things that had been broken, but some she'd had to replace. There was a proper bed where her simple pallet used to be and a wooden chest to hold her few belongings.

She ought to be sleeping in her chamber in the castle, but she liked it here better. It was familiar. Safe. Nico's presence was still here, a comfort to her always. The sneaky old man had left a part of himself behind. Everywhere she looked, in small cracks and crevices, Nico had stored away pockets of his magic. Perhaps nothing more than raw magic, perhaps some secret message left just for her. Nia didn't want to disturb them to find out. As long as they were here, Nia could pretend he was only a call away.

She yawned, weary of the day, already dreading tomorrow. She had hoped Saeran would give up on this quest for magic after what happened last time. Instead it only seemed to have made him more eager. "Why does he do this?" she asked aloud, frowning.

For you, the walls returned from all sides. Scowling, she poured water into her crystal scrying bowl and set it on the table. "Not for me," she said. "Do you know why?"

For you, the walls insisted.

She'd show them. Gazing deep into the bowl, she let her will sink into the water, seeking the future. "You'll see. He does not…he cannot…"

As images began to form, her words trailed away. Instead of an older king, she saw the boy Saeran had been years ago. He was sitting at a long table with king Halden and a number of Wilderheim's soldiers at one end. At the other sat warriors of another kind. They had shirts made of dark red cloth, and leather armor shaped like scales. They were dark skinned and black haired, in contrast to Saeran and Halden's fair northern complexion. These had to be Aegirans.

Between the two groups was a window to another place. Nia couldn't see into it, but she could hear the voices speaking from inside it. "You threaten us at your own peril, Farraj. You are beaten. Accept your failure with honor."

"There is no honor in failure!" The one called Farraj snapped. "We will come. Many more. You have magic men, we bring our own. You hide in your stone houses. Where we come from, stone crumbles into sand. Nothing will stop us!"

His warriors shouted their agreement, some reaching for the curved swords strapped to their sides. There were only a handful, the ones sent back to demand recompense for the men they'd lost in the fight. It was customary in the desert lands of Aegiros for the winning side to appease the conquered with a tribute to bury the bad blood between them. Nico had made Nia learn this early on, while the war still raged. Life was precious, and no matter how foolishly lost, it had to be repaid. To deny the Aegirans this was a great affront to them, fueling their rage at having been defeated.

"You raze our cities and expect payment in return?" Manfred demanded. "By the gods, I have never been so insulted in my life! Bring your armies, Farraj. We will water our fields with their blood!"

Halden paled as the Aegirans began shouting angrily, shoving away from the table, readying to fight.

"Wait," Saeran said. No one heard him so he stood and shouted it again. "Wait! There is another way."

"Saeran, sit down," Manfred ordered, but the prince would not be silenced.

Instead of listening to his father, he looked to the guard sitting at his left, a man wearing a bloody bandage over one eye. Whatever he saw in the man's face made Saeran's shoulders droop with a sigh. "There is a way to resolve this. Life for a life, that is what you want, Farraj, is it not?"

"*Rah!*"

Saeran held up his hands. "Then have mine."

"No!" Halden and Manfred shouted at the same time. Halden was on his feet in an instant, trying to push the boy behind him.

"When there is no wheat to pay the life price," Saeran said, "A marriage can be brokered between the clans to ensure peace."

"Saeran, stop!"

But he didn't. "I can never leave Wilderheim," he said. "But if you will accept, I will marry a daughter of Aegiros as a symbol of peace between our kingdoms."

Farraj stroked his beard, staring at the prince. His tribesmen whispered harsh words in his ear, clearly unhappy he was even considering Saeran's proposal. He heard them, one and all, nodded to each in turn, but when he faced Saeran again, it was his word alone that mattered.

Manfred was rambling, saying the boy had no authority to speak on behalf of Wilderheim or Lyria. His frantic arguments only served to convince the foreigner of Saeran's importance. That the prince hadn't dropped his gaze from Farraj's didn't help matters, either.

Farraj twitched his head to the side, indicating for Saeran to meet him halfway. Each with four men behind them, the two met in the middle of the room. The Aegiran official was tall among his people, but at sixteen, Saeran was almost of a height with him. "You are correct," Farraj said. "A marriage can end fighting. We call this *ramesh feh*. My *shansher* has two daughters. The older promised to another. You marry younger. Pay bride price. There will be peace."

"Consider carefully, Highness," the guard advised, but they both knew there was little more to consider. As prince and heir to the crown of Wilderheim, Saeran would have eventually had to make a politically advantageous marriage. Now would be as good a time as any. Aegiros was a kingdom of tribes bound by custom and each had a sort of king, called *shansher*. To marry one's daughter was equivalent to marrying a northern princess. Saeran would gain not only peace, but a powerful ally as well.

"I understand what I am doing," Saeran replied. To Farraj he said, "No more will die."

"No more." The foreigner held out his hand.

Saeran stared into his eyes for a moment longer, making Farraj's mouth twitch with amusement. When they clasped forearms, the deal was struck. Farraj touched a hand to his heart, then his forehead. He bowed to Saeran and his company before all of them walked out of the room without another word.

Nia dissolved the vision with a wordless cry, stumbling away from the table.

For you. For you. For you, the walls chanted over and over.

Nia slapped her hands over her ears. "Stop it!"

For you. For you. For you.

Torches flared to brilliant light, burning higher and brighter than they should. The flames licked the ceiling slithering in her direction, adding their voices to the walls.

"Enough!" Furious tears blurred her vision. Her magic pulsed inside her skin, leaking from her hands, creating bursts of light and heat.

For you. For you…

Nia screamed.

The study plunged into blessed dark silence. With all the flames extinguished and the walls turned mute, nothing else dared intrude on her solitude.

Left to herself, Nia found her bed by touch, laid down upon it, and buried her face in her pillow to weep in peace.

~

There were duties Saeran had to perform as king, yet all seemed to have been forgotten. Guests still celebrated, masters oversaw the servants, his father was busy packing for his travels, and Saeran was free to do as he pleased. He went to the glen.

When Nia arrived, he wanted to be ready. She'd been right last night. Saeran's future was already set. He didn't know why he'd said what he had, but was grateful Nia hadn't taken his words to heart. Perhaps the wine had gone to his head.

Today, however, was a new beginning. He'd prove to her that he was a good student and he'd make her forget about any foolish thing he may have blurted out in the heat of the moment. Saeran was resolved. He would make this work somehow. No matter how enchanting Nia might be, no matter how seductive the thought of kissing her again might become, he would be steadfast and true to his goal. She would never have reason to regret taking him on as her student.

Thusly decided, he climbed an apple tree up to the third branch and settled in to wait.

A sparrow flew circles around his head. It lighted on a higher branch and stared at him, tilting its head first to one side then the other before it opened its beak and made a shrill sound.

Saeran grinned and held out his hand, delighted when the bird perched on his finger. "Hello."

The sparrow chirped.

"What brings you to my tree on this fine day?"

The bird chirped again, this time with enough gusto to ruffle his feathers.

"I see you've made a friend up there."

Saeran grinned down at Nia. She was dressed in her usual robes, but today she'd draped the wolf's pelt over her shoulders for warmth. The head of it rested on her shoulder as an old friend. He was glad she wore it. A wizard he was not, but even he could sense its proper place was not mounted on a wall or tossed over a chair. No, that wolf was meant for Nia.

"He just came to me," he told her studying the sparrow now nesting in the palm of his hand. "You are a he, are you not?"

Nia chuckled. "Come down from there, the both of you. We have much to do today."

The bird abandoned him and landed on Nia's shoulder. Saeran shook his head. "Does all of nature obey your every whim?" He jumped to the ground, falling into step with Nia as she walked farther away from prying eyes.

"As much as the whole kingdom obeys yours, I would think." She lowered herself to sit on a fallen log.

"Such a powerful ally," Saeran mused. "I am glad you stand with me and not against me." He sat on the ground facing her. "You may begin your instruction, master."

Nia attempted a smile. It was feeble. Something weighed on her mind, and by the look of it, it wasn't good. "I've had to think long and hard about the wisdom of continuing your lessons."

"That does not bode well."

"I have decided to carry on only as long as it does not interfere with your rule and my ability to aid you."

"Nia," Saeran said softly, "the only thing that could interfere with my rule is your absence." He may have spoken foolishly last night, but he realized now he'd meant what he said. Saeran couldn't be king on his own. The restrictions were too great, the responsibilities too heavy for any one person to shoulder. Without Nia, he'd make himself mad with the games and intrigues of court. Seven noble houses already vied for his favor. Saeran didn't know what they would ultimately want, but he knew if they had their way, those nobles would manipulate everything and everyone in order to make themselves indispensable to him.

He'd seen it happen in Halden's court, the way this master or that had only to mention his displeasure at a roving tribe making camp on his lands to have the king order them immediately removed and jailed, without reason other than appeasing a man who called himself friend. Saeran had no stomach for it. He needed Nia to keep him sane.

"I am here to advise and teach you," she said. "A wizard is meant to be her king's aide. But nothing more."

"And if that is not enough?" The words were spoken before he could stop them. He didn't regret them, though he knew he should.

Nia shook her head. "No. I…"

"Nia—"

She abruptly pushed to her feet and paced around the log to the other side. "You have already learned to listen; now I will teach you to understand what you hear." She petted the sparrow gently. "Thank you for agreeing to help me." It chirped in answer. To Saeran, she said, "Listen as you already know, but listen for meaning."

Saeran met her gaze, but hers skittered away. She wouldn't look him in the eye again. Something had frightened her. Had he done this? Saeran sighed. "I hope one day we have enough trust between us for you to tell me when something weighs on you."

She said nothing.

The sparrow began to sing then, forcing Saeran's mind to the task she set him. There was a certain pattern to the chirps and trills, but no meaning that he could discern. What was he saying?

"Don't force it," Nia said. "Calm your mind and let the meaning come to you."

Saeran closed his eyes and relaxed, concentrating on nothing but the sparrow's song. He listened and simply enjoyed. After a while, a slow smile spread across his face, and he chuckled as the melody began to make sense. The sparrow wasn't singing, he was complaining! His nest was too far and his mate too fickle, his offspring perhaps not his own. He bemoaned the lack of food and the long winter cold that hurt his joints. This was an old bird as bitter as any man made grumpy by his age.

Saeran opened his eyes and looked at the bird with what he hoped was more sympathy than humor. "I am sorry for your plight, friend."

The sparrow chirped grumpily at him. *Let me not catch you near my nest, sonny. I'll peck that grin off your face, king or no!*

Nia thanked the sparrow before he could get more agitated and gave him a handful of seeds to eat while she turned her attention to Saeran. "Well done," she praised. "You learn quickly."

"Will I understand all animals now?"

Nia smiled. "If they wish to allow it, yes. If you work hard and practice often, you might even learn to understand the earth and the wind. The earth and anything of it never lies. Only humans can do that. You can trust the wind to tell you of coming riders. The earth will tell you when it is tired and cannot yield crops."

"What of fire?"

"Fire is born and dies too quickly to know anything of use. But fire can sing as well as any songbird. It can lull you to sleep or roar a warning if someone intrudes when your back is turned."

"Then I shall never be without one."

Nia hugged the wolf skin closer around her. "Perhaps we should continue indoors. The next lesson is scrying."

They walked back side by side in companionable silence. If the wind sensed his heart yearning, it did not say a word. If the earth felt the weight of his step, it held its silence.

And if his hand brushed Nia's, lingering, he chose to pretend it meant nothing.

Within the fortnight, Manfred bid his son farewell and set out on his journey. It was a long ride to Lyria, and the caravan was prepared for anything, but Manfred planned to take shelter in an inn whenever they could. Nia asked the gods for blessing on their behalf that history might not repeat itself. She prayed Manfred's journey was easy and that he arrived in good health and high spirits in his brother's home.

"I expect weekly reports," he told Nia before he left. "And leave nothing out, girl. I may not be king anymore, but I am still Saeran's father."

"Yes, Majesty."

"And you," he said to Saeran. "You grew up too fast, my boy. But you grew up well. Fret none, I will be back in a few months. We will have all the time in the world then." Manfred embraced his son, adding a quiet warning for his ears only. Nia still overheard. "Be careful," he said.

"Yes, Father."

With the old king on his way, Saeran didn't hesitate to put Nia and himself to work, and she was surprised to find that what she'd told him weeks ago was still fresh in his mind. Saeran personally met with cooks, butchers, huntsmen, milliners, merchants, and travelers to learn what winter had wrought on Wilderheim. Only when he'd made certain no one would go to bed hungry in his kingdom did he turn his attention to everything else. He held court, consulted with guards and sentries, met with the masters and the nobles, heard complaints, carried out judgments, sent messages and received them.

Nia was present for all of it. Saeran called on her to sense truths and falsehoods, to see to it his orders were obeyed, and to advise. And once the day was done, the two of them met alone in a room Saeran had turned into a makeshift library where she taught him magic deep into the night.

Saeran proved to be a quick study. Once he caught on to the makings of a spell, he didn't need it explained to him a second time. Nia taught him the rhythm of nature, how everything, from the smallest fly to the largest bear, had a place in the order of things. Often by observing a malady in one aspect of nature, one discovered the cause somewhere else. She taught him how to find leylines in the earth and follow them to points of convergence. Castle Frastmir stood on one of these points. Here, the earth lent its strength to everything and magic wrought on these grounds was more potent and powerful than anywhere else.

Nia enjoyed teaching when her student was so attentive. But more than that, she enjoyed his company, which was very ill advised. Saeran made her smile and laugh. He seemed to know when she got hungry or tired before she noticed it herself. At times she would say something exactly the way Nico had said it to her and for a moment she could think of nothing except how much she missed him. Whenever her sentence faltered, Saeran noticed. He took her hand in his and reminisced with her about the old wizard until she no longer felt so alone.

But when it came time to say good night and she returned to her cavernous study and her lonesome bed, the feeling returned. It was only then that Nia could let herself acknowledge how much she ached inside. Every night Saeran burrowed deeper into her heart, and every morning she found it more difficult to cast him out, something she had to do if she hoped to get through the day. Very soon she feared there would be no denying him any longer.

Weeks passed quickly this way until Saeran announced he wanted to reform the advisory council before the spring equinox. There were seven members on the council, old men rewarded handsomely for their years of service, who've come to enjoy the privilege of the king's audience too much. They no longer served the kingdom's interests but their own, and Saeran wanted to be rid of them. Having made the announcement without consulting her, he'd put Nia in the awful position of having to defend the king's decree while at the same time pacifying those who would be asked to return to their family lands.

If he thought this would relieve him of an unwanted burden, he was mistaken. The council was necessary, since no man, not king or wizard, could do everything on his own. Not only that, but since he'd appointed Nia to take care of the old council, he was forced to handpick the new members by himself. Nia would, of course, have to give her approval of each one he chose, but the most difficult task of sorting through the eager crowds of learned individuals was up to the king. Especially since she made her excuses every time he called her to the proceedings.

Nia didn't feel guilty about that at all.

"It is impossible, Nia!" he complained one night, dropping his head to the table with a thud. "They are coming from everywhere like locusts! Charlatans, each and every one of them! I cannot trust the ones who come forward, and I cannot find the ones I would trust. You have to help me." He slid out of his chair to the floor and knee walked to her side of the table. Grasping her hand, he looked into her eyes and begged, "Please, please. Save me from their wretchedness. It is your duty to protect your king."

Nia was laughing too hard to answer.

Saeran grinned. "Or at the very least distract me for a while."

"Now that I can do."

"Thank you," he cried with heartfelt gratitude. "What is tonight's lesson?"

"Scrying."

His head thudded to the table again.

"You wanted to learn," she reminded him.

"Can you not teach me something else?"

"Hearing the wind tell you there is an army at your door will not help you if you cannot see how big the army is. Why must you continue to fight me on this?"

"Because it amuses me to see your brow pucker every time I do."

Nia set the scrying bowl in front of him hard enough to splash water into his lap. "It is easy to listen to what is already there. To conjure something from nothing takes focus, strength of will. You must want something enough to will it into a vision." Raising a pert eyebrow at him, she asked, "Is there nothing you want, my king, now that you have everything?"

Saeran gazed at her so long her good humor waned and her face grew warm. Without a word, he lowered his head to stare deep into the bowl.

"Look beyond the water and the vessel," she guided. "They are only a window to what you seek. Hold the thought of what you wish to see in your mind, let it sink into the bowl and guide you to the vision."

Nia let her voice trail off into silence. This time was different from all the other nights he'd attempted to See. This time she felt his will as if he was working a spell without words. The intensity of it grew, filling him, leaking out of him without direction. Nia couldn't sense what it was, but she could lay a hand on his shoulder and look into the bowl with him. Thus connected, she Saw his vision without altering it.

She saw herself. Her own nightmare playing out before her just beneath the water's surface. Eirwen's face was as wrinkled as she remembered. The old woman, her caretaker, stood by the fire, listening to Nia shout. She didn't say a word, merely stood there. And then the waters came.

Her fault. Nia dreamed of water, and water tore apart the life she'd known. Eirwen was dead. Their cottage gone. Nia was alone in the forest, with nowhere to go, no one to look after her. Nine years old.

She saw herself walk away, seek out the merchants passing by. She'd hidden from their sight but followed them into the village. And another after that. Until they led her to Frastmir. By then she'd been half starved, half asleep on her feet. Hiding took more strength than she possessed. The shadows slipped from her grasp as she was stealing a loaf of bread from the baker's kitchen.

Nia's hand slipped from Saeran's shoulder. He caught it and held on as the vision continued. Nico stopped the bread thief, searched her soul and saw something there that Nia never knew. He never told her. She saw him taking her in, teaching her, giving her a home again. She saw herself smile, laugh, fall asleep in safety and comfort, but wake up screaming in the night.

Saeran squeezed her hand tighter when she tried to pull away.

The water showed her the night Saeran pledged himself to the Aegiran girl he didn't even know. Nia hadn't known it then, but the king had, as had Nico. That was the night he'd taught her how to make lights dance and cast shadows. He'd sat at the table and watched her play with them and laugh, as if her joy was the only good thing there was.

Nia saw her first meeting with Saeran, the day in the woods, their first kiss. She saw this very moment, with Saeran clutching her hand as an anchor for the vision, and her looking over his shoulder. Then another vision began to form: a dark foggy image, the shape of a man and woman in a passionate embrace, and Nia couldn't bear to see more.

With a wordless cry she knocked the bowl off the table, breaking the spell, and Saeran's hold on her. Shaken, she went to the window and braced her hands against its ledge, breathing deeply of the night air.

"I am sorry," Saeran said behind her. "You never told me where you came from. I just wanted to see."

"I came from nothing," she told him numbly. "I am no one."

"Are you angry with me?"

Nia shook her head. "No." He'd only done what she told him to do. There was nothing to fault him for. Saeran was not responsible for her past.

When he laid a hand on her shoulder, she allowed him to turn her around. "Then why do you weep?" he asked, brushing her tears away.

Nia had no answer to give him. He didn't demand one from her. Instead he drew her into his arms and held her until her tears dried. She watched the moon rise bright from behind the tree line. Its light brushed the fields and villages in silent affection. The wolves would be out to play tonight, she could feel them gathering. As the first howls rose up to the sky, Nia pulled away from Saeran. It was time to say good night. She gathered her scrying bowl and crystals and half bowed to Saeran, taking her leave.

"Nia," he said as she was passing through the door. "You are not no one."

Nia closed the door behind her without saying a word.

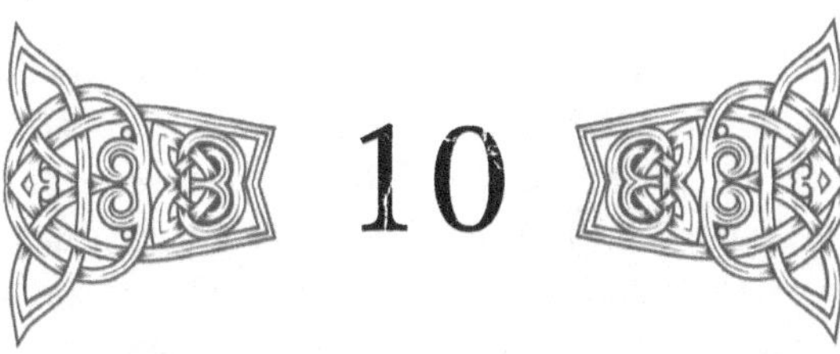

Saeran stared into the bowl of water, willing images of his father to appear. He'd been sitting there since dusk trying to practice his scrying to look in on the old man. His entire body felt cramped, his legs completely numb. Still, after all this time, there was nothing in the bowl but water. He was beginning to think Nia did something to make him see things when she taught him to scry. It was the only lesson she had to repeat almost daily, and he still couldn't do it on his own.

The one time he'd managed to catch a vision, he could hardly believe his eyes. He'd have thought it a fluke, an illusion, were it not for Nia's tears. She broke his heart that night. And he hadn't seen a vision since. Instead he did this. Sat at the water bowl for hours on end, wondering if Nia was already asleep. If she was waking up from nightmares alone in that cursed tomb of a study.

Frustrated and sore, his head pounding without mercy, Saeran shoved the bowl aside. He pushed to his feet, nearly falling back down when his knees gave out. It took long moments for feeling to return to his lower extremities, and then it felt like he was standing on needles. Saeran hobbled with as much dignity as a king could muster to the bed and sat on the edge, sighing.

Tomorrow was another day. More royal decrees and more disputes to settle. He'd have to get the new council together and present it to Nia. Again. She'd turned half of his chosen candidates away and restored three of the old members, including Allon, whom Saeran could hardly stand on a good day.

Nia had her reasons. Something about respecting tradition and wisdom guiding youth. He didn't care about why she did it. What he cared about was that the ones he'd most wanted were where he wanted them. Saeran grinned. No one but Nia had met the new council members yet. He couldn't wait to present them. One by one, he would buck every antiquated tradition his father had upheld out of laziness. When Manfred returned, Wilderheim would be a much different place.

It was too quiet. Today he'd had Nia open a window to Manfred so they could talk. He hadn't realized how long they were at it until the window began to close in on itself as Nia's strength flagged. She'd been forced to beg off from their daily lessons. It was the thing he looked forward to the most each day and he missed it. He missed Nia.

She'd taught him so much already. If he had to, Saeran could cloak himself from the sight of others. He could create an illusion of himself for a short time; he could even speak and have the air carry his words to a single person alone in a crowded chamber. He understood all things now, and they spoke to him often, telling him so much more about his own kingdom than he could ever hear from his sentries and advisors. Yet no one knew of this, save Nia.

When they were alone, Saeran was no longer a king. He was simply Saeran, a man and nothing more. But when he sat his throne, Nia proved invaluable to him. She saw things he would have missed, gave him sound advice when he needed it, and her presence alone calmed him. If he let himself, Saeran could love the wizard with her sad eyes and quick wit. But that would only bring pain to them both. Saeran had sealed his fate six years ago, and there was no going back. He'd done what he had to for the good of two kingdoms, and he prayed the gods showed him mercy enough that he never had to regret that choice.

Saeran stretched out on the bed. Nothing stirred this late at night. The windows were open, but the air outside was still, with nary a breeze to whisper in his ear. The fire in the hearth was dying down, taking its song with it. Saeran was completely alone, cocooned in silence.

It bothered him. He closed his eyes and thought of what he wanted most in that moment. "Nia," he said out loud as she'd taught him.

All at once, there was a gust of wind and she was there.

Saeran jerked upright on the bed. She was naked. Her hair pinned up, her hand holding a washcloth to her shoulder. Her back was to him, and for an instant Saeran wondered if he'd fallen asleep. He had dreamed of her so often he couldn't be sure.

But then her hand stilled and her head lifted to look around. She gasped, then growled furiously, and the sheets were pulled out from beneath him. They draped around her to conceal the expanse of skin, and Saeran nearly snatched them back again. When she was covered, Nia turned to spear him with an icy glare. "When I told you you could summon me at will, I did not mean for you to do it on a whim!"

"Forgive me, I did not realize…" He couldn't stop staring. Nia was before the hearth and the dying light was still strong enough to shine through the sheets, outlining her form as a shadow.

"Close your eyes," she commanded and his eyelids obeyed. But Saeran could still see her in his mind, so close he could reach out and touch her. Gods, but he wanted to!

There was rustling, and when he could open his eyes again, she was clad in her robes; her feet bare, her face blushing. "Here," she said, tossing the sheets at him. They hit him in the face and he grinned as he pushed them away.

"Ah, Nia," he cajoled, standing off the bed. "Don't be cross with me. I had no way of knowing you would be bathing when I called you." He reached out to pull the pins out of her hair, letting it cascade down her back and over her shoulders. "And it is your fault for not expecting this could happen when you taught me how to will you into my presence."

Her glare didn't lessen, but her lips were pale and she shivered.

"The floor is cold," he said. Reaching around her shoulders and beneath her knees, Saeran picked her up against his chest. "You will catch a chill."

The flames in the hearth blazed higher as her temper rose, but Nia was too tired to do anything other than ask, "What are you doing?"

Saeran sat her on his bed as if it was perfectly acceptable for her to be there, nearly naked in the king's bedchamber. "Seeing to it you don't die of cold and leave me without counsel," he answered, covering her bare feet with a thick blanket. "And making up for summoning you away from your bath."

"Why did you summon me?" she asked, her eyes narrowing in suspicion. She shouldn't have. Almost halfway closed, her eyelids became even heavier. Her head was already swimming. She couldn't keep this up much longer. The spell she'd done for Saeran and Manfred hadn't been difficult in its making, but in its perpetuation. There was no flare of magic and then a moment to restore herself. To keep such a window open, Nia had to channel her magic into it in an even, continuous stream. It had wearied her more than she realized. She'd been moments from bedding down when Saeran summoned her.

"I couldn't sleep and I hoped you would keep me company for a while."

"It has been a long day, Saeran, I will not be much of a conversationalist." Beltaine was almost upon them, and there were preparations that needed to be done. Nia had to rise before dawn tomorrow to oversee the villagers' efforts, and to perform some of her own spells and ritual. For many, Beltaine night would be one of celebration, and they would care for little more than that. But for those many to enjoy it, a few had to work very hard in the days prior.

Saeran caressed her cheek. "You are tired."

"Yes. Send me back." She shouldn't be here. But her mind wasn't focused enough for her to transport herself back to her own bed. If she tried magic, she might end up in a wall. And walking barefoot through the castle at night left her exposed not only to attack but also gossip.

Saeran cupped her face and kissed her eyes closed. "Don't worry, Nia. There is no need for you to stand the king's guard tonight. I will keep you safe."

Nia felt the world shift as he pushed down on her shoulders to make her lie back. Her eyes refused to open; she was half asleep already. "Send me back, Saeran," she asked him, consciousness fading. "You know how."

"No," he whispered in answer, and then there was darkness.

PART TWO

Severance

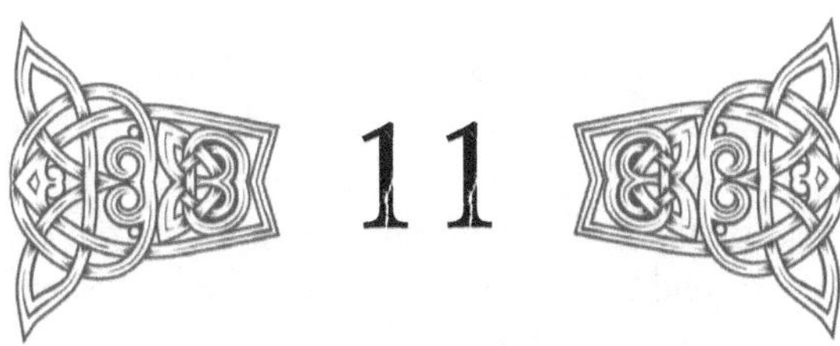

11

The breeze woke her, sighing her name. *Niaaa.*

She opened her eyes and sat up with a start. It was day, by the brightness of the sun she judged it to be nearing noon. She'd slept half the day away in the king's bed, and there was a tiny creature with a limp hat and a beaked nose almost as big as his head perched on the pillow next to her, watching her with curious brown eyes. Mortified, Nia fought the coverings to get out from beneath them. By the time she looked back, the gnome was gone.

Gods, what had possessed Saeran? Anyone could have come in here while she slept, and she didn't want to think about how the people would have mocked her for it.

Nia, I need you, the breeze said in Saeran's voice. Of course, Saeran didn't dare summon her as he had last night, he wouldn't want her to appear in the great hall half clad and sleeping.

With a thought Nia transported herself to her study. The candles had burned down with no one to tend them and it was pitch black. Summoning light, she stripped her robe and dressed in her usual clothes. There was no time to do more than splash cold water on her face and drag a comb through her hair. Mornings were when Saeran held court and heard petitions, and it was part of Nia's duty to oversee the proceedings should she be needed. She was late!

When the walls called her name, echoing each other, Nia moaned her frustration, took up her staff and disappeared, reappearing outside the great hall.

She opened the door with a wave of her hand and hastened toward Saeran. There was a crowd gathered, and several men knelt before the dais, facing the king. They were knights by the look of them, but Nia didn't recognize their crests. They must have come from far outside of Wilderheim, and by the tense set of their shoulders she could tell they've been waiting for quite a while.

Nia sent Saeran a meek look of apology. It wasn't like her to neglect her duties, as he well knew. He shouldn't have let her sleep so long. But when his mouth twitched in answer, she realized he'd done it on purpose. Nia scowled. She'd get him for that later.

"The royal wizard and advisor," Saeran announced, his voice carrying to the farthest corner of the great hall.

Nobles bowed and nodded their greetings. Nia kept her gaze on the wall in front of her, debating whether it would be more effective to summon an army of fire ants into Saeran's boots or pour sticky honey in his hair. Neither was good enough. This offense was too great to be tolerated. She'd toss him into the stream and make everything he ate taste like old fish. Yes, that ought to do it.

One of the men kneeling before the king glanced up as her robes brushed his shoulder in passing, and once he looked, his gaze snared. Nia could feel the weight of it on her before she turned to face them. He was first in his company to dare raise his head. He was not the last.

Nia spared him a glance but didn't return his open regard. Her magic reached across the great hall to take measure of the crowd.

She sensed curiosity about the knights among the gathering, one the king didn't seem to share. Saeran's agitation chafed against her mind like bristling fur. "These men are travelers from Synealee by the Sea," he said for Nia's benefit.

Nia glanced at him, surprised at his harsh tone. She'd never heard him speak that way, not even in the face of insult. Saeran didn't anger easily, but it was clear something had upset him.

"They ask for shelter and our assistance in their quest."

Nia addressed the knights. "I have seen Synealee. You have come quite a distance from the land of eternal summer. What is it you seek this far north?"

The one in the middle looked askance at the king. "Your Majesty," he said uncertainly, "surely this is a matter to be discussed among men."

"Sir Frederick duChamp," the king said by way of introduction, turning his head toward Nia without looking away from the knights. "He speaks for this lot."

Nia nodded to the knight. He was the elder of this company, a man whose pride kept his shoulders back despite his gray hair and weathered face. The simple clasp securing his cape was a circle wreath with a hand brandishing a sword in its center. They all wore a similar symbol, but his was the only one etched in gold.

"The wizard is my right hand," Saeran told the knight, daring him to argue. "You will show her the same deference you show me."

"Answer to a woman, by the grace of god inferior in every way?" Sir Frederick said, his face turning red.

"Tread carefully, knight," Saeran said. It was the only warning he would give.

Rather than leash his tongue, the knight stood. "Boys, we have come to the wrong place! The king's woman rules this land; we should have gone to her instead!" As the onlookers hummed in displeasure, Sir Frederick turned on Nia. "And where would we have found her, I wonder? In the king's bed, perhaps?"

Saeran rose from his throne, and all those with sense backed away from the dais and the man who had just incurred the king's wrath.

Nia stood her ground and held the knight's gaze without saying a word.

"Do you please him well, *wizard*?"

Rather than roar his fury, Saeran quietly dared, "One more word."

Sir Frederick sneered. "Harm a hair on my head and you will have the armies of Synealee descending on you to avenge me."

It was the worst thing he could have said. The guards filed in, arms raised, but they looked to Nia and Saeran for orders. Both shook their heads to keep them back.

All of the knights were on their feet now, trying to reason with their companion. He would hear none of it. Shrugging off their hands, ignoring their warnings, he toed the very edge of the first step. "We came to you out of courtesy, not need," Frederick declared. "This insult will not be borne. I will not yield to a boy's fancy, nor woman's whim!"

Saeran drew his dagger, but Nia stayed his hand. She brushed past him, her robes pushing him back. The gathering retreated more with every step she took, all but the foolish knight who thought himself above a king. Nia descended three steps and looked Sir Frederick in the eye to see his soul.

She wasn't gentle, and she didn't hold back. Arrowing through the haze of red temper, she found his pride and fear. Deeper still, she followed a path of determination to the heart of him, where all that he was and would ever be resided. There she found his quest, a dream of touching godhood in its purest form.

His obsession with a lone god's son, neither human nor divine, but both at once made no sense to Nia. This man worshipped what she could only call a wizard, yet he scoffed in the face of another. He sought a holy object with the power to grant eternal life. Nia had never heard of such a thing. To find it would mean great honor to him and all his descendants, a blessing he hoped to prove he deserved. Only one whose soul was worthy, blessed by his god, would be allowed to touch it, and he desperately wanted to be such a man. To fail in this meant an eternity of fiery torment at the hands of demons, but to have come this far gave him hope and made him believe he was their better.

Baffled, Nia left where Frederick was headed and sought where he'd come from. The knights didn't move while she searched him; she didn't allow them such freedom. They stood frozen, watching, waiting for her judgment while Frederick shivered before her, wide eyed, terrified of being found out.

"He lies," Nia declared. "A reckless old fool. They have no supplies left and the journey has drained them. This one is an outcast from his own lands. The others hold allegiance to no one. They seek a treasure far to the north where even our own people rarely venture. Their legends led them here, and they require a guide to go the rest of the way."

Nia released him and raised her head high as everyone present sighed in unison. Saeran issued the signal to bring the guards closer, but it was her honor the knight had impugned and she would be the one to pass judgment over him for his insolence.

Free of her spell, Sir Frederick clutched his chest as his aging heart shuddered and slowed. As with the poisoned wolf, Nia felt the knight's pain as if it was her own. She schooled herself not to show it.

"Foolish old man," she said, keeping her voice soft. "Your god has no power to protect you here. This is Woden's realm, and his children do not take kindly to such insult."

Sir Frederick dropped to one knee, sputtering, dying. Nia descended two more steps and held her hand out over his form huddling at her feet. Closing her eyes, she droned a hum and then gave it words: a healing spell which drew on the earth's nurturing magic to mend the flesh of man. It wasn't a forceful order, but rather a prayer, a petition. The earth, as all living things, could choose whether to obey. The knight stilled, breathed in deep, then straightened and stood, his eyes wide. He had finally run out of words.

"I saved your life this day," she told him. "Think twice before you slander me again." Turning away from him, she returned to her place at the king's side. "They are no threat to us, my liege. The treasure, if there is one, has value for them alone. The sooner we help them find it, the sooner they'll leave."

"What of him?" Saeran asked, indicating Frederick with a nod.

The knight still staring at her traced a cross over his chest and knelt, bowing his head. "Bless my soul," he said reverently. "Forgive me for not recognizing the great Lady of the Lake. My life is yours if you ask it."

Nia and Saeran looked at each other, equally confused.

"Lady of the Lake," the rest of them echoed, kneeling along with him, and once again those present hummed with gossip.

Saeran despised gossip, yet he always seemed to find himself in the midst of it, its subject or its audience. By tomorrow, some great fable about Nia would be making its way across Frastmir and this time he would have no explanation for what she'd wrought. Who were these knights, casting judgment one moment and then prostrating themselves the next? What utter drivel would the nobles invent about what they'd seen?

Saeran didn't like this sudden shift, didn't trust it in the least. He found himself wary of them. They were fervent in their beliefs, fanatic in their quest for what they themselves had admitted might not even be there. Such steadfast faith could be a powerful thing.

Even now, though he showed humility to Nia by kneeling, Frederick still raised his head to gaze upon her with unnerving reverence, and Saeran knew without question Nia would rather be anywhere in that moment than standing there before him.

He looks at you as if he sees a goddess given form, Saeran thought, willing the words to her. He didn't expect her to hear him, but she answered all the same.

More fool he. A goddess would pluck his eyes out for daring to meet her gaze.

Her disgruntled voice in his mind soothed Saeran.

But then he noticed the knight at the far right of the company who, much like Frederick, didn't have the sense to drop his gaze. This one was different. There was something very familiar in his eyes. Saeran had worn that selfsame look many a time when Nia either didn't notice or chose not to see. Saeran's fingers curled tighter around the dagger he hadn't yet sheathed.

Nia stepped closer but said nothing. Saeran held their lives in his hand. Knowing she would stand by him no matter the judgment made it harder to choose but easier to carry the burden of choice. Saeran leaned to the side a little to brush shoulders with her. She reciprocated, elbowing his dagger arm. Scowling, he sheathed the blade and resumed his seat.

"Beltaine comes in two days' time," he said. "There will be no talk of quests until it passes. For now I will choose to overlook the affront you've caused. Have a care, I will not tolerate another."

"We understand," one of them said. "Our thanks, your Majesty."

Saeran waved the guards to lead them out and clear the great hall. The court session was over. "I do not trust those men," he told Nia when they were all gone. "Keep away from them."

"As you command, your Majesty," she replied.

He looked up at her where she stood. "I mean it, Nia."

"Why do they bother you so?"

Saeran thought of the way the younger knight gazed at Nia and dread settled in his bones. He couldn't shake the feeling that some-how, someway, these knights would rob him of something precious. The maddening sense of portent hovered just out of reach, as visions always did each time he sought them.

"You are the one with magic Sight. What does it tell you?"

Nia tilted her head and looked off into the distance, no doubt seeing many things Saeran would never glimpse. "It tells me we are nearing a fork in the path."

Saeran reached for her hand and squeezed it tight. Whichever path the gods chose for him, he would walk it with Nia by his side. Or not at all.

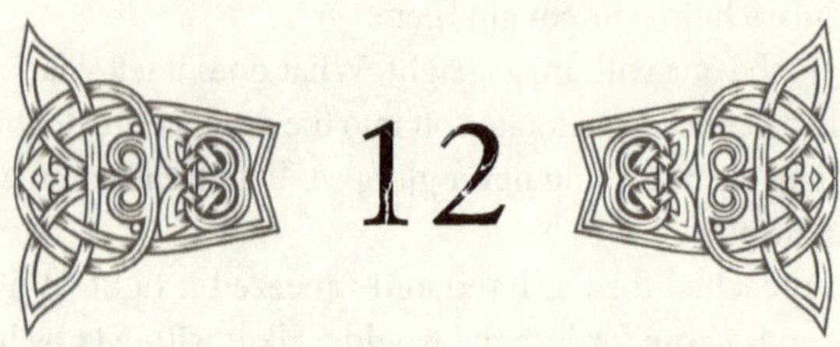

12

Sir Frederick was pacing. He'd smoothed his shaggy hair six times since he'd come out to the courtyard, and it still wasn't tidy enough to him. If he didn't stop, he would smooth what little hair he had left right off his head. Arnaud shifted in his seat, made nervous by his fussing. Frederick must have seen dozens of pagan ceremonies in his life, he ought to be used to the sights.

Ah, but this one would be attended by the Lady of the Lake, and that was no ordinary thing.

The night the royal wizard had healed him, Frederick had told them all what he had seen. He described the lady Nia without the human mask he said she wore. He said he'd seen her shining from within, draped in a glittering pearlescent gown. He'd seen her beneath the surface of a deep lake, with fish and water nymphs paying her homage. But as she was in King Saeran's court, Frederick said she'd also been out of place in the lake. Honored and revered, yet somehow greater than the nymphs around her. One of them, but separate. Her eyes, he'd said, had been like that of a doe, not a fish. A creature of land as much as water, and both at the same time.

Did she have the sword of kings, they all asked. Frederick hadn't seen one in his vision. Did she say anything of the cup, they asked next. Hanging his head, he again answered no.

What was Arnaud to make of that? If it was a vision from God, it was one that seemed to serve no purpose. If it was the workings of evil, why would it have healed Frederick when it could have so easily killed him instead? The wizard didn't lack for acolytes, and there was no service a wandering group of knights could render to one like her, so what reason could she have for deceiving them with a false vision?

Arnaud's faith in God was unshakable. He'd seen the face of his Savior and would do whatever He commanded to see it again when his life in this world came to an end. His faith in Frederick's vision was far less. They'd all been exhausted by their journey here, pride alone keeping them on their feet before the pagan king and his wizard. What Frederick had seen could have been nothing but a dream. Arnaud would not be swayed to believe otherwise unless he saw evidence of it for himself.

Tapping his foot, he chose to leave his companions to stroll about, lest he begin to pace as well. He'd heard talk in the village about this so-called festival. Despite the mystery surrounding the ritual itself, it seemed to him the rest of this day's importance lay in the fervid coupling these people seemed to look forward to with more than a little impatience.

When he'd come out to check on his mount this morning, he'd found a young maid already being chased by the hostler in the stables. Arnaud had made a hasty retreat into his sanctuary for prayer. *God give me strength to remain true.*

He was tempted, increasingly so as the sun dipped lower and torches were lit, casting shadows all around. Wickedness lurked in those shadows, wearing the face of innocence. Temptation dressed in revealing gowns, smiling with open invitation. So many beautiful wenches brushed past him with ill concealed intent that he was hard pressed not to avail himself of one of them. Yet each time he came close to succumbing to such sweet temptation, he closed his eyes and saw the golden one. The lady who'd swept into the great hall on a summer breeze and faced them with sunshine in her hair and lightning in her gaze. Sir Frederick's Lady of the Lake.

Arnaud had never seen her equal. In beauty, poise and bearing, she surpassed any queen he'd ever glimpsed, and he was ashamed to admit, if only to himself, that he was smitten. His weakness in the face of a pagan sorceress reminded him of his pitiful humanity. No matter how he strived to be pure of thought, devoted to his God and his quest alone, lady Nia had become a constant spectre in his mind, beguiling him, tempting him. He ought to hate her for it, yet everywhere he went, people loved her and sang praise enough to make a martyr blush. She was a healer among them, in every possible way. She mended bodies and minds, reconciled friendships, birthed children and cared for the old. She was their priestess and midwife, advisor and confidant.

Whether she was the Lady of the Lake the legends spoke of was irrelevant. Here, in this enchanted land, the wizard was a legend in her own right. And she was the true ruler of these people, Arnaud knew, for the king was no more immune to her beauty than the rest of them. She would guide his hand with a single word or gesture.

A child pushed through the crowd and barreled into him in his haste, dropping a handful of polished stones. "No!" he cried, diving for them, heedless of the feet so close to stomping him to death. The boy's dark eyes were wide and brimming with tears, and his wee hands shook as he gathered the stones.

Arnaud knelt to aid him. "There now," he said, keeping his voice soft. "What's this? Tears on such a happy day?"

The child looked up at him, wiping a ragged sleeve under his nose. He did his best not to cry. "They're a gift to the gods," he said, "and I almost lost 'em." His chin wobbled, but he squared his bony shoulders and pushed to his feet. "They're for lady Nia," he finished grandly, opening his hand to show Arnaud his collection.

"They are lovely," he said, "Perhaps too lovely for the wizard. You should save these for your mother."

The boy shook his head. "Every 'un gives something to the gods. But me Ma says the gods are far and hard of hearin' a wee one as me. 'Tis why the wizard is here. She's their ears and voice. She hears our prayers and tells 'em to the gods an' they listen. She sings to 'em, ye see." He glanced down at the precious pile of pebbles. "She'll pray for me Da to return. An' he'll listen an' come back to us, I know it."

Arnaud looked after the boy as he hurried away once more. "The poor child," an old woman said, following his gaze. She was dressed in gray, save for the red and yellow ribbons in her white hair. "His father died last winter. Attacked by a poisoned bear. That was before the wizard rid the woods of the poison. And before the king rid the kingdom of them what put it there." She shook her head sadly. "The boy's right to pray to the wizard. But even she can't bring back his Da."

Arnaud pushed to his feet and bid the woman farewell. If the lady Nia was worthy of such honor and praise, then perhaps she was worthy of such offerings. He would find her a bloom, the most beautiful one around. And only Arnaud would know it was meant for her alone.

~

Tonight the Veil would thin. What was unseen could easily become visible if one was willing to look hard enough. It was Nia's duty to keep the dark spirits away until the light of dawn. She would be the voice of Wilderheim as well as the gods and Others.

She had been dreading this night for a long time, since the moment the Others had appeared for her presentation at King Manfred's court. Everyone would expect her to know what to do, but how could she? Nico hadn't taught her what he himself had never known. The Others had never appeared to him. They seemed to be around Nia constantly. Even when she couldn't see them she felt their presence. They've been roaming the castle since dawn, more of them now as night approached.

Nia retreated to her study, hoping the wards would keep them away. They didn't. The great dire wolves she'd seen at her presentation paced the underground chamber as she bathed, making her extremely nervous. They tilted their heads at the walls, growled at the books and scrolls, but it was when they approached the wolf skin Saeran had given her that Nia wished she could disappear.

In her panic, she felt magic gather and pool in her chest, a precursor to her disappearing and reappearing somewhere else, but no matter how frightened she became when those feral glowing eyes turned on her, she stayed put as if her magic had suddenly become inert, a dead weight on her heart.

One of the pair, the larger, darker male shifted so close his nose touched hers. Nia closed her eyes. "I tried," she said.

You failed, his voice growled inside her head.

"I know."

And now you keep his pelt as a trophy.

Nia shrank from his terrible anger. "No, as a reminder. So I never forget that death is inevitable, but mercy is a gift."

He snarled and suddenly her bath was gone and she stood naked before him. With the female stalking behind her and the male baring his massive fangs before her, Nia had no way of retreat, but she didn't want one.

"You led him to me, didn't you?"

The dire wolf's hackles rose, making him even bigger.

"Why didn't you heal him yourself? He was one of yours. He must have called out to you, in agony, dying. Why didn't you help him?"

He snapped his jaws a hair's breadth from her face, his breath burning her. *You dare question me!*

"Yes!" she snapped. "You led one of your children on a useless chase after a human who could never hope to do what you could have so easily, had you wanted to. You let him suffer, and for what? To test me?"

His hackles smoothed down and he tilted his head at Nia to an almost impossible angle. The female woofed behind her and the two met eyes. They circled her until their positions were reversed and now the female stood before Nia, lowering to meet her gaze. Her eyes were wild, but also kind. Her gaze hypnotized Nia, made her feel tired. Her legs weakened and she lowered to her knees. *We are Other,* the female said, and her voice echoed with the sound of countless pups calling to her with infinite affection. *We can walk among humans, but we are not them.*

Before Nia's eyes, the dire wolf shifted, her great body dissolving like a vision into that of a tall, slender human woman. Her long hair was gray, her eyes golden like the moon she revered, and though she looked human enough, Nia sensed the shape for what it was, a beautiful mask for the wolf beneath her skin. *Who are you, child?* she asked, revealing teeth too sharp to be human.

The male dire wolf came around to his mate, and she stroked his fur with a graceful hand. He nuzzled into her touch, sitting by her side so close she became half engulfed in his fur. Nia was envious of the love they obviously shared for each other, something she could never have.

"I am the royal wizard," she answered. "My duty is to stand as Wilderheim does, between humans and the gods, and the Others. I walk the path of inbetween, and I know I walk it alone."

The wolf's smile was menacing, her words rough. *You know nothing. Learn.*

Nia frowned. "Learn what?"

The male dire wolf huffed and nudged her shoulder hard enough to knock her off balance. *Learn,* he ordered, and then both of them were gone. In their absence, the wolf pelt seemed to watch her from its place on her bed.

Shaken, Nia rose to her feet and donned her robes against the chamber's chill. It was almost time for her to make an appearance outside.

13

Torches were lit all at once when the sun kissed the western tree line, flooding the courtyard with blazing light. It was magic as much as fire; hundreds of hearts beating together in the same wish for children and a healthy harvest later in the year. Saeran could almost see their prayers shimmering interspersed with torchlight, floating among the sparks thrown by bonfires. It was a beautiful sight to behold.

Every house was decorated with vibrant flags and ribbons to celebrate the beginning of summer, every man woman and child dressed in their finest. The music was loud, the laughter even louder, but through it all the breeze teased him with secrets of things unseen. The Others were walking among them tonight. Saeran strained to catch a glimpse of even one, but he saw nothing.

He weaved amidst the crowds, searching for anything that was out of place. The courtyard was a melee of dancers and revelers, the great hall open to everyone on this holy night, for all were equal before the gods. Instead of formal feasts, everyone would go to the altar on the hill where offerings to the gods would be made.

Nia would lead the procession. She would weave spells around her to make sparkling lights follow in her wake and her white robes would glitter in the dying light with a magic of their own. There would be flowers in her hair and a golden mask covering her eyes and nose. She would be the embodiment of the goddess Frigga.

They come, they gather, the breeze whispered. *They come to see…*

"What?" Saeran asked.

See, the breeze repeated, swirling around him once and then streaming toward the castle. *See…*

Saeran walked in the direction of the wind. He focused his intention as Nia had taught him, willed it into a vision to See the Others among his people. It took him long moments to realize he was following a leyline, and when he saw what it was leading him to, the young king almost dropped to his knees.

In an instant, all became quiet and the crowds parted to create a passage. They bowed deeply as Nia passed, paying homage to her and the goddess of fertility she embodied. Saeran forgot to breathe. She glided along the uneven ground on bare feet, her step silent but for the tinkling of tiny bells that none could see. It was an illusion, the king told himself, but couldn't be certain.

See…

He saw.

He kept his features calm, falling in step behind her; the first in the procession. It was his right as king. The breeze wafted over him, bringing with it the scent of her. She was summer. She was sunshine and flowers, rainstorms and life.

As they passed the outer gate, a cheer went up and the music and revelry resumed, following in their wake. Nia never faltered. She led the way to the hill, oblivious to everything else. When she reached the altar, she turned to face the crowds and raised her arms above her head, speaking to the heavens and the setting sun. She called for blessings upon the land and all who lived on it, asking for a bountiful harvest and happiness for couples young and old.

When she finished speaking, she rounded the altar and passed her hands over it. Then the villagers came forward, placing their small offerings onto the slab of stone. They brought wreaths of wild flowers, pieces of fruit, if they had any, or puppets made of hay, ribbons and cloth. They brought what they could spare to please the gods, laying it before Nia and speaking soft prayers as if she truly was the goddess who looked after them.

Nia accepted the gifts formally, thanking each person and blessing them as they passed. The offerings would be left on the altar for the gods to do with as they pleased. No one was allowed to take from them, lest they incur their wrath.

The foreigners came forward at the end, each taking part in the ceremony as they would. Sir Frederick gave a silken handkerchief, saying a prayer of thanks to both the gods and Nia herself. He bowed deeply to her as he stepped away and Nia nodded to him in acknowledgement. The rest of the knights followed suit, one bringing a piece of bread, another a carved wooden horse, the third a piece of chain mail, and the last a single red bloom. She nodded in thanks and blessed all of them as well.

Finally it was the king's turn and, for him, Nia rounded the altar once more to face him without barrier. The king had no tribute to give. It was tradition for him to show respect to the gods by proving his humility.

Saeran stepped forward, grateful the ritual required no words. His mouth was too dry for him to speak. The fires sang out with the wind, even the sky added its voice to the chorus. He bowed his head before Nia and knelt. The crowd echoed with a prayer for the king, that he might find a wife soon and sire offspring, and their voices made the earth shudder beneath him.

Nia touched a hand to his chin, urging him to look up. When he did, she leaned down and kissed him, as was custom. Saeran balled his hands into fits, fighting the urge to pull her to him and kiss her the way he wanted to. He was drunk with the scent of her, the feel of her lips so chaste against his.

Too soon, she withdrew. In the darkness, only he could see the hesitation in her movements as she straightened and he wished the others would disappear. "Rise, King Saeran," she said, her voice ringing out over the hill. "May your reign be prosperous for all the years to come."

He obeyed, but he couldn't make his feet move him from the spot. For a moment they merely stared at each other, caught in an instant of pure magic. It pulsated in the air around them like a heartbeat, making it difficult to breathe.

Another cheer went up, startling them both, and Saeran forced himself to walk away. The bonfire would burn all through the night, and few would leave before the sun rose again to light their way home.

Nia faced the altar and once more raised her arms above her head, her own tribute and offering. She removed the flowers from her hair and placed them on the altar, saying a soft prayer. Then she turned in a circle thrice and dissolved into mist, disappearing from sight.

When she reappeared next to Saeran, her golden mask was gone. Instead of white robes, she wore the blue ones she'd received at her presentation and the wolf skin over it. She watched the celebrations with a smile on her face, though it seemed a disguise for something else lurking beneath her carefully composed mask of calm.

Only those too young or too old stayed to the side; the rest danced around the fire in celebration. The foreigners, Saeran noted, did not dance either. But while four of them watched the revelers, the fifth's eyes searched through the crowd until they settled on Nia. It was the selfsame knight who had gazed at her in the great hall, the same one who'd presented her with a red bloom and placed it so close to her hand. Arnaud was infatuated with the wizard, and he'd scarce seen her once since he'd arrived.

Lady Brigit spun out of the circle and caught Saeran's hands. "A dance for the fire spirits, your Majesty?" She pulled him into the throng before he could answer, obliging him to dance. She held him so close he was tripping over her skirts, but Brigit only laughed. Saeran suspected the lady had sampled the mead one too many times. It loosened her tongue enough to say, "A finer king Wilderheim has never had! Maidens are praying for you tonight, that you will choose a wife and make her queen, but each of them wants you for herself."

It was nothing he hadn't heard before, but tonight the flattery only served to remind him that he'd already chosen.

Brigit grabbed his waist and spun them around. She leaned in and said, "If you choose me—"

Saeran didn't hear the end of it because the seamstress sisters, Finna and Maeve, pulled him away, chattering one over the other. He danced around the fire thrice, and each time he thought he was free someone pulled him back into the jig. Saeran heard Nia squeal. The woodsman, Dahl, had picked her up one-armed to dance her around. Like Saeran, she was passed from one to the next, but unlike him, she seemed to enjoy it. The fire illuminated her laughing face as she spun and hopped directly across from him.

Then, out of the corner of his eye, Saeran saw the knight Arnaud step into the fray, following Nia. She was in Hundr's arms now, but before Arnaud could join them, Hundr passed Nia to Geir and away from the knight. Geir lifted Nia by her waist to spin her around while Saeran found himself with the shy Dagmar in his arms. He smiled at her briefly, but his attention was on Nia and the knight following after her from Geir to Konall, to old Sigmarr, and back to Geir.

"Your Majesty!" Brigit called, but Hundr pulled her away as Elsa replaced Dagmar. Maeve caught the knight's hand, but he shook her off and continued around the circle after Nia like a bloodhound after a scent. Saeran turned Svana around to go the opposite way. Hundr with Brigit danced quicker than the rest, past him and halfway around the circle in a few steps. And just as Nia spun away from Tannir, as Saeran was preparing to switch partners yet again, Brigit stuck her foot out and tripped Nia in the direction of the blazing bonfire. Saeran let go of Svana with gasp and made a grab for Nia as she tipped forward, arms flailing to stop herself.

He caught hold of her sleeve and pulled her upright into his arms just in time, and when her gaze met his, Saeran went deaf and blind to the world. *Nia.*

She shivered as if she'd heard him speak her name. She couldn't have. Only in the deepest, most secret corner of his heart would he ever dare to say it that way, with the whole of his soul calling out in anguished longing to the mate it could not reach.

"Lady Nia," Arnaud said close enough to startle him.

Saeran felt his mouth pull into a snarl. With Nia in his arms, he spun out of the circle of dancers. Darkness pulled around them and a facsimile of them broke off to continue in the current of dancers. The darkness was his; the illusion Nia's. Taking her hand in his, he pulled her into the woods, far from prying eyes.

He took them so far the massive bonfire was little more than a flicker, but not so far he couldn't hear the revelers anymore. Only then did he release the shadows around them. "Wait, Saeran—"

He crowded Nia against the trunk of a tree.

"This is not real," she said in a rush, "It's Beltaine. It's affecting all of us."

"No, Nia, this is us." His mouth descended on hers before she could say anything else. Too long denied, Saeran gorged himself on the taste of her. He couldn't pull away and wished with everything he was that he could stop time just once more, have this much of her at least. As if she'd whispered it in his ear, Saeran felt the same wish in Nia.

She kissed him back, her fingers grasping at his shoulders to hold him close. A strange fervor had them in its hold, demanding they give in to its power. Nia let go of everything. She willed the mischievous sprites away, ignored the shadows that weaved between the trees, watching her, waiting. If this was another test, it was the cruelest one yet. Out here, she couldn't hold back from Saeran, not even knowing it might destroy her. She yielded to her king, giving herself this one moment because there would not, could not, be another. Nia opened her mind and soul to feel everything around her breathe. The entire forest and all that lived within it leaned and bent toward them, flooding her senses and making her body sing under Saeran's touch.

She wrapped her arms around him to hold him close and everything else sighed away, leaving nothing but Nia and Saeran. Their feet left the forest floor and this time, she embraced it. Saeran's hands searched for the fastenings of her robes, slipping inside while the garment fell away. She wore nothing underneath, and his hands slid over her skin, caressing molding, teasing. She moaned, the sound muffled by his kisses.

It was dangerous to feel this way, but she couldn't stop it. With no more than a gesture, Saeran's jerkin and shirt disappeared. Her breasts flattened against his bare chest and she shivered, bringing her leg forward to hook her ankle around his calf.

Skin to skin, she could feel Saeran's mind and soul open, and she couldn't help falling into both. Joined with him this way they shared thought and sensation, feeling with each other, for each other, in a dizzying cycle. Saeran's heart beat fast and hard and Nia's matched it. Blood roared in her ears, yet she could still hear his every breath and all the words he didn't speak. She reveled in the moment, committed every detail to memory. He kissed her, touched her, gave her all of himself, and she sensed his determination to show her with his body what he couldn't tell her in words—that she was his and no one else would ever lay claim to her.

It broke her heart.

Saeran shuddered. "Don't," he whispered. "Don't hurt." But when she looked into his eyes, she could see the same pain reflected back at her. Saeran cupped her cheek, drawing breath to say what was shining in his heart. Nia kissed him, stealing the words from his lips. Words held power and once spoken, they could never be taken back.

Nia caressed his shoulders and back, her nails scoring lightly before she looped her arms around him to bring him to her heart. With one swift motion, Saeran buried himself inside her and she cried out against his shoulder as he tore through virgin flesh.

Saeran moved slowly, taking his time to bring her pleasure to take away the pain. His thrusts were deep and sure, so deep that she no longer knew where he ended and she began. She felt their souls twine together like sheens of mist over the moors and in a single moment of perfect ecstasy the mists pulled tighter, binding her to Saeran in some elemental way.

As the feeling faded, her awareness of Saeran did too, and within moments she was alone in her mind, as if none of it had happened. They descended back to earth on a current of magic, in a tangle of limbs she didn't want to leave. Saeran held Nia to him as if afraid she would disappear. They were so close when one inhaled, the other exhaled, as if they breathed for each other, their hearts beating in unison. "Beautiful Nia," Saeran said. "Be my queen, beloved. Sit by my side forever."

His words cut her to the quick, and Nia squeezed her eyes shut. Too far. They went too far. Saeran had not been meant to be hers this night. They'd stolen a moment from time, but that was all they could ever have. She knew what had to be said, though her heart broke to say it. "No," she whispered and a part of her died.

Saeran didn't push her away, knowing as well as she that he asked the impossible. Instead, he tightened his hold on her, giving her awhile longer to pretend. As long as he held her, nothing else mattered except that she was his and he belonged to her.

They stayed there until morning light. Cushioned by the soft forest grass, covered by the blanket Nia wove from the plants around them, they didn't stir and no creature intruded.

When at last sunlight tickled her eyelids and teased her awake, she cursed the light of day. Saeran slept soundly in her arms, her head nestled against his heart, but he woke when he felt her move. He smiled at her and kissed her, squeezed her closer as he stretched.

But his smile died away too quickly. "They will be looking for us," he said.

Nia nodded and slowly rose, calling for her clothing. Everything fell down from the branches above with a shower of leaves that caressed her sensitive skin. She dressed in silence, trying to ignore the cry in her heart. She had known what would happen if she got too close to the king, but she'd done it anyway. It was her own fault, and she would have to live with the consequences.

When she faced Saeran again, he was dressed, his jaw set and his eyes hard with regret. She held her hand out to him and he came to her, pulling her into his arms. For a moment, she basked in his strength and warmth. For a moment too long she remained in his embrace, wishing.

She couldn't make herself move away; her very soul protested it. And so Nia did the only thing she could. "Good morning, my king," she told him before squeezing her eyes shut and sending Saeran to his bedchamber alone.

Left holding nothing but air, Nia stood there until she could breathe again. It was almost noon when she summoned her staff and walked. She wandered the forest without aim or direction until she came to a lake hidden by thick foliage. There, she shed her clothes and stepped inside, wishing the lake could cleanse the grief from her soul.

"Where are you?" she demanded.

Silence answered her. The sprites who'd pulled her and Saeran away from the dancers last night didn't appear, but she didn't expect them to. Their mischief was finished; they had no reason to come back again.

Furious, she drew magic from so deep inside she felt it tug on her heart. "Show yourselves!" she commanded, trying to force her will on the Others. "Gods damn you, you don't know what you have done!"

Nothing stirred, not even the wind.

Nia dropped to her knees in the lake with the water up to her chest and lowered her head until her nose almost touched it. As light played over the rippling surface, images appeared. What should have been. Nia and Saeran leaving the circle in opposite directions to stand watch over the people until morning. Nia leading them all back to the castle as the sun came up and bidding Saeran a good morning by the great hall. They would have parted as friends and everything would have been all right.

Instead the wood sprites had interfered and made the drunken Brigit trip Nia right into Saeran. With the Veil so thin, magic had saturated the earth and air, and everyone capable of sensing it had been drunk on its heady power. Even by the light of day Nia still felt the effects of what the sprites had done and knew there would be no easy way back. Saeran would never be satisfied with only friendship now; she'd sensed it in his heart last night and was even more certain of it today. He would defy everything and everyone for her.

The lake rippled again, and in the light-play over its surface she saw Aegirans gathering in force. If Saeran refused the bride he'd sworn himself to they would stop at nothing to tear him and Wilderheim apart. To the last they would fight and die to avenge such an unforgivable betrayal.

Nia's tears dropped silently into the lake, marring the vision.

The water embraced her. It warmed to her and grieved with her. *Have hope,* it said.

"There is no hope, there never was."

Always hope, it replied. If only she could believe it.

Nia didn't return to the castle until she was certain she could hold her cloak of shadows and hide from everyone, including the king. Avoiding the great hall, she went to her study instead, finding what little solace there was in her tomes and scrolls.

She picked up one after the other, gazing at the words without seeing them, no matter how hard she tried to make out their meaning. Food held no taste and wine burned like acid as it slid down her throat.

She dared not sleep that night, afraid of what she might dream. When morning found her the next day, Nia's eyes stung from the tears she'd locked inside. Her jaw ached from clenching her teeth against the pain, and her body was cramped from sitting huddled on the floor.

How she wished her mentor was there to counsel her. She needed his advice, his shoulder to lean on. "Nico," she whispered brokenly. "Why did you not warn me?"

For the first time, not even the remnants of his power in the walls could console her. Heartbroken, she let the tears come.

The council of advisors met in its entirety for the first time in Saeran's presence. Nia should have been there, but she had not deigned to appear, just as she hadn't been there for the last three court sessions. She would not be called, summoned, or brought before him. She was avoiding him, and Saeran had no idea why.

The sun had set long ago, his fire was dying down, and he still couldn't sleep. Pacing his chambers, he tried yet again to summon his wayward wizard. Closing his eyes, he imagined her there with him and willed it to be so. It didn't work.

Cursing, he poured water into the scrying bowl and concentrated to conjure a vision of her in its depths. Instead of Nia's golden hair he saw a dirt road and a caravan of wagons traveling north. Dark skinned men and women dressed in colorful draping attire walked on either side of a closed carriage and armed guards surrounded it from all sides, sharp eyes on alert for any threat.

Saeran swiped the bowl off the table, his heart thudding in his chest. No, it couldn't be. It was too soon. He raked a shaky hand through his hair, looking out the window, but the breeze blowing in from the south only confirmed his vision. They were close. What few lights still flickered in cottages were going out one by one as the kingdom settled in for the night, but he could almost make out a lighted camp far beyond the towns, and all he wanted to do was disappear.

Storming out of his chambers he ran to the staircase and down to the empty great hall. The guards woke from their half slumber and stood to attention as he passed, but he ignored them. He traced the path he'd walked a dozen times today, out into the courtyard, to the small door and the stairway down to Nia's underground study. Where he would have stopped and turned back before, he shoved the door open and marched down there heedless of what he would find. If she was hurt or afraid, he could soothe her, but he couldn't go on this way anymore.

"Nia," he called, throwing open the door at the bottom of the stairway without knocking.

Nia looked up from the scroll she was writing on, and it was all Saeran could do not to sweep her into his arms then and there. Passionate words locked in his throat, foolish words.

"Yes?" she said.

Saeran started for her but hit an invisible wall halfway there. "Nia?"

"Your Majesty."

He frowned. "What is this? Release me."

"It is a ward," she said. "You are free to move anywhere on that side of it."

"Is this a test…or another lesson?" His entire being ached to touch her. Why would she deny him?

"No. The magic lessons have become a detriment to both of us. I will not be continuing your instruction." Dipping her quill in ink, she bent over her scroll again.

Her careless dismissal shocked him, but if Nia wanted to play, so be it. Saeran placed his hands on the ward and traced it left and right, searching for an edge. The cursed thing was a perfect circle surrounding her with no way in that he could discern.

Oh, but she'd taught him well. Magic was little more than will and determination. He had an endless supply of both where she was concerned. Saeran closed his eyes and listened to the ward humming its own melody. There was a pattern to it, and if he could disrupt it, he knew he could get through. He hummed until he matched the tone and felt it shiver beneath his touch. Smiling a little, he altered the tune and the wall rippled, weakening.

He pushed a hand through, ready to pass completely, but then something changed. The wall bowed inward and solidified again, shoving him away as it flexed back to its original shape. Saeran slammed his fist into it in frustration. "Nia, let me through. Please."

"If there is anything you require of me you have only to say so," she said without looking at him.

"I want you," he said. The caravan had stopped for the night. They had at least a day before the Aegiran princess arrived. He could marry Nia before then and break the arrangement with Aegiros. It would mean war, but he had fought against them before. He knew their weaknesses and no matter how many Aegiran soldiers marched into Wilderheim, with Nia at his side they could beat them back.

Her quill disappeared from her hand and she blew lightly on the scroll to dry the ink. "No, that will not be possible." She rolled up the parchment and carefully tied it off with a black ribbon.

Saeran shuddered. Nia had taught him the code for the library. The ribbon on each tome and scroll indicated the potency of what it held. Blue and green were constructive spells, descriptions of herbs and healing incantations, spells to mend what was broken. Red were battle spells for war and defense. Black was reserved for the deadliest, most dangerous of spells, the ones that meddled with dark forces and could destroy a target as easily as the wizard herself. In all the months he'd known Nia, she had never even touched a black-bound scroll.

"I love you," he said to her back as she placed the scroll back in its place.

"You are under a spell," she replied. "It will fade in time. I told you Beltaine affected everyone this way. You did not listen."

"Beltaine was one night, Nia. What I feel for you goes back a lot farther than that."

She sighed with impatience. "I do not have time for this. If I don't transcribe these scrolls the spells will fade forever. The Others have been roaming Wilderheim since the day I was presented. They have been meddling with everyone, not just you. Believe me when I say they will get bored sooner or later and this will pass. Now please leave me to my work."

Saeran drew back. "Then you don't—"

"Love you? I am your wizard. I cannot love you."

"No, I will not believe that." He'd felt her soul Beltaine night; part of it was still with him as part of his had to be with her. Everything she was saying felt wrong. This wall between them, her distance, the dispassionate tone she spoke with, it all reeked of deception.

A heavy black-bound tome thudded to the table. "You try my patience, Saeran. Why do you think you latched on to me? What possible reason could there be for a king to fall in love with his wizard?"

"You are—"

"I am not for you," she said. "Don't you see? It's a jest. This is what they do to amuse themselves; play with people's emotions and watch them implode. What better entertainment could there be than a handsome, powerful young king yearning for the one woman he can never have?"

"Stop it! If I have done something, hurt you in some way, tell me. Let me make amends, but don't push me away. This is not you."

"Oh, but it is," she countered, pulling on the ends of the black ribbon to untie it. "You just refused to see it. Well, I am done hiding. Take a good look, Majesty. This is the wizard you chose to stand by your side."

"You are trying to provoke me," he said to himself as much as her. It was working. Anger boiled low in his gut, a hot swirl of it pulling him in. He resisted, holding on to what they had because whether Nia admitted it or not, it was real.

"I am trying to make you leave! Why are you still here? There is nothing here for you."

Saeran slammed his hands on the ward. He knew he couldn't beat his way through, but what else could he do? Give up? Never. Changing tactics, he stepped back, let his hands drop to his sides. "We were friends. Was that a spell too?"

"Yes," she said. But she'd hesitated.

It was enough to bring Saeran to the wall again. "Nia, please let me through."

Her expression shuttered and he lost hope. "I have work to do and so do you. We crossed the line. It was a mistake, and I will not be making it a second time. Besides, I quite like that dark haired soldier Geir. I don't plan to take up with a man anytime soon, but when I do, it will probably be him."

Saeran's anger burned hotter. "Then he is a dead man."

Nia raised her head again, her eyes shining with fury. "You will not touch him," she said and he felt the charm slither into his core, commanding his action.

He struck the ward with all his might. "Why do you insist on making me hate you!"

"Leave!"

"I will not!" he roared back.

Nia opened the tome and a low rumble started beneath his feet, spreading outward until the walls shuddered and squealed. Rubble rained down on him and Saeran backed away from the ward, staring at Nia in astonishment.

"You will," she warned, her eyes pale like glacier ice. "Or I will bring the castle down around your ears."

For the first time Saeran saw the true extent of her magic and felt cold beneath her stare. He believed Nia would do as she threatened without hesitation. She might come to regret it, but by then it would be too late. Saeran couldn't reconcile this version of her with the lover he'd held in his arms all through Beltaine night, thanking the gods for bringing her to him. This Nia was a stranger, cold, unfeeling, and dangerous.

Seeing him hesitate, she lowered her gaze to the tome and murmured strange words that chilled Saeran to his soul.

"Stop," he said, disappointment numbing the raw ache in his heart.

Nia looked up and raised an eyebrow in question.

"I am done with you." The words sounded hollow, fitting, coming from the empty shell he'd suddenly become. Saeran dropped his gaze to escape the sight of her with that cursed tome and made himself turn away.

The ground shivered beneath his step, the disturbance following him across the chamber. Nia waited for Saeran to walk out the door and close it carefully behind him. She counted his footsteps up the staircase until he was out in the courtyard and away from her door.

Only then did she release the earth to settle. She pushed to her feet and had to grab hold of a bookcase to stay on them. Her legs had cramped hiding there and her knees felt weak. When she made it out of the library, she regarded her doppelganger and shuddered at the ice spreading through her eyes.

Her, but for the kindness of an old wizard.

Nia raised a hand to dismantle the illusion and was shocked to see how badly it shook. Turning it over, she gazed at the lines in the palm of her hand. There lay the destiny she had never been able to decipher, glowing as if to remind her there were things she could never avoid, no matter how hard she tried. It didn't matter which paths she took when all of them eventually led to the same place. She'd chosen poorly and caused unnecessary pain to Saeran as well as herself. And now here she stood, the same way she would have stood regardless of what she'd done or not done. Alone.

Nia closed her eyes and took a measured breath. When she opened them again, she moved quickly to touch the doppelganger illusion and watched herself fall apart, cracking into thousands of thousands of pieces which fell and scattered all over the floor. Like ice, the pieces melted into the ground, leaving no trace of their presence behind. The room warmed by slow degrees but Nia didn't feel it. She picked up the tome and the ribbon which bound it. In her hands, the length of silk faded to blue and she carefully retied it around the tome and carried it back to its resting place in the library.

For once, the walls of her study were silent.

She was glad.

"They have progressed," Sir Frederick noted, watching the two young knights battling with wooden swords. There was pride in his voice and a little sadness as well. Their youth reminded him of his own age. "Their skill grows daily."

Arnaud glanced at them briefly before returning his gaze to the forest line. The treasure lay that way, and he was as eager to continue on their journey, as he was reluctant. "Alec still needs to gain more courage and Jonah's footing is wrong. Practice will correct that. Let us pray it will not be needed."

"If it is," Lucca said, "they will do what needs be done." He was carving something out of a piece of wood again, his own form of worship. Lucca was not like the rest of them. He believed in God, but having lost his wife and three children in a fire, he no longer spoke of Him as the Savior. He never entered hallowed ground and rarely had Arnaud heard him utter a prayer or sing a song. The man often got a look in his eyes that worried Arnaud. It was as if this quest was one of revenge for Lucca, not salvation. What he hoped to find or prove, none of them knew, and he would not say. They've all learned it was best not to ask.

The young knights locked their swords and grunted, trying to push each other back. They were covered with dust and Arnaud wondered when he'd last gotten as dirty in practice. It seemed like a lifetime ago that he'd been forced to draw his sword. Perhaps it was the long journey that had dulled the memory of past battles. Or perhaps it was this place. He could feel something here with every step he took. Magic or the Divine, he could not tell, but he hoped it was the latter. This far north, perhaps they were closer to God than they had thought.

Perhaps it would help Lucca find his way back into His grace.

"Come, then," Frederick said, pushing to his feet. "Enough, you two. The king has commanded our audience today. Set yourselves to rights."

Arnaud stood. "Today?"

"That is what I said, boy. The king is as good as his word. Beltaine has passed. We are to be on our way soon."

"Beltaine was three days ago," he argued. "Surely the festivities take longer than this."

Frederick stopped and turned to him, his faded eyes narrowed. "The day we came here you urged me to ride through. You said you would as soon bed down with the Devil than share a meal with these heathens. What's changed?"

"A certain fair haired witch caught his eye, isn't that right, Saint Arnaud?" Lucca mocked, as he had since the night Arnaud had spent chasing after her. Days later his face still turned ruddy to recall it. There had to be magic in this land to make him lose his head like that.

Arnaud shifted his weight from foot to foot. "Nothing has changed," he said, not believing himself. "I only worry about the sort of guide his Majesty will deem to give us. Last night all of Frastmir was drunker than sailors in port. What good will they be today?"

Frederick shrugged with uncharacteristic nonchalance. "It is not for us to decide. I am certain the king will choose well."

Lucca grunted. "You did not have so much faith in his judgment a few days ago. The witch must have spelled you both."

Frederick glared at him but said, "Mayhap." Was he beginning to doubt his own vision? "Or mayhap God has chosen to answer my prayers and take away my doubt."

"What about…" Arnaud began, afraid to finish. It needed to be said. He tried again. "What about last night?"

The old man's composure faltered, and even Lucca shifted uneasily. "Saints, I thought I dreamt it."

"The whole castle shook, Frederick. Are you not curious why?"

"No," he answered, turning his back on Arnaud. His gait was slow and uneven. His knees always gave him trouble if he sat still too long.

"Cheer up, man," Jonah said with a grin, slapping Arnaud on the back and urging him to follow Frederick. "Soon the dust of this cursed odd place will be behind us, and you will need not think on it more."

Arnaud whistled to Alec and went inside. Thinking was all he seemed to be doing of late. It didn't sit well with a simple knight. All kinds of new ideas now distracted him from his devotion to God and his mission, and though he knew it to be wrong, he couldn't stop his mind from wandering where it ought not go.

~

For the second time, the knights knelt before the dais in the great hall. Their eyes no longer downcast, they waited for King Saeran to make his decree.

Nia walked toward the dais with her head high, ignoring the Others who filled the great hall instead of Saeran's court. They always gathered when there was a spectacle to be seen and Nia was beginning to resent it. She didn't spare Saeran a glance when she ascended the steps to take her place, and he didn't seem to care. It was just as well.

"My lady," one of the knights said to her, and she looked at him in surprise. Arnaud was his name. "Is aught amiss?" he asked.

She would have expected the question from Saeran. But not today.

"You will address me when you speak," Saeran said before she could answer the knight.

Startled, Arnaud bowed his head. "My apologies, your Majesty."

"I have summoned you here to grant you passage through my lands."

Nia straightened as the earth whispered to her of a nearing caravan. "Riders approach," she said to Saeran, but he ignored her.

"And because certain duties are about to render me beyond reach, I do this now, whilst I still can."

Nia frowned. The earth spoke to her of exotic places of sun and sand, where water was scarce and strange animals roamed. It sang songs so strange to Nia's ears, yet the melody was as beautiful as a thousand songbirds taking flight.

Aegiros. Nia bit her tongue to distract herself from the arrows of pain stabbing at her heart. Saeran's intended bride was coming to claim her crown.

"Wizard," Saeran called, as if she was standing on the other side of the great hall, instead of right next to his throne. "Stand by these knights and face me."

The chamber echoed with silent hisses and growls, the Others voicing their displeasure. It made Nia's head throb and her face heat with embarrassment.

Even the knights started, all and one at the insult Saeran had just delivered, degrading his right hand to the level of a peasant. It was cruel but not completely unexpected. She'd hurt him and now he wanted to hurt her back. The malicious gleam in his eyes told Nia she'd done it so well Saeran had no idea the pain he felt was hers as well. He never would, if she had any say.

Nia complied, taking the insult in stride. She would not disobey the king. Descending the steps to the bottom, she faced Saeran with her head high, eager for this humiliation to be over with. The caravan would be arriving soon. And they were expected. The Others knew it, too. Several of them loped, slithered, or simply disappeared to see the new queen arrive. But the rest stayed behind to watch Nia.

She cast a question out to them: *Why are you here?*

The Sidhe dressed in flowing gowns and robes came closer, so near she could make out the diamonds inlaid in their pearlescent skin. *What will you do?* the silver haired female asked without her mouth moving. *When the river forks and jagged rocks await you down each path, which will you choose to brave?*

Humans have their laws of honor, the male said. *We follow our hearts—that is our justice. What will you do? We wish to see.*

We wish to see who you are, the female added.

"The time has come for me to take a wife and ensure a line of succession," Saeran said and both Sidhe turned their heads to look at him.

From the other side of her, the dark male dire wolf stalked out of the crowd, head canted low. He moved just behind her, his fur bristling against her skin and the Sidhe retreated as if afraid of him. *Have you learned?* He growled in her ear.

"Under different circumstances I would be choosing from among our noble maidens the one most fitting to stand by my side." He looked at her as he said it and Nia flinched. He'd dressed in his most intricate clothes, the cloak dyed a stunning shade of blue and a thick bear skin over his shoulders. A heavy chain hung about his neck, the crown he seldom wore resting on his head. For all the splendor, he could not hide the shadows beneath his eyes. His hair was shaggy and the beginnings of a beard made his handsome face look gaunt and his gray eyes even paler. Saeran looked every bit the king he was and every bit as miserable. The sight of him pained her twice over, for she knew the cause of his despair.

He has, the dire wolf said and moved away, back to his mate. His tail struck the backs of Nia's legs and she was grateful for the staff which kept her from falling to her knees.

"Happily, I have no need of it, as I have chosen my intended bride years ago. Knights, you may be the first to hear the news. I will be taking my chosen to wife within a week." His gaze settled on Nia again, expectant. "Wizard, what think you of this?"

Nia bowed her head. "A wise decision, Majesty," she answered in a hollow formal tone. "That very same bride now approaches in the caravan, does she not?" She spoke without a wince or flinch, without any indication that she felt anything at all. Saeran's very soul rebelled at making the proclamation, and Nia stood there as if she didn't know. And there were Others around them, Saeran could feel it. Their presence set him on edge, made him feel as if he were being judged without knowing what he'd done.

"Indeed," he replied, silently damning all of them, including Nia. Did she not care in the least? Seeing she wouldn't stop this nonsense, Saeran drew himself up and made himself the king he was. "I wish to inform my father at once. The wedding will not take place until he is here to witness it. Knights, you may choose to remain for the happy occasion."

"Majesty," Nia spoke before any of the knights could say a word.

"Allow me to congratulate you on this happy occasion."

"I thank you," he said.

"And as it appears that you shall be indisposed for some time to come, it is my duty to aid you and relieve you of some of your responsibilities, this company of travelers among them."

Unease made Saeran shift in his seat. "What are you saying?"

"I will facilitate a communication to King Manfred about the arrival of your bride that he may join you and give his blessing. And then I will accompany Sir Frederick and his knights north and serve as their guide."

Saeran's eyes narrowed. "Leave us," he commanded the knights.

They picked themselves up and wisely retreated, but in their absence, the great hall felt even more crowded. Magic throbbed in the air, pushing on his mind, demanding all his secrets. He resisted, but in the effort something changed. Saeran could see currents of multicolored lights flowing left and right, whispers passing among the Others. Though they hid themselves, they could not hide their magic.

Nia stood her ground, her gaze steady on some point beyond him as if none of it mattered one way or another, including him. The king forced his muscles to unclench enough to allow him to speak. "You think to abandon your post?"

"I am confident that you will not require my counsel for the time being. The journey ahead of these men is not a short one, but with my aid, we can all be back before a fortnight has passed."

She was not asking him. The wizard was telling him she was leaving, in a way that dared him to argue. He couldn't believe the months he'd known her to be a lie, yet here she stood as if none of it had happened. She'd deceived him then, or she was deceiving him now and how could he have a wizard he didn't trust giving him counsel?

How could he have anyone but Nia at his side?

Trumpets blared, announcing the caravan's approach and Nia flinched, light flaring out of her skin briefly before she pulled it back and Saeran's eyes widened. She was hiding. He made himself push his emotions aside and truly look at her. He had never seen Nia as anything but composed in the great hall, ever the calm, steady strength at his back. Now she was tense, her posture rigid. She clutched her staff in a white-knuckled hold and her wolf pelt was gone. She looked tired, haunted and lost.

She looked as if she would rather be anywhere but here, and Saeran didn't have the heart to force her to stay. "So be it," he said and it felt right, though he could barely admit it to himself. "You leave by sunset."

~

With the exception of last night, holding the window open for Saeran to tell his father he was getting married to the Aegiran girl was the most excruciating thing Nia had ever endured. Manfred knew the moment he saw his son that something was amiss, but he attributed it to the impending ceremony. No one wanted Saeran to marry the girl: not Manfred, not Halden, and certainly not Saeran, that was obvious.

He would do it because it was his duty, and because Nia gave him no other choice. By the time she let go of the spell she was exhausted and she still had to prepare for the journey into the most inhospitable land known to man. There was a reason why no one ever ventured far beyond Wilderheim's northern border. Nothing lived there but creatures humans ought not tangle with.

Saeran sat forward in his chair, staring at the ground by her feet. His fists were clenched tight enough to shake the slightest bit, and she had to stop herself from reaching out to him. Rubbing her tired eyes, she rose from her seat and turned for the door.

"Don't go," he said. It was so soft Nia half thought she'd imagined it.

She turned back to face him. "I must." There was no other way. She could tolerate being in the shadows, she could stand his anger or indifference, but she could not stand there and watch Saeran take a wife. When he did, Nia needed to be as far away as possible.

He smiled bitterly. "I remember when you spoke your oath to me; I believed every word you said. *As long as need be, until death or longer.* Do you know, I believe it still? I just never realized the one thing you would not be able to save me from is myself."

One more time, Nia focused her Sight to scry the air and looked into the future, seeking any way to avoid this. What she saw was war. Hundreds of horses trampling fields, sowing salt in their wake and setting crops aflame. Swords clashing, magic burning through the night, and blood. So much blood. Death and disaster waited down every path she chose. An arrow through the chest. A blade across the neck. Poison in a chalice of wine. Treachery and deceit. She flinched each time she saw Saeran meet his end. Frastmir would burn to the ground one way or another, unless Nia did what she already knew had to be done. There was no other way. "This is the way it has to be."

Saeran nodded, his eyes bleak. "I suppose it is."

She was at the door when his voice stopped her a second time.

"I know you will not want to," he said. "But come back to me anyway."

~

Close to sunset the gates opened to admit the caravan. Over twenty riders entered, followed by a great tent-like carriage and an entourage of another twenty people on foot. Nia and the knights watched their progress from the stables. Their horses ready and their supplies packed, they came outside, to join the curious crowds in the courtyard.

A single wind instrument played in the tent-carriage, its melody sounding their soft fanfare. These were desert people. They wore long robes and cloth wound about their heads, their horses' reigns adorned with tufts of ribbons and cords. The women were draped in robes from neck to foot and they wore veils to cover their hair and face. Nothing but their hands showed. An odd way to dress, Nia thought, but then they must be thinking the same about the northerners.

Wondering what Saeran would think of this, Nia glanced up at the catle windows. She could just make out his shadow in one of them. But he didn't seem to be looking at the caravan. As soon as she caught sight of him, he stepped away from the window and out of sight.

No good to be leaving in pain, Stardust told her, gently butting his nose against her shoulder.

"I know," she replied. "But it would be even worse if I stayed."

The caravan stopped and the men dismounted as Nia swung into her own saddle and made ready to ride out. As she nudged Stardust forward, a bright glitter caught her eye. One of the men in the entourage was not a southerner. He dressed in robes, yes, but he wore no cloth around his head, and his hair was as fair as her own. About his neck hung a pendant. It was a glittering black stone as big as her palm, set in pale gold. Curious, Nia tried to get a better look, but with so many people milling in the courtyard, it was of no use. She gave up for the moment, shaking her head at her own silliness.

But when they passed close by, the pendant once more caught her eye as the man bowed. Her gaze became unfocused as she watched the pendant sway back and forth and in the haze, she saw a vision. No longer in the courtyard, she watched the dream unfold before her.

There were two women, the older teaching the younger her craft. She was a midwife, well liked and respected in her village. But soon, the vision showed her, the younger woman surpassed her mentor and fearing the old woman was no longer trustworthy, the villagers turned from her, to her apprentice.

The old midwife ran on stiff legs to a great rock that served as an altar and dropped to her aged knees. With her arms raised above her head, she beseeched the gods. She cried to the heavens, invoked incantations she had no knowledge of, shouted for all the gods she could name until one of them answered.

Lightning struck the altar, frightening her into fleeing for her life, but when she found her courage again and cautiously returned, she discovered a jewel. Taking it into her bony hands, she turned it to the light and Nia saw through her eyes the wicked gleam of Loki's gaze in the depths of that black crystal.

In the next blink Nia was in the young apprentice's cottage. The woman was asleep in her bed, wearing the pendant around her neck, a treasured gift from her mentor. The gleam of a knife by candlelight was the only thing to betray the old midwife before she plunged the blade into the sleeping woman's chest. The apprentice died quietly, with no one the wiser and her murderer retrieved her gods given trinket with shaking hands. As soon as she put it on, her posture straightened and she sighed, walking away with an easy step. Too easy for one so old.

Stardust jolted her and Nia blinked, finding herself the object of a curiously knowing gaze as the man with the pendant grinned at her. Before she could approach him, Stardust took off, leading the way out of the castle.

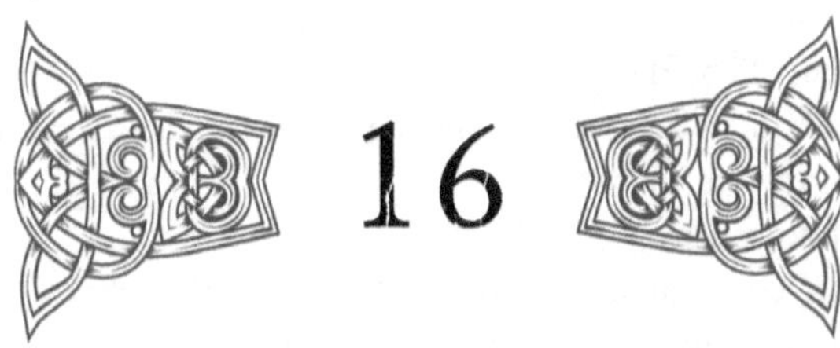

16

The first stretch of the path north was easy enough, and they rode hard to make headway before the sun dipped low. The wide, well used dirt road wound through the forest for miles until it ended abruptly as if whoever traversed it suddenly decided they'd gone far enough and turned back the way they'd come. Beyond this point, there was nothing but trees.

Nia would have ridden on, but the knights grew wary of riding in the dark of night. The moon wasn't bright enough to touch the forest floor and lighting torches would only blind them to the shadows. They made camp under a giant oak and lit a small fire to stave off the chill of night. Once everything was done, they retreated together for prayer, leaving Nia alone to stare into the flames. Shapes danced within them, slender, sensuous waifs moving to the music of the night. Fire sprites.

They danced and they beckoned to her, smiling when she refused to join their play. "What do you want?" she asked, tired of being made a source of amusement.

The sprites laughed, making the fire crackle and spark.

Nia blew on the flames, banishing the sprites in lieu of a vision. Scrying flames was different than air or water, the images obscured by ash and smoke. It was also more difficult because fire touched Spirit and Soul. Asking something of the flames meant opening oneself to them, and more often than not, the fire pointed in two different directions. One leading to the object sought, the other to the one most desired, without revealing which was which. It was as close to deceit as an element could get and even then it was self-deceit which sent a petitioner the wrong way. Some desires ran so deep a person was not always aware of them.

"What do you see?"

Nia blinked through the flames at Lucca. She thought he'd gone to pray with the others. "I seek guidance to the treasure you are after," she said.

"And?"

Nia gazed into the fire. From opposite sides two hands raised a chalice in a salute. One silver, inlaid with blood red stones and engraved with runes, the other gold with elaborate silver filigree depicting a winged man with horns and a tail. Both were reaching toward her, a choice between the two. It could mean any number of things and with her heart still bleeding over Saeran, it probably had to do with her choice to leave rather than stand by his side as she'd sworn to do. Red stones for her aching heart, wings to symbolize the freedom of flight. "I see two cups raised in offering."

Lucca smiled somewhat sadly. "Our legends say there is a cup which once held the blood of our savior. It is said this cup is one of judgment. To those who serve god without question, it has the power to grant salvation. But those who serve only themselves get cast into damnation."

"Do you believe this?"

"No. Man was given thought in order to question everything, even god."

"But you just said only those who do not question will have salvation."

He grinned. "Yes, well, not everyone interprets the words as I do."

Curious, Nia studied the knight who spoke so little but said so much. "You are not here for the treasure of eternal life, are you?"

"And you are not here to lead us to it, are you?"

"Why else would I be here?"

"Why indeed?" Lucca stoked the fire. "Perhaps to run away from something? Or someone?"

A twig snapped, announcing the return of the others and Nia was grateful for the interruption. For the rest of the night, Alec played a thin wood whistle to entertain them and Nia stared into the flames, seeking guidance.

But every time she asked her silent question, only the two cups raised in answer.

~

The moment he lost sight of Nia and her company of knights Saeran felt hollow. He welcomed the Aegirans in the great hall as was his duty, meeting his intended for the first time and receiving the wedding gifts they'd brought with them, all while silently wishing he was anyone but himself. A small army had accompanied the girl here, many of whom would stay behind to ensure her well being and comfort.

Farraj, Saeran was relieved to learn, would return to his *shansher* as soon as the deed was done. He liked the man well enough, but he didn't want him to linger. A warrior whose honor bound him as surely as any of Nia's spells, Farraj would give his life to protect those he served and Saeran could see how he doted on his princess. Should Farraj ever suspect Saeran of wrongdoing against her, he had no doubt he would find himself without a head.

To marry her at all felt wrong when his heart belonged to another. No, he did not want Farraj to stay long enough to discover that.

The girl's name was Mari and there was never a moment when she was not surrounded by handmaidens, all cloaked and veiled to hide everything but their eyes. Saeran could not pick her out of a crowd if he tried. And they would remain estranged this way until their wedding night.

Saeran spoke the words, acknowledged the oath he'd taken years ago and sealed the pledge with another to ensure the Aegirans' good will. He could not look away from the girl's eyes. They were so very young.

When all the ceremonies of greeting were finished, the Aegirans were led to their chambers to rest after a long journey and Saeran escaped into the glen. His chest ached with each breath he took and all he wanted to do was mount a horse and ride as fast as he could out of the castle, away from the life of a king. Anywhere but here.

"Your father is not here."

Saeran felt the earth tremble at Farraj's footsteps but he could not face the man. "He rides this way as we speak," he replied. The moment Manfred had heard the news, he'd ordered a carriage. If he changed the horses often and never stopped for the night as he intended, he would be here in two days time.

"It is good to see you well."

"And you, Farraj."

"Now noble talk over. We speak as men."

The words felt like an order, compelling Saeran to turn and face the southerner. "Say your peace."

In the years since the war, Farraj had changed. He'd acquired new scars in battle, and adornments to mark his victories. His hair was longer, graying on one side, but his eyes were as shrewd as Saeran remembered. "Where we come from the women are treasured."

"They are bartered with," Saeran said, instantly regretting his words.

Farraj drew himself up, but chose to overlook the insult. "They are protected and given to worthy men who can keep them safe. It is not so here. Mari is not strong like your women. She has lived only with other women and never known a man."

Knowing he would be the one to change that made Saeran want to turn back time, undo the foolish deal he'd struck and take his chances down another path. "I expected as much," he said with difficulty. "You have my word I will treat her gently."

"She can never know you do not want her as wife."

Taken aback, Saeran could only stare.

"In Aegiros she would have been one of a noble's many wives, but cherished. Here she will be lonely queen. But her children kings and queens after her. For her it will be enough. But she cannot know she is reason for another's heart pain. It would bring too much sadness for her to bear. Better she believe you will not love her than that you cannot. I ask this for favor. For Mari."

Saeran blanched. "How did you know?"

Smiling a little, Farraj laid a hand on his shoulder. "I look in your eyes and see the woman you want. She is in your soul, and she is not my *idrah* Mari."

"I will honor our agreement. I will be true to Mari."

Farraj grunted. "This I know," he said, stepping back. "You are man of honor. It is not an easy thing to be. Many winters ago, when you offered a life for a life, I knew then you would regret it. You bargained bravely for your people, young king. Bravely, but foolishly. For life of another you gave up your heart. A heart without life will sleep until it breathes again. But what is life without heart?" The Aegiran wise man touched a hand to his chest then to his mouth, and finally his forehead and he bowed at the waist. He returned to the castle, leaving Saeran alone in the dark glen.

17

They made camp in the forest on the third night. The knights gathered wood for a fire and Nia lit it for them before she walked away, needing the comfort of solitude. It was difficult to find in a place where everything was alive and singing. Dozens of voices spoke to her, asking questions she didn't want to dwell on and giving her advice she had no wish to hear. Well meaning creatures, they were, and their presence infuriated her. How dare they broach the subject when they had no knowledge of what they were saying?

The trees wanted to know why she was here when her place was at Saeran's side. The sparrows told her to go back and speak to him. The earth hummed to her that the woman he was to wed was not his true intended; that she did not belong. And the brook she crossed sang to her that it knew her heart and knew that it was no longer inside her.

With each new voice her anger rose. It was easier to confront than the pain. Nia had chosen this path. It had been her choice to teach Saeran and learn his heart in the process. Her choice to share her evenings with him, countless witching hours when sitting in silence next to him began to feel like the most wonderful thing in the world. She could have turned Saeran away countless times; could have refused him Beltaine night, but she hadn't. And so it was her own fault she was here when he was miles away, wedding a southerner out of obligation.

You did not have to turn him away from your embrace, the earth whispered and the words stabbed at Nia.

She'd had no other choice. Not turn him away? Nia shivered. The king's happiness might mean the world to her, but it would have mattered little to a kingdom torn apart.

No, Saeran had chosen this fate long ago, as had she. Wilderheim had to come first.

That she'd done what was right for the greater good, however, meant little when her soul howled in anguish at the crescent moon.

Knowing it was a mistake but unable to help herself, Nia weaved her hand through the air to conjure the castle. Just one peek, she told herself. A brief glance at Saeran and then she would put him out of her mind and finish what she'd started.

Light followed her movements, creating a window, and in its depths she saw the throne and Saeran seated upon it. He was somber as he watched the celebration in honor of his bride, but his gaze strayed often to the woman at his side.

A child. She was draped in colorful silks, the bottom of her face covered with a transparent veil. Her eyes were beautiful. Dark and exotic, both innocent and sensual. She was a beauty, to be sure. And Saeran had noticed it as well. When he turned to gaze at her, his eyes became dream hazed and a small smile pulled on his mouth.

Nia turned away with a whimper. She let the spell dissolve and sank to a fallen tree trunk, burying her face in her hands. She couldn't breathe; didn't trust herself to release the air in her lungs, lest it take her voice with it. If she cried now, she would never stop.

It was done. Saeran was married. He had his queen just as Nia had wished for him the night of his coronation. She would sit by his side, guide his hand, and ease the burden of ruling a kingdom. She would be his friend and hold him when he needed to be held, kiss him when he came to her each night. She would give him heirs unlike any Wilderheim has ever seen.

It's as it should be, she told herself. *My place was always in the shadow.* Hugging the wolf skin closer around her she lifted her gaze to the stars. Not for the first time she wondered what Nico would have wanted her to do. But then her thoughts turned dark, wondering why the old wizard had even brought her to the castle, made her face things she'd never wanted to see, and then abandoned her when she needed him most. He must have foreseen this as a possibility.

In the shadows, a dark form stirred. It was Lucca. This morning when she'd greeted each of the knights he'd coldly informed her that he was not truly a knight and that he did not wish to be addressed by the title. She'd heard him cry out in his sleep the night before and knew he suffered his own nightmares which made him surly in the mornings. But whatever he dreamed, he never told her and she never asked.

Now, a fair way from the camp fire and the rest of their company, he kept his distance, hiding in shadows rather than stepping into the light of the moon. He addressed her from that darkness as if its embrace was the only reason he could speak the words at all. "I know your pain," he said, his voice so hollow it called to her, and she reached out unbidden to his mind. "It is the pain of loss, same as mine."

His memories rose like mist in her mind, pulling her into his past without being invited. She saw a child suffering with fever, his worried mother sitting by his bedside while Lucca hunted like a madman for a healer, a priest, a witch, anyone who could help his dying son. She saw a kindly old priest enter the house in his absence to console the mother and light a candle by the child's bedside, saying a prayer for his recovery. Then the priest left. Exhausted, the praying mother fell asleep on her knees. The candle tumbled, sparked a flame in the thresh and within moments the entire house was ablaze.

"They tell you it will pass," Lucca said, banishing her back into herself. "They tell you to give yourself to god and let him take the pain away. It is all a lie, wizard. Pain like that never goes away. And it only becomes worse with time."

"Among my people we believe our loved ones await us beyond death," she said.

"Your gods are not mine. The one I worshiped took my wife and children from me because I loved them more than him." His harsh tone made her flinch. "You cannot imagine the hatred I hold for him, and for that he will keep me from them forever."

Nia's heart broke for him. This was the torment he lived with day and night, mourning his family, cursing his god. Lucca had lost everything, and in his despair the pain had become all he had. It was overwhelming, the kind of grief that scarred the soul. It went beyond her ability to heal and she wasn't fool enough to try. "I am sorry," she whispered.

Heavy rustling footsteps put an end to their conversation. Lucca retreated deeper into the night and then disappeared all together.

"Lady Nia."

Nia did not face Arnaud. "I told you not to call me a lady. I am not noble."

"You are something," he said coming closer. Lowering himself next to her, he plucked a sleeping flower to toy with. "May I ask you a question?"

"You may not."

"Why have you decided to join us? It is because of the king, is it not?" He pulled on the flower, forcing it open and tearing off its petals. Nia's hand twitched every time she heard the delicate rip. Still raw from Lucca's memories, it aggravated her much more than it would have under normal circumstances. Where she felt an odd kinship with Lucca, Arnaud's presence was forceful, bothersome. She wanted him gone. "Matters of the heart are—"

"None of your affair," she snapped. "My reasons for coming with you are my own and you have no need to guess at them. Rest assured, I will get you to your treasure, and I will lead you back again. But my obligation to you goes no further than…" She never finished the sentence. Her skin prickled and the wolf pelt's hackles rose as if he was still alive and scented danger.

Power was in the air; not her own. It controlled the wind and made it spy. She stretched her senses to find the source but it was beyond her boundaries. Its magic tasted different than her own or anything Other she had thus far encountered. It made her shudder, for she knew that this grand display was only a hint of its true potential.

"What is it?" Arnaud rose to his feet, hand on his sword, looking for an enemy to slay.

"Hush for a moment," Nia told him and knelt on the ground to bury her hands in the earth. It was a stronger medium than the air, and through it she would be able to reach farther. Closing her eyes, she concentrated, using the power's scent to track it as a predator. She separated herself from her body and streaked across the forest floor with incredible speed. She felt nothing in this state, not grief or pain, not love, anger or regret. Only the freedom of flight. Nothing restrained her, and if she wanted to she could disperse to eternity and never return. It was a temptation Nia forced herself to resist. She had her target and she was getting closer.

The earth was cold, covered with ice and it sped her progress. She was vaguely aware of what was around her. A field of snow and ice, a sparse forest and in its depths a cave. This was where the spy dwelled, hidden away from the world where no one would think to look for him. She slowed as she neared the cave, her limits stretched as far as they could go. If she went too far she wouldn't be able to return to herself.

Nia pushed a little more. It hurt to move, but she put it from her mind and approached the cave. There was light. A fire burned in the back, but the light of magic was much brighter. So bright it blinded her, though she had no eyes. She reached for it and just managed to brush the core.

Pain exploded in her physical body, merciless talons ripping into her mind so deep she screamed. Her essence pulled back with such a rush that it knocked her back against a tree. And still she screamed, trapped in the clutches of a being she couldn't identify. It probed her, searched her mind and soul with cold efficiency, leaving no secret undiscovered. Nia burned. Her blood was on fire, scorching her from the inside, yet her skin was freezing from the Other's touch.

At last, it touched upon something that made it still. For a moment, lucidity returned to her. Instead of the forest, she was suddenly in her study beneath Castle Frastmir. Everything was tossed around as if a great wind had swept through the chamber, and then her gaze fell upon Saeran. Nia squeezed her eyes shut, refusing to allow the creature tearing through her to see with her eyes. It was useless; it was in her memories, not her body, and it saw everything as clearly as she remembered it.

For a terrible moment, all she could do was breathe and hear it breathe with her, inside her.

Then, all at once her torturer released her from its clutches and disappeared. Nia fell to the forest floor as many footsteps rushed toward her. She heard the knights, their voices so far away she couldn't make out their words. They touched her, but she felt nothing.

And then everything went dark.

She awoke by the camp fire, her entire body aching as if she'd been stomped to dust by Stardust's hooves. Arnaud and the others stood over her, all of them wearing identical expressions of fear and concern.

One of them, she wasn't sure which, helped her sit up. The simple motion brought her so much agony she almost cast up the meager contents of her stomach. The remnants of that strange power still lingered inside her. She felt seared with it, branded. Her hands were stiff and she couldn't hold the cup Arnaud handed her. She saw their mouths move, knew they were talking to her, but couldn't make any sense of their words past the ringing in her ears.

It didn't matter. Such immense power had a source. It was a territorial being, dangerously intelligent and cunning. It relished its seclusion and did not tolerate any trespasses on its land.

It knew who they were and where they had come from.

They were heading right for it and the creature knew.

It was waiting for them.

Wilderheim would never suspect the sacrifice Saeran had made for the safety of his people. Manfred had known the day his son shook hands with the Aegiran delegate that one day he would have to stand by and watch the boy's heart break. It was a thousand times worse than he'd ever imagined now that Saeran sat next to his young queen, and Manfred would give anything to spare him this; to give Saeran what he'd had with his mother.

Manfred had come riding in with two hundred of Halden's finest soldiers to tell Saeran he had only to say a word and he would have two armies at his back to defend Wilderheim and its king. But his son would hear none of it. With Manfred at his side, he'd wed the southern girl at once and fulfilled the foolish bargain he never should have struck. Now he sat his throne with her at his side, watching over the feast but Manfred knew he wasn't seeing any of it.

"A fine pair they make," one of the border lords begrudged. There were many who shared his disgruntlement that the king had chosen a foreigner over one of their daughters.

Manfred motioned to one of the servers. "Where is the wizard?"

"She's gone, my lord," the serving girl said, blushing. "She rode out days ago with a company of knights."

"For what purpose?" What could be more important than this? And how dare she abandon Saeran when he needs her the most? If anyone could have put a stop to it, the wizard Nia could have done it.

"No one knows, my lord. All's I know is that the night before she left the castle shook as if the very earth was set to swallow it whole! And she looked none too pleased to be leavin', her and his Majesty."

Manfred closed his eyes and sighed, dismissing the girl with a wave. He should have known. Reaching for his chalice, he drank deeply of the honey mead, but it did nothing to sweeten the bitter taste in his mouth.

"Hail King Saeran and Queen Mari!" someone shouted and dozens of voices echoed the toast.

"Hail the king and queen! Huzzah! Huzzah! Huzzah!"

Saeran met eyes with him and Manfred fisted his hands against the urge to give an ill advised order. Instead he rose from his seat and climbed the stairs to the dais and his son. "You spoke to her before she left," he said for Saeran's ear alone.

The boy nodded.

"Did she tell you anything of use?" He knew the way of wizards all too well. Nico had spoken in riddles so often Manfred still gritted his teeth to remember it. He could only imagine his apprentice was likewise disinclined to reveal what she thought his son was not prepared to know.

"She said this must be so."

"And you believe her?"

Saeran looked away, his jaw set. "She is the stronger one," he said after a while. "Regardless of the king's happiness, Wilderheim must hold. One of us had to put the kingdom first, and three days ago it would not have been me. Yes, Father, I believe my wizard spoke the truth, though I wish to the gods it was not so. With all my heart I believe it."

Then there was little hope for either of them.

Manfred sighed and bid his son good night, feeling every one of his many years in his bones as he descended the stairs and retreated to his chambers to rest. Of all the many wishes he'd held for Saeran in his heart since the day of his birth, none were greater than that he grow up hale and strong and find someone to make him as happy as Rhys had made him. Now he wondered whether he'd called down some sort of curse upon him instead.

Better that Saeran never know that kind of happiness existed than live the rest of his days with it just beyond his reach. Better that he never know love than ever pine after one that could never be matched.

For if ever a woman lived to make his son lose his heart and soul in love, the wizard Nia was she.

~

The music was overwhelming. Three different groups of musicians played three different songs, several of them plucking tunes Saeran had never heard before. The entire kingdom was rejoicing, celebrating his marriage to the Southern princess. Saeran sat his throne as tense as a statue, feeling the same way he had the first time he'd seen the Aegirans on the other side of the battlefield. Cornered.

He wanted to howl his anguish, willing to make an utter fool of himself because maybe, just maybe the sound of his heart breaking would carry far enough for Nia to hear, loud enough to call her back to him. But what could he do once she was here?

The princess, his queen now, had barely moved since she'd sat next to him. She was a beauty to be sure. At ten and five she was a vision in silks, no matter that he couldn't see more than her eyes. Dark skinned, with raven hair that reached almost to her knees, Queen Mari watched the feast through wide, exotic eyes. Those eyes held magic as hot as the desert sun.

If only it scorched Saeran as it seemed to burn all his nobles. Old lechers, the lot of them.

He tapped his foot to a particular rhythm, straining his ears for the breeze. It was difficult enough to concentrate with music blaring and everyone shouting congratulations his way, but everything seemed more difficult without Nia close by. She must have witched him somehow, made him see and hear things that were never there when she was absent.

There lay true magic. Not in the eyes of Mari, but in the presence of Nia. She wore power like a lady wore a cloak, yet she rarely called on it. Magic came to her, eager to do her bidding, eager to be touched by her and to touch her in return.

Eager for her as Saeran was desperate.

A breeze tickled his neck and he sat up straighter. *What news?* he asked it, hoping to catch word of his wizard and her companions.

The breeze wavered with silent laughter and tickled him once more. *I bring news from the south,* it said, *and your wizard treads not here.*

Frustrated, he sat back once more. He needed to walk out into the night and question the trees, the earth. Anything at all. There'd been no word of her since she rode into the woods. No one had seen her or the knights pass through a single village. No one could tell him where she was, whether she was safe. Saeran didn't trust a single one of those knights; he never should have sent Nia out with them.

He needed his wizard back.

In her absence, Saeran had nowhere to turn but to Mari. "Does this please you?" he asked, striving for at least the appearance of civility.

She blinked her dark eyes at him as she slowly deciphered his words. Someone had taught her his language, but she still had much to learn. At last she nodded.

Saeran returned the gesture and turned his attention back to the revelry. She'd not said a word to him yet. It annoyed him, her silence, more than the musicians, and more than the nobles. He missed Nia's prickly tongue. Never had that woman lacked for something to say, whether to anger him, amuse him, or teach him. She'd have risked her neck to speak out of turn rather than hold her silence when the stakes were high.

The timid creature next to him now was her exact opposite. If she had strength in her, any spirit at all, Saeran couldn't see it.

With Nia, he'd felt it. From miles away he'd felt it.

Now all he felt was a void where she'd once stood, keeping watch over him and his reign. His trusted advisor and beloved friend. Friend, for he could never now call her by a name more dear.

Clenching his hands into fists on his knees, Saeran forced his thoughts away from the wizard. He had a wife now. A queen. He should be among his nobles, dancing and rejoicing with them. But though his feet ached to move, it wasn't to dance. Though his gaze was watchful, it wasn't to take in the spectacles. And though his ears were sharp, he didn't care for the bard's ballad. Despite his best intentions, Saeran couldn't help but search for what he knew he would not find.

His nose tickled and for a moment he thought he smelled summer blooms. *Nia.* He had but to think her name and all of a sudden the music of a thousand hearts beating at once made his own beat faster. Colors seemed brighter somehow, everything more beautiful, and he felt as if she was there, causing this change in him. His frown gave way at the fanciful thought, imagining things he knew could never be.

In his mind, he was well and truly wed—to the woman who'd taught him to hear the wind sing through trees. And when he glanced to the honored seat to his left, it was a golden haired nymph he saw sitting there, proud and regal, draped in robes instead of silks, with a wolf skin hugging her shoulders. She wore no gold, or adornments, but for that. He saw her red lips curve into a smile and his own curved in answer.

And then, as quickly as it had come, the feeling was gone, as was his wizard. In her rightful place now sat a southern girl of ten and five, no doubt petrified at being wed to a northern king.

Saeran pushed to his feet to leave, not realizing his mistake until the music stopped. There was only one thing he could say, the thing they all expected to hear. "It is time for us to retire." He choked on the words. As tradition dictated, he bowed to his young queen and offered his hand. He told himself he didn't see her glance uncertainly at the guards who had accompanied her here. He told himself he didn't feel her hand flinch when his fingers closed around hers.

And later, when he left her chambers, he told himself he didn't hear her weeping softly in her bed.

Nothing would compel him to sleep after that. Saeran could not close his eyes to escape knowing he would have to open them in the morning and return to the same world he'd left tonight. It would break him all over again. The briefest moment of hope for relief could make any torment that much worse.

Instead, he slipped outside into the glen. All was still in the castle now to give the king and queen their privacy, but he could hear laughter and dancing carrying on in the town of Frastmir.

Taking a knee, he caressed the ground. *Tell me, mother earth who birthed us all,* he beseeched, *tell me of my wizard.*

The earth sighed beneath his touch. *The wizard's wish is stronger than yours, king Saeran. She bid me hold my peace.*

Stunned, Saeran recalled Nia's lessons about charms and commands. The larger or older a thing was, the more difficult it was to command; a sapling was easier to bend than a full grown tree. Sometimes charms worked better than spelled commands, but even so there were few who would ever try to move a mountain, let alone succeed. Yet somehow Nia had compelled the vastness of earth itself to keep her secrets. He couldn't fathom it.

A cold wind made his shirt billow and he shivered at its touch. *Have you any news, wicked breeze? Have you news of my Nia?*

It swept by him again, playing with his hair and trailing between his fingers when he held his hand up to it. *I do indeed,* it hissed, twining around him like a cat asking to be petted.

Tell me, then.

The wizard travels north, the wind told him, sweeping once more into his hair and making him shiver with cold. *She travels with armored knights, seeking treasure.*

Saeran rolled his eyes. *This I already know. Tell me...* He hesitated, unsure of what he would hear. *What is she doing now?*

A moment's rest in the air silenced the north wind and he feared he'd missed his chance. Saeran wondered if his summoning spell would work. Could he simply call Nia to him as he had before?

No. If she'd charmed the earth into silence, she wouldn't come to him for the asking. He could shout himself hoarse and Nia would not appear. She was well and truly gone.

But just as he was about to lose hope, the wind returned, sweeping past him with renewed strength and chill. It rushed at him with such force he nearly fell off his feet and it spoke to him four simple words:

She screams in pain.

The first snow began to fall on the twelfth day. Arnaud pulled the hood of his cape over his head and watched the wizard ride out front to scout their way. They should have reached their destination by now, yet she kept leading them farther north.

It was getting colder by the day, the landscape more and more barren. Where before they'd hunted for their dinner to ration supplies, there was now little game to be found. Lucca and Alec had returned empty handed the night before and Arnaud himself had had no luck this morning. If something didn't change, they would freeze or starve long before they ever made it back. If they made it back.

The wizard returned to confer with Frederick and Lucca. Arnaud might have savored the sight not long ago. Now chills ran down his spine, and they had nothing to do with the snow.

Arnaud had faced armies before. He'd felt the blade of a sword kiss his neck, moments away from death but for the grace of God. He'd brought lawbreakers and sinners to justice, looked in the eyes of monsters wearing a human mask, and never felt a twinge of fear for he'd always had God on his side.

The night he'd so foolishly sought the wizard alone, he'd felt his Savior abandon him. Demons had been out to play that night. They'd clawed their way inside the wizard, and Arnaud could still feel their taint lingering. He felt it each time she rode near, whenever she looked his way. The ice in her gaze now frightened him.

And no one else seemed to see it.

"What do you think they are talking about?" Alec asked.

"Planning the easiest path, no doubt," he replied, but the way Frederick frowned, shaking his head, he couldn't be sure.

Lucca separated from the group to come to the rest of them. "We camp here," he said.

"It is midday!" Jonah protested.

Lucca glared at the young man. "Dismount and make camp," he ordered.

"What's happened?" Arnaud asked.

"Nia says there is a squall awaiting us not far ahead. We need to wait it out before we can ride on."

"We have our winter gear," Alec argued. "We have ridden through storms before."

Lucca shook his head. "Not like this. We cannot risk it."

"Especially when not even our guide knows where we are going," Arnaud added with venom.

Lucca speared him with a hard look. "You two, do as you are told. Arnaud, a word."

Arnaud dismounted and followed Lucca a fair distance off. Though the land was slowly turning white, the blanket of snow was not thick enough to cushion his step and frozen grass and foliage crunched beneath his boots.

"Something is bothering you," Lucca said.

"I—"

"I do not care what it is. Look around you, Arnaud. This is as far from what we know as we have ever been, and if we cannot work together this land will kill us."

"I put in my fair share," Arnaud snarled.

"Then do it without questioning every step of the way," Lucca snarled back and stalked off.

Angered more than he ever remembered being before, Arnaud returned to his mount to retrieve his pack. As he tossed it to the ground, the hairs on the back of his neck stood on end and he turned around to see the wizard watching him. He shuddered. Taking his crossbow from his pack, Arnaud went east to hunt for their midday meal. Anything to put some distance between him and the wizard.

He didn't return to camp until the growing darkness forced him to the warmth of their fire. His hands were empty. The snow had begun to fall in earnest, hiding any tracks there might have been. Even creatures of the air were sparse here; he hadn't seen a single bird in days.

Someone had unrolled his pallet and unpacked his winter gear. He nodded his thanks to Jonah and Alec, knowing that Lucca and Frederick would not have bothered, deeply engrossed as they were in their conversation with the wizard.

"No luck?" Alec asked, handing him a little piece of stale bread and old cheese. Jonah had the flask of wine, which had days ago been refilled with water.

"Nothing moving out there," Arnaud told them. "It's as if the animals know to hide from us."

Jonah breathed on his hands and rubbed them together for warmth. He took out his whistle and held it up. "Shall I play?"

"Not tonight," Arnaud said. "Get some rest. We will all need it for the days to come." And pulling the furs around him up to his ears, he bedded down to sleep.

When morning came, they didn't wait for first meal. Frederick gave the order to mount up, and he and the wizard took the lead going north. Ever farther north. Arnaud kept his complaints to himself. He filed in rank beside Lucca and held his peace.

They rode over even ground for a while before heading up an incline. Arnaud's mount wasn't as well shoed as the others. He hesitated and fell behind the rest, struggling up that hill. Arnaud picked his way with care, mindful that if they lost a horse now it would mean trouble. Better that he fall behind now than rush and meet his Maker too soon. The others wouldn't leave him; he would take his time now and catch up with them on the other side.

But before they could crest the hill and head down, the front riders pulled to a stop not far ahead. "What is going on?" he called. "Why have we stopped?"

No one answered him.

Arnaud spurred his mount to join them and stopped as they had, lining the cliff. Breath left him at the sight. The valley at his feet was frozen, everything covered in a thick layer of glistening ice. The trees, the ground, even the animals stopped forever in their tracks stood there as if encased in glass.

Frederick crossed himself. "God have mercy, this could have been us."

"It was not God who made us stop," Jonah returned. "You saved our lives, Nia."

Arnaud was speechless. His mount fidgeted, but the reins slipped from his numb fingers when he tried to subdue him. Saints, he could see the animals' eyes wide with fear, their mouths open to scream. Deer, rabbits, squirrels, they all must have sought shelter here. As sheltered as the valley was, it would have been warmer than the rest of the forest before that squall swept right through it.

Arnaud looked at the wizard to find her watching him in return, and he felt no gratitude, only deeper unease.

Lucca dismounted and drew his sword. "Take what you can," he said. "It may be all we will have to sustain us from this point on."

~

"He says the orchard is infested with mice."

Saeran looked up from the report at Kvaran. "Mice?"

"Yes, your Majesty." The man looked left and right at the other advisors, but none of them spoke while he addressed the king. "They are destroying the flowers, and Robert says if it continues there will not be any apples left come harvest time."

"But *mice*?" Saeran repeated. "Can mice even climb trees?"

"I do not know, your Majesty."

He groaned and rubbed his aching forehead. Half the day gone and they hadn't even touched on two thirds of the issues the council of advisors had brought before him. He'd never known so many things could go wrong at the same time. The apple harvest was being destroyed, the bears were breaking bee hives to get to their honey, the huntsmen had their hands full with too many wild boar which were digging up all the mushrooms and root vegetables to take care of the bears. The weather was dry, forcing farmers to carry water in pails to keep their crops from dying, and though the lake was filled with fish, the fisherman couldn't catch anything because his nets fell apart every time they touched water.

And Nia had only been gone a fortnight.

Saeran had given orders to be informed the moment she and the knights were spotted returning. It should be any day now, thank Woden. He didn't think he could handle this much longer.

"Your Majesty?"

"Yes, what is it, Liam?"

The servant bowed. "Forgive the interruption. I've been sent by her Majesty to inquire whether your business is finished."

Did it bloody look finished? "Tell her no."

"Yes, your Majesty."

"Wait," he said. "What does she want?"

"I do not know, your Majesty. Shall I inquire?"

He frowned. "No. No, that will not be necessary." He'd told Mari many times if the matter was urgent she could interrupt him no matter what he was doing. But though she nodded each time he told her, she always sent someone else to ask for him and never insisted on his presence. He could only assume it wasn't important.

After Liam left, Saeran turned back to his council. "Send word to the farmers that anyone handy with a bow or spear is free to hunt as many boar as they can slay until further notice. Anything they kill is theirs to do with as they please. That ought to free up the huntsmen to take care of the bears and save our honey, as well as compensate the farmers for the drought. Call together the carpenter guild to come up with a faster way to bring water to the fields and send someone to investigate the mysterious, tree climbing mice."

"What of the fishing nets?" Allon inquired, snickering beneath his moustache.

Saeran closed his eyes and focused to hear the earth speak. It was exhausting this far up and he rarely used the trick, but at times like these, he trusted the earth far more than his own messengers. People lied to achieve their ends. The earth did not. What it told him made Saeran raise an eyebrow. "The fisherman's wife is a weaver?"

Kvaran consulted the scribed message before him. "I believe so, your Majesty."

"Send the midwife Kata to talk to them both. She is almost as good a peacemaker as Nia."

Kvaran frowned. "Why do they need a peacemaker?"

"Because if I heard correctly, the fisherman Neal has been eyeing the weaver Sidda's apprentice, Maeve. And if Sidda found out, I would not put it past the woman to take apart all her husband's nets in retaliation."

While many of them chuckled, Allon asked, "Where might his Majesty have heard such a thing?"

Saeran, in no mood to explain himself, made a grandiose gesture. "The wind told me." Not a lie.

The old advisor harrumphed.

"Enough for today," Saeran ordered. "I will trust you to take care of the rest. You may go, and have someone send for general Orri." He wanted to know how the Aegirans were getting along with his troops. Most of the ones who'd stayed for Mari were trained warriors. At least two guarded her day and night, but the rest were housed in Saeran's army barracks. In times of peace the building was mostly empty, but whenever new soldiers joined, they slept there while they trained.

Happily, Orri reported only a few disagreements, all of which have already been taken care of. Good. One less thing to worry about. After hearing the report on the soldiers and making sure all was in order, Saeran dismissed the general and took the first moment of quiet he'd had all day to stand up and stretch.

He went to the window and looked out across the courtyard to the northern woods. Nia was in there somewhere, hopefully already on her way back. Not a moment went by when Saeran didn't miss her. He dreamed about her nightly and cursed the light of day that stole her from him every morning.

Someone knocked and Saeran sighed. "Enter," he said because he had no other choice.

When no one spoke, he turned around to see Mari come in with a covered tray. She set it down on the table and waved him over with a slight bow-nod she always did whenever they met. The first few days he could not make her meet his gaze for longer than a moment. But as time passed, she became more at ease in his presence and Saeran found he didn't resent her as he thought he would. Mari was a kind girl. She spoke little, embarrassed by her difficulty forming their words, but she listened intently whenever he spoke and he found himself talking to her more and more each day.

It didn't make him miss Nia any less.

"What is this?"

Mari uncovered the tray. She'd brought him a hearty meal and a pitcher of wine and seeing it, Saeran realized he hadn't eaten a thing all day. "Thank you," he said.

Mari bow-nodded again.

"Will you not join me?"

She shook her head and touched her stomach, indicating she didn't feel well. From what he'd managed to get out of her and her people, northern food was much different from what they were used to back in Aegiros, and it didn't always sit well with them. Saeran understood. He'd instructed the cooks to do their best to prepare simple dishes and use the ingredients the Aegirans brought with them as gifts to ease the transition.

"Are you feeling all right?" Since she insisted on wearing her veil whenever she was outside of her chamber, he couldn't tell from her face.

Mari bow-nodded and touched her stomach again. Then she did something he'd never seen her do. She reached up and untied one side of her veil to reveal her face. She was smiling. "Magic-woman tell me I have child."

The great hall was bursting with people and Nia, caught in the midst of them, couldn't find her way out. Everything around her was spinning madly out of control. People's faces blurred together, but she recognized them all.

There was the new queen, her lovely face uncovered and smiling in the afternoon sun.

There was Saeran, staring moodily out the window in the royal study.

Nico, no more than a shadow, danced all around her, just out of reach. She tried to speak, to call to him, but no sound would come out.

The familiar faces disappeared into the crowd and colorful gowns blinded her for a moment. This was a celebration of some sort, but the faces were grotesque masks of malice, not joy. They had fangs filling their mouths, monstrous grimaces contorting their features.

The jesters and jugglers came so close to her she could feel their rancid breaths on her face, yet her feet would not move. She had no body here and no way to leave.

The crowd shifted, and from its depths emerged a man. His golden hair was shorn much shorter than was common, and his gentle face was clean shaven like a boy's. But his eyes were ancient. They were the eyes of an old man. He approached her with fluid steps and, though she couldn't hear him humming, she felt the impact of his silent melody. It moved through her in waves, making her sway.

The black crystal was in his hands. He held it out to her and she couldn't take her eyes off it. So beautiful and unusual. It looked to be incredibly heavy, but not because of the stone's weight. That pendant glittering so enticingly in his open palm held ancient magics. Countless separate energies swirled inside, each singing a different tune, yet each a mere imitation of the true wielder's power.

He came closer and Nia reached out, though she had no arms.

A silent scream shuddered through her and broke the spell, allowing her to look away. The sorcerer shouted his fury, but her attention was now on the queen. She leaned over the body of a man, her frame shaking with heartfelt sobs.

Somehow, Nia floated closer. Only the man's hand was showing, but she recognized the ring on it at once. It was the royal seal of Wilderheim. The crowd rushed at her again, taking her along, away from Saeran and his queen. She was carried on the current of countless people until she couldn't tell up from down.

And then the creature made its presence known.

"Nia," it hissed…

"Wizard, wake up!"

She jerked awake and reacted on instinct, shoving with all her might and not a little amount of magic at the man leaning over her, shaking her shoulders.

Arnaud went flying and landed several feet away, his breath knocked out of his chest.

She didn't apologize. Since her contact with the creature, she'd had terrible nightmares every night. Though she remembered little of them when she awoke, the feeling of dread remained long after the dreams faded.

Nia had made her wishes clear. She slept away from the camp they set up each night and told them she was not to be disturbed. The only way she would make sense of these things was if she could do so in her sleep.

Rising from her pallet, she winced at the ache in her shoulder.

There was snow everywhere. It was their constant companion this far north, the air so cold all the knights had donned their thick woolens and animal skins for protection. Nia still wore only her cloak and wolf skin. It was all the warmth she required.

With a thought she dried her clothes, wet and frozen from sleeping on the snow-covered ground, and stretched out her spine.

Straightening her cloak around her, she took up her staff. Arnaud was on his feet again, though his breath was still uneven. He had a look on his face that told her he was cursing himself a thousand kinds of fool for trying to wake her. "It is late," she told him. "We need to be on our way."

More than a month since they'd left the castle. At least ten more days until they reached Sir Frederick's coveted treasure. This journey was stretching much longer than she'd anticipated. It was, in part, because of her dreams. She slept late and wasted daylight so none of them could cover as much ground as they wanted. But there was no help for it. It wasn't only that she needed the sleep. Once she fell into those dreams, she became trapped in them and couldn't tell how much time has passed. Her mind became so absorbed in the scenes that it took her longer and longer to relinquish the unsolvable mystery and return to the waking world.

Nia feared there might come a day when she wouldn't wake at all. It was as if a sickness had taken hold of her, and she knew nothing of its source to fashion a cure. It was placing all of them in danger.

The land was so silent she could hear her heart beat like a drum as she led the way back to the camp. The absence of animals unnerved her. It had been weeks since she'd heard a bird's song or a predator's soft whisper. Even the earth sounded different here, its voice sharper and colder than Nia was used to.

Her feet buried in the snow as she walked, making her shiver, but she continued on, longing for the surety of Stardust's company.

"You were screaming," Arnaud said and coughed as he caught up to her. "We heard you in the camp."

"I was perfectly all right," she said, though her shaky voice left something to be desired. She wasn't all right. Something was draining her in a frightening way. It felt as if she was using her own essence to work spells without realizing it. Not only did it leave her weak in body, she found it harder each morning to simply cleanse herself.

And it was getting worse the closer they got to their destination. If she was left completely drained by the time they got there, the lot of them would be left defenseless against whatever was waiting for them.

But that wasn't all of it. Her magic was tied to her soul, her essence. It could replenish itself if she used too much, but if it drained out of her completely, it would take her life force with it.

Arnaud caught her arm, pulling her to a stop. "Enough of this," he said. "I don't know what is happening to you, and I no longer care. But you have a duty to us that will not be so easily dismissed. We all know something is awry. If you are ill, all of us are in danger, and you need to tell us."

"Arnaud," Lucca said, his voice hard. "Release her."

"You know I am right!" His hold on her arm tightened.

Lucca drew a long dagger from his belt loop. "You are in a temper. You are not thinking clearly."

Arnaud stared at the blade a moment, and Nia almost feared the two would come to blows. The others were already on their feet, keeping their distance, but ready to step in should they be needed. "What is this?" Arnaud said. "Are you all so blind that you do not see what is happening?" He shoved her toward Lucca. "Whatever happened to her back there, it has left a mark. Can you not feel it? The evil has tainted her. She is not the same wizard who rode out with us."

Lucca's knuckles turned white, clutching the dagger.

"I am well enough to lead you where you need to go," she grated, stepping in front of Lucca to get between him and Arnaud. "But be warned, Sir Arnaud, if you touch me again, you will regret it."

"You will walk today," Lucca told Arnaud. "It seems to me you have a need for exercise to clear your mind. Were I you, I would use the time to reflect." Sheathing his dagger, he turned his back on the man. "Mount up," he told the rest of them. "We have a long way ahead of us."

When their company rode out, Nia took the lead. Lucca was behind her, and behind him rode Jonah and Alec. Frederick took up the rear with Arnaud's mount, keeping pace with the unhorsed knight to lecture him. Such was their arrangement for the next three days.

There was no path here to follow. No animal tracks to mark the white snow. The trees were bare of not only leaves, but sometimes entire branches. The absence of life was worrying. What happened here? Why did nothing live in these woods?

"There was truth to his words," Lucca said, coming up to her right. "We have all noticed something is not right with you."

"I am well," she returned, keeping her eyes on the ground in front of Stardust.

"You mistake me. I did not say I believed you have made a pact with the devil. But there is something troubling you. Gravely, if your sleep is so disturbed."

"Be careful, Lucca," she told him. "Any more of such kind words and a lass might think you care." A sharp breeze laughed at her. It pierced through her clothing, stabbing into her body until she had to suppress a shiver.

Lucca smiled. "You are an extraordinary woman. If I did not know your heart to be engaged elsewhere, I might come to care." He held his hand up to silence her when she would have spoken. "I know, I know. No need for your lovely voice to carry harsh words. I will leave you in peace. But you should know, Lady Nia, that we do not take something for nothing. You have provided us with direction, and for that we are grateful. In return, we are honor bound to protect you against whatever lies ahead. We will do it, whether you want us to or not."

Nia would have told him there was no protecting anyone from what lay ahead, but he'd already slowed to fall back and give her space. She considered telling them something, preparing them for the possibility that they might all die, but in the end thought better of it. If she was being overcautious, there was no need for them to fret. And if she wasn't, there was no reason for them to fret and tire themselves needlessly. If they were to die, better it be a surprise.

Knowing one's end didn't make the remaining days any sweeter. Rather, it killed a man before he was even dead.

They passed through nine days of snow. Nine days of battling the wind and knocking ice from their belongings. Nine days of absolute misery during which a fire once lit had to be shielded and watched over the entire time to burn. If Nia so much as glanced away from those flames, let her concentration slip for an instant, the fire went out. It took effort and energy to keep a flame burning. It took even more to get one started when everything was too wet and frozen to catch the flame.

As cold as she and the knights were, the horses were colder. They had no woolens to keep them warm, and the more skittish of them could not be cajoled closer to the fire for anything. They'd already lost two to this bitter winter, and they all had to walk the rest of the mounts to spare them as long as possible. When they made camp for the night, humans and animals slept huddled together, sharing what warmth they could.

Their food had run out, and melting snow for water took hours in this weather. Arnaud and Jonah had taken to praying whenever they stood still, seeming to derive some strength or courage from ritual. Even Frederick and Alec joined them every so often. Lucca alone refused to say the words, warming himself instead with memories of his wife and children. Whenever the wind died down a little, he sought Nia out to speak to. He told her stories of his past for his own comfort and allowed her to lean on him when the weight of her staff became too much of a burden to carry.

It was more often than not now that Nia needed to lean on something or someone. She'd stopped sleeping because she was needed to keep the fire burning at night. It was just as well; it kept her from her nightmares and whatever was casting them over her. But the effort was taking a terrible toll. Already she was stretching her powers thin. Keeping everyone and herself warm took precedence, and so she'd stopped casting a glamour over herself. The knights could now see how badly she was faring.

It wasn't only her magic that was draining, it was her body as well. Her legs were always weak, and though she didn't want to, she was forced to lean on Stardust to stay on her feet in the harsh winds. They ought to have turned back days ago, but none of them would hear of it. Whatever it was they sought, it was more important than their lives. And she'd pledged to lead the way. So long as they had the will to continue, she had to as well.

On the tenth day, the storm finally died down. They made camp at the foot of a slight hill which provided at least some shelter from the wind. The fire needed only wood to keep burning that night, but Nia kept watch over it nonetheless. Several times she caught herself casting her will into the fire to bring up a vision. She was too weak to complete it, but the intention kept resurfacing, as if it was a habit she couldn't rid herself of. Those dancing flames kept singing their lullabies, making her yearn for her home, her bed.

She missed Saeran. There were times now when her mind recalled memories of him without Nia having any say in it. She would pat Stardust's neck and feel Saeran's hand squeezing hers. She would sit before the fire at night and feel his arms around her. Nia couldn't be sure if it was her imaginings or something entirely different, but she felt as though Saeran was there with her, hiding in illusions. His presence comforted Nia for a short while, but then she remembered everything that happened before she left, and since, and she was left aching and weary, tempted to lay her head in the snow and simply sleep.

Sleep until this wretched winter passed. And if it never did, then so be it.

Staring into those flames, she didn't notice when night turned to day. Lucca's hand on her shoulder startled her out of her trance and she struggled to her feet to help them ready to move on again. For all her good intentions, she couldn't make her body obey. It was all she could do not to fall back down once she'd stood.

The knights did everything on their own, telling her to mount Stardust and wait. Even Stardust agreed with them, butting his nose against her back until she nearly fell over. Nia couldn't argue after that, so she did as she was told.

After hours of riding at a steady pace, Stardust halted at the edge of a clearing. *I go no farther,* he said, ears back.

Nia swallowed past the lump in her throat, her gaze fixed on the cliff face before them. It towered up to the sky, a dark barren rock face rising from a level clearing big enough to hold an army. Even the wind didn't blow here.

This was it.

She dismounted, taking care to find her balance before she let go of Stardust's saddle. She felt weak and what little magic she had left, she was using to stay on her feet. Her body shivered in the cold she could no longer keep away and the wolf skin hugged itself tighter around her. Nia was grateful for that little comfort.

The knights tied their horses.

"We are here," Sir Frederick said, his eyes feverish as he looked for something that clearly wasn't there to find. "Where is it?"

Nia listened. The effort made her head pound, but she had to know what was around her.

There.

In the shadows of a deep cave it stood still. It waited to see what they would do, ready to strike, should they be so foolish as to approach. "This is madness," she managed to say.

"This is what we came here for," Sir Frederick countered, moving forward.

"No!" Nia caught his arm. Bracing herself, she spoke the words she knew would spell all of their dooms. Death waited for them where the knights expected to find treasures untold. Death by means no mortal could imagine. "I will go first."

Sir Frederick hesitated, but half bowed in ascent and backed away from the edge to allow her passage.

Nia took a step into the clearing, carefully placing her foot to make as little noise as possible. She fell through, knee deep into the snow. The beast did not stir. Shaking, dizzy, she took another step and almost collapsed.

Come back, Nia, Stardust pleaded, sensing her weakness.

She couldn't reply.

Instead, she focused all her energy on wading through the snow. Nia felt the knights following her, and she knew they worried. She heard Lucca swear under his breath each time her knees buckled in the deep snow.

It became shallower the closer they got to the rock face and Nia would have sighed in relief if she didn't know something far worse was waiting for them there.

At last, she reached the face of the cliff. It hummed with power, its own as well as something else's. The knights lined up on either side of her, their weapons drawn. They treated her now as what she was, a deathly ill woman, shaking and hunched over, her hair frozen and her face bloodless. Nevertheless, they didn't say a word. As the warriors they were, their eyes didn't linger on her, but searched for enemies to slay.

Not much energy left in her. No more time to waste.

Reaching out with one shaking hand, Nia touched the jagged rock.

All at once, a terrible roar shattered the wall before them, the earth shuddered and shook. Boulders rained down on them, and they fell to their knees for cover as the beast in the cave rushed out of the darkness.

Nia couldn't defend herself, much less the knights; couldn't even shield herself from the horrendous sound. She felt, rather than saw, one of the knights being lifted off the ground and tossed carelessly back toward the tree line. Two more met the same fate, and then the beast reached for Nia. It lifted her up by the shoulders so high she couldn't tell how far off the ground she was. She dared not look.

But then the beast stilled and became quiet, and Nia opened her eyes to behold Saeran's beloved face just beneath hers.

She fainted.

21

A fortnight had come and gone. It's been almost a month since Nia and the knights had ridden out, and still there was no sign of them. Saeran had sent a trio of soldiers north to where the road ended, marking the border of his kingdom. They'd returned with no news whatsoever. He was beginning to worry, and he wasn't the only one.

Nia's absence had been noted and was much remarked upon in all circles. Some were saying the wizard had abandoned him and took it as a bad omen for his reign. Without confirmation, rumors had begun to spread, one more outlandish than the next. The wizard had died. She'd run off to join the knights' order. She was battling monsters in the north. She'd been abducted into the Otherlands, never to return.

It was the last which bothered Saeran because of all of them, it was the most believable.

Something had changed.

His people grew discontent, the elements spoke to him less and less. It had been days since he'd heard even the wind speak of Nia. It was as if she had disappeared from the face of the earth, and in her absence Saeran saw how important a wizard truly was to the wellbeing of Wilderheim. Without her to interpret the weather, the winds, the changing seasons, Saeran felt blind and dumb, at a loss as to what needed to be done.

But it was worse than that.

At some point, even his mind turned against him. Where not long ago he went to sleep each night eager to see his wizard in dreams, now he dreaded the time when he had to close his eyes. Nightmares tormented him, dark portents of disaster and death. He saw it everywhere he turned, even in himself. For days now he'd dreamed of everyone he knew dying in some horrible way, yet there seemed to be no rhyme or reason to any of it.

Wary without knowing why, Saeran had ordered Manfred away for his own safety. His father had protested, of course. Now that Mari was with child, he'd wanted to stay for both of them and the birth of his grandson or granddaughter.

But the more insistent he'd been, the more nervous Saeran had felt until he'd put his foot down and ordered a contingent of soldiers to pack up his father's belongings and escort him back to Lyria. The sense of dread only left him when his messenger returned with news that the company was well beyond the mountain pass, and his sudden relief assured him that he'd done the right thing. One life, at least, he could save.

But what to do about the rest of them, including his own?

Half crazed with worry, Saeran struggled for control, but it proved elusive. With a foul curse he made a circuit around the chamber before falling back into his path from window to door and back while his advisors watched him as if he had lost his mind.

Saeran's step slowed, and his gaze snared on the floor, refusing to be moved as his latest nightmare came back to haunt him in his waking hours. His vision blurred until he could see it unfold in his mind's eye and he shuddered, unable to call out, unable to escape the sights.

He saw his queen lying dead in a pool of blood, his own hands covered with it. Shock held his body still, but his hands refused to stop shaking. When at last he looked up, he saw Nia, doubled over in tremendous pain. He felt with her, his own body contorting, muscles locking until he couldn't draw a breath. Terror made ice of his blood, but he kept looking at her, fighting his fate and trying to reach her, touch her. Help her, though he himself was dying.

"Majesty?"

The tentative voice brought him back to the present, and Saeran found himself staring at his own shaking hands. Gods, this had to end. He had to get Nia back. If for no other reason, than to ensure that she was safe. If he could just see her, even from a distance…

"Majesty."

A little stronger this time. Despite his torturous thoughts Saeran felt a smile pulling on the corner of his mouth. He glanced at the frail-looking girl with her cloud of unruly russet hair and made an effort to soften his gaze. "Yes, Braith?"

She blushed scarlet to be addressed directly. "Has our business been concluded?"

Her impatience charmed him. Braith would be a hellion as soon as she found the courage to speak her mind more often. Saeran almost looked forward to it. He would enjoy the presence of more confident women among his advisors. The only trick would be to find them. Braith sneaked a glance at the window. No doubt she was eager to get out and join her cousins in their mischief. Saeran decided to be merciful. "It has," he answered her, dismissing them all with a wave of his hand.

He sighed as he watched the oldest shuffle their feet out the door and stroked his beard. Something important was about to happen. He needed to be prepared, and it was damned difficult to prepare for something without knowing what it was.

"If only I could talk to Nia," he said aloud.

Call, the walls replied.

"Do you think I have not tried?" Oh, how he'd tried.

Soulcall, they said.

"What?"

Soulcall.

Saeran shook his head and scowled.

He wished he could speak to Mari; truly speak to her. But unlike Braith, his queen wasn't so eager to demand her voice. She rarely held his gaze for longer than a moment, and though she has learned his language well, she refused to say more than a handful of words whenever she was required to speak. To get her to say that much was a task in and of itself.

"Pregnant," he said, still baffled by the news. Four different mid-wives and a witch had confirmed Mari's news and the chambermaid told him his queen had asked for a witch to visit her every day since the wedding to see whether she'd conceived. He wasn't sure what to think about that.

She was a mystery, his queen. Saeran had been mistaken to think her weak. On the contrary, there was strength and courage running deep inside her, and he was beginning to admire her for it. True, she didn't speak much, but in her silence she heard and observed so much more than anyone else he knew, besides Nia. She could sit by his side when he held court, listen to the petitioners speak and see into the heart of their dilemma. Saeran could tell by the way she tilted her head whenever she'd heard enough to make up her mind, and her decision, when he managed to drag it out of her, was always wise and just. It was the getting her to voice it to anyone but him in anything above a whisper that was the problem.

"Easier to talk to walls. At least you answer."

Call.

"Even if you are somewhat flat."

Perhaps it would help if he told Mari about his nightmares. He would risk frightening her, but a show of trust might inspire the same in her. And if she still couldn't bring herself to speak to him, he could at least be safe in the knowledge that she wouldn't repeat what he said. "It is as good a plan as any." And it would give him something to do besides sit around and wait for the gods to strike him their blow.

Rubbing a weary hand over his brow he set out in search of her.

He hadn't gone five steps outside the chamber when someone called to him. Saeran turned to acknowledge the magician who had ac-companied Mari's caravan and stayed when the rest had departed. It baffled Saeran how a born northerner could end up so far from his homeland. Jasper was such a man. Though his skin was now darkened by the hot Southern sun, his hair still gleamed gold, and his eyes were sharp and blue.

Cold eyes, he had. No matter how much he smiled, he could never disguise that. Saeran was uneasy beneath his direct gaze. He could sense Jasper was not all together sane, but he'd thought better of mentioning it.

Now, the man bowed. "Forgive the intrusion, Majesty," he said politely, but something dark lurked behind his too easy smile.

"Be quick about it, whatever it is," Saeran said, impatient to find Mari.

"Of course, Majesty," Jasper said, rummaging in his pockets with well practiced haste. "I have overheard the maids speak of a wizard."

His tone put Saeran on guard. "And what have you heard?"

"Nothing of import, I am sure," Jasper replied with an easy shrug. "But they mentioned, too, your Majesty's interest in magic tricks, and it so happens that I am in possession of a rather clever one. I thought your Majesty would appreciate it."

Saeran tapped his foot as the boy continued to search for his trinket, but curiosity kept him from dismissing Jasper. Truth be told, he missed talk of magic and spells. Saeran continued to practice what lessons Nia had imparted on him, though it was never the same without her.

At last, Jasper pulled a chain out of his pocket and Saeran watched as the dark, shining stone pendant settled on its loop, swinging enticingly back and forth. Back and forth. So beautiful and dark, Saeran felt as if he was falling into it. Back and forth. Back…and forth…

"Merely a first step," Jasper was saying, but Saeran was too distracted to follow his words. Something cold and ravenous dwelled in the depths of that stone. He couldn't see it, but he could feel it. It swam in circles, trapped by the pendant, enraged and distraught that it could not get out.

Then Saeran felt its gaze snare on him. It stopped and stared, singing a tune to lure him closer, even as invisible bands slithered around him and pulled taut.

"You see, I need to find the wizard. She hides better than most I have come across, but she cannot hide her love for you."

Saeran swayed forward, as the dark chill of magic spread around him, and, of its own accord, his hand reached out to the black stone, so shiny it seemed like ice.

"She will come back for you," Jasper said with malicious determination, all pretense of innocence gone. All at once he sounded far older than he looked, and for an instant, fear gripped Saeran and he fought against the binds, a last ditch effort to free himself. It was too late. His call for help never made it past his lips. "Oh, aye, she will come. And when she does, I will be waiting."

At those terrible words, Saeran's vision went dark and then he was falling through emptiness with barbed spikes stabbing into him, turning his blood to ice…

~

Nia woke slowly, fighting her way through layers of fog to find that her body was warm and languid, cushioned by something much softer than her mattress roll. It shocked her how difficult it was just to open her eyes and keep them that way. She could not move more, no matter how much she wanted to.

Before her, a fire burned merrily in a stone hearth built into an almost smooth wall. Bright banners covered the walls around it like tapestries to keep out the chill, and there were furs strewn about the floor to protect bare feet. She was lying on a nest of pillows, covered with several of those furs.

Had she dreamed it all?

No. Nia still felt echoes of the pain she'd endured to get here, and her essence was barely glowing—a reminder of how close she'd come to dying. She made an effort to rise, but even raising her head proved to be too much. Too much effort. Too much pain. A helpless sound escaped her before she could prevent it. Her mouth was parched and her eyes felt dry.

Strong arms came around her to help her sit up. The man they belonged to was a shadow against the fire's light, something she thought was very deliberate. He retrieved a goblet and held it to her lips, and that was when she noticed his hand. It was covered with scales that shimmered in the firelight, his nails more like thick claws.

Nia struggled to raise her arm to push him away, surprised to find his skin was warm to the touch. Rough, as if he wore armored gloves, but warm as any human flesh. Nia was shivering even with the many furs covering her, but this creature, whatever he was, seemed comfortable enough.

He growled and twitched his hand to get away from hers, then pressed the cup to her lips again and tipped it, giving her no choice but to drink or have its contents spill all over her. The tepid herbal brew choked her at first, but she made herself swallow more, recognizing its power. Three gulps later she felt her strength returning, and after four she felt overheated and had to wrestle several of the furs off her just to breathe.

When the creature decided she'd had enough, the goblet disappeared behind him and he sat back on his haunches, studying her. "You are strong," he said, his voice as deep as it was menacing. Nia got the impression that this was a whisper for him, his way of tempering his presence. She was grateful. "Most would not have taken more than a sip."

"Where are the others?" she rasped, then coughed.

"Asleep," he answered, "as they have been for the greater part of a month. I thought it best to keep them that way until you were well enough to mediate." Then he leaned closer and she could almost make out his features. "Understand me, wizard, if one more raises arms against me, I will burn them all."

"They fought you?" She struggled to comprehend, but her mind wouldn't work properly.

"Thinking they were defending you, no doubt," the almost-man said, sounding amused. "I will admit I was a bit gruff when you arrived."

"A bit," she agreed. Squinting in the dark chamber, she tried again to make out his features. "Who…what are you?"

Though he'd not moved much since he'd sat, Nia somehow felt him grow still. "You don't know?"

Nia shook her head. "I have never seen anyone like you."

There was silence as she felt him study her and Nia caught herself reaching for the furs to hide. Though she couldn't see his eyes, his gaze felt piercing sharp, as if he could see inside her skin into her soul and found her lacking.

But when he answered, there was no distain in his voice, only something she might have called surprise. "I am a dragon."

22

Nia's head swam as the light in the room intensified, aided by magic, to reveal the dragon as well as his dwelling. He looked so much like Saeran, but there were also marked differences. His hands were scattered with scales, his fingertips clawed. Though he was tall for a human, he seemed uncomfortable in his own skin, as if it didn't quite fit. And why would it? He was, after all, a dragon.

His hair was black, reflecting many colors when light touched it. The strands fell below his shoulders, but couldn't disguise the smooth horns growing out of his temples. He had glowing silver eyes, slitted like a reptile's, and even his features seemed sharp, hard somehow, as if his skin was stretched taut over stone.

He allowed her to study him without comment, and didn't speak even when her gaze slipped past him to glance at the chamber. But it wasn't exactly a chamber. Though there was furniture aplenty, they were still in a cave. The dragon had made it as comfortable as possible, but at the border where the burrow ended and cave tunnel began, all luxury stopped. Nia could make out the sleeping outlines of the knights in the darkened corridor. They slept on the cold, hard ground, with nothing but blankets to warm them. The dragon's hospitality, it seemed, didn't stretch that far.

As if reading her mind, he spoke again in a deep gravelly voice that made her think he was growling, "Their comfort was not my concern." He pronounced the words carefully, as if unused to the need to form them.

"Then why am I not among them?" Nia asked, not certain she wished to know the answer. From what little she had read about dragons, they were very few and very solitary creatures. But although they despised crowds of people, singular companions, usually chosen for their charm, or wit, were almost a necessity to them. Nia had read stories of maidens choosing to remain with a dragon and giving up everything else. If that was what he wanted from her, Nia might have to fight him to leave.

"You are a wizard," the dragon replied with an elegant shrug, his ancient eyes taking in everything about her. "Wizards are kin to dragons, in the same way wolves are kin to foxes."

"Does that mean you are only being polite?"

He nodded.

Nia shook her head. "You are lying."

The dragon's mouth quirked, but he didn't smile. She wasn't certain he could. "I will admit there were other reasons for keeping you alive."

A knight stirred in the tunnel, drawing Nia's gaze. "Wake them," she said, before she could temper the order into a plea.

The dragon didn't seem to mind. "Not yet. I expect they might give me trouble for what is about to come." He studied them for a moment longer before shaking his head. "Fools," he scoffed. "They risk their lives for something they cannot even use." When he looked at her again, Nia felt him probing her mind. "You do not know what they seek. But how could you? They themselves have never seen it."

Nia pushed off one more layer of furs. Her strength was returning quickly, but even with the dragon's help it would be awhile yet before she was back to herself. It worried her. How long had they already been gone? She thought of Saeran alone in the castle, then remembered he wasn't alone anymore, and never would be again. She cast her worries aside and settled. Nia was in no rush to get back.

"What is your name?" she asked, then winced when he raised a mocking eyebrow. Names held power over their bearers. To name a thing meant to have control over it. Of course he wouldn't tell her. "What do I call you?" she asked instead.

Rather than answer, the dragon reached behind him. When he faced her again, he held a wooden chalice. "Behold, your knights' coveted prize. One of man's most wondrous inventions."

"What is it?"

"A cup."

"What does it do?"

The dragon huffed with impatience. "It holds drink," he retorted.

Nia gaped. "That's it? That is what we have almost died trying to find?" She'd seen little more than ideas in their minds when she'd searched for their treasure. Nothing but myths and legends, stories of miracles and great power to those who found it. "We came all this way for a cup?"

Before her anger could manifest in the air, the dragon waved his hand down, forcing her power into submission. "They came here for the cup. A cup which is useless without something to drink from it, though they would not believe even me, should I decide to tell them. You, Lady Nia, are here for the drink itself."

Leaving her to ponder that mysterious proclamation, he rose and walked to a table near the far wall. He made no sound at all as he walked, making Nia wonder whether he was there at all, and his long, reptilian tail swished left and right in his wake. Taking up a pitcher, the dragon man returned to his seat before her and poured deep red wine into the wooden cup.

"At least tell me it's the magic one. The one they said once held the blood of…I forgot his name."

Again, that almost smirk. "Humans," he said as he set the pitcher aside and placed the cup before her. "Always twisting everything to serve their own purpose." He uncurled the fingers of his right hand and pressed a black claw into its center, drawing blood. He allowed three drops to fall into the wine before the wound closed and the wine boiled and sizzled, giving off black smoke.

Nia swallowed with difficulty, but accepted the cup when he held it out to her. Staring into the dark liquid, she imagined she could see shadows in its depths. "It will hurt," she said, knowing it was true.

"You have and will yet endure far worse," he replied. This was a gift, as well as a test. She knew nothing about the magical properties of dragon's blood, something she was sure dragons kept a close secret. Combined with her own magical essence it could do any number of things: permanently alter her physical being or even mark her soul. If she drank, it would mean submitting fully to the dragon's will. Blood bonds created a link between beings, allowing the stronger to control the weaker if he so desired.

If she refused it, he might simply move on to another topic of conversation, or he might burn her to ash where she sat. There was no telling what mysterious thoughts compelled a creature so old and powerful to give up three full drops of his blood for a lowly, human.

"You wished for answers. They are in the wine. Drink."

She took a bracing breath before bringing the cup to her lips. Her hands shook, but she made certain not to spill a single drop. The wine flowed smoothly down the back of her throat, leaving warmth in its wake, a mere taste of what was to come.

She'd no sooner handed the cup back to him than fire exploded in her belly, sending tendrils out into her blood to scorch her from the inside out. Nia doubled over, unable to draw breath to cry out. Her tears turned to steam before they could be shed, and the inferno inside her kept growing, burning, changing her. Her muscles locked until she couldn't move, but that wasn't the worst of it.

When the fire reached her mind, she choked on a scream as her vision went black and the shadows she'd thought to have seen in the wine took shape. Dozens, hundreds of images flew at her, too fast for her to understand, but they ingrained themselves among her own memories, as if she herself had lived them.

There were thousands of years the dragon had given her—his years, his memories. In them, she saw a beautiful, fair haired woman. She laughed as she spun around a pyre, looking back at the dragon many times with so much emotion in her gaze that even the mighty dragon's heart squeezed in his chest. Nia felt his love for her.

But in an instant, the strength of that love turned to agony as she saw through his eyes the beautiful, dark haired child held in his big, rough hands. Only memories of the child's mother remained, and each brought with it equal measures of pleasure and pain. All he had left was his daughter, his beloved's final gift to him. And he adored that child more than his own life. The girl grew up and ventured into the world, and met a man Nia recognized, though he was still young and full of all the joy he'd lost when his queen died in childbirth.

And then it was the widowed king who stared at a child in his arms, his beloved wife far and gone. The boy opened his big gray eyes and uttered soft coos, mourning his mother as his father did.

The dragon caught her against him when she would have collapsed. "Saeran," she whispered, fighting for breath and shivering as the fire slowly died down inside her. "He's your grandson." It all made sense now. His thirst for spells and magic, his aptitude at both—it was in his blood. Why had she never questioned it before?

"Humans," the dragon said, his voice thick with emotion, "cannot carry our seed. A dragon's life essence is too powerful to be contained in a human vessel, too ravenous. It needs magic to feed on and in its absence, it drains its mother's life."

"It takes dragonblood to birth dragonblood," Nia said, beginning to make sense of what he'd shown her. She could feel the effects of the drink. Her essence was brighter than before, and more volatile as well. Nia would never again be as she'd been before. Dragon's blood was now a part of her.

Why hadn't the dragon changed his beloved mate this way?

She already knew the answer. By the time he'd realized the danger, it had been too late. She would have risked her child, and had refused to do that. The dragon had been helpless to change her mind, forced to live out her remaining days with the constant knowledge that each hour was one closer to losing her. The mere thought that he could save her, but she wouldn't allow it for the sake of their child had driven him mad time and again, and when his daughter was born, and he felt his mate slip away into eternal sleep, the little girl's gentle presence had been the only thing preventing him from becoming a monster.

"But Saeran's mother—"

"Was only half dragon," he said. "She would have lived for a while, in agony, had she survived the birth. No one can live for long with only half their being."

Nia's arms crept around him. She wanted to offer some comfort, but there was nothing she could do or say that would take away the torment he carried. "What do you want me to do?" she said, knowing he hadn't done this to her without good reason.

His hold on her tightened for an instant before he pulled away and resumed his seat. Now, when she looked into his silver eyes, she could see his love's shadow dancing in their depths. His mate was always with him, if only in his mind. And he could never forget, never leave it all behind. "Look after my grandson," he said at last. "He needs you more than he will ever admit, even to himself."

Nia hesitated. "I will stand as his advisor," she said. "I have sworn that much and will stand by my oath."

The dragon cast her a look full of sympathy. "He needs far more than your counsel, Nia. And you do as well."

"The kingdom must come first," she insisted. The future of Saeran's rule was only as stable as his people's trust that the hand of their king was guided by one outside the hierarchy, who would judge fairly for not having anything to gain from another's loss. If they betrayed that, if she ceased to be neutral to his reign, there would be war. It would take so little to incite a battle, merely the suspicion that Saeran was unfaithful to his Aegiran queen.

"Nia," the dragon said, his voice echoed with another—Nico's. Her heart fluttered in her chest at her mentor's familiar rasp, even while she knew it was nothing but a dragon's trick. "Saeran rules with his heart. If it breaks, his kingdom will as well."

"Nia?" Lucca's voice sounded from the tunnel, an unwelcome reminder that soon she would have to return and face her king again. The dragon held her gaze, refusing to release her, weighing her soul and judging her strength.

"Do not fear this," he told her as the others began to rise. "He needs your strength to lean on, as you need his. You are well-matched, Nialei of the Streams. It is only your fear of love that hold you back. Let go. Leap and he will catch you."

"He is wed," Nia told him, her voice harder than she'd intended.

The look in the dragon's eyes revealed what he would not voice.

Not for long.

23

There were clouds in the sky again, as there have been most days since she'd arrived. The sun tried valiantly to reach out to all those beneath its bright majesty, but was thwarted time and again by those cursed clouds. The sometimes harsh winds snatched away any warmth that might descend upon the earth, and with each step she took, Mari's entire body jarred at the impact with hard packed earth and stone. Travelling north from her homeland, she'd seen rivers so powerful their waters were forever white with foam and lakes so vast it would take a day to walk around them. Everything in the north was green and wet, cold and hard; it was a wonder the people here managed to survive in such a bleak place. This world simply did not feel right.

Mari gazed out the window, ensconced in an abandoned tower room from which she could see over the fields and forests to the mountains in the distance, their peaks brilliant white in a stray patch of sunlight. She told herself to ignore the draft and the ever present chill in her body, despite being cocooned in layers and layers of cloth. Lifting her unveiled face to the sky she strove to ignore the wind's bite.

She missed her homeland. Her eyes longed for the glistening gold sea of sand that stretched far and wide. Her skin yearned for the loving touch of the searing desert sun, and her ears, so sorely abused these past weeks, wished for nothing more than the absolute silence of a clear, moonlit night. But her heart, treacherous beast that it was, longed for something else.

Mari settled onto a hard bench, taking care not to lean against the cold stone wall at her back, and sighed softly, her gaze turning inward. Down a long, winding staircase, at the heart of this monstrous castle, the king slept fitfully in his grand bed. His brow glistened with sweat, though his skin was icy and his lips pale. He tossed and turned, crying out in fevered dreams, his mind as tormented as his body.

And he would not wake.

Mari had tried everything, every remedy she had ever learned from the women of her tribe, every foul smelling herb these northerners favored. But she knew nothing of his illnesses and could not help him, save to hold his hand.

The healers had come and gone. So had the priests. They spoke amongst each other quietly, as though they didn't mean for her to hear. In that way they were far worse than the men of her tribe who, in the absence of her royal father, treated her as though she didn't exist. As brazen and heedless as Aegiran men were with their words, so these pale-skinned northerners were secretive. They would not speak to her, lest their gaze was lowered as hers had used to be all the time, and Mari knew that they did this to spare her. For the truth was that they knew no more about King Saeran's illness than she, and they could no more advise her but to tell her to "cleave to him." Mari surmised it meant she should keep him company, hold his hand.

As a dutiful wife, she had sat by his side for days and days, at first in silence and then speaking to him, secretly relieved when he seemed to quiet at the sound of her voice. But then the illness had taken a turn for the worse, racking his body with horrible shaking fits which had sent many a maid fleeing.

And he had called out. Not for Mari. No, not for his wife who'd sat by his side and tended him, fed him broth, even held council with his advisors there in the sick room. Not for the woman who'd never before known anything but obedience yet was now expected to rule a kingdom until he recovered—if he recovered.

No, the fever stricken king had called for Nia, his voice tormented, as if his soul needed hers to be whole. At first Mari had understood, having heard of the great wizard who served as the king's advisor. A female advisor. The news had been so wondrous upon hearing that Mari could scarcely believe it. From what the others have told her, the wizard was so powerful she could appear out of thin air, from miles away, if the right person were but to call her name. She could heal almost any illness or injury, in people, animals, or the earth itself. Mari could almost believe this woman to be myth. How could any person, leastwise a woman, hold so much power?

She reminded herself to breathe as she once again pondered the amazing tales she'd heard. It was no wonder King Saeran called out to her; he had to know, even in this state, that Nia would be able to heal him. But, of course, that was not why he called for her. Mari had not seen the wizard with her own eyes, but she knew her to be a beauty, one who walked tall, certain of her place among these people as their elder, despite being very young still. She knew, though people have tried to keep it from her, that there was a powerful bond between the advisor and her king. Only a fool would fail to see how each of the king's cries for her now echoed with soul rending grief—one that Mari recognized to be the result of cursed love.

It was why she cowered here, unable to stand hearing it any longer. Each time he called Nia's name, Mari cursed it, aching in her heart, her treacherous heart, to hear him call for her instead. It was not her place to want, she knew, but how could she not, when at every turn the king showed her kindness; strove time and again to convince her she was among a different people here. She was their queen now and ought not look down in front of anyone. He wanted her to speak her mind and seemed to truly wish to hear her thoughts, as if they were important to him.

He wanted her friendship, but no more. For in his heart he longed for his Nia the same way she longed for him. It was precisely why she kept silent, for it was futile to try for something Mari could never have. She would only gain his pity in the end, and, indeed, they were both to be pitied.

Mari's hand settled on her stomach and she sighed again, feeling a new life stirring within her. It seemed her midwife's fertility charm had worked its magic. Part of her rejoiced at the thought of cradling her child in her arms. But the other part of her died slowly to remember that its father would love it far more than her. King Saeran would welcome the babe, an heir to the throne and his own flesh and blood, but there would forever be only one woman queen to his heart, and Mari was not her. It was this cursed land that made her feel this way. In the desert she would have thought nothing of being one of a man's many wives. Why, then, did it pain her to be the only wife of a good man, a lofty station by anyone's standards, without his love?

The door creaked loudly in the cavernous room, and Mari jumped to her feet, fumbling with her veil to cover her face once more. Her heart raced with dread, and she prayed that it wasn't one of the healers come to bring her news of her husband's death. But it was Jasper's face that appeared when the door opened, his smile stretching across his stone face, a grotesque imitation of true happiness. "My queen," he said in greeting, though he did not bow, holding her gaze, expecting her to submit to him.

His presence, in the past so eerie and daunting, now angered her, and she straightened her shoulders to meet his empty gaze with confidence. His brows rose in surprise, though his smile never faltered. "I have come searching for you," he said, his voice at once smooth and sticky, like a camel's spit. "They told me his Majesty is not improving. I thought I would try to bring cheer with a trick or two." He spoke her language, as well as a native, but on his tongue the beautiful words sounded sullied.

Mari was in no mood to tolerate his presence. When he reached into his pocket for one of his "tricks," she stifled the urge to scream and brushed past him as grandly as she had seen King Saeran do so often. "I was just on my way to my husband's side," she told him, evading his touch as he reached out to stop her. "Find someone else to entertain with your play."

She felt a cold shiver run up her spine and knew he was watching her leave. Why had he stayed behind? The entire caravan, save her personal guard and hand maidens, had departed the very day after her wedding, yet Jasper refused to follow them. Mari supposed it was King Saeran's unfailing hospitality that made Jasper think he could stay as long as he wished. She would give him the moon's cycle to leave on his own. If he did not, she would have him removed. It was, like as not, his very presence that prevented the king from healing as he should.

A sharp pain stabbed through her belly and up to her chest. She had to stop and brace herself against the wall to stay on her feet. Cold sweat broke out on her brow and fear shivered through her, for her child as well as herself. But within moments the pain was gone and she could once more stand unaided. Casting an apprehensive look behind her, she was glad that Jasper was nowhere in sight, but not willing to take the chance she hurried down the stairwell and to her king's bed chamber. There, at least, she felt safer. But there, instead of fear, sorrow weighed on her ever more until she could do nothing other than what the healers had advised. Sit by him and hold his hand.

~

By the time the knights joined them the painful effects of the dragon's blood had passed and Nia shoved off the rest of the animal furs in deference to the heat burning within her. Her cheeks warmed and her limbs strengthened until she felt sure she could run for miles without rest. The feeling of power was at once intoxicating and frightening. One little slip and she could do a lot of damage. It was as if she was nine again, just awakening her power and all that came with it. Only this time, she had no mentor to teach her how to control it.

"It is the wine," the dragon told her, ignoring the knights completely. "With my blood it weakened your guards. It will pass."

Nia believed him.

"What happened?" Lucca asked, the only one of his company not staring all around them. He reached out to her, but the dragon caught his hand, his eyes glowing with menace. "Do not touch her," he warned.

Nia was grateful for the intervention. Her skin felt unbearably sensitive, and she had a feeling that if she were to touch someone, she would not be able to stop the flood of knowledge from overwhelming her. Even at a distance she could feel the knights' confusion, their worry and anxiety. When Lucca spoke, his voice echoed in her mind as if she was hearing it twice. Nia had no doubt that with his touch he would unwittingly share every thought, sight, emotion and sensation.

"Nia," the knight said. "Are you well?"

"Much better," she replied with a nod, glancing at the dragon. *I know your name now,* she thought in surprise. He'd gifted her with his memories as well as his strength. And in the process left himself vulnerable to her.

His mouth quirked the slightest bit. *So you do.* There wasn't even a hint of worry in his mind-voice. *But do you know how to use it?*

"Can you travel?" Lucca questioned, still looking as if he wanted to reach out to her, but the dragon's closeness kept him wary.

"Yes, I can," Nia said, confident in her physical ability to ride, but unsure if she was ready to return to Saeran's side. To step into shadow once more and watch him smile at his queen the way she'd seen him do before, to become a spectre over their reign as she was bound to do—no, she wasn't keen on riding back to Frastmir with all haste. But for her king, she would.

"Then we should be on our way at once."

The dragon eyed him curiously. "You will not claim your treasure?"

Sir Frederick's gaze snared on the dragon, and Nia heard his breath catch. "So you do have it, then," he said in awe.

The dragon nodded and produced the cup he'd given Nia to drink from. When she would have expected their faces to fall in disappointment, their eyes grew wide with wonder. They knelt before dragon and cup, whispering a prayer and bowing their heads. She could see Lucca's jaw clench, and his eyes shimmer with unshed tears. He knelt with the others, bowing his head, but did not speak the prayer.

Behold, the dragon said inside her mind, *the power of a lone god's dominion. Willing or not they bow to him, not even knowing what he is.*

Can you help him? Nia asked on Lucca's behalf. His grief was so strong she was suffocating with it. How could he live each day with such a burden?

The dragon eyed her a moment, then transferred his sharp gaze to the knight in question. When he handed the cup to Sir Frederick and the knights huddled around it, each wanting to touch the sacred object, Lucca stayed behind, watching them. He was angry with them for their devotion to what he considered a cruel monster, yet at the same time envious of their unshakable faith. The dragon laid a scaly hand on his shoulder and coaxed the man to meet his gaze.

Nia didn't know what transpired in those silent moments when the two simply stared at each other, but after a while, Lucca's shoulders collapsed and he broke into wretched sobs.

Grief shared is grief lessened, the dragon said, his voice strange. Of all of them, he understood the best what Lucca had lost. And while he couldn't return those lives to him, he could at least help him heal. *A lesson you have yet to learn, child.*

Long after he'd composed himself as best he could, Lucca and the dragon remained removed from the rest of the company, deep in conversation. Nia didn't intrude. Instead, she kept the others engaged, asking questions of their god and telling stories she'd heard since childhood. A full night and day passed unnoticed in the dragon's den until, once more exhausted, the knights fell asleep.

While they slept, Nia pondered the strength of their faith. It baffled her. They spoke reverently of a god all good and noble, one who was everywhere, knew everything, and loved everything. He could work miracles, he was the creator of all, yet he didn't scorn those who turned their backs on him. Sins could be forgiven, enemies could be destroyed, and kingdoms could be saved with his power and his power alone.

They held fast to such silly beliefs, even while they had no proof. Save the cup. She held it again, now that it was empty, and felt none of the power that had thrummed into her hand while it was filled with wine and no more than three drops of the dragon's blood.

When she asked the dragon if their lone god could truly exist, he'd not given her an answer. Her people lived every day with the reminder of the gods who ruled them. Kind gods, fickle gods, gods who reveled in toying with people's lives. Gods who feasted on war, drenching the earth in blood. Gods who could bring a man back from the dead, grant him immortality and divine strength. Though one had never ventured into Wilderheim, stories of berserkers traveled to them from far and wide on the wings of messenger birds; on the wind itself. Beautiful maidens in shining armor walked the battlefields, choosing from among the fallen only the strongest, bravest, to take their place of honor in Valhalla.

To these knights, stories of her gods had seemed as strange as their god seemed to her. Perhaps it didn't matter what one believed in, but that they believed. Having someone to revere, or even fear, kept a person humble.

In the morning, when she walked out of the cave with the dragon and told him this, all he said was, "The mind feels what it needs to." Puzzled twice over, she tried to come up with her own answer as he led her over the frozen field to a sturdy stable she didn't remember having seen before. Inside the mounts happily chewed on clumps of hay, clean and warm, though they fidgeted when the dragon approached.

"You wish to ask me something," the dragon man said.

"Do you not already know what it is?" Nia asked, surprised.

He shook his head, gazing into the mount's eyes. "You grow strong with my blood. I can only get impressions now, unless you allow me entrance to your mind."

He seemed completely unperturbed about that. An ancient and powerful being, a dragon, had given her a weapon against him without batting an eyelash, and even now showed not a hint of unease, as if the mere fact that she was who she was should keep her from using it against him. How could he trust her so?

Or was it that Nia was so weak and puny that she posed no threat to him at all, even with the added strength of his own blood? That seemed far more likely and she nodded to herself, satisfied with her own conclusion for the moment.

"Ask already, I grow impatient."

"I wanted to see your true form."

He faced her then, something akin to surprise on his handsome face. "You have seen it. In my memories."

"But only through your own eyes and we never see ourselves as we truly are," she said pragmatically.

The dragon's mouth quirked. "Perhaps another time," he said. And before she could reply, he made his manner brisk and nodded to the horses. "I have procured mounts to replace the ones you have lost. You should start getting ready. They will not let me near them and the sun is rising. It is time you kept your promise."

PART THREE

Convergence

# 24

On a good night, the king slept undisturbed, lying still as death, his chest barely rising and falling with breath. On a good night, the priests and magic men and women lit black candles in his bedchamber, surrounded his bed and chanted prayers in ancient tongues, terrifying Mari and making her wish she had never come to this cursed place. Tonight wasn't a good night.

King Saeran screamed as if his soul was being torn out of him and Mari started awake from her slumber. She must have slept longer than she thought. The fire had died down to embers and she was chilled to the bone. Heart pounding, Mari rose from her hard seat by the hearth and went to her dying husband.

Saeran tossed and flailed on the bed, screaming louder than anything she'd ever heard from him. She caught his arm, but he shook her off so violently she fell to the floor. From there she watched her husband scratch at his neck and chest, still screaming. Helpless sobs tore out of her and she covered her ears to block out his cries, but it didn't help.

Guards and healers rushed in and took hold of Saeran's limbs to subdue him. They called his name, tried to tell him to stop, that he was safe, that they would get him well again, but the more they spoke, the more he thrashed and Mari couldn't stand it.

"Stop it," she whispered. Then louder, "Stop it. Stop it! *Stop!*"

Saeran's body bowed off the bed on a blood curling bellow: "*Niaaa!!*" The fire blazed to renewed life, and Mari screamed in fright. The guards and healers fell away from Saeran and she gasped. He was glowing. The fire didn't simply illuminate his sickly pale skin, it was inside him, burning beneath the surface like a lantern.

Saeran collapsed back onto the bed and the fire dimmed, in the hearth and inside him. Muttering prayers, calling on all the gods they could name, the healers approached him carefully and touched his skin.

Mari became light headed and sucked in a breath. She'd forgotten to do that. "Is he dead?" she demanded.

The healers looked to each other and shook their heads with sorrow. "No change," they proclaimed.

No change? Were they blind? Saeran had glowed!

Becoming aware of the noises behind her, Mari turned to see the servants spying through the open door. "Out," Mari commanded, picking herself up off the floor. "All of you out!"

The guards took charge, herding everyone back as the healers made their exit. The hallway cleared slowly, but just before the last healer closed the door, Mari saw Jasper standing there, smirking at her.

Shuddering, she quickly barred the door from the inside and backed away from it, all the way to Saeran's bed. There, she fell to her knees and prostrated herself, praying and begging her gods to have mercy; bargaining with them to demand whatever price they would of her, but spare the king she loved.

She cried and sobbed, pleaded and made promises she wasn't certain she could keep. She even prayed for Nia to return, for if anyone knew how to help him, the wizard was she. And when she finally ran out of words and tears, she became aware of noises coming from the bed. Whispers, harsh and broken.

Mari stood up and faced Saeran, watched his parched lips move to form the words, but she couldn't make them out. Drawing closer, she leaned in to put her ear almost at his mouth.

"…kissed you…time stopped…love you, Nia. Please…until death or longer."

Mari's heart broke at his words and she clutched her chest to soothe a pain almost too great to bear.

She kissed his brow, caressed his icy cheek and pulled the covers up to his chest. Feeling fragile as an eggshell, she went back to the hearth and stoked the fire until it blazed. It was for him more than Mari; the cold no longer bothered her. Nothing did anymore.

The maids had brought trays of food for them both. All of it sat untouched by the door, as it had all day long because Mari was too unsettled to eat a thing. She retrieved a bowl of broth and set it near the fire to warm while she adjusted the pillows beneath Saeran's head to raise him up a little.

Then she sat next to him and patiently fed him a spoonful at a time until he would take no more. He must have been hungry. By the time she was finished, most of the broth was gone and very little had spilled. Mari cleaned Saeran up, settled him back on the bed and laid down next to him. She knew now what needed to be done.

Tomorrow she would write a message to her father. Saeran had fulfilled his duty to the *shansher*, and there was no more need to keep up this pretense. Whether he lived or not, there was no place for Mari in his heart or his kingdom. She didn't blame him; how could she? Saeran had been nothing but kind to her. But it wasn't enough. Her father would understand. He was a proud man, but not a heartless one.

He would take her in even if, by returning, she brought shame to the family. Mari could make her father see why she had to come back, but to everyone else she would forever be the abandoned wife, a cast out, pitied or reviled, never to marry again. Perhaps it was for the best. Mari didn't want another husband. All she wanted was a little tent of her own, far from prying eyes and wagging tongues, to live out her life in peace. She would fulfill her own duty to Saeran. She would stay by his side and nurse him until she gave birth to the child who would one day become a king or queen after him.

But once Mari was fit to travel, she would go back home where she belonged.

25

Ten days after they rode out, the company of travelers came to the edge between the dragon's territory and the rest of the world, a clear line of demarcation across the land. It was at this border that the snow gave way to green grass in such a way that trees straddling it were half green and half barren. Nia spared it a brief glance as they crossed, noting absently that the transition hadn't seemed so sharp going the other way.

They rode at a slow, steady pace, rarely stopping for food or sleep. The knights might be in a hurry to return home as heroes now that they'd found their coveted cup, but Nia felt no such compulsion. Her mind was weighed with thoughts of what she had discovered. There was so much she had to tell Saeran, and knowing he wouldn't want to hear any of it made her as reluctant to return as the idea of meeting his young queen.

It hurt. More than it should, far more than the dragon's ordeal, the surety that her voice, no matter how needful, might fall on deaf ears hurt worse than any physical pain. Saeran was angry with her for having refused him and would turn to his queen for the advice Nia ought to give. The king knew his people, but Nia knew his lands.

She sighed. Fighting a battle with herself was useless. Of course she had a place at his side; she was a wizard. Nico had not chosen her for nothing. She was meant to advise the king and aid him, no matter how stubborn he was.

Nia held her hand out before her and gathered magic into her palm. Aided by the dragon's blood and her own emotion, the pool of light was red with a mixture of love and anger. It came to her so easily now she had to be careful not to draw too much. She watched the surface move like a lake, glistening pure. Curling her fingers, she tipped her hand sideways and let the power pour out. It laid a path in the air alongside her like a trail of fireflies.

When the last drop fell, she swirled her hand and the ribbon of red light curled in on itself to form a circle that kept spinning, following her progress down the little used forest path. She touched the bottom edge with a fingertip, pulling on it to alter the circle's shape. The dip she created filled up and formed a bubble. Then the bubble changed, sharpening at the edges into a five-sided disc, a pendant for the chain. When at last Nia was satisfied that all five sides were equal, she blew on the pendant, searing the shape of a dragon in flight into its surface.

Holding her hand out to her creation she whispered an ancient word of protection into its depths and sealed it. The finished pendant and chain dropped into her hand, formed in pure silver. Nia lifted it to the light to inspect her handiwork. The chain was heavy, as befitted something so elemental. As for the pendant, the dragon had ruby eyes and each visible fang was a diamond chip. The play of light over him gave the dragon an illusion of motion, as if he truly lived and the fire he breathed changed color like oil in water. It stayed warm to the touch, even after the rest of the pendant had cooled in the chill air.

The pendant was a work of art, mesmerizing and entrancing. A powerful tool. It could be used for any number of things, acting as protection, defense, enchantment, and warning. Whoever looked upon it would know at once that its wearer was not to be trifled with. It could be used to channel energy or create a living shield that could withstand any magical assault, except, perhaps, a true dragon's.

And to what purpose will you use this tool? The dragon's voice in her mind was unexpected but soft, unlike his earlier, painful trips into her thoughts.

I will give it to someone worthy of it, she replied. Stardust tossed his head, as if he felt the dragon's presence and didn't like it. She patted his neck to soothe him.

The dragon was silent for a moment. *It has been a long while since anyone has trapped dragon essence in an object,* he mused. *Even the little you used could be turned against you by one like me.*

You sound almost worried about me, she said, smiling to herself.

I worry for myself, he said and she got an image of his scowl. *If anyone harms you through it, I will have to intervene. Then everyone will know where to find me. I do not like this plan, not one bit.*

Then I will simply have to be more cautious when choosing its keeper.

Give it to Saeran. He'll wear it as well as anyone. And it will serve him well. Especially now.

Nia stilled at the odd comment. *What do you mean?* But she could already feel the dragon withdrawing. He would not answer her.

Sir Frederick rode up beside her. "My lady," he said politely, nodding a bow. "Perhaps we should stop for the night. The shadows grow long and the men are tired."

Though they rode slowly, they rode almost without cease. Nia couldn't feel her legs anymore and knew that as soon as she dismounted, she'd crumple to the ground. She looked at the other knights, noting the shadows beneath their eyes and the set expressions that hid any weakness they might feel. They were strong men, and brave. Perhaps they ought to stop.

But the worry she'd begun to feel would not leave her. Something was very wrong if the dragon felt the need to warn her of it. They were still three days' ride away from the nearest village, and from there two more to Frastmir. Did it matter?

Nia pulled Stardust to a halt. There was a small clearing sheltered by a rocky cliff. The wood was dry and the grass soft. This was a good place to rest for the night. Sensing her weariness, Stardust took her all the way to a tree so that she might use it to steady herself when she dismounted. "Thank you, my friend," she told him.

Sir Arnaud caught Stardust's reins as she dismounted, saying, "I'll care for the mounts."

Nia, holding on to the tree to keep upright, could only nod ascent.

By the time she could stand unaided, the others had gathered wood and tended the mounts. They only waited for her to join them and light the fire. The provisions the dragon had given them were laid out and ready to eat and Nia's mouth watered for the bountiful offering.

But she was too weary of sitting to join the others. Instead she lit a fire for them, took up her staff and an apple and went for a stroll to stretch her legs.

The dragon's words wouldn't leave her. Could Saeran be in trouble? Needing to get away, Nia had closed herself off from him completely, rendering even his calling spells useless. He could not have reached her, save by a messenger, and he would not have known where to send one. She'd left him completely stranded, without counsel or aid.

Regret stabbed at her, and she lifted the magical veil she'd cast over herself the day they rode out.

All at once her blood turned to ice. Saeran's calling tolled like a massive bell inside her, amplified each time it had fallen on deaf ears. It wrenched her out of time and space in a mad swirl of colors and darkness. Red for danger. Blue for cold. Black for oblivion.

Saeran was dying. She felt it as she spun end over end in a void where not even her voice would carry its frantic call. When she started falling, she braced herself, but even so her cloak tangled around her and she fell in a heap on the cold stone floor of Saeran's bed chamber.

A soft gasp. Hurried footsteps. Then delicate hands grasped her arm to help her stand. Nia was disoriented and dizzy and the entire chamber, with its dozens of candle flames dancing, spun and dipped around her. And all the while her heart thudded in her chest for herself as well as Saeran. Even with her hearing focused on the sound, his heartbeat was almost too weak to find and his breaths came too slow, too far apart.

"You come," the woman said in a heavily accented voice. The girl, the queen, was holding her upright. "Finally you come."

Nia made every effort to steady herself and slow her heartbeat. She wanted to ask what was wrong with Saeran, but her jaw was clenched against a wave of nausea.

The queen told her without being asked. "He fell ill with fever, but is not fever." When she couldn't think of the right words, she began speaking in frenzied sentences in her own tongue. Nia understood her perfectly. "He's cold as ice. We cannot warm him, and he will not wake. He called for you!" The accusation rang with despair and the small hands on her arms clenched as if to shake her. "He called all the time, and you would not come. You are supposed to help him! So help!"

Nia took a deep breath and reached out to something, anything, to steady herself. Her staff lay by the window, too far to reach. She didn't need it. The queen helped her to the bed and she sat heavily on the soft mattress. Next to her, Saeran didn't move. His breaths were shallow, and each was a sigh—her name. Tears stung her eyes. How many times had he called out to her and met with emptiness?

You know what to do, the dragon said in her mind, his voice banishing the dizziness. At last, Nia was able to look up without the world spinning around her.

Her gaze fell onto the queen's young face. The girl was beautiful, with dark skin and big round eyes. She wasn't wearing a veil and her thick, raven hair fell to her hips, plaited through with golden adornments. She looked as if she'd been crying for days and hadn't slept for weeks. Her lips were bloodless and dry, not a good sign, especially with the babe in her womb already crying out for nourishment.

Nia's heart sank for the girl, and the child. She couldn't help either. "Eat something," she said.

The queen drew back in surprise at hearing her native tongue. "I cannot leave him," she said. "He needs me." In the small moment of silence that followed her words, Nia was pulled into the girl's thoughts and memories, and she came to understand how much Queen Mari had changed in the months since her arrival. The shy, fearful young maiden was gone. In her place was a true queen. She stood tall now, when before she had cowered. She spoke up, when she hadn't in the past, and she had ruled the kingdom during Saeran's illness. She'd done it well. So well, in fact, that nobody, save those closest to him, knew that Saeran was ill, maybe dying.

The queen squared her shoulders with steely resolve. "He needs you more. You will make him better."

Nia wasn't so certain.

But when the queen made her exit, she had no choice.

26

The door closed. Nia shook all over, too scared to look at Saeran; scared she would see only a withered shell of the strong man she knew. Scared she wouldn't be able to heal him. Even now, listening to everything around her, she knew this was nothing she had ever seen before. The candles sang their sorrowful melodies. The walls mourned the dying king. The wolf's pelt pulled tighter around her, as if in encouragement.

Steeling herself against the stab of pain she knew was to come she turned her eyes on Saeran and sucked in a sharp breath at the sight of him. His hair was soaked with sweat, his eyes swollen and red, closed and still. He looked frozen, his skin pale and his lips blue. His beard had been shaven, revealing a gaunt face once so handsome. Blanket upon blanket covered him from the neck down, but she knew what they hid; a skeleton covered with skin.

"Saeran," Nia whispered, unable to believe this was the man she loved. She laid a shaking hand on his brow and gasped at how cold he was.

The noble king breathed in a true breath, his brows twitching as if he sensed her presence. Even his heart answered the touch, beating a little stronger.

Nia bit back her tears, struggling to her feet so she could examine him. She drew all but one blanket down to his waist, feeding magic to the hearth fire when he started shivering. Then she laid a hand on his chest and closed her eyes, Seeing with her essence into his.

Breath left her when she found the source of his illness. He was ensorcelled! A ball of sinister darkness, like a coiled spider's web glowed in his core, sending out tendrils that stretched into his entire body. It was in his heart and his mind, racking his body with pain and his thoughts with terror. He was too weak already to fight it much longer.

Nia drew back and opened her eyes. The spell was a powerful one, borne of several essences entwined together. How could that be? Who could wish such a thing on the king? And how could Nia have missed it?

It was too strong now, too deeply embedded in Saeran for her to draw it out. She would kill him in the process.

You know what to do, the dragon repeated, his voice revealing an uneasiness that frightened her.

The pendant won't be enough to banish this, she replied.

But it will allow me entrance.

Nia squared her shoulders, pulling the pendant from her pocket.

You do not hesitate? Even knowing what you will need to do, what it will do to you?

She lifted Saeran's head so she could put the chain around him. *I will keep him with me. Do what you must.* When the chain was in place, she removed the blankets, leaving him in nothing but his night shirt and the pendant. He hissed when she opened his shirt and placed the pendant in the center of his chest over the infection, his icy skin turning red around it as if burned.

Are you ready?

Nia took a deep breath, laying one hand over Saeran's brow, the other over the pendant. She closed her eyes and drew on all the magic she possessed, the dragon's power, and the light of her very soul. She held nothing back, pouring it all into Saeran to entwine her essence with his as tightly as she could, surrounding him. The cold, dark taint inside him made her shiver but instead of pulling back, Nia held on tighter, determined not to let him slip away. She nodded when she was done, knowing the dragon would see.

My blood will protect you, but not completely.

Do it now.

Very well, the dragon said after a small pause. *Do not let go.*

She felt the first wave of heat like a tendril of smoke winding around her and Saeran. It was no stronger than the heat of a hearth fire, but already Saeran bucked and she winced. The smoke twined around them until it created a cocoon from which the infection couldn't escape. Nia's hands shook, but she planted her feet and refused to move.

In the next instant, fire blasted the cocoon, blue and hotter than anything even Nia could conjure. It came rushing in through the smoke and became trapped inside it, just as Nia and Saeran were. Both screamed, and Saeran arched on the bed, every muscle in his body tight. His soul bucked, tried to escape her hold, but she wouldn't let it. He screamed and raged against her hold, begged and pleaded to be released from the scorching flames. Nia hardened her heart against his cries and held on.

And all the while the infection squealed like a living thing, burning like embers in a dying flame. Its tendrils pulled back into the mass at its core, giving it strength, and the fire intensified, determined to scorch every last bit of it.

Nia felt her flesh burning, giving way, but she would never show a sign of this torment on the outside, just like Saeran. Already his body was filling out, reclaiming the strength the infection had leeched from him. In a pained spasm, his hand shot to cover hers on his chest. She thought he might try to pull it away, but his fingers curled around hers, his magic mixing with hers, and he held on to her, gaining more strength and courage as the infection grew weaker and smaller.

The fire swirled around them, inside them in a vortex of blinding heat that drowned out their cries with its roar. The infection sparked and lashed out, trying to find another place to hide, to seed and grow anew. There was nowhere to hide.

Do not fight it, the dragon told her. *Give yourself up to the fire or it will burn you alive.*

Nia opened her watering eyes to squint through the flames at Saeran. His eyes were like mirrors, reflecting the blue fire, and for a moment she recognized in them that which had always been part of him—dragonblood. She managed a small nod and saw him grit his teeth. He squeezed her hand, then closed his eyes and did as the dragon had told them. Nia followed suit. She let the fire in, let it do with her as it pleased. The white hot flame cut off her cry, burned her tears away before they could fall. It embedded itself in her core, the place where the dragon's blood had merged with her life's essence.

But instead of searing her, it fed her strength. The burn turned to warmth, the transition so sharp that it weakened her and her knees almost buckled beneath her. She'd felt this before with the dragon's blood, knew what she had to do, but Saeran hesitated, refusing to accept it completely. It trapped the flame in his body, but outside of his soul, and it could do nothing but burn him. It was killing him as surely as the infection, and Saeran was frozen in uncertainty.

Let it in! she wanted to tell him, but couldn't make herself heard. Saeran was beyond hearing anything. He clutched her hand, fighting the terrible draw pulling him away from her, but it wasn't enough. He was slipping.

Nia cried out. She climbed onto the bed to kneel next to Saeran. *Please. Please do not fight me.* Then she leaned over him and pressed her lips to his, forcing the fire that had become part of her into him through a kiss. The door it opened was small, but it was enough. She felt Saeran gasp against her lips as the flame bonded with him completely. As if awakened from deep slumber, his own fire flared and joined the dragon's, and together they burned brighter, hotter, searing the infection until nothing remained but ash, and then not even that.

The dragon pulled back as soon as it was safe to do so, leaving Nia and Saeran shaken and cold without the fire's heat, but safe. Nia sat on her heels to keep from falling on top of Saeran. Head swimming, eyelids heavy, she was moments away from passing out.

Faint voices intruded, guards and healers entering the chamber. Though her eyes were open, she couldn't make sense of what she was seeing. There were only colors and lights dancing before her, making her dizzy and tired.

Something brushed her cheek. Someone said her name.

Strong arms closed around her and then everything went black.

Nia collapsed against Saeran and for a moment the shock of waking up to see her there turned into blind panic that the fever had passed from him to her. But Saeran felt her breath puff against his skin, heard her heart beat.

He clutched Nia to him, his heart thudding in his chest as it hadn't done in weeks. His limbs were weak, his body still stinging with the memory of fire, but there were no scars on his skin. He felt stronger than he ever had in his life, and knew it had little to do the fire the dragon had lent him. How Nia had managed to find a dragon, let alone persuade him to help Saeran, he would never know and, at the moment, didn't care. She was back in his arms, and this time he wasn't letting her go.

His hands were clumsy, but he managed to pull on the ties of her cloak and take it off her shoulders. The wolf skin left her with a caress as if it still lived, and it stayed on the bed when the cloak slid to the floor.

"Your Majesty," one of the healers said, breathless, as if he couldn't believe his king's rapid recovery.

"Leave," Saeran said, surprised at the strength of his own voice.

"But your Majesty—"

"Now."

They left. The door closed again, shutting out the murmurs and grumbles and outlandish rumors being born while the chamber filled with the soft music of candle flames and whispered secrets, a lullaby to ease Nia's slumber.

Saeran smiled down at her sleeping in his arms. He arranged the pillows behind him so he could sit against them, then settled back with his beloved wizard in his lap and laid his cheek against the top of her head. In the morning, he would ask her what happened, where she'd gone, and how she'd gotten back. He would ask about the dragon and her quest, and the chain he now wore about his neck. But for the moment, he was more than happy to simply be. Saeran closed his eyes and, with the dragon's fire still burning inside him, warding away the chill of death, allowed healing sleep to claim him as well.

In his dreams, he soared high above mountains and streams, playing among the sun-warmed clouds. And wherever he flew, though he couldn't see her, he felt Nia at his side.

Mari walked out into the courtyard, wandering toward the kitchens. She had no appetite, but for the child's sake she would eat as the wizard had told her.

The sounds coming from the king's chamber were horrible. It was as if a great thunderstorm had become trapped there. Things were crashing, guards, priests, and healers shouting and running to lend assistance. They didn't yet know their efforts were of less use now than they had been before the wizard returned.

Now that she has, Mari knew precisely why the king adored her so. The wizard was a beauty beyond beauty, and her eyes were ancient with knowledge so profound that mere humans could never grasp it. Mari was a creature of the desert, of hot sands and burning sun. The wizard had been created from air and water, at once mysterious and familiar. Where Mari was a shadow, a ghost, the wizard shone like a star, guiding and brilliant.

How could the queen ever compete with such a creature? She, who had not even been born here, when the wizard seemed part of the land itself. And she was as much part of the king.

The queen steeled herself not to sigh. The king would recover, that much she now believed. And when he did, he'd have the wizard at his side without cease to ensure he would not fall ill again. And Mari would fade into the background, into their shadow, as had always been her fate. It was useless to fight it. She'd been reared to defer to others, why should she have come to believe that would ever change?

She paused beneath the stone archway, in shadows cast by her castle home. Mari didn't envy the wizard her magics. Aegiros had its own magic men and women, and she had seen them struggle for years on end to learn how to channel the will of the gods. They could do much harm before they learned. Many did not survive at all; the terrible power turned on them with such force no one could stop it.

Mari had no magic of her own, but she could sometimes feel it in others. The wizard Nia was far more powerful than any other she had ever met. Yes, the wizard would heal Saeran, of that she had no doubt. But even now, through the din and noise inside his chamber far above, Mari could hear their pained screams, and she shuddered to think about what was happening in there. The wizard was welcome to her gifts. Mari had no desire for them, or the pain that came with them.

Someone fell through an open doorway across the courtyard. Mari started and, remembering she had not veiled herself, shifted deeper into the darkness. But she kept watch in case she was needed. The man on the ground curled in on himself, groaning, then shot straight and arched as if he was a puppet being moved by some greater force. He cried out in pain, echoing the screams within the castle.

Mari was about to go to his aid, but then his fingers curled to claw at the hard packed earth as he thrashed. His body smoked, though Mari could see no flames. The sight frightened her; she recognized the workings of evil spells even from this distance and hid behind the corner. The wail he let out terrified her. It shifted like some demon from the depths of hell, as if several voices cried out from a single being.

And then his appearance began to change, flickering between short-haired youth and a shriveled, gray-haired mass. He was ancient one moment, a woman the next, then a man, his body contorting in ways that made him writhe in agony.

He clawed at his chest and then tore away a chain with a heavy pendant, flinging it aside. But it would not leave him. It slid back toward him until it was in his hand once more, glittering in the night like a black star.

Mari whispered a soft prayer of protection. Whatever the wizard was doing, it was affecting this creature, and there could only be one reason for that.

She ran into the kitchens and closed the door before the man-demon could rise and sight her. Her heart raced and her belly ached with fear. A brave woman would have stayed to discover who had poisoned her king. A strong woman would have confronted him, regardless of the danger to herself. Mari was neither.

Another of those sharp, burning pains stabbed through her, and she collapsed into a chair, fighting the darkness threatening to overwhelm her. Something was wrong with her. The pain in her womb was a bad portent and fear for her unborn child made her shiver.

When the wizard finished with the king, she would ask her aid. Surely, if Nia helped the king, she would help Mari as well. All she wanted was for the child to be safe.

But there was to be no speaking to the royal wizard.

When Mari felt strong enough to stand once more, her gown came away from the chair soaked. The last thing she saw before she fainted was the pool of blood where she had sat a moment ago.

~

Ali al-Hassan, third son of the third son of Melorn the True, loyal warrior of *shansher* Dhakir the Conqueror, and faithful servant and protector of *shensari* Mari of the North could not sleep. He had stood his watch from sunup until sunset, guarding his *shensari* and her husband as was his duty. Now it was his time to rest, yet he could not.

The *shensari* was troubled. She would not rest or eat while her husband lay dying, and it was beginning to take a toll on her. It was no good for her to do this, especially now that she was with child. For her sake Ali wished the king's torment would end, one way or another. No warrior wanted to die in such a way. There was no honor or glory in withering away from disease. A man should die by blade or arrow. In battle, protecting his family, serving his *shansher.*

If the *shensari* would allow, Ali would end the king's life the honorable way. But she loved him and would not hear of it. And so she tended him day and night and prayed for his recovery, while the rest of them guarded day and night and prayed for her well being.

A great noise erupted in the castle. Ali drew his sword but saw no enemy to slay. The noises were like a terrible demon dervish raging inside the castle, striking fear into his soul. He retreated, though he kept a watchful eye for the *shensari*. When he saw her strolling in the courtyard, he was relieved.

Sheathing his sword, he turned the other way toward the stables. No matter that these people were so strange, they bred magnificent horses and cared for them quite well. Their stables were clean and well tended, their horses never wanted for food, and no rider was allowed to mount one without proper gear.

Ali liked horses. They always soothed his troubled mind.

Tonight, even the animals were disturbed by the noise. A small mare snorted in her stall, stomping her hooves and shaking her head. The male next to her kicked back at the wall, his eyes wide with fear. A new mother nosed her little one who cowered against her side, hiding his head beneath her neck. Ali shuddered and stroked a beautiful steed's neck, pretending he did not hear.

But then someone screamed outside, and that he could not ignore. Drawing his sword once more, he ran toward it and burst through the kitchen door to see the *shensari* falling to the ground. "Mari!"

Ali caught her, saw all the blood, and his bones turned cold. He shook her, called her name, but she would not wake. "Help," he called. "Help! Someone!"

No one answered. Ali scooped her body into his arms, terrified at how small and light she was. He carried her outside to where they all slept, bellowing for his comrades. "Hamdan! Bakri! Najjar! *Shensari bahran sephri!*"

They came running, as they'd been trained. Hamdan took one look at the *shensari* and swore a vile oath. "Fetch the midwife," he ordered Najjar. "Bakri, help me."

They cleared one of the beds and laid their mistress upon it. Hamdan lit candles for light and Bakri gathered linens and rags. None of them would dare touch her skin; to see her face bare was bad enough. But

Ali was most worried about how pale she was, how bloodless her lips. She had been cold in his arms before and now she would not stir at all.

When Najjar returned with the midwife and Mari's hand maiden, the men left the room and let them tend her.

"Who did this?" Hamdan demanded.

"I saw no one," Ali answered, though he wasn't certain himself. His main concern had been the *shensari*. He had not searched for whoever might have harmed her.

"Could it be the babe?" Bakri said. "My sister lost a child once. I was the one who found her. It was much the same as the *shensari*, but Sibaal was awake, and she was in great pain."

They stood in silence awhile. Ali did not know what to say. If it was as Bakri said, then the *shensari* was blessed to have fainted rather than endure such pain. But that she would not wake worried him.

The midwife, Wurud, came out then. Her gaze was downcast and she would not look at any of them.

"What is it, woman? Speak!"

"It is not good."

"What do we do?"

Wurud looked at Ali, met his gaze, and he could see tears in her eyes. "Pray," she said.

Ali met eyes with Hamdan and saw the same helpless anger in him as well. There had to be a villain to slay for this. Ali intended to find him.

With a curt nod, he stalked back to the kitchen where he'd left his sword. The sight of his *shensari*'s blood on the floor made him sick to his soul, but he steeled himself. He was a warrior. He would do what he did best. Kill the enemy.

He was headed for the opposite door when it opened and a man stumbled in. He looked as if he'd gone through a great battle, barely keeping his feet under him. Gasping for breath, he reached for a chair but seeing the blood on it thought better of sitting. "Is the bitch dead?" he rasped, his voice almost unrecognizable.

But Ali knew this man. Or thought he did. "You? You did this?"

The man harrumphed and groaned. "Then she lives. Pity."

Incensed, Ali roared his rage at him, brandishing his sword.

The man only laughed.

Ali charged him, ready to take his head but with a wave of his hand, the man sent him flying back. And still he laughed.

Ali got back to his feet, his sword arm shaking. What witchery was this? He came forward a second time, intent on the demon despite his fear. For his *shensari*, he would do this. He would kill the demon and avenge her.

Laughing harder, the man pointed a finger and Ali's sword clattered to the ground. Baffled, Ali looked down at the weapon and then at the hand which used to hold it. It was gone, his wrist turned to ash. And the ash was spreading up his arm.

Gods help me, he prayed, watching his other arm disintegrate. There was no pain, only fear, and the feeling of his self falling apart, body and soul. When he fell to the ground, desperate prayers slipped past his lips, useless whispers no one would ever hear. No one would ever know who he was or how he'd died.

His last prayer was for his *shensari,* that she wake and heal, and live a happy…

28

Nia woke to Saeran's call. She opened her eyes, though they wanted to stay closed, and rose to her elbows. She was in Nico's study. How she got there, she didn't know, nor how much time had passed since she'd collapsed. Her head pounded and every bone in her body ached. Her legs would not support her and without her staff, she had to brace herself against the walls and table to stay on her feet.

Someone had dressed her in a night gown. She didn't care. With a swirl of her hand she hoped to conjure clothes, but nothing happened and the action only made her sway more. She leaned precariously to the side and took the blanket that had covered her, draping it over her shoulders for warmth. There was no time to waste. Saeran's call came again, stronger than the first one, which had somehow managed to wake her from a wizard's sleep.

It gave her strength enough to make her way to the staircase, but she was forced to crawl up to the courtyard. She was winded and shivering by the time she made it there. *What is happening?* she thought to the dragon, but was too weak to reach him. There was no answer.

"Micah," she called softly, willing her voice to carry to the stables. That much, it seemed, she could manage. The boy came out frowning, looking around for the person who had disturbed him from his duties.

When he spotted Nia, sitting against the wall, his eyes widened and he came running.

"What's happened?" he asked, helping her up and then holding her up when she couldn't stand on her own.

"Don't know," she said. "Need to get to the king."

"Aye, then, at once," Micah said with a nod and turned toward the royal chambers. "Would you have me carry you?" he asked when her dragging feet snared on a stair.

Nia shook her head. "Dignity, my friend," she told him, attempting a smile. "I would like to keep what little I have left." Her words were slurring. She didn't have the strength to speak with her usual authority.

"You turned the castle upside down night before last. Brought a dying king back to roarin' life. There's much dignity to be flaunted."

The assurance made her feel little better. A full day and night she'd been unconscious, and should have stayed that way longer to heal completely. Her chest still ached from the dragon's fire, and the memory of it made her skin sting and burn. It was too much too soon. Whatever Saeran wanted of her, she was sure she wouldn't be able to grant. Not in this state. And knowing he wouldn't have summoned her for any trifling matter, she dreaded what awaited her.

There was a crowd gathered before the queen's bedchamber. Nia planted her feet, stopping Micah's progress. Every healer she knew was standing before her, chanting and praying, looking at her with both hope and defeat. She smelled incense burning inside, heard the walls whispering, but couldn't make sense of any of it.

She didn't need them to know what the matter was.

Two armed Aegiran warriors guarded the door and between them, a woman draped in all white, a veil hiding her entire face.

Nia squeezed her eyes shut as sorrow overwhelmed her.

"You are weak still," the healer Padraig said as he approached. "We can aid you in this."

She shook her head weakly. "It will not help."

The man's eyes flickered to the queen's chamber door and then back to her and he paled. Bowing his head, he returned to the others and told them something that made everyone quiet. They turned to Nia, expecting something she could not give them. Miracles, perhaps, or an explanation. But they could plainly see she was at death's door herself. What the dragon had wrought to heal Saeran would have destroyed her had his blood not been in her veins. As it was, it had nearly done her in, and she had a long ways to go to recover her strength and magic.

The queen would not last long enough for that.

"Nia."

She looked up at Saeran. The king stood in the doorway of his wife's chambers, looking pale and tired, but otherwise hale. His hands were clenched at his sides and his eyes, more than anything, revealed his soul's struggle. He didn't want to ask this of her, but he had no other choice.

He didn't yet know.

The Aegirans made way for Saeran as he came to Nia and took over for Micah, helping her the rest of the way into the queen's bedchamber. "She's fallen ill. I think…I think it was because of me."

Nia took in the queen's still form, lying in the middle of a bed that dwarfed her already small frame. She looked so young and serene, so close to slipping away. "Your illness did not cause this," she said with difficulty. Her eyes stung, though she could not shed a tear.

"Then, you can help her?" She could tell Saeran struggled to keep his voice even. He might not love his queen, but he cared for her very much. She was under his protection and had ruled in his absence. The affection he held for her was obvious.

Though it broke her heart, she shook her head, no. She could not voice the word.

"Are you too weak? The healers can aid you. They can lend you their strength. If you can heal her, then you must!"

"Saeran, I cannot," she whispered, unable to look at him. "Nothing I could do would save her."

"Why?" he demanded. "The healers said she is…bleeding. What is wrong with her?"

Nia's shivers became too much and she fell against him, unable to support herself any longer. Saeran helped her to a chair and then knelt before her, catching her hands in his. "You can help her, I know you can," he said, and every word he spoke was a dagger in her soul. "You are the greatest wizard I have ever heard of. What could be wrong with her that you cannot heal?"

Nia looked at the bed once more. *I am sorry,* she whispered to the queen, hoping the girl would hear her, though she was too far gone already. The girl was too young. Her body too weak to care for the essence of a dragon, no matter how far removed. The child demanded too much that the queen could not provide. It was draining her.

"She is dying."

The words, spoken on a whisper, shuddered through the chambers, silencing the walls.

A log split in the hearth, startling them both, but neither said a word.

The Aegiran guards stepped into the chamber with the woman, Mari's midwife, chanting a quiet dirge for her mistress. They couldn't have heard Nia's quiet admission, but only a fool would need to hear the words to see the truth of them.

Saeran was such a fool. Against everything telling him otherwise, he'd hoped Nia could work just one more miracle. He could see in her eyes now how wrong he had been, and his face grew cold, all the blood drained out of it. He let go of her hands and forced himself to his feet; locked his knees when he would have fallen to them again. Back to Mari's bedside he went, where he'd sat for an entire day, watching her breathe. Strange, he could feel vibrant life inside her, even as he was watching her die. "She did this for me," he said. "I do not remember much, but I remember she was with me."

"I should have been here," Nia said.

"Hamdan told me one of their own is missing. A man named Ali. He disappeared the night she fell ill." The night Nia had returned to save his life.

"Are you blaming him?" she asked them, but the Aegirans didn't know her and would not answer.

Saeran shook his head, surprised that his voice was so steady; that he could speak at all. "They think someone or something hurt Mari, and that Ali died trying to protect her. But no one knows anything for certain. There were no witnesses."

"Your Majesty," Padraig said, braving his way between the warriors into the chamber. "What will you ask of us?"

Saeran didn't know what to say.

"Help me up," Nia said. With Padraig's help she came to Saeran and held out her hand. "I don't know what this might do, if anything. But I am willing to try if you are."

The midwife fell silent and rushed forward. "What will you do?" she demanded, the first sentence Saeran had heard her speak.

"Whatever I can," Nia replied, but her eyes were on Saeran. Because she was too weak to do anything, but Saeran wasn't.

He took her hand without hesitation.

The midwife hurried around the bed to the other side and took Mari's hand in hers as the warriors came closer. "I will feel what you do," she warned. "If harm comes to my *shensari,* there will be retribution."

Nia nodded her understanding and then looked to Saeran. "Do not let go," she said, closing her eyes.

Saeran felt a tug on his heart, Nia drawing strength out of him, through herself, and into Mari. Her hand was over Mari's belly and her unborn child, and for a moment he could almost feel it. That tiny spark of life was so bright it stunned him. So strong, eager for all that life had to offer. As Saeran's strength poured into it, it grew brighter, stronger, and he heard a cry worthy of a warrior in his mind.

But even as he did, Saeran felt himself grow weaker. He swayed on his feet, almost let go of Nia's hand, but she held him fast, drew a little more on his strength.

With a gasp, Mari opened her eyes.

The warriors cried out, rushing forward to witness the miracle for themselves.

"Gods all bless," Padraig whispered, reaching for the queen, but without his support, Nia's legs gave out and her hand slipped from Mari.

Saeran felt the connection break, watched his wife and queen blink twice at the ceiling and then release the breath she'd taken and close her eyes. He felt her soul fade away, and the child's followed. He knew when the midwife wailed her grief, falling to her knees by Mari's side that his queen was gone.

Saeran collapsed on the floor next to Nia.

"It would have taken…that," she said, struggling to form the words and he knew they were all listening, all but the poor, heartbroken midwife lost in her grief. "Constantly, all the days until the child's birth…just to keep her heart beating. I am sorry, Saeran. I'm so sorry. I could not have saved her."

Saeran pushed to his shaky legs. "Padraig," he said, his voice hoarse. "Assist the wizard to her chambers. And have…have the priests take care of the queen."

"No," one of the warriors growled. "We will tend to the *shensari*. She is one of ours. We will look after her."

Padraig looked to Saeran, and he nodded his ascent.

He didn't know how he managed to walk to his chambers; wasn't aware of anything going on around him. People spoke, but he heard no words, only the buzz of their voices. They touched him, but he could not feel their hands. The door slammed shut, closing him away from everything out there, and then his world plunged into total silence and he was alone.

Completely and utterly alone.

29

The funeral pyre burned higher than the tallest trees, but the smoke curling up toward the sky was white. Pure, as the queen had been. Her personal guard, three strong men who had not uttered a word since she died now roared their grief as they beat their chests. They had seen the queen born, had stood guard over her from that moment until she'd breathed her last. She'd been more than a queen to them. The three guards mourned Mari as if she'd been family. No longer did they refer to her by the formal title of *shensari*. If they spoke of her at all, she was always *idrah* Mari. Dear one, beloved.

One after the other, each unsheathed his sharp, curved blade and pulled it across his cheek, drawing blood. It was a sign of great devotion and grief. They stood so close to the flames their skin was beginning to turn hot, yet they would not move until the last embers were cold. This was their final duty to their queen. They would take her ashes back to their homeland and scatter them across the vast desert planes so she might always feel the sun on her face and the hot sand beneath her feet.

There was to be no feast this day. Though it was custom here to celebrate when a person returned to their ancestors, the Aegirans practiced the opposite and would be offended if they saw the kingdom rejoice at the queen's death.

Nia watched everything from where she would not be in the way. In Nico's study, she felt safe from reproach, but not guilt. Whenever her window spell showed her Saeran, standing still and silent at the edge of the gathering, she could think of nothing but the look on his face when she'd told him the queen would die.

He had not argued, cajoled, or threatened. He'd simply looked into Nia's eyes and read the truth of her words there. Then he'd turned away from her and gone to the queen's bedside to sit with her and hold her hand so she might pass peacefully. He'd not said a word to her when the queen died. He'd not even looked at her again.

And so Nia had returned here and mourned the queen by herself, in too much pain to sleep again.

She had not slept the wizard's sleep yet, though it weighed on her every waking moment. She was still weak, only capable of working the most basic of spells. Nia would not risk Saeran's safety now. When she was in the wizard's sleep, she couldn't perceive the world, nor react to it, more vulnerable than anyone else. And now that she knew someone wished Saeran harm, she couldn't take the chance they would strike again while she was helpless to stop them. It would mean a much longer recovery, but what choice did Nia have?

The gathering was breaking up. The villagers descended from the hill, slowly returning to their homes, the healers and priests following after one last prayer. The knights, now returned from their quest, came after them, once again asking about the wizard. They wished to thank her, but Nia was in no shape to see them. They would leave on the morrow and, having found what they'd sought, never again cast their gazes north.

Saeran was the last to turn away. His face showed no emotion, but his step was heavy as he followed the path toward the castle, leaving the Aegirans behind.

Nia watched his progress until he reached the castle's gate. When she was sure he was safe within, she turned away from the window and let it dissolve into firefly sparks to scatter into every corner of the chamber. Nico's magic still lingered here, and Nia now thought he'd left it to make sure she was never weakened completely.

She had yet to draw on any of it. Its presence was a comfort she didn't want to relinquish, and as soon as she absorbed one pocket, she knew it would be gone forever. Nia might never call on that power now. She needed the reminder of her mentor, however faint. *I am tired, Nico,* she thought, wishing he could hear her.

The door groaned open, admitting the king. He paused just inside, hesitating. Then he closed the door behind him and joined her at the table. Though they sat opposite each other, neither of them moved or looked up, and the silence stretched on while they seemed suspended in time. There was some comfort in that. They could still be in the same room this way without feeling the need to escape. She'd feared otherwise.

"Did you know?" Saeran finally asked, his voice soft and unsteady. "When you sensed her caravan approaching, did you know then?"

"I knew there was a chance…" Words failed her. Would he even believe her? Suddenly the whole idea of looking into the future disgusted her. "Chances, probabilities, that is all the future is. There are always risks. But they change with every blink. A thing so small as pausing to greet a friend could change the rest of a man's life." Nia splayed her hands on the surface of the table, tracing a groove. "There was a chance she would meet with disaster. There was also a chance that the rest of us would. I didn't…I didn't know it was a certainty until it was too late."

He gave a slight nod, but made no other move, still staring at the floor. "Why did the dragon help me?"

"You are his grandson," she told him without skirting it. "Dragonblood is in your veins. That is why you can master spells more easily than others. Magic is part of you."

Something flickered in his eyes. "Then why did he not help Mari?"

Nia drew a bracing breath. This was what she'd been dreading. "Mari would have died in childbirth, had she survived this. You would have had an heir, but lost your queen."

"Why? Why is that a certainty? Stop hedging, wizard, and tell me!" His hands curled into angry fists, but he still would not look at her, as if he wanted to spare her his wrath. He was not angry at her, she realized, but at himself.

"Mari was too young," she said with difficulty, "far too young and unprepared for any child. She had been weakening for weeks because her body could not sustain both her and the babe, and she tired herself out more caring for you."

"So it is my fault."

"No! Saeran, she loved you. I...would have done the same."

Saeran shoved to his feet, making her flinch. "Go on," he demanded. "Tell me the rest, I know there is more. With you, there always is."

Nia clasped her hands together. "Human vessels cannot carry dragonblood," she said. Not knowing how to temper her words, she repeated to Saeran what the dragon had said to her. "Dragon essence, no matter how diluted is too powerful. It needs magic to feed on, and in its absence, it drains its mother's life to save its own. If Mari had survived this, the birth would have killed her."

"Enough," he rasped, plunging his fingers into his hair as he paced around the chamber like a caged animal. His chest rose and fell in harsh breaths, and his jaw was clenched so tightly she could hear his teeth grind against each other.

When he came back to the table he lashed out and sent the water pitcher flying with an angry swipe. It flew end over end, but though it stopped at the wall upside down, it neither fell, nor spilled its contents. It was not Nia's doing.

"Why would my father not warn me of this?" he asked, staring at it. That, more than anything Nia said, proved the truth of what she was telling him.

"He did not know," Nia answered. "Your mother never told him. She was half dragon and must have hoped it would give her strength enough to survive. She died before she could tell anyone."

The pitcher fell and Saeran's head lowered. "You are telling me I cannot take another wife. I can never have heirs without sacrificing the woman's life." He was no fool. Though he wished he could argue, to call Nia a liar, he felt the truth of what she told him. Something had changed him, though whether it was the cursed illness or the dragon's fire Saeran couldn't tell. But whatever it was, it awakened a fire inside him he'd never felt before. The bright, shining flame gave him strength as he'd never known and enhanced his senses beyond anything Nia had ever taught him.

He no longer strained to hear the elements or summon a vision; they came to him for the asking. When he slept, he dreamed visions so sweet he was loath to open his eyes in the morning. Saeran had only to think of what he needed and it appeared before him as if summoned and earlier, standing witness to Mari's funeral, he thought he'd glimpsed white shadows moving among the crowd. The Others had been in attendance. While he embraced the changes within him, they also sometimes frightened him.

And so he understood what Nia was telling him, and it nearly killed him. He mourned Mari as a friend and companion. She hadn't deserved to die at all, let alone because of him—and no matter what Nia said, it was his fault and his alone. From the moment he made the pact to end the war, to the moment he took her to wife and gave her a child, all his fault. Each and every one of the choices leading to her demise had been his and he would have to live with that for the rest of his life. He ached and missed Mari.

But he had never felt for her what he did for Nia.

The wizard was the very beat of his heart. She was why Saeran lived.

But if there had been boundaries between them before, they'd been nothing compared to this. He'd rather die than risk her life.

When Nia didn't answer, a memory suddenly struck him and he turned rigid with fear. Beltaine night. Saeran forced himself to face her, though everything in him resisted broaching the subject. "You would," he said, then had to clear his throat to continue. "You would know if you were with child, would you not?"

Nia blinked up at him as if the thought had never occurred to her. She nodded. "I can control that. Prevent myself from conceiving."

Relief made him sway dizzily and he took a chair, closer to her this time. Her eyes were bright and her posture slumped. "I can see how weak you are." And he knew it was because she wouldn't sleep, though she desperately needed it.

"I am well enough," she replied, but the smile she attempted only made her condition that much more obvious.

"Sleep, Nia," he told her. He didn't like seeing her vulnerable this way. He'd give her his strength, the way she'd tried to give it to Mari, taking none for herself, but Saeran knew without asking that she wouldn't let him. He knew because the walls grumbled to him day and night about the magic she poured into them for protection. Someone had tried to kill the king, and the last thing she would do was take from him and leave him vulnerable.

"Can't leave you unguarded," she said, rubbing her forehead. "The spell that was cast on you was no trifling matter. If there is another attack while I am sleeping, I will not be able to protect you."

Hazy memories of a glittering object and incoherent words floated across his mind. It would make sense that someone had enchanted him. Saeran had always been strong and healthy. He'd not have succumbed to an illness so easily. But the healing Nia and his dragon grandfather had performed had wiped away any memory he had of his attacker.

Saeran tugged on the silver chain around his neck to pull the dragon pendant out from beneath his shirt. He wore it next to his skin now, sensing its power as he could his own. "This might do a passing fair job of it," he told her.

Nia smiled a little and reached out to trace the dragon's image. "It likes you."

Saeran caught her hand and brought her palm to his lips. "Sleep, Nia. I need you strong if I am to rule forever and without heir." The ease with which he spoke the words gave him pause. How quickly he'd given up a future with a wife at his side and children bouncing on his knees.

But he realized he didn't regret the loss. He still had Nia. Until death or longer. The words bound them both better than any marriage ceremony devised by man or god. He had Nia by his side now. Nothing mattered more.

Nia frowned, gazing at the swinging pendant, and he felt it grow hot enough to warm the chain it hung from. She looked entranced by it, her shoulders slumping a little more. "I am a wizard," she mumbled.

"Yes, the greatest wizard Wilderheim has ever seen. And the prettiest. Now let's get you to bed."

"Of the Streams, he said."

"Who said, sweet?"

"The dragon." She struggled to raise her gaze to look him in the eye. "He knew things even I don't. He said *of the Streams*. I was not… paying attention…" Her eyes closed, but she shook her head to wake herself up again.

Losing patience with his stubborn wizard, Saeran picked her up, tucking her against his chest. "Enough of this, Nia. You will sleep whether you want to or not. I order you to sleep. And I am king." He felt her smile against him and his own lips twitched in answer.

"Can't let you walk about alone," she murmured sleepily.

"Then I will just have to stay close to you."

"I could send you away."

He laughed as he laid her on the bed. "Try it."

And she did. But either he'd grown too strong for her to command, or she was too weak to force him away.

Saeran grinned at her attempts to banish him and pulled the covers over her. "Give up?"

Nia scowled. "Stubborn royals." He felt her magic flare again, creating a bubble that expanded until it melted into the walls. Once the guards were raised, added to the ones already in place, he doubted he would be getting out again until she took them down.

Saeran couldn't say it bothered him overly much. He kissed her on the brow. "Sweet dreams, Nia."

She sighed, already fast asleep.

30

There were shadows, and within them pools of darkness so thick they could hold portals to other worlds. It was through these secret, sacred doorways that a pale, red haired creature chose to travel. He was not one for fanfares or great processions. No, he preferred to remain unobserved when he watched the seeds of his mischief bloom and bear fruit. He uncurled his long bony fingers to watch the lines on his hands change yet again.

Destiny for ones like him worked in odd ways. Nothing was ever set in stone; no eternal pathway lay ready to be walked for always. Only those with an end got the pleasure of reaching it. He cocked his head to the side, black eyes narrowing when the pendulum of his fate swung wildly to settle in an unexpected way.

Merely by appearing here, he'd changed his destiny. His temporary destiny. The darkness that had been spelled out in the center of his palm, the centuries of pain and destruction, the end of all things he'd been foretold to cause were suddenly gone. In their place now lay mist. Balance. A point from which he could move either way.

The legendary Trickster found this new turn of events unnerving. Crossroads and convergences could be distorted, but when there was a clear, straight path, he had nothing to play with. Left to his own devices this way, he usually chose to cause more mischief. It didn't suit him to have a reputation for doing good deeds when plagued with indecision. Faced with such a decision, and the choice he always made, his destiny tended to change instantly, just for the intent of a dark deed, plunging him right back into that blackness he found so reassuring.

It failed to do so now. Instead of dwelling on it, a tiresome thing to do, he stepped out of the doorway and into shadow, casting his wild black eyes about the room. It was plain, unless one possessed the ability to see through illusions. Nothing plain would do for his ambitious sorcerer. His ego was big enough to rival a god, and that his pride and vanity were so wholly undeserved made the Trickster chuckle in delight.

Great golden and silver shields covered the walls to act as mirrors. They reflected the lights of a hundred candle flames, only three of which would be visible through the illusion's cover. The floor, hard packed earth, was covered with animal skins that overlapped each other so that the sorcerer's toes might never touch the ground. His grand bed was bigger even than a king's, with posts reaching the ceiling and heavy velvet drapes hanging from the top as canopy.

"I can feel your presence, Ancient One," the man himself said from that bed, and even his voice sounded different without the glamour he cast on himself. "*It* feels your presence." It was a good one, the glamour. It even made him feel young. But beneath that polish he was an old man already. The power he held so tightly was too much for him to bear, though it was contained for the moment, it still drained his years away and he was far too drunken with it to care. His skin was withered like an autumn leaf, scarred from the pox and boils he could not treat, his teeth were rotted, and what was left of his hair was pure white and matted from lack of washing.

It was the height of rudeness for a creature so low to address a deity in such a way. And Loki didn't take kindly to it. The Trickster narrowed his eyes at the pathetic pile of bones and decided to put the withered prune back in his place.

The heavy bed frame shook and shuddered, a mere hint of what he could do, but it would be enough to get his point across. The mattress lifted toward the ceiling so quickly the sorcerer had no time to draw breath for a scream. He did scream later, all the way down, when Loki let the mattress drop, slightly out of place and balance, just enough to jar the sorcerer until he began sliding off the side. So far off the floor, the fall might have proven fatal. A shame his grip was still sturdy.

Deprived of his opportunity to spy, Loki stepped out of the shadow and into the flood of candlelight. He rushed the bed, coming nose-to-nose with the cantankerous wretch, brushing away the meager spell the sorcerer spat at him. "Manners, mortal," he hissed and then disappeared as quickly as he had appeared, removing himself to the other side of the room.

The sorcerer clutched his chest and wheezed. Even from so far away, Loki could hear his heart thundering, and it amused him enough that his temper dissolved like a snowflake in the sun.

He should have known the stone would reveal him. He squinted at it from a distance. A fine piece of creation, he wasn't too modest to admit. A work of genius. It drained the wearer of his magic without draining him at all. What got sucked into the black ice crystal was a mirror image of the power, just as potent, but forever trapped in the pendant. It had to be touched to release its magics and became so bonded with the wearer that it would forever find its way to him, eager to share what it held, and absorb more.

A ravenous wee thing, it was. Always wanting more.

The sorcerer sputtered, attempting to cast yet another spell. All it took was for Loki to toss a small windstorm about himself to make the fool fall silent. With wide eyes the sorcerer watched him, that precious little gem clutched in his gnarled hand. It was the same look he might give to a ravenous beast that had him cornered. Good.

Loki was used to such reactions. He made no attempt to use a glamour to hide his true appearance, saw no reason to do so. He was, after all, a god. Why should those who look upon him not see it? He knew full well that he exuded energy so potent it made lesser crea-tures shrink back in fear. His appearance was as it should be; at once beautiful, and dangerous and terrible. His hair was as pure copper, shining and sharp, his war braids merely proclaiming him that much more of a threat. His skin was pale, nigh sickly, but magnificent to behold, and his charcoal black eyes were opaque, without the wet gleam of human eyes, or the whites.

Perhaps his teeth were a little sharp as well, too often displayed in a wicked toothy grin. That very same grin he wore now. "I see you were not expecting me," he said with mock disappointment and clucked his tongue in censure.

"What would you want of me?" the withered sorcerer rasped and coughed, surprised that his glamour was faltering. One gnarled, shaking hand reached for the goblet of wine by his bedside. Half of the liquid sloshed over the sides as he brought it to his pale lips and drank greedily. When he was finished, he let the goblet tumble from his grasp, spilling what remained.

"It has been a very long century since the day I deigned to answer an old woman's prayer," Loki said, holding the sorcerer's gaze. He enjoyed the man's squirming. "One hundred years of waiting and watching from afar as one after the other powerful mages destroyed each other and then themselves in the name of grandeur."

With a careless shrug, he wandered around the room to examine its contents more closely. "A very boring century. You see, my creation was so beautiful and self-sustaining that it no longer needed me to move it along. It wrought its deeds very well without me. I am…displeased."

Another wheeze. But this time, his brows lowered defensively. He would fight Loki for the trinket, should he think it necessary.

Loki smiled at the sorcerer's reflection in one of his shields. Its shape offended him. Perfectly round and ordered, perfectly shined and centered on the wall. With a thought, he warped the metal, crumpling it like a piece of parchment, the sound sharp music to his ears. When it was nothing but a jagged ball, he straightened out half of it and stepped back to survey his handiwork. Better. "And so I have decided that it might be time to intervene and have a little fun of my own."

"You want to reclaim it?" The mere thought of losing it made the sorcerer clutch his precious pendant to his chest.

"Perhaps," Loki said with a thoughtful look. "I have not yet decided."

"Let me keep it awhile longer," the sorcerer said, as if his very life depended on the trinket. The sad truth was, by now it probably did. "Let me claim the wizard's power, and then you can have it."

The crumpled shield went flying off the wall at the sorcerer. With a loud gasp, the sorcerer threw up a barrier to deflect the warped metal and send it slashing into the opposite wall. It became buried there. "It is not your place to barter!"

The sorcerer cowered. What Loki wouldn't give for someone with a solid backbone. "Forgive me, I meant no disrespect." He pushed up to kneel on the bed. "I meant only to suggest an alternative. If you would but consider, it might prove engaging."

An attempt at the royal wizard's powers? Intriguing.

But pointless.

"Forget the wizard," Loki said. "She will never yield her power and far too many forces stand guard over her." Something he disliked greatly was being told he could not play with a shiny new toy.

"I can do it," the sorcerer insisted. He was far too weak to make it to his feet to stand, though he did try. And fail. "I can get her power and take it from the stone for myself."

Loki laughed, an ugly sound that resonated in the bright, bright room, and the remaining shields crumpled where they hung. The black crystal sparked with a sinister light in answer, sensing its creator, calling out to him like a long lost favored pet wanting to return.

The sorcerer's ire rose and his face gained some color, though it failed to fully express his feelings. "I can use it to restore myself and live forever."

And again, he spoke out of place! Loki was losing his patience with this puny man. This time, when he made the mattress fly, he dumped the sorcerer off it. When he would have moved, the furs came to life, curling limbs and claws around him to hold him down. Loki took his time crossing the chamber, giving the sorcerer an opportunity to remember his place. He put one foot on the man's chest, lightly, just enough to make it near impossible for him to draw a breath. From the night stand he summoned a trio of sharp, gleaming daggers. He leveled one at the sorcerer's eye, one at his throat, and one at his hand, still clutching the pendant.

"If I gave you a choice," he said thoughtfully, "which would you want part with, your sight, your voice, or your hand with the toy in it?"

The sorcerer was turning blue.

"Indulge me, if you will. I am curious about how that mind of yours works. If I take away your sight, you will have an excuse for your insolence. How are you to know whom you are speaking to when you cannot see them? If I take your tongue, you will no longer say anything insolent. You will not say anything at all. But if I take your toy,"—he drew the blade over the inside of the sorcerer's wrist—"you will no longer have reason to believe you can be insolent."

The sorcerer freed one hand and grasped onto Loki's ankle, pulling with all the might he possessed to save himself. Even with the pendant aiding him, he could not budge Loki an inch.

The Trickster leaned a little more weight on that foot, feeling the boundary past which bones would break. He skirted it closely, but did not cross. Instead, he leaned down to meet the mortal's gaze, letting him see the vast, swirling darkness in his eyes. "Speak to me once more in that tone of voice, and I will give you the immortality you crave. I will give you forever to regret your words."

By the time he removed himself again to the other side of the room, the sorcerer was in his bed, on a righted mattress, coughing wretchedly. "I can do it," he said between ragged breaths.

Of course, there was no possibility of that. The other gods would never allow it. Not that it would ever get so far. Daughter of a demi-god and a water sprite, Lady Nialei of the Streams would never yield without a fight. And now, with the dragon's blood, she might even be powerful enough to not only stop the sorcerer, but destroy him as well.

The sorcerer would burn like tinder in the face of her terrible wrath, never knowing how he had failed, still trying to capture that fire inside the stone—in himself, the fool.

But watching him try and fail might prove entertaining. And if the fight came to sway overwhelmingly in the wizard's favor, he could always step in and make it a little more equal. No one had ever said he could not meddle in a mortal's affairs. That it would affect the Lady was simply a tragic coincidence.

It was bad politics to anger everyone around him. Like them or not, he still had to live with all those other gods. If he defied them, they'd become insufferable, and there weren't enough hiding places in all the dimensions to avoid them for long enough. Better to keep them content. For the moment.

This little rebellion would undoubtedly feel quite satisfying once it was under way. And he was certain that as soon as he left the sorcerer, his destiny would once more turn dark. How could it not?

The sorcerer watched him, scarce breathing. He was still, save for the shaking of his hands and lips. It seemed the older humans got, the more difficult it was for them to not move.

Loki held out his hand. The stone tore out of the sorcerer's grasp, and he cried out in helpless anger. It came to the Trickster, rubbing over his palm as if to appease him. He had but to think about wishing it and it opened to him, displaying all the pretty shinies it held within.

Powers and magics no single being should ever possess. Nearly all of what humanity had to offer bottled in a small black crystal, neutral as long as its wearer remained so. They never did. From their influence, the magics were turning dark and evil.

Though Loki was ever one to cause mischief, this darkness in the power made him uneasy. It warped his creation, changing the design and slowly forming a hole. It was not yet finished, he could see. It only waited for that one last bolt to crash through the warp and leave the crystal open wide.

So this was how the sorcerer hoped to become immortal. Once again, the fool didn't realize what he dealt with. Black ice could hold not only magics, but traits as well. Thoughts and feelings, hopes and dreams. Perfect imitations of the wielders' true souls. So many lay within that they would overwhelm the sorcerer, make him crazed. The shock would strip him of his control and the powers would destroy him.

Win or lose, the sorcerer was already dead.

But if the powers held within the stone drained into him instead, his body would not be a strong enough prison for them. They would burst out of him and, dark as they were, wreak havoc on the human world. *Woden would not like that,* Loki thought with a dejected sigh. The god king would know the stone's origins and hold Loki responsible, even though he'd not interfered a single time since the pendant had come to life for the old woman.

And that meant that his choices had just been whittled away to only one. He closed his fist around the pendant, searing it shut for the moment. It would not hold for very long, the warp in the structure was weakening it already. When he tossed it back to the sorcerer, happy tears sprang up in the old man's eyes.

"I knew it," he said.

"Knew what?" Not that he cared.

"I knew I was right," the sorcerer cried. "You'd not have returned the stone to me if I was to fail. There is too much at risk." He cackled madly, crawling on hands and knees back to the center of the bed to curl into a ball with the pendant clutched to his chest again.

Loki watched him rejoice for a while, allowed him to gain more and more confidence in himself, and begin celebrating the grand victory he imagined in his future. He built the sorcerer's hope into a firm belief. Before he shattered it. "You forget who it is you are speaking to."

Silence descended upon the garishly appointed chamber as the sorcerer realized his fate was no more certain than the outcome of a coin toss. His face turned gray, his eyes opened wider, and a small wailing sound escaped him. Doubt. Fear. He would carry them next to his ailing heart for a day or two, as he carried the crystal, but soon both would fade, conquered by his greed.

Satisfied for the moment, the Trickster melted back into shadow, back through the portal to await the grand battle.

31

Nia dreamed of walking through a beautiful forest. The sky was bright blue above her, the grass soft and warm beneath her bare feet. Woodland creatures watched her from all around, their large, curious eyes unblinking. Nia smiled at them, sent them her greetings, but they didn't respond. Thinking nothing of it, she continued on her path and came to a footbridge across a forest stream.

There, her step slowed. It was a plain enough bridge, three flat, even planks laid side by side across the stream. Nothing to cause alarm. Yet she felt the tension in the earth as it waited. The stream glistened like magic, singing songs she could almost understand. It called to her, beckoned her closer. But the sight of the bridge held her back.

It didn't belong. Whatever it was, it ought not be here.

But, though she knew this, Nia couldn't stop herself from stepping closer. The grass hugged her feet, the blades sliced skin, but the sting was soothed by morning dew. Another step closer. Close enough to see the grooves in the wood.

Close enough to see the planks had rooted themselves into the bank as though still alive. As she studied it, puzzled by this unnatural magic, the roots groaned and strained. The ground bulged and then broke apart as a long, thick root tore out with enough force to snap like a whip.

It lashed back again and Nia jumped aside, but she wasn't quick enough and the tip cut her skirt open across one thigh. Blood marred her white skin and the roots groaned again, laughing.

One after the next, the bridge planks tore out of their moorings across the stream and stood on end before her. They melted together into a solid pillar, and then what used to be the center plank collapsed in on itself, pulling the others around it to form a frame. The center plank twisted tighter, became darker. So dark it was like black glass, reflecting the world back to Nia, but she couldn't see herself in its surface.

The stream sang louder, a warning this time. It went unheeded. Her gaze on the crystal in front of her, Nia came closer. The forest hissed, creatures crying out; she heard them fighting to come to her. She thought about releasing them, but the idea was as fleeting as a rare southern breeze.

Another step. Reaching out to touch the beautiful, dark thing, wondering at its secrets.

The root whip snapped again, lashing at her wrist and around it, squeezing like a sharp vise. It snatched Nia forward off her feet and into the air. She cried out at the searing pain, tears stinging her eyes. Yet she was still unable to look away from the crystal, searching for her reflection, desperate to see it and…there! An image began to form.

The stream roared; she heard its fury uncoil from deep underground and the crystal's pull intensified. She could almost make out her face.

The stream exploded into the air and broke the root binding her in half.

It jarred her out of the enchantment and Nia fell to the ground, scrambling away. The forest creatures swarmed her, big and small, hackles up and teeth barred at the black glass and the bridge. The stream battered the crystal without mercy. It fought back, growing in size, but the bigger it became, the harder the water beat at it until it began to break apart under the onslaught. It screamed like a wild thing, and the animals gathered closer around Nia, pushing her away from it.

Nia shuddered. It sounded human. Human, and filled with dark rage. This was no ordinary dream.

The stream didn't let up until the crystal reverted back to wood and broke apart into small pieces to be washed away. As it did, the root still twined around her wrist withered and fell away, turning to dust.

Nia opened her eyes and gasped for breath. She was in her own bed, the stillness of earth telling her the world had not yet awakened to morning. Hands shaking, she brushed her hair away from her face and felt wetness smear across her cheek. She frowned and summoned light.

The skin of her wrist was chafed bloody.

~

The sorcerer screamed his rage at the crystal and hurled it across the chamber. It struck the earthen pitcher and shattered it to dust. He tore the warped silver disc off the wall, slammed it on the floor and then stomped on it again and again until his foot slipped and he fell.

The furs weren't thick enough to temper his fall, and a bone in his leg snapped like a twig. In his fury, it mended in an instant, but the pain remained and enraged him further. He struggled to his feet, gasping, and hobbled back to the bed. By the time he sat, the crystal was slithering like a snake back into his hand.

He stared at it while he caught his breath. It was a thing. It didn't think or feel. But staring into its depths, the sorcerer admired its imitation of regret.

And then it sang.

In the first few months after he acquired it, that song used to terrify him. Haunting, sinister strains, like those of a reed whistle, would fill the night, bringing him nightmares of demons wearing human skin. They tore into each other, fed on their own innards and drank their own blood. He would wake up in a sweat, screaming and weeping like a child afraid of the dark. But no matter how many times he took it into his head to get rid of the crystal, he could never make his fingers uncurl from around its chain.

It owned him, not the other way around.

But in return for his service, it gave him the world. It showed him the mysteries of the south, the beauties of the west, the treasures of the east and the magics of the north.

Then why, with all its power and cunning, could it not bring him the gods damned wizard?

Thrice now it had failed, and the sorcerer was beginning to think the Trickster had spoken true. Each time he set a trap for her, something snatched her right out of his grasp.

"Why?" he asked the crystal. "Why can't you bring her to me? You want her as much as I do, I can feel it." The stone was ever ravenous for power, and the wizard had so much she all but shone with it. Never had he encountered one so strong.

He wanted her. Oh, yes, he wanted her very much. If he possessed such power he would no longer have need of this pathetic human shell. He could create a new one, in any form he fancied. He could change faces as he did clothes. He could be truly immortal; walk among the Others who hid from his sight.

The wizard is no fool, the stone whispered, not in words but thoughts and ideas the sorcerer understood. *She will not yield easily.*

"Then help me!" he screamed at it. "Tell me what to do!"

She will not surrender her mind. You must draw her out where she is most vulnerable.

"Yes," he said, thinking fast. "I understand. I do." The wizard was human and as any other human, her biggest weakness was her fragile body. If he wanted to bring her to her knees, he'd have to do it himself. "You always lead me true," he crooned, cuddling the stone to his chest as he laid down to sleep. He would have his wizard.

And as a treat, he would have the privilege of feeling the life drain out of her body.

32

It was the first time in four months that Nia made it up the stairs from Nico's study on her own. Bright sunlight blinded her in the courtyard, the autumn sky clear blue and the air crisp. She turned her face up to the sun's warmth, listening to the earth and the trees begin preparing for their winter sleep. Summers were short this far north. Already the leaves were turning brilliant shades of red and yellow.

The harvest was being gathered; the people sang as they worked. The earth had given them enough to fill their stores; there would be no empty stomachs this winter.

Nia thanked the earth and sent a little wave of power into the ground to replenish the fields. It was a simple spell, one she'd done many times before. The power would lay sleeping with the earth, grow on its own until spring and then awaken to nourish everything in the kingdom.

She wished she could ride out across the fields to see for herself how everything was faring.

Alas, as the royal wizard, her first duty was to the king. The only reason she'd even made her way above ground was because Saeran was meeting with his advisors yet again and required her presence. Though she had her suspicions that he'd only asked her to attend to make sure she would breathe fresh air again.

Sometimes she wondered who was looking after whom.

Nia smiled at the stable hand who'd called a greeting to her. Time to see to her duties. She inhaled deeply one more time and then turned toward the king's council room. The way wasn't long, but it was arduous. The halls were filled with people, servants and guests, all preparing for Samhain. Nia would have to lead a procession to the altar again to thank the gods for a bountiful harvest. The celebration afterward would be no smaller than Beltaine night.

There was a faire in the village, with merchants from all over the kingdom and farther come to display their wares. Though the queen's passing had saddened many, she had only been among them for a very short time. What the people mourned more was their king's loss. The news of Saeran's illness and recovery was slowly spreading throughout the kingdom, though no one but those closest to him would ever know the full truth it.

Nia doubted anyone else would believe it if they knew.

She nodded to the guards at the top of the stairway. There were more of them throughout the castle, keeping an eye on the king. They had strict orders to come for her if they saw or heard anything suspicious. She knew Saeran chafed to be so closely watched, but until she could be sure the threat to him has passed, he would have to endure it.

Once she mounted the stairs, there were no more crowds. The doors were all closed, all but the one to the council room, where she could hear men speaking.

Nia frowned and slowed her step.

"There will not be another queen," Saeran was saying, his voice strained, as if he'd said it several times already.

"But Sire," one of the advisors argued, "the realm will need an heir. It will tear itself apart if you should die without one!"

Saeran hadn't told them the reason for his decision. Who would believe him? Even with a powerful wizard at his side, performing magic in plain sight, no one would take talk of dragons seriously. Until she'd met one herself, Nia had thought them to be no more than legend, and she had Others shadowing her step almost every day.

"Was it the fever?" a timid voice asked. "We thought, all of us, that the wizard healed his Majesty."

"She did," Saeran said tightly. "That is not the reason."

"Then what is?" the first advisor demanded.

Nia pulled her shoulders back and entered the study. "Mind your tone, advisor Allon," she told the old man swathed in purple robes.

Allon was one of two advisors Nia had asked Saeran not to replace. He was old and pampered and often forgot his place, but he remembered a time most of them had forgotten, if they'd lived through it at all. His wisdom on the council was worth these brief spurts of insubordination.

At least that was what she told herself.

"You have heard of this, I assume," he said, his face turning ruddy. "His Majesty has decided not to take another wife. What do you make of it?"

Nia met Saeran's gaze. "It is not my place to question a royal decree," she told Allon without looking at him. "Nor is it yours."

"That is precisely your place! You are the only one he will listen to." His words fell silent at the sharp warning look she cast him. He blushed deeper and straightened in his seat, adopting a more measured tone when he spoke again. "What I mean is King Saeran has no siblings to provide a line of succession. If he dies heirless, the royal line will die with him. There are several noble houses eager enough to see one of theirs sit the throne that would go to war. If there is no one to take his Majesty's place, the kingdom will be torn apart. You know this is so."

"There is also the matter of the Aegirans to consider," Kvaran added.

Saeran drew himself up. "What do you mean?"

"The marriage was a bond of peace between Wilderheim and Aegiros. That bond is now broken. Queen Mari, may she be at peace, died in the land of the people who nearly destroyed an entire tribe."

"And what would you have had us do? Bow down to the Aegirans?"

Kvaran steepled his fingers. "I am simply trying to point out that the circumstances of her death are not clear, and the wizard's involvement might sow seeds of suspicion. Should they decide that Queen Mari's death was deliberate, the tribe will retaliate."

There was silence after he finished speaking. It was a possibility Nia hadn't considered.

Only the midwife who'd held Mari's hand as she died knew what Nia had done. She was the only one who could tell Mari's family the truth of her death; that they'd done all they could to save her. But would they hear her? And if they did, would they believe her?

A woman in Aegiros was expected to hold her tongue and defer to the men of her tribe: warriors, men whose only purpose in life was to fight for their *shansher* and conquer in his name.

As a people who revered bloodlines as much as the royals of the north, the Aegirans might forgive Saeran for taking another wife directly after Mari's death, but they would never forgive the murder of one of their own, one entrusted to Saeran as a symbol of peace.

Braith, the young girl with wild red hair, cleared her throat. "Perhaps Lady Nia could look into the future?" she suggested.

"No," Saeran said at once. "Whatever she sees there will not affect my decision. If an heir is all you concern yourselves with, I will be sure to appoint a successor before breath has left my body. I may not have siblings, but there are cousins aplenty, King Halden's children, any of whom would do right by Wilderheim, should it come to that."

The advisors spoke up, one and all, except for Braith.

"That is final," Saeran said, silencing them.

Everyone looked to Nia. They expected words of wisdom when she had none to give. She and Saeran alone understood why this had to be so, and Saeran didn't want them to know; therefore, Nia couldn't tell them. Instead, she made her way to his side, taking her place as his right hand without a word. None were needed.

The advisors didn't take it well, but they held their peace. "Be at ease," she told them. "Should the unlikely happen and leave the kingdom without a ruler, it will pass to King Halden's heirs. His Majesty has learned much from his uncle, as I am sure, have his cousins, all of them honorable men and women who owe Wilderheim their lives. That debt alone will compel them to do right by us."

You complicate things far too much, the dragon said, amusement and exasperation lacing his words.

"Let us move on," Saeran said. "What of the Samhain preparations?"

Braith was the one to answer, and Nia smiled to herself. It was about time there were more women telling the king what to do. She sent the thought to Saeran, and he shifted in his seat, subtly elbowing her in retaliation. She hid her grin behind a delicate cough as Braith spoke.

By the time the advisors left, the plans for Samhain were set, the harvest cataloged, news relayed and official correspondences dictated. Saeran leaned back in his seat and rubbed his face. He looked tired, understandably so. "They will not let up on this," she warned him.

Saeran chuckled without humor. "They are more concerned about royal lines than I am."

"Perhaps one of them ought to be king. Or queen." She took a seat, still weak, though gaining strength every day.

Saeran's eyes twinkled. "Perhaps I should name Braith as my successor."

Nia grinned. "I have always said every kingdom needed a woman's touch."

He made a rough noise. "That is the last thing a kingdom needs." Nia laughed.

Saeran smiled. "And how do you fare, my lady?"

"Well enough, my lord."

So many words remained unspoken between them, words that couldn't be voiced. Not now; perhaps not ever. They lay heavy on Nia's heart, making her feel ancient with sorrow.

What pained her more, Saeran seemed to see it, and his own smile dimmed in response.

"Come," he said, rising. "We will take a walk."

She took his offered hand and let him lead her down to the gardens. After being in the warm study for so long, the cold air chilled her, but she breathed in and accepted it. It was merely another part of life. Sometimes people had to get cold to appreciate the warmth of a hearth fire.

She walked beside her king in silence, enjoying every breeze. All around them life was thriving. Animals scrambled about, making stores for the winter, preparing their nests and burrows. Soon snow would cover everything, erasing memories of a year gone by. The land would start anew, without the burdens humans carried with them.

Sometimes she envied that.

Close to the edge of the forest, the gardens were empty. No one ventured here since the flowers have begun to wilt. The path led past a tall hedge, sculpted into a wall onto an open field. In the summer it was covered in wild flowers and herbs that midwives used to brew their teas and remedies. There was a stream running through the meadow. Its waters were clear enough to drink, and the stones lining its bed were polished by sand and time.

By the banks lay logs to serve as seats. They were nigh invisible in the tall grass, but those who knew where to look would always find them.

Many a noble had sat here with their beloved and spoke vows of everlasting love. They did so hoping there was magic in this place to grant them a long and happy life together.

Rarely did such vows hold true.

Saeran led them to one of the logs and pulled Nia onto his lap when he took his seat. He embraced her tightly. "I miss you," he said, breathing a sigh into her shoulder.

"I'm right here." They shouldn't be like this, but Nia didn't move away. Instead of leaving his embrace she weaved an illusion around them. In case someone happened by, they'd see the king perching on the log and Nia sitting by the creek, playing with the waves.

"Not always."

"No one can spend every moment of every day with another person," she told him, half smiling at this strange conversation.

"You could. But you won't." He caught her hand in his, tracing her palm, and then twining his fingers between hers. "I offered you the crown once and you refused. Would I risk the same disaster to offer it again?"

"I can't, Saeran." Though all she wanted to do was stay with him this way forever, she couldn't ignore the feeling of disaster looming ahead.

"Why?" he asked roughly, and this time the dragon echoed him, puzzled.

33

Do not tell me you still harbor a mortal's fears, Lady Nia.

Nia left Saeran's lap and took her illusion's place at the creek, blending into it until they matched. The illusion turned into mist and blew away on a breeze. *Will you be spying on me for the rest of my days now, Dragon? Simply because you can?*

You are my window to my grandson, he said. *It is my only amusement in this place. Though I cannot see why you frustrate the poor boy so.*

Saeran was silent, his features tense, waiting for her to speak. It was clear he'd like nothing better than to say more, but it was a moment's passion that would pass as soon as he remembered why he ought not wed again.

I cannot speak to him with you in my head! I do not need you to take his side in this.

But you do, the dragon replied. Then, after a pause, his tone changed. *Child, do you still not know who you are?*

Nia shut him out of her mind. "Someone's coming," she said softly, sending her words to Saeran alone.

Within moments the intruder came into view on the path from the castle. Saeran pushed to his feet and his jaw tensed when he saw the slight man with gleaming blond hair and an empty smile. His instant dislike was obvious and put Nia on guard. *Is something wrong?*

There is something about him, Saeran replied. *Something not right, but I cannot remember what.*

Jasper, the northerner from Aegiros who had accompanied Queen Mari here, had not departed with the others. Not even after the queen had met her end. This land might be his home, but the castle wasn't.

Nia came to stand by Saeran as Jasper approached.

He bowed deeply to them both, that same smile still plastered on his face. He spoke, but Nia didn't hear his words. She stared at his face, which seemed out of place to her. She looked at him again with a dragon's gaze and saw an illusion. It was powerful, carefully constructed, and very detailed, but an illusion nonetheless. What worried her was that she couldn't see through it to what lay beneath.

Nia blinked, trying to adjust her focus, and her gaze snared on something lying hidden in the man's pocket. Her senses returned to it each time she thought to look away. It was at once smooth and sticky, like a perfect little trap. Nia could feel the cold seeping out of it and shivered, but she couldn't look away. Behind her, the creek screamed. Beneath her, the earth shuddered. Her vision clouded over, and in the dark mist she remembered the nightmare from which she'd awakened bleeding, a scream caught in her throat.

The ground shuddered again, hard enough to throw them all off balance. Saeran caught Nia against him, breaking her concentration, and she shifted her sight back to normal so she could once again see Jasper's false face. Dark laughter, sharp as a blade, sliced through the autumn air.

"Nia?" Saeran's said, but she didn't answer him.

She searched with her senses for the threat she could feel saturating the air, careful to avoid the trap, but found no one; no one was around them, except for the man hiding in illusion. The dragon was restless, wherever he was, trying time and again to reach her, to speak to her, but she wouldn't let him.

"Are you well, my lady?" Jasper asked, his voice polite, but beneath it she could hear the edge of glee.

Nia found her feet again and faced him. "I do not know who you are, but I know what you are doing. You have outstayed your welcome.

Leave, or I will make you."

The king frowned. She could already feel questions burning inside him. He would ask them later, but for now he didn't say a word.

Jasper's eyes turned assessing. His smile returned, this time with a calculating edge to it, as he looked Nia over. "My apologies," he said, backing up a single step. "I had not realized my presence offended. If the lady wishes me out of her sight, I can oblige. But surely, your Majesty, banishment is too harsh an order in this case." There was a lilting note to the end of his statement, as if he was asking, not saying it outright, and Nia caught the faintest slither of compulsion. It infuriated her that he would dare. But before she could do anything about it, Saeran spoke.

"You waste your charms on us," Saeran said with difficulty, as if he had to fight to speak the words, but speak them he did. "I agree with the wizard in this. Your queen is gone, and you have no more reason to stay. You have until the day after Samhain to depart."

Nia winced. Samhain was in two day's time. A reasonable stretch, by anyone's standards, yet Nia couldn't shake the feeling that it was precisely what Jasper had wanted. Not to prevent himself being banished, only to postpone it a little while.

Jasper bowed. "As my liege commands." Before he left, he spoke his last. "I regret that I have caused you any kind of discomfort. Please, allow me to make amends. I am a fair hand with magic tricks. Perhaps I could provide entertainment for the Samhain feast." His gaze encompassed them both, and Nia felt another push of compulsion.

The wolf skin at her back moved, hackles rising until it made her own tickle. She suppressed an uncomfortable shudder. "No," she said at the same time as Saeran decreed, "I will permit it."

Jasper's glee followed him like invisible smoke back to the castle and out of sight.

Saeran rubbed his chest over the dragon pendant. "It's burning," he said. "I suppose that means I have made the wrong choice."

Nialei of the Streams.

Nia flinched at hearing the words whispered on the wind. She turned toward the source, back to the creek. *Niaaa…*

Drawn to the dancing waves that shimmered in the sunlight, Nia went back to the bank and knelt there, taking off her cloak. The wolf skin remained, refusing to be discarded like a garment. It hugged her shoulders instead.

"What is it?" Saeran asked, coming to kneel by her side.

On the other side of the stream, shapes shimmered into being. Glowing mist swirled around a gathering of Others of all shapes and sizes. Nia recognized the Sidhe and the dire wolves among them, but there were so many others, too. Creatures she'd never seen before, beautiful and terrifying, childlike and ancient, creatures of air, water and fire, earth and pure magic, all gathered there together, watching.

"Gods," Saeran breathed, "look at them all."

"You can see them?"

He nodded. "Why are they here?"

Have you learned? the female dire wolf asked.

What will you do? the Sidhe inquired.

"I think they are here for me."

"What? Why?"

Nia closed her eyes and felt the dragon nudge her mind. "I think it is time to find out who I am," she said, opening her mind again to the dragon. She let him in, but didn't let him speak. The creek looked fuller, eager somehow. Nia placed her hands flat over the stream, just close enough to feel its cold, but out of reach of the water itself. Closing her eyes, she concentrated for a moment and then cupped her hands. They cut into the stream without touching it, and a perfect ball of water separated from the rest, hovering a hair's breadth above her skin, nestled in her hands.

It was still moving, swirling 'round and 'round, still a creek, even caught in her hands. Nia had read about water creatures. They didn't understand words, didn't use them. They communicated with their minds and bodies. These creatures had powerful voices and didn't use them unless there was no other way. Their songs could kill as easily as bring a thing back to life.

Nia searched her memories as far back as she could go, looking for a spell. There had to be one and it had to have been there since she'd been a child. What she found was a dream, and in it a melody.

Nia hummed to the ball of water in her hands. The song echoed, a double voice so strange it couldn't be human, yet it was hers. How could it not be?

Do not tell me you still harbor a human's fears, the dragon had said to her.

The ball of water quivered to be struck by her voice, but it was not a defensive movement. It was dancing to her tune, responding in motion when it could not in voice. It swirled faster and faster, until it resembled a ball of yarn. A single ribbon detached and stretched up from the ball, creating a small vortex.

It grew and splashed outward, straining against her hold. Nia released it to float just above the surface of the stream and sat back to watch it, still singing, letting her instincts guide her when the memory faded away.

At last, Nia ran out of notes to voice and the vortex as big as her now collapsed, leaving in its place a creature so strange, and so beautiful, that Nia could only stare.

The female was shaped almost like a human, but her fingers were webbed and her ears were tiny. She had gills on the sides of her neck and brilliant scales scattered down from her neck all over her body. Her hair was not hair at all, but some sort of water plants. Her eyes were enormous in her face, the color of stars and emeralds, and her eyelids closed sideways, not up and down. She had only two small slits where a nose ought to be, and her lips were full and feminine. When she opened her mouth to draw breath, Nia could see a row of tiny, sharp teeth.

Nia pushed to her feet and bowed to the creature, recognizing royalty when she saw it. She nudged Saeran to do the same.

The female blinked a couple of times, and then Nia's mind filled with images, sent to her on a sigh. She saw a beautiful castle made of shells and pearls, crystals and flowers, deep beneath the water. Creatures like this one swam all around, playing and laughing, singing together to help fish and plants grow. They were the guardians of the world's waters. She was showing Nia where she'd come from, a way of introduction.

When Nia acknowledged this, the images changed to show another female, this one with eyes more white than green. She was floating serene by the edge of a lake but a dark cloud of blood was spreading around her body. She was dying. With her last breath, she sent a shrill call into the air, a summons.

An impossibly tall man came running out of the forest. He had antlers growing from his head, and hair like spun gold. He wore only a pair of tattered pants and his skin was darkened from the sun. Drawings and symbols covered his chest and arms, patterns that changed as he approached the female in the water.

His sapphire eyes were filled with pain at the sight of her. He dropped to his knees at the edge of the lake and caught the water sprite's face in his hands, searching her eyes.

The female brought forth a bundle of water plants and handed it to him with shaking hands. He nodded to her silent pleas, tears of blood running down his beautiful face as the sprite closed her eyes, sinking beneath the surface of the lake where she dissolved into the element which had birthed her.

The male unwrapped the bundle to expose a naked babe, a little girl with eyes almost as bright as his own.

His daughter.

Nia.

But she was too small, too fragile to stay with him. His people were a powerful lot who reveled in contest and battle. Though it broke his heart, he took the child to an old woman who lived at the edge of his forest. Nia's eyes welled with tears as Eirwen took the child into her care, but she made her father swear on the love he held for his water sprite that he would never approach the girl.

Understanding passed between them. Halflings were extremely un-stable. Born with human bodies, for that was a shape easily adoptable by all Others, they could change as they grew to favor either of their parents, or both. It all depended on who raised them.

Had Nia stayed with the water sprites, she might well have become one herself. But more likely, she would have drowned in their world before developing the ability to breathe under water.

She could not have survived with her father, either. In his demesne she would have been less than half the size of other children, weak and disadvantaged, easy fodder for everyone to prove their dominance by fighting her into submission.

No, her only hope for survival was to stay human, but she could only do that if she never knew Others existed.

The male gave his word and swore to look after her from a distance to keep her safe.

The old woman nodded, and by the time she raised her gaze again, he was gone.

Nia was shaking by the time her vision cleared, and she could see the water sprite again. The female's eyes were sad. She'd waited a long time to be summoned to show Nia these things. A long time to carry so many memories not her own. She reached out a webbed hand, caressing Nia's hair without touching it.

Water creatures and land creatures rarely mated. Nia's mother had died giving birth to her because she'd been forced to do it near the surface to make sure Nia survived. And to keep her away from her father's people, Eirwen had taken Nia far away, to a no man's land between Wilderheim and its western neighbor Ravetia, where she would never hear anyone speak of magic or Otherlands.

Nia remembered little of her time there. Only that they'd traveled from village to village for years until Eirwen had been too old to go any farther. By the time Nia's magic flared in her sleep and took Eirwen's life, Nia had been on the border of King Manfred's realm, and she'd made it all the way to Frastmir on her own, only to be found by Nico.

Saeran caught her hand in his and held on, his presence warming her cold insides.

You were brought here for a reason, the dragon said. *Do not fear it, there is no need.*

The water sprite tilted her head to hear another's voice. She blinked and sent her greetings through Nia.

The dragon responded with assurances that she was relieved of her burden. He would look after the pair from now on.

The sprite nodded and looked at Nia again. What might have been a smile transformed her face for a moment, before she twirled around and changed into water, splashing back into the creek.

Had it not been for Saeran's arms coming around her, Nia would have fallen to the ground.

# 34

Nia spent the next day in her chambers. Not of her own will. She had yet to sleep a wizard's sleep since the healing she'd channeled for Saeran and Mari, and the summons of the water sprite had undone what progress she'd made.

She thought about her father. If he'd ever been around, even at a distance, would she have sensed him? Nia couldn't remember if she ever had. She couldn't even be sure of what he was. He could be a wood sprite, an animal spirit, or anything in between or beyond. Far too many creatures dwelled in this world to know them all, especially when most never revealed themselves to humans.

The only thing she was now certain of was that she was not human. That was what Nico had seen in her the day he'd caught her stealing from the castle kitchens. That was why the Others let her see them—she was one of them. An Other at the right hand of a human king. Or as human as a dragon's descendant could be. Nia chuckled. What a pair they made, Halflings governing a human realm, and no one the wiser. But Wilderheim had always been a kingdom of Others as much as humans, and if Nico could have done it, she could do no less than prove worthy of his faith in her ability to do the same.

Nico. She sighed. Another mystery. Her mentor had served three generations of kings, prolonging his life as much as his human body would allow. Toward the end, Nia had felt the toll it had taken on him. Through practice and sheer force of will, Nico's essence had grown to make up for his withering body. For her sake he'd waited longer than was wise, but now, at least, Nia knew what had happened to him.

For all his power, Nico had been human. With age and wisdom, his soul had begun to outgrow its vessel, dissolving it completely as soon as Nia had taken his place. No one had seen her mentor since then because his bodily form no longer existed but, as with the pockets of magic he'd left behind in his study, his soul was still whole.

By her estimates, Nico had been nearly a hundred years old when he'd disappeared. What did that mean for Nia? How long would she walk this world? The thought of centuries passing her by, everyone she knew growing old and dying while she endured unchanging filled her with sadness.

The ancient ones grow weary of life after a while, the dragon told her. *Some have been known to go mad without an anchor to the world.*

An anchor like a loved one, Nia guessed.

The dragon didn't answer. He didn't have to; he'd given her his memories.

A sudden shiver ran down her spine. There were shadows in her chamber that ought not be there. Her senses sharpened, her Sight shifted, and she could see that the darkness had mass. "Show yourself," she said, feeding what little magic she had into the command.

The sharp laughter she'd heard in the gardens the day before cut through the air again, severing the spell mid-stream as if it were a piece of string. "You dare command a god, Halfling?" said a voice from the darkness. It was like nothing she'd ever heard before. "The audacity of it is…intriguing."

"Who are you?"

"Cannot say," he said easily. "I can be many things or nothing at all." His tone turned conspiratorial as the dark shadow floated closer to her. "I choose to be nothing, you see, because nothing is allowed to interfere."

Nia smiled a quick, sharp smirk. "I know you."

"I expected nothing less."

"Why are you here?"

"To spy."

"And what have you discovered?"

He chuckled, the shadow quivering to mirror the sound. The more she heard him, the less his voice bothered her. "What kind of spy would I be to divulge all my secrets?"

"But they are not your secrets. They are mine. Hence there is no harm in telling me." She enjoyed verbal sparring and sensed that he, too, was reluctant to abandon this little amusement. As the dragon had said, the ancient ones grew weary of life.

"A secret is only a secret so long as it remains hidden. A secret, once uncovered, is nothing more than gossip. Boring. I do not waste my time with such things."

"I thought gods had nothing but time."

"Yet we still know how to make better use of it than you who have so little. Humans." There was a sound, like a hiss, and then he breathed, "Ah, but you are not so insignificant as that, are you, Halfling?"

Nia adopted as innocent an expression as she could, struggling not to laugh. "I am no more significant than a shadow in a dark chamber."

"And we both know what monsters those shadows hide."

"A monster is only a monster so long as it is fearsome. A monster, once accepted, is nothing more than an oddity. Do you think me odd?"

Another chuckle, and with it, the shadow drew back until she almost thought it would reveal its owner. "Most definitely odd. In the way a flame is, enclosed in a watery cocoon. Oddly strange and unnatural. Especially when the flame can reach out and bite the unwary sorcerer."

"And what of the cool watery well within a fortress of fire?"

"Stranger still," he groused. "A strange world indeed it is we find ourselves in, where the well protects the fire and the fire nurtures the well. You weaken yourself needlessly with your sentimental spells. The balance keeps tipping, the clock is ticking, and the sorcerer is not tripping over his own feet the way you are. It spoils my fun."

"Sage advice," she said dryly.

The shadow rushed her, and a face emerged so close to her that all she could see was a pair of opaque black eyes in a grayish pale face, with coppery hair to frame them. "Have a care, Halfling. Your infinite protectors will not be around forever, and I can make your existence quite unpleasant if I choose to."

Nia nodded in wordless ascent, not trusting herself to speak. She kept respectfully docile, but would not drop her gaze from the Trickster's. He smiled at that, though the expression never reached his eyes. Empty eyes, he had. Empty and endless, dark and dangerous. "I have not met one such as you. Even the sorcerer quivers at the sight of me. Yet here you are, with little over a score of years to you, looking at me as nothing but another...oddity."

"Why are you here?" she asked again, softly.

The Trickster's thin mouth contorted. "The amulet is flawed beyond repair. It will not heed my call, and any magic used on it is sucked in to warp it further. The jest goes too far, and I cannot involve myself beyond this point. I risk much by simply being here, conversing with you, Halfling."

"Are you asking for my help?" Nia strove hard to conceal her surprise, but it showed regardless.

"Much as I loath to," the Trickster replied. "Rid this world of the thing, and in return I shall tell you where to find your sire."

Nia's breath left her. "Why should I trust you? I could be walking into a death trap."

"You will be," he said. "But if it will ease your weary mind, I vow on Woden's lifeblood that I will keep to our bargain. And if you do as I say, and precisely as I say, then all will end as it should."

"And how is it that all this should end?"

"With the amulet gone, its evil destroyed and me beyond suspicion."

How like a god to see only his own ends. "What will happen to this kingdom and its people?"

"They are not my concern, hence they will not be affected."

"And me?"

"You have little enough to lose, and even less to fear. Is your life so full that you fear leaving it behind?"

She swallowed. "Yes."

The Trickster studied her for a moment, and what he found seemed to unsettle him, but he regained his composure quickly. "Then you might yet survive the trials to come."

35

The music began well before sunset. Though she couldn't see it from Nico's study, Nia knew there were people on the castle green already singing and dancing to their hearts' delight. Nia didn't share in their revelry. Her mind was burdened with weighty thoughts, her soul weary of this weakness.

The Trickster's plan troubled her. She'd sensed no falsehood from him, but having never spoken to a god before, Nia couldn't be certain of anything. Whether he spoke the truth, or whether he chose to change his mind didn't matter. What he asked of her would endanger not only her life tonight but everyone else's as well.

For the third time since noon, Nia made a circle with her hand to trace one in light. Just as with her last two tries, the circle blazed white hot and then cleared in the center to show gray mist. The future remained hidden, veiled by some force or another, though she had an idea about whom to blame. It wouldn't amuse the great Trickster to have her know precisely how to play this grand game of his.

Frustrated, Nia swiped her hand to dissolve the circle and then brushed her hair back, clutching it in her fists until the tension snapped a few strands. *I may lose this game,* she thought, something akin to fear coiling in her belly, tying her into knots.

She pushed to her feet slowly and made certain everything was in order. The books and scrolls were all arranged on their shelves, no parchment out of place. The table was clean, a single candlestick gracing its center. The pitcher and chalices stood on a tray in the corner, covered by an old piece of cloth so as not to gather dust. She'd asked the servants to take the bed and all her personal belongings out and back to the chamber she ought to be sleeping in. Nothing more remained here except all the knowledge Nico had gathered over his very long life. And if she never returned, the one burning candle would stay lit to guard it all until someone worthy of it came to claim this place. Forever, if need be.

Nia ran her hand over the grooves of the table, tracing a pattern. She would miss this place. This library was her sanctuary and training ground. The stone was scarred in places, marked by spells gone awry, the domed ceiling black with ash and soot from countless days and nights spent down here by nothing but the light of a hundred candles.

Every chink and groove had a story to tell, and the pockets of magic Nico had left behind shone bright from within, without shining at all. They held his essence like a page in history, proof that he had walked these halls and left an impression on an entire kingdom. There would be more such pockets here, and everywhere in the castle within the hour—hers.

With a few whispered words, Nia sealed the library nook so no one but the king would know it was ever there. A small smile pulled on the corner of her mouth to remember the very first time she'd worked the spell. She'd sealed herself inside that small space with what should have been an illusion. Bitter sweet memories of the past. She had to remember them; remind herself she still had much to live for.

Her mask this eve was a simple one made of leather and dyed to resemble tree bark. It would cover her face so only her mouth and chin would show. She tied it in place and gathered all the charms she'd made the day before. One of them attached to the top of the mask, another hung on a chain at her breast. She put on bracelets wreathed with night blooming flowers and rings made of water reeds and magic. Two more stone charms would fit into small pockets in the seam of her cloak and there was a protection spell written on the sole of each of her shoes, as well as on her staff. It wouldn't be enough, but it was all she could have.

She couldn't make such protections for any of the people present tonight. If the sorcerer suspected anything, the entire game would shift and not in Nia's favor. All she could do was hope that he would be intent on her and no one else.

That was her hope and prayer.

Nia searched the shadows for movement. She hadn't seen any Others in a while. "If you are here, I ask that you grant me one wish. Keep those present from harm. You need not involve yourselves with the sorcerer, but all those people filling the castle tonight are innocent. They will be helpless against him. Please…" She sighed. It was no use to beg someone who wasn't there.

Her cloak and staff waited for her by the door. With one last look around, she clasped the cloak around her neck and lifted the hood to hide her hair. The wolf skin pulled tighter around her back and she grasped her staff. She would need it in a moment or two, just to climb the stairs.

Nia hesitated only a moment before she closed her eyes and envisioned the core of her magic. In her mind's eye, it was a glittering ball of bright light. Slowly, carefully, she melted that ball into the consistency of smoke and let it seep out of her body, shivering at the heat it created. For a moment, her mortal shell glowed like a star in the night as tendrils of brilliant magic curled up and around her, filling the air with sparks like fireflies.

She directed them with her mind to coat the walls of the study and seep into the stone. Once the chamber was saturated with as much as it could hold, Nia sent her power up through the castle, filling strategic places where it would shield the most people from any attack. The king's bedchambers, his study, the great hall, the kitchens and the stables soaked up her magic eagerly.

There wasn't much left by the time she was certain the castle would be safe. Whatever else she could spare without killing herself she gave to the earth to ensure bountiful harvests for years to come.

Drained, tired and weak, she whispered a prayer for luck and left the study, locking the door behind her. Going up the stairs took a while with her knees aching and protesting the strain, but she climbed on until at last she reached the castle green. After locking the second door as well, she made her way to the bonfire to begin the procession up to the gods' altar.

"What's the matter?" Saeran asked, grasping her elbow through her cloak as soon as he caught up with her. His dragon pendant would allow him to see past the illusions she'd woven the night before because it had been made by her and recognized her spells. To all others, Nia looked to be clad in a gown of brilliant green, with autumn leaves and wheat in her hair. She would wear a mask of bronze and bells and chimes would trail in her wake.

"All is in order, my liege," she said. She hadn't told him anything about the Trickster's visit, or his plans for this night. Until it was absolutely necessary, she saw no reason to worry the king. Should something happen to her, Nia had made sure he would be well protected within the walls of his castle. It would have to be enough.

"You do not lie well, wizard," he retorted, aware of the nobles following close behind. Though the music and drumming concealed their conversation, Nia was proud of her student for being careful with his words. "I sensed the magic you sent out. It was too much, especially now when you are so weak. What are you up to?"

"I fulfill my duty to you and your kingdom, Majesty."

"Not at the cost of your wellbeing!" he whispered furiously.

The emotion in his voice gave Nia pause, and she stopped in her tracks to look at him. His eyes were like blue flames, glowing in the night. If anyone saw, he would forever lose a vital advantage. For now, no one knew of his dragonblood, or his aptitude for magic. It was an essential piece of information to keep secret from his enemies, in case he ever had need of it in battle.

Saeran's chest rose and fell with harsh breaths, and his fists were clenched at his sides. This was not good. "Majesty," she said, trying to sound reasonable, "My life was forfeit to your rule the day I made my vow to you and you accepted my place at your side."

Saeran didn't look pleased to have this pointed out to him. He urged her on again. "Keep going before the others notice we have stopped."

"What is the matter with you?" she whispered to him. "Are you regretting your decision now?"

"Father was right," Saeran said, keeping his voice low. "I was not ready to see the wisdom in his doubt back then. Not until it was too late. Had I understood…I never would have allowed you to put yourself in danger to protect me. Not when it should be the king's duty to protect those who serve him; a man's duty to protect those he loves."

"Now you are being silly," Nia told him, but her voice was not as steady as she wanted it to be.

"I know you are up to something," he said, without looking at her. "I know it will be big and, knowing you, probably very dangerous. And I know I cannot stop you." It didn't seem to occur to him that he was walking by her side, when he ought to be following her. In this and all processions, the wizard became the embodiment of a god or goddess, and it was symbolic for everyone, even the king, to follow. Nia knew that a handful of nobles and a couple of advisors had already noticed, though they had said nothing yet.

They were almost at the altar. "You can trust that whatever I do will be for the good of the kingdom."

"That is precisely what I am afraid of."

If she hadn't been so worried herself, Nia would have smiled at that.

Saeran finally took his place behind her as they reached the altar. The procession cheered and the music rose louder. Nia was glad for it. She performed the ceremony, moving her mouth in the right places, though no sound left her lips. She silently thanked the gods for a good harvest, and prayed for protection from bad spirits bent on mischief this night. The revelers were mostly oblivious, caught up in their own celebrations, observing only the necessary prayers for the sake of ritual.

Nia was so drained she could no longer understand the earth, or the breeze. Both hummed and whispered to her, and she sensed their worry but couldn't answer to soothe them. The shadows moved with a mind of their own. There were beings all around them, lured closer out of their hiding places by the sound of celebration. Nia had no way of knowing if they were benevolent or not, and without the ability to see them, she could do nothing to warn the others.

She concluded the rituals with haste and began to lead everyone back to the safety of the castle. The bonfire was lit there tonight because Samhain revelry was always longer and wilder than any other. This way the castle guard could keep an eye on the people and make sure nothing from within or without harmed them.

Nia shed her illusion and joined the dance for a round or two, enough to show the people she was one of them but not more. She couldn't risk losing even more of her strength.

The Trickster had told her very little about what she needed to do. It was his way of making sure she was ready without giving her any kind of advantage. But not even a god could foresee everything. From what he had told her, Nia knew exactly what she would be fighting. She'd seen the pendant born of hate and greed, of a dark prayer on a darker night, to a god who cared little about the fate of mortals. She knew she couldn't use magic on it, because it would only make matters worse.

She couldn't risk having her magic turned against her and had never trained in physical combat. But there were ways to use magic without using it directly. Loki's stone could only absorb powers straight from the wizard directing them at it or through physical touch. Nia planned to do neither.

The king called to his people, catching Nia's eye. There was a warning in his gaze, and his posture was rigid, as it always got when he didn't want to show weakness or fear. He worried, and he should.

Nia came to his side, and the two of them led the nobles back to the great hall. It was ablaze with candlelight. Everything had a golden glow about it, even the lavish feast laid out on three long tables, one that ran alongside the dais and two others at each end to form a U. Many nobles were present for this occasion, some even from the neighboring kingdoms. Saeran wanted to make an impression, and Nia had to admit he had succeeded. The foreigners would think this kingdom strong and bountiful, wanting for nothing.

They would be right. Nia, and Nico before her, had made sure of that.

The guests exclaimed in delight and sighed in awe as the castle bards began a different kind of music. Everyone took their place at their seats and politely waited for the king to make a royal motion before they sat. Nia remained standing behind Saeran's right shoulder to keep everything in sight.

Saeran reached for his fork, hesitated, and then shook his head and rubbed his eyes as if they stung. "Your magic is everywhere," he said, "even in the tables. I will go blind before the night is through if you do not do something about it."

"What would you have me do?"

"Take it back. If it's back where it belongs, it will not make my eyes water where it doesn't."

"I cannot do that," she told him, her heart squeezing at his tactics. Saeran wasn't above dirty tricks when he wanted her to do something for her own good.

He shook his head and ate a little from his plate. A moment later, he stopped again, his fork clattering from his grip as turned to look at her, his face gone pale with horror. "You can't hear me anymore, can you? In your head. I just…gods, Nia, what have you done!" He grabbed her wrist and squeezed hard enough to make her bones scrape together.

"Your Majesty," Jasper's voice carried from the other side of the great hall. "My lords and ladies." He bowed to all sides, but that cold, empty smile never fell from his face. He was puffed up with self-importance, walking on his toes as he came forward, one hand over his heart, the other behind his back. When he was before the king, he bowed again in a mockery of respect and announced, "I have come as summoned to entertain the masses."

36

There were shadows, and within them the Trickster god paced, a caged beast impatient for the play to begin. The other gods had caught a whiff of his dealings with mortals, and they were searching the worlds for him. So long as he remained in Shadow, he was safe. But so long as he remained there, he could do nothing but stand by and watch. Any interference would draw the others' wrath down upon his head, and he wasn't keen on their punishment, especially when, for once, he didn't plan to cause any harm.

He looked at the palm of his hand again and scowled. The lines had changed, just as he'd predicted they would. Yet, thanks to Fate's sick sense of humor, they'd not changed the way he wanted them to. Curling his fingers into a tight fist, he struck out at the darkness around him. It reverberated like a great, soundless bell, making his bones shudder.

The Trickster was at the edge of his patience, a rare instance in time when he was not in control of whatever trick he'd played. He'd let the jest go on for too long. Loki's shoulders fell in what might have been a sigh. He hated admitting defeat.

A sharp pang of uncomfortable awareness made him tense, and his gaze turned to the great hall. It was filled with Others. Incensed, he rushed the barrier between darkness and light, snarling at the congregation. Did the wizard think to cheat him of his victory? Loki almost laughed. She should have known better than to expect the Others to involve themselves in human affairs.

Tilting his head, the Trickster watched them awhile, wondering at their intentions. Others always wanted to be entertained. But this felt excessive. It felt… What was the word? Deliberate. Yes, that was it. Deliberate. He could tell by their number, the way they moved—or rather not moved—that there was a reason for their presence.

They knew he was here. Perhaps not his true identity or his exact location, but they knew something was here which did not belong. Countless sets of eyes were trained on his Shadow, trying to guess at its secrets. He grinned savagely. They never would. Not even other gods could find him where he now was, a world of his own; a construct of the Trickster's imagination.

Eyes trained on the Others directly before him, Loki stepped away from the barrier. If they interfered with the game, he would wipe their clans from this land and every other.

A commotion broke his stare and brought his attention back to the matter at hand. The ambitious sorcerer was making his entrance. Lofty as ever. To look at him, one might think he was the king. Every gesture, every word from him was a jibe the monarch seated before the dais couldn't possibly misunderstand.

The Trickster's gaze turned to the king. Or perhaps he could, he amended. Perhaps he'd noted other things amiss, such as the bright glow of his beloved wizard's power everywhere, but within her. Perhaps he'd already discovered the state to which she'd brought herself, draining every last drop of her magic from her mortal shell. Perhaps, at this very moment, the king might possibly have other things to fret about than some stranger's manners.

Loki's curious gaze settled on the girl wizard. She leaned on her staff, drained magically and weak physically. There were those who likened magic to a warm cloak of comfort. The wizard had shed hers for the occasion. He wondered how she bore such separation. Did she feel lighter? Or perhaps heavier, weary, without the brace of her power.

The air shifted, though it should not have. Distracted away from his musings, the Trickster glanced over the great hall once more. The noble guests were stirring. They didn't need magic to know something was amiss when a peasant approached a royal gathering without being summoned outright. Some grumbled, some subtly shifted farther from the table, and to his surprise, the Others in attendance drew near, an Other to each noble like guards against bad spirits. Curious.

Loki had no need to look at the king and his wizard to know they were alert. Lady Nia would lean closer to her king's ear to whisper a few words. He would acknowledge with the slightest of nods, hiding his unease very well, circumstances being what they were. He would touch a hand to his chest, to the dragon pendant that lay beneath his shirt, and the muscles in his jaw would bulge and jump, the only outward sign he was displeased with his wizard. She wouldn't notice.

The sorcerer began performing his tricks. He spoke nonsense to ease the nobles' minds while his hands moved to hide the actions of his magic. The Trickster's mouth pulled into a sharp smile at this sight. How utterly frustrating it had to be for the little old young man to try time and again to send his magic out and have it return to him without sticking to anything. He couldn't See. The pendant had not absorbed the power of Sight, or Hearing, and he had not been born with them, so he couldn't See the great hall glowing with the wizard's magic. He couldn't Hear the ancient stone around him laughing at his efforts.

For the smallest instant, his smile skewed in anger, but he smoothed it out quickly. He met the king's gaze as he juggled an illusion of balls, his eyes sparking the same way the crystal at his chest tended to do. The Trickster straightened. The sorcerer was losing patience, and that was when he usually started to make mistakes.

He did not disappoint this time.

His power flowed from him again, sliding down his waist and legs to the floor, like slime with hundreds of hues. It slid and slithered in every direction toward the tables and the nobles sitting behind them.

The Others countered but their magics slid off the spreading mass. They looked at each other and tried again. And again. And once more before they realized it was of no use. Loki smiled. A god's creation, however warped, would ever carry its maker's mark, and there was no creature, human or Other who could counter a god's wish with anything but a god's power.

When they realized this, the Others changed tactics, laying hands, vines, paws or wings on their charges. It wouldn't shield the mortals from the sorcerer's spell, but it would keep them alive until he was finished. Several of the nobles shivered, but none of them moved. Soon the writhing mass of dark magic engulfed them and it was too late for them to try.

The sorcerer tossed the balls high into the air, making them explode in a shower of sparks. It was to disguise the cries of those around him as awe, while his power sealed them to their seats. They were now sufficiently under his spell and wouldn't cry out again unless he allowed it.

But he had been foolish. He'd left the king and his wizard free. Had he bothered to imprison them as well, he would have sensed the protection spells on their persons. The king didn't wear the dragon pendant for decoration, after all. Nor had the wizard stuffed charms and pendants into her clothing for nothing. Clever, clever little cat. She'd known, or gathered, that black ice couldn't draw magic from anything that did not live. She would have warned the king to refrain from casting spells, and she'd drained herself of her own magic to keep it from the sorcerer.

The entertainer let his arms drop to his sides as he sucked in a breath of premature victory. "Now, then," he said, his smile taking on a fragile, vicious edge. "The spectators are stuck to their seats in anticipation. They wait for the players to take their place." He held his hand out toward the king and his wizard. "Come, magicker, let us give them a performance they will not forget."

The foolish king pushed to his feet, sweeping the lady behind him with an arm outstretched. His guests didn't move to stand with him, as propriety dictated, and he finally looked at them. Could he see the Others filling his great hall?

Lady Nia grasped his arm to free herself, but he would not budge. "Stay behind me." He barked the words at her, though his gaze never left the guests. Loki shaped his will and consciousness to See everything through the king's eyes, with his mind.

The monarch was furious. He'd allowed himself to get distracted by the stranger's display, and hadn't noticed the subtle sheen of his power. Nia's magic had blinded him, bright as it was. Now he could see his nobles covered with a multicolored veil and he couldn't free them; Nia had warned him not to. Though she was often foolish with her own life, she had never been with his, and so he had no choice but to trust that she had good reason for keeping him back.

His free hand rubbed over his chest. The pendant burned him. In his mind, he could hear the great dragon shifting restlessly. Saeran could sense him, but he couldn't understand yet.

Nia tried to move past him once more, speaking, though he couldn't hear her through the thundering of his own heart. Loki pitied the king at this crossroad. His royal duty was a double-edged sword in its own right, but his love for the wizard added a third edge, the sharpest. For, as king, he had a need both to protect his people, and to survive to beget an heir. As a man, his being screamed at him to keep his mate safe. But against these forces, he was powerless.

The sorcerer laughed at the look on the king's face. "Still you protect her?"

Thoughts raced through the young king's mind, so many and so fast that Loki didn't bother trying to make sense of them. Memories he couldn't recall itched in his mind, but with each word the sorcerer spoke, the wall around them chipped and cracked a little more.

"You try to hide your love, and it only makes it so much more obvious. I never had to guess whom to use to force the wizard back from her quest."

At this, even the wizard tensed, ceasing her struggles to get free of the king. When his hand on her tightened, hers responded in kind, letting him know she was still there, perfectly safe. For the moment.

Yet, even without her magic, Loki could feel through the king how the air changed around them both. Drained or not, power was in Nia's very blood. She could no more get rid of it than she could live without her heartbeat. The king shivered, and within him the Trickster did as well. The air pulsed with her wrath, a whirlwind built around her and the king, snatching at his robes. With a slight nudge to his consciousness, Loki made Saeran turn to look over his shoulder.

The wizard was as he had never seen her before, and even the king had to suppress the slightest twinge of fear at the sight. Never before had Lady Nia lost her composure this way. Ever the calm lake in the storm, now she was the storm, her hair wild in the wind, her eyes shining like sapphire stars.

The sorcerer grinned, satisfied to have found a weakness. And now he would milk it for all it was worth, to his own peril.

The Trickster sighed, and left the turmoil of the king's mind to watch the battle with his own eyes.

"Nia," King Saeran said softly.

The wizard didn't look at him, but spoke with a voice not her own. "You may use illusions, but do not use them on him directly."

Without further question, the king nodded, and a moment later stepped out from an illusion of himself and took up a place in the shadows opposite Loki. He pulled out his pendant, rubbing the surface to draw strength from it as he worked his spells.

"I lose my patience, woman," the sorcerer said, beckoning. "Come and give me what I want. Or I may just decide to play by myself for a while." One of the noblewomen pushed back from the table, toppling her chair. Clumsy as a puppet on strings, she came around toward the sorcerer, her eyes wild, tears streaming down her face, and her determined Other guardian holding her hand. Her efforts to scream came to naught.

The king's illusion leaned back, as though to say something to the wizard and then sat down to watch.

The sorcerer smiled again. "Have you obtained permission to die?"

Lady Nia stepped through the table, as if it was no more than mist, the wolf skin at her back bristling. "Before this night is through," she said without emotion, "You will know suffering like no other."

The noble woman stopped in her approach, quivering with silent sobs.

Eyes blazing with madness, the sorcerer's smile finally died, his illusion wavering to reveal just a glimpse of what lay beneath. "You do not know the meaning of suffering," he snarled and the noblewoman fell to the floor in a faint.

In his Shadow, Loki's smile turned dark. "Let the games begin."

37

Nia felt power gathering within her, fueled by her emotions. She was livid, intent on the sorcerer's death as she'd never been on anything before. She couldn't keep the magic at bay, and at the moment she didn't want to. It gave her strength enough to advance on the sorcerer and make her stand.

Jasper's eyes shone black as the crystal he wore. He watched her approach, his anticipation rising in palpable waves, so focused on her that his glamour began to waver over him. He expected to make short work of her, and Nia would use it against him.

Words whispered over her, a warm breeze of magic settling around her like a cape—Saeran's magic. She'd told him to use illusions; it hadn't occurred to her that he would use them on her. The feeling was alien, though not unpleasant. What was he up to? For all that she could feel the spell, sense it taking shape, she couldn't see its result.

Can't think about it now. She curled her hands into fists at her sides, then opened them, sending the tables and those who sat around them sliding across the floor as far as the walls would allow. The tables turned on their sides, spilling food and creating a barrier for the nobles to hide behind, meager though it was against a magical assault. Nia would simply have to keep Jasper occupied fighting her.

Jasper grinned. "That's it," he taunted. "Bare those claws." Power as black as the night pooled in his hand. He grew it into a sloppy sphere and threw it at her with all his might. It shattered on an invisible shield an arm's length from her. Her charms were holding. "Ah," he breathed in understanding. "I am glad. I would have been disappointed if you had let me win so easily."

Another sphere formed, and he launched it, building another straight away. The volley of blows bombarded her shields, weakening them. There was only so much power an inanimate object could absorb. When it wore out, she'd be left defenseless.

Nia didn't give him the satisfaction of seeing any concern on her face. Instead, as the assault continued, she stooped down to run her hand over the smooth stone floor while Saeran's spell slid over her. So that's what it did. She looked up to see herself standing there, hands held out against Jasper's attack. The sorcerer wouldn't have seen her move at all.

Nia caressed the polished boulders, waking her own magic to life. There was plenty of it all around her, though Jasper didn't seem to realize it.

She hummed a soft tune and it filled the chamber, deafening her to everything else. The floor thrummed under her hand, eager to do her bidding. Turning her hand palm up, she made a scooping motion and a dozen boulders the size of a man's torso tore out of the floor to float at eye level all around the sorcerer.

He altered his assault. Each sphere he created split into two, then two again, flying in all directions. Three out of four shots scored their mark, but the stones were unaffected. As a warning, she launched two of them at him as she rose to her feet. The first turned him about with the force of impact. He avoided the other.

Nia stepped out of the illusion of herself, meeting Saeran's gaze long enough for him to nod in encouragement. The sorcerer wouldn't see her. Good. She had a score to settle with him.

Jasper recovered from the hit and gathered power into himself, more and more, until his mortal shell was bending double and his back began cracking under the pressure.

Oh, no. Nia ran forward, pulling more boulders from the floor and raining all of them down on Jasper at the same time with as much force as she could muster.

They never touched him. With a hoarse yell he released all that power at once, an explosion of darkness that shattered her shields and sent her skidding back. What was left of her boulders, dropped harmlessly to the floor.

He was breathing heavily when he faced her again, but though his face was beginning to crack and his eyes were flooded with black, he was still on the offensive.

Nia didn't understand the word he screamed at her, but she felt its vibrations and knew it was bad.

She dived to the floor, rolling away, and continued to roll as he struck the floor with enough force to dig through it like a plow. Saeran's illusion was gone. He could see her now and Nia struggled to keep a meager step ahead of his assault. Not fast enough like this. She took a chance when her hands met the floor, pushing with all her strength and not a small amount of magic to launch herself into the air.

She flew up almost to the ceiling, but Jasper's power followed and pierced the walls too close to Saeran. The attack stopped when he had to catch his breath, just long enough for her to fall back down. She landed on her hands and knees and immediately launched herself at Jasper. This might be the only chance she would get. She wasn't a trained fighter, but she was of a height with him and physically stronger.

But Jasper recovered faster than she could move. Before she could reach him, another shouted word caught her, sending her flying back against the dais steps. Her back carried the impact and her spine screamed in pain. Tears welled in her eyes as she fought to breathe again, but the effort it required was too great and the pain too much.

She couldn't move. Her back was broken, rendering her legs useless and her lungs nearly so. The sorcerer cackled, approaching her on shuffling feet, in no hurry now that his opponent was incapacitated. Nia reached for something to help her drag herself away but her hands slipped on rubble. She was stuck unless…no. She couldn't risk it.

Her body tilted forward as Jasper's magic caught hold of her, slowly pulling her toward him. The agony of it was unbearable. Nia screamed, the sound cut short as her voice broke on a sob. A female Sidhe appeared at her side, her eyes glowing and enchanting. *There is no other way.*

Nia's head swam. She blinked and the Sidhe was gone. But behind Jasper, the male dire wolf paced back and forth, head canted low, watching her and snarling. *Get up,* he growled. *Get up, or they all die with you.* She looked around the great hall; saw the nobles cowering behind the overturned tables, behind a row of Others who were keeping the destroyed floor from buckling beneath them all. They'd heard her.

Move! the dire wolf snapped viciously. *Fight!*

No other way, the Others whispered all around. They were watching her, willing her to do something other than lie there and wait for the sorcerer to get her close enough to finish her off. She had to do it.

If she wanted to survive, she had to call her magic back.

She slid another pace closer to Jasper, toward a massive hole in the floor. He was matching her, moving toward her as she was pulled to him, but he wasn't walking. Instead, his feet hovered off the floor, over thin air where parts of the floor were gone. A waste of power if she'd ever seen one. He was very careless for someone so close to destroying himself.

"Come on, magicker," he said, his voice distorted by many others. "Get up. There's only one way to defeat me, and you know it. Get up and fight me. Get up!"

There was flicker of movement behind him, and then a flash of metal stabbing through his heart. Nia heard the sorcerer groan, a sound not of pain but annoyance. Black magic poured out of the wound instead of blood; she could feel it. It was heavy and sought the floor rather than disperse into the air the way natural magic should.

He clucked his tongue, turning from her to face whoever was behind him. Only one person was still capable of moving on his own, the only one Jasper hadn't enchanted. He grasped Saeran by his shirt and bodily tossed him into the throne. His impact shattered it and the floor beneath it, and Saeran didn't get up again.

Nia screamed louder than she ever had in her life. The sound hurt her ears; made the humans and Others double over in pain and, were he not floating, the sorcerer would have dropped to his knees at the force of it.

The very air shuddered. Like an out of control river, her magic came rushing back into her, all that she'd drained herself of and more, from the great hall and Nico's library; taking his power as well, and Saeran's and some from the Others. It filled her near bursting, forcefully mending injuries and lifting her to her feet, though she'd not commanded it. Her scream ended as she drew a breath.

Without thought or intent, she started moving, step after step, stalking the sorcerer as he backed away from her, wide eyed. She was in a whirlwind that didn't exist, her hair and cloak whipping around her. She was glowing like a lantern as her power leaked out, illuminating the great hall better than the torches she'd extinguished. Nia felt herself on the brink of losing control. If she let go now, she could destroy not only herself and the sorcerer but everything and everyone within miles.

Two of the tables flew at the sorcerer without her conscious command. No more warnings. They flattened him between them, as far as his power would allow. It was still shielding him, though he fueled it now with his own life. It wouldn't last much longer; he had very little physical strength left, depending on magic to sustain him.

The tables shattered as he screamed.

Nia tore out more boulders, hurling them all at once. He had no chance of defending against all of them. Several scored a hit and the sorcerer staggered and fell to his knees, his body broken and his power raging out of control. He gasped big, pained breaths, but still launched another volley of magics at her. She swatted them away without breaking her stride.

By now there was little left of the floor but what pieces there were arranged themselves before her to pave an easy path to her target. The Others were retreating, one by one drawing back from the awful sight of the two of them. The dire wolf was the last to depart, still snarling.

Strange growling words spilled from Jasper's lips, sinking into the ground, making it recoil. He shot at her everything he had. What little part of her mind was still conscious of strategy discerned a pattern to his attack. He never aimed a fatal blow. This was all a studied lure to catch her magic.

At the last moment Nia stopped herself from touching him, physically or magically. Instead, she called to the banners hanging from the walls. They tore themselves to strips and wove together to form ropes that wound around the sorcerer's arms and neck. She used those binds to lift him from the floor as she continued her forward press. He hung before her as she dragged him out of the great hall, out of the castle.

The revelers in the courtyard had dispersed. Only the bonfire remained, burning high and bright. Nia didn't hesitate to send the sorcerer through it. He shouted and screamed; cast burning embers back at her. Nia didn't waste her defenses on such trifling things. She let them sear her face and hair; the burns healed instantly.

Jasper was still ablaze when she pushed him past the castle walls and started up the hill toward the altar. He put the flames out at the cost of his own body. More cracks appeared in the shell of his mortal form, his legs so damaged already they could no longer hold their shape. His limbs shattered, scattering pieces of him over the hill, leaving behind nothing but sloppy, dripping blobs of flesh.

He spat more spells at Nia, though most of them dissipated before they reached her. One or two made her falter, and forced her to heal herself again or risk setting him loose. It was too much. She knew this, felt the strain on her own body. Nia couldn't handle much more of his assault before she, too, began to shatter.

Saeran.

The sorcerer had hurt him. The image of him unmoving in the great hall squared her resolve, and she forced her body to endure. Almost there. Almost at the altar. Her hands were shining like stars at her sides, as were her feet where they peeked out from beneath her robes with each step. The wind howled at her to stop, the earth rose around her feet to slow her, but never quick enough to trap her foot before she lifted it again.

The Others had gathered again, keeping their distance, but watchful. Nia felt their apprehension, but for the safety of their people they would stay and see this through. They would do whatever was necessary to contain this uncontrollable flare of magics. As much harm as those magics could do to the human realm, they could destroy Otherlands in an instant. It could not be allowed. They would kill Nia if they deemed it necessary, and knowing that gave her the courage to keep going.

Jasper was beginning to look demonic. The watery stumps of his legs had touched at some point and melded together, forming one liquid mass below his waist. His fingers were breaking as he kept trying to bend her will to his, but she had to hear his commands to obey, and Nia was past listening to him.

"Loki," she called into the night when she reached the altar. Her voice was not her own, and in the depths of the forest wild beasts howled in fear.

Fear for her.

Fear of her.

"*Loki!*" She made it a summons, imbuing it with all her will. Her power flared, searing her insides, and she doubled over, briefly loosening her hold on the ropes that held the sorcerer. It was all he needed to break free and drop to the ground. The grass died where he touched it, and the death spread out from him, poisoning the land.

His teeth were gone, his mouth filled with darkness. Though he still had a voice, it growled rather than spoke. He couldn't give his words any shape. One hand clutched the pendant, the source of his powers, as the black liquid he was turning into gathered around it.

And still Nia felt its pull. It could sense her power; called it out. Nia fought to keep her magic reined in, but her control was tenuous at best and she was tired, so tired of resisting. Part of her was curious at this strange toy, wanted to reach out to it. Wanted to kill the sorcerer to possess it.

She found herself drawing closer before a chilling screech in her mind made her fall back again. The dragon's warning had come almost too late. And the sorcerer cackled madly, his cheeks breaking off, taking the lower half of his face with them.

In the absence of a spoken command, his dark power spread out across the earth, killing everything in its path. It was almost close enough to touch her.

The wolf pelt at her back shivered, dragging at her neck as if it could pull her away. Nia couldn't leave. If she didn't stop it, the darkness would cover all the land and everything would die.

She cupped her glowing hands together and gathered light into them. It pooled and then rose, shaping a sphere that grew larger and brighter. In the back of her mind she noticed that the sorcerer had fallen silent. She felt his rapt attention on her, sensed his anticipation and impatience.

The sphere swirled with currents, magic trying to arrange itself so that more could fit into a smaller shape. It became so heavy it almost had a physical form.

Like a crystal ball.

The fanciful thought became a spell and shadows moved across the sphere, forming into shapes. Nia saw the great hall and the people still trapped therein. It fascinated her. Eager to see what else the sphere might reveal, she fed it more power.

The light was so bright it illuminated the ground where she knelt. As the sorcerer spread death, Nia's light brought the earth back to life around her. The light, too, began to spread, overlapping and then banishing Jasper's darkness.

He cackled, staring at the approaching well of power. He was ravenous for it.

Entranced by this thing she had wrought, Nia's attention never wavered from her crystal ball. Curiosity made her deaf and blind to the world outside of it. *What secrets will you show me? What will you teach me?*

Shadows swirled in its depths, and Nia squinted, bringing it closer to her face. She saw a mother giving birth, a mighty dragon circling high in the air, breathing magic fire. She saw a young woman bursting into flames and a young man walking in illusions.

Nia's body began to shake, but she didn't care. Looking deeper she saw demons dancing a horrible dervish in the desert night. A vast army gathering beneath the banner of a blood red cross on a grassy field. Ice slithered up her arms to her heart. Nia didn't mind; she had the cloak and the wolf skin to warm her. And the light spread ever farther.

The wolf pelt whined softly at her ear.

Nia frowned, resenting the distraction.

The crystal was showing her a drop of blood. It splattered on a shining wall of magic and shattered it, erasing the Veil between the human realm and the Otherlands and from that explosion arose a people who would carve a new order into the world.

Oh, to walk among such giants!

Nia's light touched the edge of Jasper's withered form. He screamed with glee, even as the blob of black that was his body began to solidify into rock. As the light moved up to engulf him, the pendant in his hand shimmered with white, shining through the black slime. The sorcerer's laughter died abruptly as rock sealed shut around him and the night became quiet.

Claws sank into Nia's back, fangs bit into her ear. She cried out and almost dropped the crystal ball. Through watering eyes she looked up at the rock that had once been the sorcerer. She cocked her head, puzzled by how this could have come to be, or when it had become day. Everything was so bright, colors so vibrant they blinded her.

The wolf whined again. Nia looked over her shoulder to see the wolf pelt she'd worn restored to life. He tilted his head at her and Nia reciprocated. Hadn't he died? She recalled as much. Yes, poison. She'd felt him leave his mortal shell, yet somehow he was back, flesh and blood, or at least he looked that way. Could it be an illusion?

The wolf shifted uneasily and then lifted his head and howled. Nia looked up. The moon was big and bright, the sky clear and glittering with stars. It was still night.

The wolf whined and barked, got to his feet and jumped forward and back. Nia reached out to pet the beast, only to have him shrink from her touch. Her hands were still glowing. All of her was.

The wolf sniffed the ground, backing away from the spreading light, lifting his paws high as if it bothered him.

And then the ground shuddered and the rock began to crack.

38

"Foolish girl," Loki hissed in furious whisper, appearing just before her. "Look what you have done. This was precisely what I wanted to prevent!" He snatched the glowing crystal ball out of her hands, making her gasp. "*You doomed all of humanity to make a toy?*" he boomed.

Nia reached out to take it back, but before she could, part of the rock behind Loki crumbled to reveal the shiny black crystal and her hand changed direction. It was too far. *Must get up. Must possess it.*

Loki followed her gaze and straightened an arm out to stop her as she struggled to her feet. He flinched at touching her, but held firm. "Do not go near it," he warned, though he, too, sounded distracted.

Nia couldn't tear her gaze away. It was so shiny. Even from so far away she could see her own reflection in it. And every so often, it breathed! Its breath was as dark as its core. Puffs of black smoke emanated from its depths to disperse in the air. It was alive. And so beautiful and dark. She felt on fire with the light. It filled her, made her shine like the sun and it hurt. She needed that darkness to soothe her.

I might die otherwise.

"It's the magics," Loki said by way of explanation. "This is only the beginning. It will keep weakening until all of them are released."

"Pretty," she said on a sigh, not recognizing her own voice.

"Well, can't have that," Loki said brusquely and whistled. The pendant tore itself out of its cradle and as soon as the last contact was severed, the rock that used to be Jasper crumbled to dust. The pendant floated toward them, still puffing gently, and Nia's eyes opened wider and wider the closer it got. So close she could almost touch it. It felt as if it wanted to come to her. She wanted it to. She reached out to it in welcome, undeterred even when Loki slapped her hand down. Nia tried to shove him out of her way, but she may as well have been pushing at a mountain. The Trickster didn't budge a hair.

He caught the pendant by its chain before she could grasp it and turned to keep it out of her reach. Infuriated, Nia watched through him as he dipped the pendant into her crystal ball. The black stone screeched as it sank into the light. Nia could feel its pain, and it made her angry. She shoved her arm through Loki's body to take it from him, making him yell out, but it was too late. The pendant was fully submerged into the light, and the ball became solid, encasing it forever. Even some of its glow dimmed until she could see the pendant's dark outline in the middle.

It was a strange sight to behold. Nia could still sense the black ice within the orb, but it was getting weaker and weaker, as if the light was slowly destroying the darkness. Soon, she lost all awareness of it.

Loki yanked at the chain, breaking it off, and growled, "Take your arm back, or you never will again."

Nia shook her head to clear it. What was she doing? She pulled her arm free of him and stepped back. Her entire body was shaking, and she felt as if her skin was stretching, trying in vain to accommodate the power filling her. She would burst with it soon. "Can't hold this much."

Though she wasn't looking at him, she saw Loki glare at her. "I should let you shatter," he said. "If not for you, it never would have gotten this far."

Nia hunched her shoulders, trying to keep together. Just a little longer. It was becoming unbearable. The light made her feel at once heavy and light as a feather. If she managed to hop up into the air, she'd never come back down. But she was too stiff and fragile to make that leap, rooted to the ground like a tree.

Loki tossed the orb into the air and caught it in his other hand.

"Then again, if you had not made this little toy, I would have had a much tougher time sealing the damned thing. I suppose that balances things out. And I can't very well leave you as you are. You are as much of a problem now as the black ice was."

"Fix…me," she managed to say, having to shift all of her body just to make her voice work. Nothing was where it was supposed to be anymore. She couldn't feel her heartbeat; couldn't breathe, either, but she didn't seem to need it any longer. That frightened her.

Loki scowled again. "I can't. You did this, you have to undo it. And you can't do it here."

He expected her to solve riddles now? A burst of light escaped her body and she screamed, though no sound came out. She hugged herself to keep from breaking apart. The pressure was too much. It was killing her.

"I said not here," Loki snapped. "Fly up—far up, mind you—and release it there. The stars won't mind. And you had best hurry up. Any longer and you might as well join them."

Up? He meant fly. But how?

When she didn't move, Loki heaved a sigh. "I hope one day you appreciate all this," he said. Turning his face away, he came to her, bending double. She could feel his hands slipping beneath what should be her feet. "Safe journey, Lady Nialei," he said and, with a grunt, launched her into the air.

She flew up fast as a shooting star, just as she'd thought she would. No stopping now. Thousands and thousands of lights sang to her. The stars. The higher she went the better she understood them. They were welcoming her among them, eager to hear stories and to tell their own. Their voices were so beautiful, listening to them felt like coming home.

For a moment she embraced this strange place she was flying through, even let herself enjoy it. There were entire worlds filled with people and creatures she'd never seen before. She could peek into them, watch from afar as they went about their lives; watch them like players on stage.

And the plays would never end. She knew this. Eternity beckoned to her with all its charms and Nia was curious to see it.

Saeran.

He will not be there.

Her memory returned, shocking her back to what was really happening. Going too far. Nia willed herself to stop.

The stars were puzzled. She only had a little way to go, why was she stopping?

I am sorry, she thought to them. *I cannot stay.*

The stars sang to her to keep going. They wanted to welcome her as a sister, share their world with her. She was almost there, almost home.

Nia stopped listening. There was one thing she had to do before she returned, but she had to return. *Saeran is waiting.* She hesitated for a single moment, just one moment to feel fear and doubt. Then, praying she was doing the right thing, she released all of the light, pouring it out in thick, brilliant white streams. The force of it sent her spinning, and the faster she spun, the faster it drained out of her.

As it dispersed in the sky, the pressure inside her body eased. She could feel herself returning to the way she'd been before. Her heart beat strangely in her chest, but it was beating. Her limbs began to ache, strained and tired, and her lungs expanded, filling with icy cold air. Nia shivered, but it felt wonderful.

She could move with ease again, and her stomach growled for food. Her eyes were stinging with the cold and her mouth felt parched. Wonderful. She laughed into the still night, delighting in the sound of her own familiar voice. It was even better than the stars. She couldn't hear them anymore, and that was as it should be. The smallest hint of regret faded with the anticipation of everything that was yet to come. An entire lifetime she had here. She would fill it with wonders of her own.

At last the streams of light slowed to a trickle, and Nia started descending back to earth. She used just enough magic to slow her fall, and landed softly on the hill, dizzy, but in one piece. Her ears were ringing, and she walked like a drunk as she made her way down the hill to the castle. She had no way of knowing if Jasper's spells died along with him. There might still be terrified people frozen in their seats in the great hall. Or what was left of it.

The villagers who had braved coming out silently moved out of her way. The bon fire in the courtyard had been reduced to glowing embers. Nia didn't know how much time had passed since she'd left the castle, but she was tired enough to guess it was nearing sunrise.

She mounted the stairs and gasped to see what had become of the great hall. The stone floor was all but gone. What remained was a narrow walkway, surrounded by shattered stone and enormous holes. Nia could see straight down to the cellars and there were no pillars to support the walkway, yet somehow it held.

The noble guests were where Jasper had left them. Not because they were enchanted, but because there was nowhere for them to go. Many of them were in tears, all of them looking at her as if she were a demon come to take their souls. She didn't know how to ease their fears. Instead she weaved her hands through the air to move the remaining tables. They created bridges to the walkway so the guests could escape. "They will hold," she assured them.

As soon as one stood, they all were scrambling to get outside, giving her a wide berth. She slowed them just enough to keep them from trampling over each other. What they had seen of the battle would have frightened anyone. Nia didn't expect them to cheer her and write ballads in her honor.

Once the walkway was clear, Nia approached the dais. It looked as horrible as she remembered. The throne was in splinters. Rubble and debris was everywhere, and the floor was sunken where Saeran had landed. He was still there. Nia sank to her knees by his side and carefully turned him to lie on his back.

Noises intruded, robes rustling with hurried footsteps. Now that the danger was over, the royal advisors were coming to ascertain the king's ability to sire heirs. She had no time for them. Saeran's face was bruised and bleeding and the rest of him was in no better shape.

Nia laid her hand on the center of his chest and let the rest of the world fade away. Without closing her eyes she Saw inside the king. His body was battered and broken. He was bleeding, in terrible pain, but he was alive. Barely. The dragon pendant might have saved his life, but it wasn't powerful enough to keep him alive for much longer.

Nia called Light into her grasp, but this time she did it the right way. She called it slowly and let it pass through her and into Saeran. She shaped it into the tools she needed to mend his bones and close his wounds. The light settled like a blanket over tears and cracks, healing them layer by layer. It burned away bruises with gentle heat, warming him where his wounded heart could not. Nia was meticulous in her task, repairing every injury, no matter how small with infinite patience. She took no chances, left nothing to fate.

Some of Saeran's injuries were too severe to heal right away. Broken bones needed time to mend. There, she let the Light seep into him and remain, glowing softly. It would speed the natural process of healing and, though he would be weak for some time to come, he'd be able to move about without splints and crutches.

She looked over her work twice before she returned to herself. Saeran slept. He would wake on the morrow, aching and ravenous, but alive.

Behind her, Braith was the first to speak. "My lady, what is to be done?"

"Have the king taken to his chambers," she replied, surprised at how difficult it was to form the words. She was exhausted again, and this time she wouldn't be able to keep from sinking into a wizard's sleep when she laid her head down. Already the need weighed on her so much she couldn't bring herself to stand. "He will sleep for the time being. See that he has all he needs, but do not disturb him."

"I suppose you will wish us to redecorate the great hall as well."

It was the first time Nia had heard Allon make a jest. She smiled at him. "I insist the floors be inlaid with diamonds."

He returned her smile. "Come then," he said, holding his hand out to her. "I shall see you to your chambers. It seems to me you are in need of some healing sleep yourself."

She nodded and allowed him to pick her up. The old man was stronger than he looked. He never once complained, taking her weight easily as he carried her up the stairs to her rooms. "You gave us quite a fright tonight." He sounded amused.

"I have paid the price for it, as you can see."

"What should we expect for tomorrow, then?"

When he laid her on the bed, all she could do was sink down and close her eyes. "I will sleep for some days. Do not burry me, old man. I will be very angry if you do."

He chuckled. "I shall warn the others."

The snow came up to Saeran's knee, but he didn't mind; didn't feel the cold. He was so tired each step felt impossible. Every time his foot sank into the snow all he wanted to do was sit down and stay there, but he kept going, compelled by some force he couldn't understand toward the dark cave up ahead.

At last he made it out of the snow, into the pitch black tunnel. He knew this place. His feet moved from memory, leading him down into the depths of the mountain without faltering a single time. When he emerged into the cavern, Saeran breathed a sigh of relief. He was home.

Fire pits were carved into the walls like massive torches, illuminating treasure. Giant crystals sparkled in the ceiling, streams of gold were inlaid forever shining in the floors. Shadows played over painted tapestries, making them move as if they were alive, and diamonds the size of his hand glittered in piles all around.

And in the middle lay a massive sleeping dragon, his tail curled around his body, wings folded to his sides. His scales were like shined steel, reflecting firelight, and long black horns adorned his head. His claws were the size of a man's torso and each breath he puffed was black smoke.

Saeran wasn't afraid. "It was you," he said. "You called me here." He remembered the great hall, the battle of magics. He remembered the fear that had gripped him to see Jasper closing in on Nia.

He remembered dying. And the dragon commanding him back to life.

A great, slitted eye opened to look at him. "I thought it was time we met."

~

There was a blurry red cloud before him when he opened his eyes. "If the wizard were here, she'd say that was a stupid thing to do." Braith's face slowly came into focus.

"Where is she? What happened?" Saeran's mouth was parched and it was difficult to speak the words, but he managed.

"She is sleeping," Braith told him. "Jasper is gone and the great hall is in ruins. Be glad the castle has not come down on top of us yet." She helped him sit up and brought a chalice to his mouth.

Saeran gulped the water down, and glared at her when she took it away.

"Slowly," she said.

"So you have finally found the courage to order around your king."

The girl blushed and looked away.

His mouth twitched. "Well, don't lose it now, I was beginning to enjoy myself." Braith glared at him, much the way Nia did and Saeran grinned.

"You would not be so cheerful if you knew what has been happening in your kingdom for the last two days."

"Tell me." He winced when she arranged the pillows behind him so he could sit on his own. His entire body pained him, but it was a healing ache. He felt warmth where he knew he'd broken bones. Saeran should be dead now and instead he felt better than ever. Aside from the pangs of hunger and the many twinges in his still healing wounds.

Braith took a chair by his bed. "It was bad," she said. "Those who were able ran at the first sound of trouble. Those who could not... well, they saw everything. Most of them are terrified of the wizard now. She spent so long showing them the gentle, healing side of her magic, none of them realized what she was truly capable of until they saw it for themselves."

"She has done nothing but defend them!"

"As a blade defends the soldier. But he never forgets how easily it can be turned against him if he lets his down his guard. The wizard is a powerful weapon, Majesty, but a weapon nonetheless."

"No, she is much more than that."

Braith lowered her gaze. "Yes. That, too, is quite obvious now. After what happened in the great hall, even those who kept the secret of your illness can't hold their tongues anymore. Rumors are spreading far and wide. About both of you."

"What rumors?"

"That the wizard is not human. That she has enchanted you somehow to gain control of Wilderheim. There are some who say they saw you move like a wraith that night, your eyes glowing like a demon."

Saeran flushed. They weren't far off the mark. He hadn't hesitated when he saw Nia go down. He'd moved, and in the blink of an eye he'd been at the sorcerer's back, a sword he didn't remember reaching for firmly in his grasp. If questioned by one with truthsense, he couldn't honestly say he hadn't used magic that night. Nor could he say he regretted it.

"I am afraid you will have greater issues to contend with when you reclaim your seat than the continuation of your royal line."

"It would seem so."

The foreign emissaries would no doubt be returning to their royal courts with wild tales to tell. Halden would understand but Saeran knew Queen Genevieve of Synealee to be dangerously superstitious and King Gavriil of the western kingdom of Ravetia abhorred all magic. He'd outlawed its practice and anyone even suspected of it faced immediate execution. Both regents would consider Saeran a threat if they believed him to be anything more than ordinary.

And then there was the matter of Aegiros. Saeran didn't want to think about what would happen when this news reached them.

"What will you do?"

Saeran snorted. "What can I do?"

Braith's brow puckered in thought and Saeran crossed his arms, amused despite himself and very much curious to hear what the girl would come up with. "I would not worry about Aegiros yet. Lyria will ally itself with us no matter what, and their armies as well as ours are well trained now, thanks to you and King Manfred.

"The threat of Synealee lies in their faith and superstitions, but their queen is ancient and not quite right in the head, if you ask me. Their lack of organization and forethought will be their weakness. We can exploit it if need be.

"Ravetia would be my biggest concern. King Gavriil is a warmonger, too eager to draw his sword at the smallest provocation. If they choose to take up arms, we will need every able bodied soldier on the front lines to defend Wilderheim."

Saeran gaped at her. Hadn't he just thought the very same thing?

"But with the unrest brewing right here, we will end up fighting a battle on multiple fronts no matter what," Braith continued with a wince. "I think the situation can be salvaged. It will be tricky, but the people love you, and if you meet them halfway with the truth you can regain their trust. We can win favor for Lady Nia back with diplomacy. The post of royal wizard has been created for an emissary for the Otherlands so that there can be peace between us. It has been held by human wizards until now because there has never been an Other willing to live so openly among us, but with Lady Nia here, it is finally as it should be. Now, if we can explain your dragonblood without inciting panic that the Others are taking ov—"

"What did you say?"

Braith's mouth snapped closed and she blushed deep red. "Umm…"

Saeran sat up straighter. "Repeat what you just said."

"A-about the battle on multiple fronts?" She wrung her hands together. "It is something I read in the Histories advisor Allon gave me to study—"

"No, after that. Dragonblood?"

Her eyes grew impossibly wide and she dropped to her knees, grasping his hand in both of hers. "Please, Majesty, forgive me. I did not mean to, it just happens. I swear I will never say a word."

"For all the gods' sake, get up."

As giant tears flooded her eyes, Braith hiccupped and stood, her head bowed. She was shaking with the force of her sobs and trying so hard to be quiet about it.

"Stop it," he said, keeping his voice low so he wouldn't frighten her more.

"I am s-sor-ry."

Saeran rubbed his brow and bit back a sight. "You have done nothing."

"But I—"

"Sit."

She sat.

"Now take a breath, and tell me the truth."

She looked as if she'd rather be anywhere but there in that moment. Saeran knew when someone was trying not to tell him something. He narrowed his eyes at her and Braith cringed. "M-my ma was a midwife in Ravetia." She said this as if confessing to some crime. "She had a gift with all kinds of herbs and potions. Sometimes, people felt better just for touching her.

"And my gran knew things. She would know what was happening in other villages, and she would tell us when something bad was about to happen, long before it did. But they kept it secret, see? They were afraid for us. When I was old enough to travel, gran brought us all here. The whole family. So we could be safe."

Saeran guessed where this was going, but he let her speak. If Braith stopped now, she might not finish what she'd been about to say.

"It is only a little magic," she said. "Nothing like Lady Nia can do. But all the women in my family have it." She looked up as if to judge his reaction but quickly looked away. "The other advisors do not know. I never told anyone. And then there was so much to do after Samhain they had their hands full with the castle and the villagers, but you were not to be left unattended. Since I am the youngest, they said I ought to stay here, for when you woke up."

Again, she paused. "Braith," he said, "we do not have much time before someone interrupts. Whatever you have to say, say it."

"I know you are descendant of dragons. And that it is why you refuse to take a wife and sire heirs." She flinched, as if she couldn't believe she'd said it. "I can sense the dragonfire in you."

Saeran said nothing. It was most uncomfortable, having this young girl know so much about him. Braith, he imagined, was what Nia must have been like before Nico had taken her under his wing. Untrained, unsure of herself, yet in possession of something no other had. He tried to see Braith as another wizard, not a girl child. He'd appointed her as one of his advisors, after all. It would not do to lose confidence in her now.

"Only dragonblood can carry dragonblood," she said softly. "My gran used to tell us stories." She smiled a little. "I thought they were just that until now."

"Does anyone else know?"

"Oh, no, Majesty. I would never tell." After a pause, she added, "But I think you ought to."

"And give my people more reason to fear?"

"They already do anyway," she argued. "But better a kind, mostly human king they know, than a strange inhuman thing they imagine. And you could wed Lady Nia then. Begging your pardon, Majesty, but after Samhain, no one else will have you."

Saeran laughed. He couldn't help himself. "Is that so?"

Braith nodded.

"Simple as song. Wed the wizard and completely destroy the balance Wilderheim stands on."

"No," she said. "Solidify it."

"Braith…"

"Don't you see? Who would be foolish enough to stand up to a dragon king and his mate? King Gavriil despises magic because he fears it. As a king apart from your wizard, you will always be at odds, an easy target for someone like him. But if you form a united front, he will not dare challenge you. Not with Lyria and the whole of Otherlands at your back."

Saeran gritted his teeth against harsh words. "And Synealee?"

Braith shrugged. "They might try, but they will have to go through Lyria to get to us. King Halden will not be beaten twice, especially not by pampered zealots."

"And what of Aegiros."

Braith's growing winsome smile faded. "I do not know. Queen Mari's death complicates everything where they are concerned. They might care, they might not. There is no way to tell what they will do until they do it. Aegirans do not plan their assaults, they simply carry them out."

"And how do you propose we circumvent the riots in my own kingdom?"

"Do as you have always done. Be the king you have always been and prove to them that the well being of Wilderheim and its people is still your highest priority. I cannot say it will be easy, but you have won them once, it can be done again. You descend from a long line of kings, Majesty, good kings, sometimes foolish kings, but never cruel or heartless. Show them the goodness of your heart and they will love you for it."

Saeran sighed, weary of this. "Which leaves the ever important chore of siring heirs and continuing that long royal bloodline. Tell me, young Braith, what magical solution do you have for that?"

"Lady Nia is Other," she said quickly. "She might—"

"Enough," Saeran snapped. "Thank you, Braith." He'd meant it as a dismissal. His head ached like the devil, and he was in no mood to discuss whether or not his hypothetical dragon spawn would drain the life from Nia as he'd watched it do with Mari. His eyes closed of their own volition and he leaned his head back, half drowsing already.

But Braith didn't leave. "Sire, there is more. I looked in on Lady Nia while you slept."

Saeran cracked one eye open to look at her. "So now you know all of her secrets too?"

Braith stood and arranged a tray of food and the chalice where he could reach them if he wanted to. "I do know what you fear," she told him. "I also know that with her you would not need to."

"She can keep from conceiving, you mean."

She said nothing.

"If you are talking about the Other thing again, don't. I will not risk her life on the possibility that I might be wrong."

"No, that is not what I meant at all."

"Then what?"

Braith wouldn't look at him as she backed away to the door. "Perhaps you should ask her," she said. "Ask her what the dragon did."

Saeran frowned as the door closed behind her. Left with that mysterious pronouncement and no idea what she was talking about, his mind immediately seized on the possibility that there might be even the smallest chance for…something. He rolled his eyes at himself even as sleep began to weigh on him once more. Even if he was willing to believe it, which he wasn't, and even if no one else ever offered their daughter or sister in marriage to him again, which might or might not be true, and even if a marriage between them didn't cause the chaos he knew it would, Nia had already turned him down twice. And he'd thought he'd accepted her decision with grace.

But content as he'd told himself to be with Nia by his side as friend and companion, Saeran's heart had never stopped hoping for more. Nia was part of him; he felt it even now when she was worlds away in wizard's sleep. He felt her heart beating and the world made sense.

Saeran sighed and closed his eyes. He imagined she was there with him, nestled against his side and he smiled, allowing sleep to pull him under.

He dreamed of the dragon flying circles high in the air, breathing fire at the clouds, and a pair of babies swathed in embroidered blankets, looking up at him with big, curious eyes.

40

Out of total darkness Nia fell into blinding light. She rubbed her eyes and squinted. There were giant orbs floating in the air, their light bouncing off the crystal walls and golden pillars. The chamber was enormous, with a ceiling so high she couldn't even see it and windows big enough to fit a castle through.

"Do you know where you are?"

Nia turned around to face the female Sidhe seated on a delicate white throne.

"Do you know why you are here?" the male beside her asked before she could answer.

"No," Nia said to both questions.

The king of all Sidhe scowled. "I expected better from you by now."

Nia looked around at the hall suddenly filled with faeryfolk. "I was sleeping," she said. "How did I get here?"

"What does that matter?" the queen said. "You were elsewhere, now you are here. What you should be worried about is why you are here and how you will get back."

"If you will get back," the king corrected.

"Why would I not?"

The queen folded her hands together in her lap. "There is a matter of great concern we must discuss. You will not leave until we are satisfied that it is resolved."

"Who do you speak for?" the king asked.

Nia didn't like his arch tone. "Everyone who needs a voice. And you?"

His eyes narrowed and vines burst out of the ground at her feet, twining around her legs and body. Nia kicked and ripped at them but the more she fought, the faster they grew until she couldn't move at all.

"Disrespect will not be tolerated, Halfling."

A mass of black fur hurtled over her head with a vicious snarl. The dire wolf male took a stand between her and the Sidhe, hackles up, and growled, "She is not one of yours."

"Then who does she belong to?" the queen questioned. "The water sprites? She does not look like one. Or her sire's people? Or humans? Or the dragon, perhaps!"

Behind Nia the female dire wolf huffed, and the vines withered at her feet. Nia stepped out of them and faced the royal Sidhe. "I belong to no one—"

"Still you don't know who you are," the queen said.

"—and my people are who I choose them to be."

"Your ignorance grows tiresome."

"Everyone must belong to someone," the Sidhe king decreed.

"Why?" Nia challenged. "Because you decided?"

"Because without someone, you are no one," the queen said.

Even the dire wolves had no defense to offer against that.

"Enough of this. The sorcerer's amulet damaged the Veil between our lands. Humans are passing through where they should not, and our people are becoming stranded in your world. What do you intend to do about it?"

"Me?"

"Yes, you," the king said, rolling his eyes. "The girl without clan, without a name, the nobody standing before royal Sidhe without the sense to kneel. You. The sorcerer came for you, so it is your fault that this has happened."

Nia was speechless. "You want me to repair what gods have created?"

"Are you unequal to the task, she who speaks to gods?"

The dire wolves growled and the female shifted into her human body next to Nia. "You go too far Eilwyn," she said to the Sidhe queen.

"You dare speak my name!"

"You know I will dare much more if you vex me," the female growled.

The Sidhe king stood. At his full height, he was enormous, and pale white shadows moved at his back like gossamer wings. Nia had never seen anything like it. "Remember your place, wolf."

"You would do well to remember yours," the male dire wolf said. "You do not speak for all of us. You only speak the loudest."

"See what she does to us," Eilwyn said, her voice resounding throughout the hall. "Scant moments among us and we turn on each other like humans." She turned to the dire wolves. "And Roukan and Lyall would have us welcome her in our midst."

Accusing stares turned on her from all around. No longer only Sidhe, the hall was now filled with all clans of Others, big and small.

"I do not want to be in your midst," Nia said. "My place is in Wilderheim."

What of the Veil? Nia turned to face the speaker, a male water sprite, looking out from a lake that wasn't there before. *Humans in Otherlands get lost. Humans in our lakes and rivers drown.*

"I don't know how to repair the Veil," Nia said. "But if we agree to a compromise, I can help to mend the rifts."

"Compromise," the Sidhe king said with disgust.

"Sit down, Ruari," Lyall commanded, shedding her human skin in favor of her dire wolf form. "Let the girl speak."

The Sidhe king scoffed, but no one spoke up for him, and with a snarl he sat.

"Go on, Nialei."

It was strange hearing her full name. No longer was she an orphan from the woods, she was Nialei of the Streams. Daughter of a water sprite and…well, she wasn't quite sure what her father was, but what she knew was enough. Squaring her shoulders, she addressed the crowd. "Our legends say the gods wove the Veil from the blood of each clan of Otherlands and gave it the power of illusion. It was never meant to be a gateway to be opened or shut, but a shield to hide the worlds from each other. But they were never truly separate, were they?

Not with curious Others passing through whenever they pleased to spy on humans and amuse themselves meddling in their lives."

King Ruari pushed to his feet again, but Nia held up her hand to silence him. "I mean no offense," she said politely. "What I mean to say is that it took all of us to create the Veil, and it will take all of us to mend it. But Otherlands will never again be a mystery to humans, not in Wilderheim, not after everything that's happened. The compromise I propose is that we work together to mend the rifts, all of us, even humans. Because if Others refuse to stay in Otherlands, then humans should not be forced to stay in human lands. Fair is fair, after all. Balance must be kept, yes?"

"How dare you suggest we allow mortals to walk our worlds!" Eilwyn said, outraged.

"How dare *you* assume mortals will continue to fight, bleed, and die to defend your precious worlds without having anything in return?" Nia replied. "It has been thus for centuries. Wilderheim stands bastion to protect *you. Your* worlds and *your* secrets. They are the only ones who still believe in the old legends, and it is that very faith which is keeping the Veil fluid. You know as well as I that the moment the people of Wilderheim stop believing, and wondering, and praying, the Veil will slam shut and no one will pass through it ever again, human or Other."

She paused for breath and chanced a look around. It was a bluff, a wild guess on her part but from the looks of those around her, Nia had guessed right. The Others needed humans as much as humans needed them. Nia swallowed with difficulty, wondering what would happen to those stuck on either side who did not belong. She couldn't be the only Other living among humans. And as fascinated as the Others seemed to be about them, Nia was certain there had to be humans living among Others somewhere as well.

"Those with Sight have always known and will always know there is more to Wilderheim than meets the eye. You cannot hide and expect mortals to fight for what they cannot see."

"They have done it this long," Ruari said with a careless shrug. "Why should they not continue?"

Nia took an angry step before she could stop herself and the ground shuddered beneath her foot. "Because I will not let them."

The Sidhe king and queen leaned toward each other and spoke in whispers a moment. Then Eilwyn stood from her throne and said, "Who will speak for the Halfling?"

The dire wolves stepped up to her without hesitation. "We will," Lyall said.

And us, the water sprite added.

"And us," the fire sprites chimed in.

One after the other the great majority of the Others voiced their support. Nia nodded her thanks to each of them and then turned to the Sidhe, the only ones who had not yet spoken. "And how have you decided?"

Ruari scowled at her and pushed to his feet next to his queen. With a regal nod, he answered for both of them, and then Nia was flying, spinning, dropping away, back into the darkness from which they'd taken her. Back into the wizard's sleep.

Before she even awakened fully, Nia felt the presence of another in her chamber. "Trickster," she said, in no mood to spar with him. When she opened her eyes, he perched at the foot of her bed, his black eyes crinkled at the outside edges with mischievous laughter, though his thin mouth betrayed not a hint of humor.

"At last, she wakes," he said, matching her dry tone. "I was beginning to think a dousing with cold water was in order."

Nia sighed and sat up. And immediately frowned. "This is not my room."

"Indeed, it is not," Loki said and disappeared, reappearing again on the sill of a very large window. The drapes were pulled back and Nia had an unobstructed view of the castle grounds, and far beyond to the forests. She could see the road out of Frastmir from here! And the village it led to.

"Where am I?"

The Trickster chuckled, mocking her. "You have been asleep for quite some time now, Halfling. The king has been a busy little bee in your absence. Poking around in his own mind, tasting new magics on his tongue, listening to whispers denied to him for long years. Sniffing out secrets. Always the secrets. Pecking, pecking, pecking away at mysteries best left untouched, if I had any say. It would have been more fun that way."

Ignoring him, Nia slipped out of bed, touching her bare feet to thick bear skins strewn over the floor. She padded to the door and opened it a crack to peer outside. Still in the castle. Near the king's chambers. What was the man up to now?

She closed the door again and leaned against it. "What do you want?" she demanded of Loki.

He scowled at her, as though she'd taken away his plaything for no good reason at all. "I have brought you a stray," he said. With a snap of his fingers, he conjured a wolf. Her wolf. The wolf that had been no more than a pelt hugging her shoulders not so long ago. "He has no place among the living, yet he is not dead."

The creature's eyes did seem different. They were pure white, as if he ought to be blind, yet he seemed to see perfectly. He got up and began pacing around, sniffing everything, fascinated with this and that.

"You don't remember?" Loki said. "I suppose you were a little pre-occupied at the time. You brought this poor beast back from the dead. Not completely; his true spirit is free on the other side. This one is, shall we say, a mirror image. His body is not flesh and blood, and thus cannot age or die. His mind remembers everything of his past life, and all that has happened since his death. And he is a very annoying heap of fur! I do not want him in my realm. He is your charge. You take care of him."

The wolf eyed Nia warily, head low, ears pricked forward. He ap-proached her with caution, turning left first, then back toward her, then right again, as if he couldn't decide whether he wanted to get closer or not. Nia kept still, let him make up his mind.

When he finally reached her, he sniffed at her night shirt and her hands, and at long last, his tail began to wag and she felt the rasp of his tongue against her fingers. Nia lowered to her haunches to scratch him behind the ears.

"The sorcerer is gone," Nia said, not looking at the god.

"I am aware."

"We had a deal, Trickster."

"Indeed, we did. I vowed to tell you of your sire if you rid me of the sorcerer."

"Well?" She looked at him.

Loki grinned sharply for a quick instant before smoothing his features out again. "I do not recall specifying when I would tell you, only that I would." Nia scowled and he laughed. "In time, wizard. You have plenty of it. Learn a little patience."

Nia had half a mind to put him to the ceiling and keep him there a good long while. She resisted only because she had no wish to be around him any more than was absolutely necessary.

The wolf rolled onto his back and pawed the air madly, demanding a belly rub.

"Tell me something else, then," she said. "What is this about the king? Tell me of these secrets of yours."

"They are no secrets of mine he has been learning," he said with an easy shrug.

"What do you mean by that? Enough of your games, Trickster. Tell me what it is you want so badly for me to know and leave. I have duties to attend to." And she was famished. Considering how hungry she was, Nia guessed she had to have slept for at least a fortnight.

"The kingling's feet tread far in sleep. He sought a link and found it. Now his grandsire can speak, tho' the king's hearing is weak, and summonses have been sounded."

So Saeran has found a way to speak to the dragon. Did that release her from his presence in her mind? She hadn't felt him since she'd woken. It was a relief to have her thoughts to herself again. But she'd gotten used to the dragon's presence. Even when he'd meddled, he'd at least been someone to talk to.

Not knowing why she did so, Nia reached out to the dragon. She felt his presence instantly, warmth, and kindness, and welcome. "She's awakened," she heard him say, and, realizing he wasn't alone, she withdrew immediately.

"Well, now you have done it," Loki said, rising from the window sill. The afternoon sun reflected off his hair, making it glitter and shine like sharp, polished copper. "They will pour in here in droves now to see to you. A thing I have no wish to be part of, so I shall bid you farewell."

Nia narrowed her eyes at him. "You are hiding something," she accused.

"Always," he replied with another quicksilver grin.

Her mind raced with possibilities. Whatever he was withholding would be of great importance, and he was doing it simply to spite her and amuse himself. "Saeran knows about his grandsire. What else? What other secrets?"

The Trickster's eyes gleamed wickedly. "You will find out soon enough. I would not dream of spoiling the surprise."

"Loki!"

It was too late. He'd disappeared. And while Nia thought she might be able to summon him back, there would be no point to it. He would prove no more obliging than he had thus far.

The wolf came to his paws again, barking at the nothing that remained where Loki had been. It would seem the beast didn't like him any more than Nia did. Then he turned on Nia, or rather, the door behind Nia, and he barked once more, his tail wagging wildly.

With no more time to think or debate the Trickster's riddles, she conjured her robes about her. Her hair pleated itself back as the walls and the floor all but shivered with anticipation. She could feel it in the air, and so could the wolf, if the way he shook himself and grumbled was anything to go by. There were people coming. And she had a very bad feeling that she ought not be found in this room. At the very least she needed to meet them outside in the hall. There, she could think of some reason for her presence.

Needing to escape, she opened the door—

—and walked into Saeran.

They froze, staring at each other for long moments, while the wolf barked and pranced around them and then bounded off to someone else. Nia didn't know where he went. She knew there were others behind Saeran, but all she could see was him. He was dressed in his official kingly garb, his crown heavy upon his brow. His eyes were clear and sharp, with no lingering shadows from his ordeal. He seemed younger, somehow. As if a great burden had lifted from his shoulders. He stood tall and proud, radiating heat and strength in a way that reminded her of his grandsire. Saeran was more dragon than she'd realized.

Nia heard his heart racing in his chest, and her own heart matched the rhythm. The way he was looking at her made heat bloom in her cheeks. She knew she wasn't breathing, but couldn't find a pressing enough reason to inhale.

Then Saeran's mouth pulled into a smile, and then that smile grew bigger, more dazzling as he took her hand and bowed over it, holding her gaze all the while. "Welcome back, my queen," he said, his voice low and full of mystery.

Nia blushed at the endearment aware of the others present. "Majesty," she answered uncertainly.

"It is a shame you did not wake this morning," he said. "We missed your presence at the ceremony."

"Ceremony?" Nia frowned, listening to what the walls could tell her. For once, they were silent, watching everything with rapt curiosity. There was no breeze to speak to her, and if the earth itself knew anything, it wasn't telling. "How long have I been asleep?"

"Nearly three weeks," Saeran said. "We were worried for you at first, but your color improved daily so we waited. But after everything that's happened there were those who believed that we could not wait much longer. Something needed to be done, and so a wedding ceremony was held this morning."

Nia swayed back, and were it not for Saeran's hold on her hand—both her hands—she would have fallen over. Saeran wouldn't be dressed this way for anyone's wedding but his own. "You married?"

That smile remained on his lips as he studied her reaction. Whatever he deduced from it seemed to hearten him, but he frowned as he dropped his gaze. "Sadly, my bride was not yet present, and so I was forced to marry her by proxy." With his head still bowed, he looked up at her, his mouth twitching.

This time, Nia pulled her hands out of his grasp and backed away from him. "You didn't," she whispered as understanding dawned. "Tell me you did not—"

"It is done," the dragon said with his familiar deep voice.

Nia looked to where he stooped by the gleeful wolf, playing with him. He wore dark breeches and a deep red shirt, with a brown leather jerkin. His hair was combed back, but his horns were gone, as was his tail. He looked older as well, though not near old enough to be Saeran's grandsire. There was a sharpness to his gaze when he looked at her, but warmth as well. It was a duality not easily affected by normal people.

Saeran must have summoned him out of his icy isolation, and while he didn't seem unhappy to be there, Nia could tell he wasn't comfortable with his fully human form. His essence was still that of a dragon, and she felt it fill the hallway, though the advisors behind him seemed oblivious to it.

The dragon didn't stop playing with the wolf, but his attention was on Nia. He was waiting, she realized, not for her answer, but for her acceptance. "A proxy still needs to be finalized by the bride's consent."

"It is done," repeated the dragon simply.

"What have you done?" she whispered, her heart beating too fast and her breaths coming too slow. She was beginning to feel light headed.

"What I should have done months ago," Saeran said, following her retreat. He grasped her shoulders firmly and she was glad of the support, even while she pushed against his chest to be released. "Placed you where you belong. At my side. As my queen."

"The people won't accept—"

"We will sort it out."

"Aegiros, and Ravetia…"

"Braith?"

"They will not dare challenge a royal pair as powerful as you, Majesties," Braith answered.

"Your advisors…"

"Gave their unanimous support," Allon said.

"All but shoved me to the altar," Saeran added wryly.

"Heirs?" she ventured. He couldn't possibly have the answer to every question. There were too many! Too much could go wrong, especially now with the Veil damaged and Others looking for an excuse to lash out. There would be fighting, possibly riots, to say nothing of war.

"My decree still stands. Should I die without heirs, the rule of Wilderheim will pass to Halden's children and the two kingdoms will join into one." He softened his tone as he continued. "As to the matter of children, my love, you have yourself told me that it takes dragonblood to birth a dragon. Blood that runs in your veins now. The decision will be yours."

At this last, the advisors hummed unhappily, but they didn't say a word. The dragon, still watching her with his inscrutable eyes, gave the slightest of nods. The wolf now sat beside him, another member of their rapt audience.

Nia shivered beneath the weight of their scrutiny. She was fighting not only them but herself as well. But she couldn't give in to the treacherous part of her that so longed to say yes. Why couldn't they understand? She was trying to keep them all safe! A pair of Others ruling a human kingdom would be disastrous. Her duty was to safeguard Wilderheim. She was trying to protect them! She was…

Lost for her king. And had been since the day they'd first met.

Nia had always known she would never take a lover or become a wife. She'd sworn her fealty to the king, knowing that, for her, such fealty carried a great deal of heart as well. And she'd known what it would mean. A lifetime spent in shadow, dispensing wisdom while keeping to herself. Nia was the royal wizard. She'd accepted her duty as the power behind the king.

Her heart had never been free to give.

"Sweet Nia," Saeran said, drawing her closer, despite her silent protests. "Beloved soul. The beat of my heart. There never was another way." His arms came around her, holding her close. "You were my destiny from the first."

"I am your wizard," she tried, but couldn't voice it with conviction.

Saeran noticed. He smiled again. "You must accept me," he said. Not accept this. He wasn't asking her to rule his kingdom, or bear him sons. He was asking her to let him into her heart. Nothing more.

He didn't know. She'd never told him. Her heart had always been his to begin with. Never free to give, because he'd already held it.

Saeran nuzzled her temple, his voice dropping to a whisper at her ear. "You must," he repeated, and the whole of Nia's being responded to his words. "Because the first time we kissed, time stopped."

When his lips brushed hers, Nia stopped fighting. It was done, had been for a very long time. She simply hadn't allowed herself to admit it. No matter the path chosen, this would always have been her destination because there were some things in this world not even a powerful Halfling Other with dragon's blood in her veins could overcome, nor did she want to. Nico must have known. He would not have brought her here if he hadn't been absolutely certain it was the right thing to do. It gave her the courage to believe that whatever the future held she would weather it as long as she had Saeran by her side.

And so the royal wizard acknowledged the inevitable convergence of two mate souls, accepted her beloved king as her husband, and gladly opened her heart to him, telling him with all of herself what she could not speak in words, lest she break their kiss.

And when time stopped again, she was more than happy to let it.

EPILOGUE

"You doubted me."

Freki surged to her feet. Head low, hackles up, she snarled at the shadow and the figure emerging from its depths. As Muninn took flight and alighted on Loki's shoulder, cocking his head from side to side, Woden breathed a quiet sigh. Here stood the most beautiful Halfling ever born. Beautiful and flawed. "Yes," he replied simply.

Loki's reckless smile skewed, darkness leaking from his empty eyes. "You, who knows all, doubted a future set in eternity?"

"Nothing is ever set, Loki. You should know that better than anyone."

Muninn cawed, unsettled by Loki's growing anger. "I destroyed the stone, did I not?"

"You created it in the first place," Woden reminded him. "And what of the Veil?"

A burst of darkness flared out of Loki. Where it touched, the world changed. Grass coiled like a nest of snakes, pebbles grew spider legs and crawled, jumping onto trees and logs which suddenly groaned like ravenous beasts. "*That was not my doing!*"

"It came about as a direct result of your actions. You will be held accountable."

Loki shouted to the sky, and his new creations screamed with him.

Woden fisted his hand and slammed it down on the smooth stone surface of his armrest. A deafening boom made the earth shudder, knocking Loki to his knees and startling Muninn into flight. Everything Loki had brought to unnatural life reverted to its inert form, though it would forever carry his dark taint. Chest heaving with wrath-filled breaths, Loki glared at Woden. He would not stand until Woden allowed it.

The All-Father rose from his seat and looked around, breathing in the serenity of this place. It would not last much longer. Loki's interference had set in motion events which could not be stopped by an act of the divine. The Veil was not only a separation between the human realm and the Otherlands, but also the vessel of divine power. Even now that power bled out of Asgard, dispersing into the aether and very soon it would leech from the gods themselves.

Though he was far removed, Fenrir's howls echoed on the wind. The monster knew his time was nigh. He fought his binds, bit at the delicate ribbon tied about his neck. For now it held. A product of Dwarven magic and skill, it was yet unaffected by the change. But if Nialei and the Others failed to restore the Veil, the ribbon's magic would drain and Fenrir would break free and devour the world as had been foretold.

Loki closed his eyes and smiled to hear the eerie sound. There was something akin to pride in the set of his shoulders. Even subjugated to his knees he showed no humility. "Listen," he whispered. "My son sings to me of freedom. Is it not beautiful? His agony will be your end, All-Father. It's coming, can you feel it?" When he looked at Woden again, his smile was sharp as a blade, promising terrible things.

"Get up," Woden commanded.

Like a puppet on strings, Loki rose to his feet. "You so like your Shadows, Trickster? Good. You will stay in them henceforth."

His black eyes widened. "How long?"

"Until you learn that your actions have consequences. Forever if need be."

"No!" Loki lunged at Woden, but the binding spell held him back. The Shadow from whence he came grew and reached out, wrapping smoky tendrils around the Trickster, drawing him back into its depths.

"I'll kill you! All of you!" He screamed ancient words and curses, his voice echoed by Fenrir's rising frenzy. He could feel his father's wrath, as Loki felt his. "*Avenge me, son!*" When the Shadow swallowed him whole, its stain dissipated and peace settled over the land once more.

It took a long time for Fenrir's maddened howls to die down. When they did, mist poured into the clearing, swirling up and taking shape. From its center emerged Frigga, a worried frown marring her brow. "How long will it hold him?"

"Not long enough, I fear."

"Nialei will need time."

"She might not have it."

Frigga nodded. "Then we will have to speed things along."

"Frigga," Woden said, taking her hand in his. "You cannot stop the inevitable."

His beautiful wife smiled. "So you say. But did you not also say that nothing is ever set?" Before he could answer, Frigga turned to mist and blew away.

With a weary groan, Woden settled back in his seat. "Deserted again," he told Freki.

She tilted her head at him and whined.

"What's wrong? What isn't? The Veil is down, Others sit the throne of a human kingdom, magic is spilling everywhere and..." he sighed. "And the worst of it is this is only the beginning. Darkness grows outside of Wilderheim. Can you feel it?"

Freki shook herself out.

Woden nodded and closed his eyes. Unbidden a vision formed in his mind, a portent of both light and dark. The great dragon flew through the air, breathing massive plumes of fire at the clouds. The desert moon rose on a shriek of demons rioting through the night. A vast army gathered beneath the sign of a blood red cross. He opened his eyes and rubbed his aching head. "Whatever you plan to do, my love," he said to the winds whisking her away, "do it fast."

The End...?

AUTHOR'S NOTE

Okay, so when I said The Royal Wizard would be a stand-alone book I lied. Well, no, I didn't lie. I just didn't anticipate the nefarious wickedness that is my friends.

"You have to make this into a series!" they said.

"No, it's done," I replied. "The story has a happy ending, it's finished."

And then one of them asked the most dangerous question there is: "But if you wanted to, how would you continue it?"

Well, I thought, it couldn't be Saeran and Nia's story again, because they are finished. It would have to be their child. Probably a girl who is nothing like her level-headed mother. But better make it twins, a girl and a boy. And, being that they are children of Halflings, naturally they will have issues, and with everything Nia and Saeran had done, they won't be the only ones and…

I hadn't even formed the first sentence to answer this meddlesome friend before I had the outline of an entire book in my head and half of one for the next book after it. So instead of saying all that, I turned to my friend, eye twitching and said simply, "I hate you."

She laughed and said, "I love you too."

So now I am stuck with a pair of royal dragonblood twins who can't seem to get their magics under control, a kingdom in shambles with Others roaming in plain sight, and, oh yeah, there is the little matter of an Aegiran assassin come to kill Saeran and Nia because he blames them for the death of his sister and the plights his tribe suffers as a result.

Whatever else may come, this one is going to be one hell of a ride. I hope you're ready!

ALIANNE DONNELLY was a wordsmith long before she became a reader. Driven by an insatiable curiosity about everything from history and mythology to science and philosophy, she grew into a fiction writer who hates coloring inside the genre lines. Her books all have elements of romance, with different series sorted under paranormal, science fiction, fantasy, and erotic. And then there's *Wolfen*…

Alianne lives in California, doing hard time in a corporate 9-5, while secretly scribbling away any chance she gets. She loves pizza, hiking, and avoiding small talk, and hopes to one day win the lottery jackpot. To find out more about Alianne's books and works in progress, visit her website at AlianneDonnelly.com.

www.ingramcontent.com/pod-product-compliance
Lightning Source LLC
Chambersburg PA
CBHW030611170726
48283CB00002B/563